SHAWNE STEIGER

Hi Fristina,

Thank you so much for agreeing
to review my book!

games
we
played

Games We Played

Red Adept Publishing, LLC

104 Bugenfield Court

Garner, NC 27529

http://RedAdeptPublishing.com/

---

1.   http://StreetlightGraphics.com

For my grandmothers, Ann Margolin Steiger and Sophie Os-trov

Chapter 1
Rachel
1991

The night before Grandma Gladys moved in, Rachel and her father performed their final magic show. They had been doing the shows since her father had given her the magic kit for her birthday a few months before. They always started in his study, rehearsing the patter they were supposed to use to distract the audience so they wouldn't notice what the magicians were doing with the balls or cards.

Her father closed his fist around her hand, showing her how to release the foam balls that had started out squashed together and hidden. His wedding ring left a painful dent on her knuckle, and the scratch of his beard tickled her cheek when he leaned in close. The balls felt like living creatures that could squirm away if she relaxed her grip.

At the last minute, before they went to the living room, her father placed a black magician's hat on her head. "Now, you're ready," he said, and she felt special. That feeling mingled with his pipe-tobacco smell and the hazy desk lamp and his psychiatry books. A picture of Rachel and her parents, posing in front of the lion cage at the San Diego Zoo, smiled at them from a wooden frame on his desk. In the photo, her father had covered his thinning blond hair with a San Diego Padres hat, and her mother had pulled her dark curls into a ponytail. They were squished close together. They had all laughed so hard at her father's dumb joke just as the zoo attendant snapped the photo. They hadn't yet known that Grandma Gladys would be moving in.

Rachel's mother was the audience for the magic show. She sat cross-legged with her hands clasped in her lap and a pinched smile on her thin face. Rachel opened her hand, revealing the multicolored balls that had duplicated in her closed fist. They tumbled from her hand and settled on the fluffy beige carpet. She usually felt a swell of pride when her mother clapped, and her father usually beamed. But that night, already, the fog of change had invaded their living-room ritual.

"By the time you're seven, you'll be performing on real stages," her father said.

Her mother looked at her watch. "It's past her bedtime, Aaron. Tomorrow's a big day for all of us."

"Your grandma's moving in with us tomorrow," her father said in his fake-happy voice.

They'd been saying that every day for weeks, and she didn't need reminding. Earlier, she'd helped her mother make Grandma Gladys's room special, putting flowers in a vase and the new blue comforter on the bed.

"Are you sure she wouldn't be just as happy in an apartment nearby?" her mother asked again. Rachel had heard that question several times too.

"I'm her only living son." Her father ruffled Rachel's hair and winked at her, but he didn't smile. "She asked specifically to live with us. You know that. I don't see how I can say no. We'll make it work. It will be fine." His voice had acquired that reasonable tone he used when Rachel didn't want to brush her teeth or turn off the television.

Rachel's mother pulled her knees up to her chest and wrapped her arms around her legs. "But you know she only asked because she thinks I'm doing such a terrible job with you-know-who. It isn't like Gladys can't take care of herself. She isn't that frail yet."

Rachel was confused by the bitter tone of her mother's voice and the broken expression in her father's eyes. She wasn't stupid and knew that "you-know-who" meant her. But she wanted to take a bath and get a bedtime story and be tucked in. She wanted tomorrow to be just another day.

She gathered up the balls and started in with the patter. "Hey, look! I have only one red ball in my hand, right? One red ball, but watch. I'll close my fingers and squeeze real hard..." She closed her fist around the red ball and squeezed until her knuckles turned white, but her parents were focused on each other, her mother sitting curled into herself and her father standing with his hands open, helplessly spreading his fingers, no longer good for magic at all, wide.

"I wish you could get along," Rachel's father said.

Her mother pressed her lips into a tight line. "I'm not the one who can't get along."

Rachel opened her fist and let the balls slide away. Her fingernails had left painful crescent-shaped dents on her palm.

Chapter 2
Rachel
2016

Rachel felt the wall against her back, the bend of her knees, and the floor under her feet. She focused on her breath. The last-minute backstage bustle of stagehands dragging props and actors running lines transformed into the peaceful murmur of a meditative river.

She became Louise—Louise, the abortion protestor, Louise, who dreamed of killing an abortion doctor, Louise, who only wanted to save the babies so she could believe she was worthy of love. Rachel hunted for and found Louise. She might have disagreed with everything Louise believed in, but she could channel the core longings they shared.

She had worked with actors who vomited every single night, others who self-medicated, and one who regularly fled the theater. But Rachel always stayed calm and fully present before going onstage. People often told her she came alive up there, to which she would respond, "It's more like I come home."

One more breath in. One more breath out. Pete's voice on the loudspeaker dragged her out of the meditation. "Ladies and gentlemen, please take your seats and silence your cell phones."

Two hours later, she strode upstage, gazed at the audience, and delivered her last few lines. "I dare you to judge me. I have not forgotten how I stood outside this very clinic with my picket sign. I have not forgotten that I maybe accused some of you of being baby killers."

She had tried playing it with tears early on, but she preferred the angry and defensive version of Louise. She placed her hands on her belly. She made eye contact with several audience members, finding faces she knew. Liz smiled. Joshua Matheson, the theater critic, nodded. Pete winced. She knew he still wasn't happy with that final monologue.

She sucked in air. "Judge if you must, but you'd do the same," she told them. "It's easy to have convictions when you have nothing to lose. We say abortion is a silent Holocaust. Now, I am silenced." She turned her back on the audience, picked up her pro-life sign, which featured a mother holding an infant and the words Your Baby is a Gift, then exited stage left.

Rachel had just finished changing out of the conservative Louise jumper and into her jeans and sweatshirt when Liz burst into the dressing area and wrapped her in a hug. "You were great, as usual," she gushed. Rachel leaned back so she could gaze up into Liz's perfectly highlighted blue eyes. When Liz brushed a strand of red hair out of her eye with a manicured red fingernail, Rachel noticed, as she always did, how Liz transformed even that small gesture into a graceful dance.

"Thanks." Rachel immersed herself in Liz's spicy fragrance and its promise of stolen kisses, illicit and hot. She let her hand slide over Liz's hip and brush her bare thigh, just below the hem of Rachel's favorite purple sundress. She loved those tight dancer's muscles, the way they tensed in response to her stroke, the soft intake of breath that signaled arousal.

"Hey." Pete's familiar touch on her shoulders dragged her out of the moment, and she reluctantly stepped back, hot with both desire and embarrassment.

"Something about that final monologue just doesn't feel right," he said, rubbing his dark, shadowed eyes. The bit of Kleenex he'd used to blot a shaving cut still clung to his cheek, and his bleached hair lay flat against his scalp. That was all Rachel needed to know he'd spent most of the night obsessing about that monologue. Pete never cared that much about how he looked, but he always at least glanced in a mirror and added hair gel before leaving the house... unless he had spent several late nights worrying over some scene that was not perfect enough.

"I can play it sad if you insist," Rachel said. "But I don't think that's Louise."

"I think it was perfect." Liz tugged Rachel away from Pete and hugged her again. When Rachel shrugged out of the embrace, Liz kept a possessive arm around her waist and glared at Pete.

"No, it's not your acting. It's my writing. I'm not convinced her motivation is clear." Pete picked up the protest sign Rachel had leaned against the wall. "Do you think it's enough? Maybe we should use one of those awful dead-baby pictures they're always putting on signs. Do you think?"

"I think Rachel could take anybody's bad writing and do great things with it." Rachel could feel the tension in Liz's arm around her waist.

"A problematic scene here and there doesn't mean the writing is bad," Pete retorted.

Rachel felt a flush color her cheeks. Pete and Liz together always complicated both relationships for her. "It's fine." She tried to ease away from Liz's grip. "Pete isn't criticizing my acting. You know how it is with your dancing. We're just exploring options for the part."

Pete kept his eyes on the protest sign, and she knew it was so he wouldn't have to look at Liz. "I never said a word about Rachel's acting. She's always good."

"Yes, she is." Liz glared at Pete. "She deserves a Broadway-caliber playwright." She tightened her arm around Rachel.

Pete brought the sign to the door and leaned it against the wall. "I'm going to mess with it tonight and see what I can come up with.

I'm sure my writing will never live up to *your* standards, though." He finally focused his gaze on Liz, who met it with venom in her eyes.

"Come on, guys," Rachel said, finally pulling away from Liz so she could move toward the middle of the room and stand between them. "You're my two favorite people. It'd be great if you could get along."

Pete shrugged. She'd mostly given up on imploring him to be nice to Liz. "I'll be nice to a girlfriend who treats you right," he would say.

He didn't see the Liz that Rachel saw. *Look at her tonight,* she thought, *at the way she's one hundred percent here for me.*

"Ever heard the phrase 'addicted to someone's potential'?" Pete had asked the last time she'd tried to explain herself.

Pete shrugged into his motorcycle jacket. "So, your birthday is tomorrow. We don't have a performance. You should come for dinner."

Rachel glanced at Liz and shook her head. "Liz and I are going out. We're having dinner at Arad Evans in Syracuse then going to Prism."

"Are you?" Pete asked, and there was no missing the skepticism in his voice.

Liz tensed and stepped toward her.

"We are," Rachel said, and Liz smiled.

Someone knocked on the dressing room door, and Joshua Matheson entered with his usual flourish, unlit cigarette in hand, ludicrously overdressed for the small local theater. He tugged his tie and smoothed his jacket.

"Ugh," Pete said. "I know. I know it isn't ready. But that's why we start small, right?"

"Well, act one is strong. I just don't buy that she goes from virulent pro-lifer to getting an abortion. Also, it seems a bit too pointed. Your politics are showing, Peter." Joshua spoke with a slight British accent, and nobody knew if it was real. He swept Rachel's stage makeup aside and set his laptop on her table. Then he picked up the notebook Rachel used for character notes and flipped through the pages as if he had every right to her personal thoughts.

"Hey," Rachel said, moving toward him.

Pete beat her there and snatched the notebook from Joshua's hands. "I'm fine with that," Pete snapped. "I don't worry about hiding my politics." When he handed Rachel her notebook, she touched his arm. He mouthed something she couldn't make out then sighed and softened his tone. "You're right that it isn't there yet. Stan and I are headed to P-town for some R and R this week. I'll work on rewrites on the beach."

"That's fine," Joshua said. "I shall look forward to seeing the finished play. In the meantime, I was hoping I could grab an interview with this lovely lady." He offered Rachel a smile that seemed too big.

"Don't you want to wait till Pete's had a chance to fix some things?" Rachel asked.

"You, my dear, do not need fixing."

"See?" Liz hugged Rachel again. "I told you, you're stunning. Give your interview and send the recording to me. I'll get it on your website for you. I have to hit an Al-Anon meeting then relieve poor Michael, but I'll see you later for birthday fun." She sashayed out of the dressing room, and it felt to Rachel as if the room got a little bit darker.

"I'm headed out," Pete said. He hated anything to do with publicity and had pushed back on all of Rachel's attempts to help him build his own website or even get on Facebook. "Let me know if your birthday plans don't work out."

"I'll be fine." It angered her that he was always so sure Liz would disappoint her, even if he was often correct.

"Just the same," Pete dusted the sleeve of his motorcycle jacket. "If anything goes wrong, we'd love to take you out."

"You guys can take me out when you get back from Provincetown," Rachel told his receding back. Then she sat at her makeup table, which Joshua had already claimed as his studio.

Joshua dragged a stool to the table and perched on it, crossing his legs at the ankle. He opened his computer, plugged a mic into the USB port, and checked the sound. "Ready?"

Rachel nodded.

"I'm Joshua Matheson, and today in our weekly series, *Minute of Theater*, we're speaking with Rachel Goldberg about her performance in Peter Quinn's new play, *It Happened to Me*. The play, which will officially open this fall, had its first few performances this week at the Lotus Theater in Pineville, New York. Rachel, thank you for joining us today."

Rachel sat on the edge of her chair with her feet planted, seeking the calm she'd felt before going onstage. She didn't enjoy interviews, but they were necessary if she hoped ever to have a real career. "Thank you, Joshua."

Joshua intensified the British accent when he spoke on TV or the radio. Rachel and Liz had once spent a hilarious hour hunting for anything on the Internet that proved he had ever lived in England but found only his own self-written résumé, which cited his early years in London.

"So," he continued, "your character, Louise, is an evangelical Christian who is involved in anti-abortion activism and then gets pregnant herself and decides to have an abortion. What has it been like to take on that role?"

"Well," she replied, "as with any role, I dug inside myself to find the part of me that is Louise. There are many things about her that are universal, such as her desire to be loved and her need to belong."

"How do you do that? How do you identify with someone like Louise? She seems very different from what we know about Rachel Goldberg."

She wished she could pace. It was easier to think when she moved. She straightened her spine. "I think much of theater is an attempt to articulate those universal feelings of longing and loss that so many people walk around with every day."

"Explain?" Joshua slid the mic closer to her.

"Humans are social animals. Louise might have different politics and a different belief system than I do, but at her core, she longs to be accepted and loved and wanted." She breathed to slow herself down. "That's what drives most of us."

"I don't know, sometimes a really good English breakfast is what drives me."

They both laughed, and Rachel couldn't tell if his laugh was as phony as hers felt.

"Okay," he continued, still chuckling. "Tell me more about Louise. What drives her?"

"Louise feels terribly alone, and she learned as a child that in order to be safe, she had to fully embrace whatever she was told to believe." Rachel pressed her lips into a thin smile. "She joined the church, looking for meaning in her life, and they told her to how to think. Then she met Daniel, and as the preacher, he had all that power. He made her think that she had to be with him if she wanted to stay, if she wanted to belong or to be loved."

"How about the abortion?" Joshua asked. "A core dynamic in this play is the sort of *Sophie's Choice* around her personal beliefs and her relationship."

"Yes. She has to decide if her love for Daniel and her desire to belong is more important to her than the core beliefs about abortion that brought her to Daniel's church in the first place. If she wants to stay in the church, if she wants to keep his love, she can't have the baby."

"Okay." Joshua slid off the stool and leaned against the table, turning so he could speak into the mic. "I think I get what you're saying. But this play is not just about love or dependence. It's also a political statement, so I'm curious to know your personal beliefs about abortion."

It should have been easy, but Rachel hesitated. The school year had ended only a week before, and she wasn't sure the upcoming summer months would provide enough time for the kids to forget she'd expressed an opinion on such a hot topic. She worried their parents would notice and care. High school teachers, at least in the rural county where her school was, weren't supposed to have controversial political opinions. "I've never personally been in a position where I had to make such a difficult choice. I think it haunts many women. I don't think it's ever an easy decision."

"You're hedging." Joshua offered a smile that was probably meant to be encouraging but appeared hungry. "Are you telling me you don't have an opinion on abortion?"

"Well, yes, I guess I am hedging." *Why not say it? Why not have an opinion?* She imagined Liz cheerleading her, the way she had in the early days of their relationship. *Speak up for yourself. Don't let that asshole principal tell you how to teach your class. Have opinions.* "I am pro-choice." *Louder. Say it like you mean it.* "I probably wouldn't do this play if I wasn't." She released a breath.

Joshua nodded. "Thank you very much for your time. And before you go, I understand it's your thirtieth birthday tomorrow, so I do want to say happy birthday."

"Thank you."

"I've been speaking with Rachel Goldberg about her role in the new play, *It Happened to Me*, written by Pineville's very own Peter Quinn."

After they said goodbye and Joshua left, Rachel returned to the stage. She stood in the center and gazed out at the recently occupied chairs, inhaling the odor of sweat and stale air. Then she called Liz. "I asked Joshua to send you the audio file of the interview."

"Great." There was the blare of a horn and a distant siren. "I'll put it on your website for you."

"Facebook too," Rachel said. She could have handled it herself, but Liz had helped her set it all up the year before, and it was an excuse for some of the time they spent together.

"Of course, and I'll link to it on Twitter. Get out of my way, asshole. Sorry—car cut me off. I'm on my way home from Al-Anon."

"Was it a good meeting?" Rachel paced the stage. The question sounded forced. Liz had started going after her therapist told her she was an adult child of an alcoholic. Sometimes, Rachel thought she would rather Liz drink too much than spout one more Al-Anon slogan.

"It was. We talked about having the courage to change and detach from the alcoholic. It's helping me see my parents and my childhood differently."

"That's good. We're definitely on for tomorrow night, right?" She made herself stop pacing and looked out into the empty theater.

"Definitely," Liz said. The siren grew louder. "I should go, but I'll definitely see you tomorrow at Arad Evans. I'll meet you there at eight, okay?"

"And dancing at Prism after?" They hadn't been to the only women's bar in Pineville since Rachel's birthday a year before, and she missed dancing with Liz and the way they took every opportunity to touch, to build the sexual tension for later.

"Prism after," Liz replied.

"Promise?"

"Promise-promise," Liz said. That had started as a joke, one of those things between couples who had been together a while. Liz would say, "I promise I'll pick you up right at three," and Rachel would say, "I know what those promises mean. That means eight forty-five at the earliest," and Liz would say, "Well, this time, I promise-promise."

After ending the call, Rachel left through the back door and walked around the building to her car. The usual Westboro Baptist Church people clustered near the entrance to the theater. Pete had decided not to do anything about them, since they fit so well with the theme of the play. But Rachel hated pushing through them to get to her car, so she left through the back. She still had to deal with them, but at least she didn't have to rub shoulders with them between the door and her car.

One young woman carrying a sign that said God Hates Proud Sinners! strode toward Rachel. "You are going to hell!" she shouted. "Hell!"

"I'm sorry you feel that way," Rachel replied, infused with the calm brought by years of acting training and practice from a week's worth of similar encounters. She shut herself in her car and locked the doors.

The woman knocked on the window but backed off when Rachel started the car.

Her headlights swept across the protestors as she drove through the parking lot, and she thought there were more of them than usual.

A young man stepped toward her car. His sign said Build the Wall. She could clearly make out the words on his hoodie: Pro-Life. Pro-God. Pro-Gun.

She swerved to avoid him. That did not seem like a Westboro Church protestor. She would have to tell Pete. Maybe he'd finally listen to her and hire security or something.

Chapter 3
Rachel
2016

It was nine thirty, and no Liz. Rachel had walked out of Arad Evans without eating and was at Prism, drinking white wine on an empty stomach. On the dance floor, women writhed under pulsing lights, pressing against each other and kissing.

Her phone vibrated against her thigh. *Don't look.*

She'd already dealt with a series of texts from Liz: *Running late. Order without me.*

Michael's migraine seems worse.

And finally, *Not going to make dinner. See you at Prism.*

She would have looked, if she could have been sure the text would turn out to be Liz saying she was on her way, nearly there, would be there any second, or maybe just finding parking. But it was more likely Liz texting to say she wasn't coming, and Rachel wasn't drunk enough for that.

Her phone buzzed again. *Do not look.*

She looked, but it wasn't Liz. *Deplorable1 sent you a message,* the notification read. She clicked through to Messenger, wondering who the hell Deplorable1 was.

You dirty Jew dyke bitch. We're gonna hunt you down and gas you.

Before she had fully absorbed the message, she pressed the side button to shut down the screen on her phone. She looked around, feeling exposed, but nobody had seen. Nobody had read those words over her shoulder.

The music slowed, and she tried to match it with her breathing. *Who is Deplorable1? Some crackpot who probably doesn't even know for sure I'm Jewish. Or gay.* She went back into Messenger and deleted the message. *There. Gone.* But she felt dirty, as though she'd done something to deserve that attack.

The two women nearest her on the dance floor pressed close, working their hands down to each other's asses. Rachel felt it in her own body, the anticipation of later with Liz, dancing, going home, spending the night. If it happened.

Her phone played the opening bars of "I Could Have Danced All Night." She answered.

"Hey, happy birthday."

"Hey." Rachel let her tone go flat. She knew what was happening.

"Listen, Michael's migraine isn't gone. Twins both have fevers. I can't leave."

"Okay." All around her, women kissed and hugged and were happy to be there together.

"I'll stop by tomorrow. So sorry. I love you. Happy birthday."

"Thanks." Rachel kept the phone to her ear for another second before pressing End. She should have yelled at her, made Liz feel guilty, something. So much for promise-promise.

The DJ switched the music to "It's Raining Men," and the couples separated and began gyrating on the floor. She wondered why they always played "It's Raining Men" at women's bars. Rachel started a text to Liz: *Fuck you.* She stared until the words blurred then deleted them. Instead, she tried, *This is not okay.* She knew how it would go. She would say, "This is not okay," and Liz would say, "I'm sorry, but you know how it is. The kids need me." Rachel would say, "But I need you," then feel guilty, because who was Rachel to think she should be more important than Liz's five-year-old boys? But Liz had never bailed on her birthday before.

She deleted the text, finished off her wine, and ordered another. The throng of women coupled up and moved together again for an unfamiliar slow song. The wine went down easy and fast, and she knew she should leave, just go home, call a friend, do something other than sit alone, watching other couples make out on the dance floor.

She slid off the barstool and pushed through the sweaty throng and the press of flesh on flesh, the heat reminding her that it wasn't Liz touching her, pushing into her, or wanting her. Once in the bathroom, she stayed on the toilet in the tiny stall longer than she needed to, reading love notes and jokes carved and inked on the wall. *Jenny loves Mindy. All my heart to Nicole.*

At the sink, she splashed cold water on her face then glared into the cracked gray mirror, watching damp trails slide from the ends of her dark curls toward the subtle laugh lines that marked the corners of her bloodshot eyes. "Happy fucking birthday," she said out loud.

She returned to the bar and ordered another glass of wine. The DJ put on a Melissa Etheridge song, and she considered dancing by herself, imagining swaying alone in the midst of all those couples. But they couldn't all have been couples. There must have been other women who had come alone. Even some of the women together on the dance floor must have been faking it, squashing all the inside feelings that said *you are just not quite it.*

Back in her early twenties, when she first came out, Rachel had been all about the T-shirts and the jewelry and the women's music festivals. She'd fidgeted in impatient lines, checking out the other women, buying the CDs, swaying to Melissa Etheridge, Indigo Girls, and Tegan and Sara. But it had always felt like an act. It always felt just like her being alone at a bar, watching everyone else belong.

She guzzled the wine, ordering herself to stop immediately but feeling fuzzy and careless. The couple in front of her kissed again, and she considered going out there, wrapping her arms around them, and telling them they were beautiful. If she got drunk enough, she would. She ordered another.

Her phone vibrated again: *Deploarble1 sent you a message.* She went into Facebook instead of just opening Messenger. Her Facebook profile described her as "Actress and Drama Teacher." The photos linked to videos from plays she'd performed in, reviews of plays she'd been in, plays she'd directed, plays Pete had written and directed. It was her public profile, and she'd put nothing there about her sexual orientation. It might have been 2016, and gay marriage might have been legal, but parents still thought any member of the LGBTQ community would corrupt their kids, and school boards still got twitchy.

She looked at the comments on her timeline. Someone had tagged her in a bunch of photos. There she was, carrying her Out and Proud sign in that pride march she'd gone to ten years before. There was a party picture from Pete's twenty-fifth birthday with her in the background, smiling while Pete kissed Stan with all the passion of new love. Then came an ancient newspaper photo of her dressed up as Esther at the synagogue's Purim play when she was six. She hadn't even known such a photo existed. *Why would someone care that I was Esther in the Purim play when I was a kid?*

She dug her reading glasses out of her purse and looked more closely at the picture. A yellow star had been photoshopped onto her costume. Under the picture, Deplorable1 had written, "Rachel Goldberg should have been exterminated before she turned seven, the same way she wants to exterminate little babies." The music was too loud. Her head throbbed. *What is going on? How do I get this stuff off my Facebook page?* The music picked up into a dance song with relentless pounding, and the women swirled and merged. The wine tasted stale, like a wet dog. She would not throw up. Comments appeared on her wall as she watched.

ImaNazi: *You Jew Dyke bitch. We've got an oven waiting just for you.*

Librultears: *You wanna kill babies? We'll kill you. Go to fucking Auschwitz.*

She blocked them both.

Deplorable 1: *Baby killer.*

Block.

Hitler36: *Kike. Whore.*

Block.

Her entire body quivered. *Block it. Breathe. Block it.* The phone refused to respond to her shaky taps. She tried to slow her pulse. *Who are they? Why have they suddenly targeted me? What if the parents of my students see? Will I lose my job?* She hailed the bartender and had her glass refilled. That time, the wine tasted like nothing, but the first sip went down fast and warm. It left her numb.

1488: *Get on your knees, you dirty Jew. I'm going to fuck you like the dog you are.*

The comment terrified her and turned her hot with shame. She pressed the wineglass to her forehead and curled against an unwanted spark of arousal deep in her belly. She felt small and helpless, and the words intensified the empty feeling Liz had left by not being there.

She knew she should leave, but the DJ put on wordless dance music with a beat. She slid off the barstool and swayed in place. The women writhing on the dance floor doubled and spun, and she couldn't tell whether it was an illusion from the lights or her eyes playing tricks. The phone vibrated in her hand.

I'm so sorry to miss your birthday. Love you. XXX

"Fuck her." She said it out loud. It felt good.

"What if I'd rather fuck you?"

Rachel turned. The woman standing next to her looked familiar, but she couldn't place why. She was a little shorter and a few pounds heavier than Rachel but not fat. Straight dark hair tumbled to her shoulders, and she met Rachel's gaze with warm brown eyes. Her full, kissable lips curved into a smile.

If Liz had come, they would have danced then maybe gone back to Rachel's house and opened another bottle. They would have spent the night together. But Liz was not there.

"Hi, Rachel," the woman said, smiling again.

Who the hell is she? Rachel smiled back. "Hi." She finished her wine to hide her confusion.

"Dance?" the woman asked, offering her hand. Rachel took it.

RACHEL WOKE TO THE sound of the shower and Liz standing at the foot of her bed, a package wrapped in bright-red paper in one hand and a Bruegger's coffee in the other. The blinds were open, and the sunlight hurt Rachel's eyes, which were crusty and dry in the wake of her hangover.

"Who's in the bathroom?" Liz sounded calm, almost flippant.

"Um." Rachel rubbed her eyes. Her head throbbed in time with her heart, which was beating too fast.

Liz dropped the gift on the bed and squatted. When she came back up, she held a black bra that did not belong to Rachel. "So, I guess we can establish it's a woman?" Her pale face was inflamed, the way it got when she danced under hot lights and the way it got during sex.

Rachel pulled herself up to sit against the headboard. She was wearing the T-shirt she vaguely remembered putting on before she went out last night. *Does that mean nothing happened? Do the sheets smell like sex?* Her memory was full of black holes. She had danced with someone, someone she knew from somewhere, and apparently, she'd taken her home.

"It was my birthday," she said, purposely keeping the note of accusation in her voice. She didn't have to say the rest. They both knew that if Liz had shown up, the scene would not be happening as it was.

"Yeah, it was your birthday, and I wasn't there. I guess I don't have a right to be upset," Liz said, but coffee sloshed onto a shaking hand, Rachel's new white comforter, and the wrapped gift.

The shower turned off.

"No, I guess you don't," Rachel said softly.

"But you could have warned me. If you're going to bring some random woman to your house, you could at least text me and tell me not to let myself in." Liz tossed the bra onto the bed. Her voice was shrill with anger and something else—maybe fear.

It twisted a knot of regret through Rachel's gut, and she pulled the comforter closer, tucking it under her chin. "She wasn't random," Rachel said, fighting to keep the tremor out of her voice. *How is it that I can perform any scene when I'm playing a part but lose all self-control in real-life situations?*

"What do you mean, she wasn't random?" Liz asked, spilling more coffee.

"She was a decision," Rachel said, wondering if that was true. She must still have been drunk to be saying all that so openly.

"Decision about what?"

"You have to decide what you want. Me or him."

Liz stared at Rachel. "Who is she?"

"Me or him."

Rachel had never seen that look in Liz's eyes and wondered again whether it was anger or fear. Liz carried the coffee to Rachel's bedside table and set it down hard. Coffee sloshed over the edges and pooled on the table next to the lamp. "We've talked about this over and over," she said, her voice unexpectedly steady. "You know it isn't about Michael. You know how I feel about this. Divorce is hell on kids. My Evangelical mother..."

Rachel resisted the urge to walk down the familiar path in which she reassured Liz that she understood how badly her parents' divorce had affected her and was willing to wait for the sake of the kids, blah, blah, blah. Instead, she said, "I'm tired of being alone. Maybe it's selfish, but there it is."

"So what? You're going to leave me for some stranger you spent one night with?"

Rachel was saved from answering by the woman's emergence from the bathroom. She was dressed in the same jeans and tank top she had been wearing at the bar, but her hair was pulled back into a ponytail, and of course, she was not wearing a bra. Rachel watched Liz watch the woman's breasts jiggle, her nipples erect against the slightly damp top. She was curvy where Liz was angular. She was sexy in a very different way than Liz with her dancer's body.

The silence stretched long enough that Rachel could hear the bass from a passing car's stereo.

The woman broke the silence. "Is there coffee?"

Liz's face had progressed from red to white. She stared at the other woman. "But I know you. You're the cop. The one who does the drug talks at school."

"And you're the English teacher." The woman stood with a hip cocked and looked relaxed, as if she was having a perfectly normal morning.

Rachel mentally placed her in a police officer's uniform and suddenly understood why she had seemed familiar. With her hair in a ponytail, it was easier to see.

"I can make a pot," Rachel said, but she didn't move to get out of bed. The cop stepped back to lean against the doorjamb, her mouth flirting with a smile. Liz walked to the bedroom window and stood, looking out. There was something fragile about her erect back. Rachel had wanted to hurt Liz before but felt overwhelmed with shame.

Liz spun around. "I'm not just an English teacher. I'm a dancer. I'm a choreographer."

The cop offered a tight smile. "Okay. And I only do the drug talks sometimes. I also get to play detective now and then."

Rachel wondered whether it would be weird if she drank the coffee.

"So," Liz said, glaring at Rachel. "You went out to Prism for your birthday." Each word was clipped. "You took a cop home and fucked her. Did she bring her handcuffs? I bet you liked that."

Rachel bowed her head so neither woman would see the heat flooding her face. Nausea gripped her, and she swallowed hard.

But Liz continued. "She likes it kinky. Did she tell you that? She gets a little crazy sometimes, our Rachel."

"I don't know what this is," the cop said. Her voice was contained, almost gentle.

Rachel suddenly remembered the first time she had seen the cop—it had been maybe the only time she'd noticed her. The year before, one of Rachel's students, Caitlin, had written an essay for her freshman English class about being molested at home. Rachel had reported it, and they'd sent the cop in with a social worker to talk to the girl. The cop supposedly had a psychology background, which was why they sent her to the school so often.

Rachel had sat in while the cop met with Caitlin. Rachel remembered that she was gentle and warm, and she had wondered how it might have been if someone like that had been around when she was a kid. *Jane? Jeri? No, Jo. That's her name. The cop's name is Jocelyn, but she goes by Jo.*

"I don't know what this is," Jo, the cop, repeated. "But I didn't mean to make any trouble. I didn't know you guys were a couple. Rachel and I ran into each other. It just happened. It didn't mean anything."

Of course it didn't mean anything. It was a one-night stand. But still, the words gut-punched Rachel. It never meant anything. She was the other woman, the one to have a fling with, a mere one-night stand. Women moved on, went home to their hubbies, and Rachel let them. Because she didn't need things like normal people. She didn't need the white picket fence. But something welled up inside her, and she let it out. "We aren't a couple. Liz is married. It's just a fling." *Definitely still drunk.*

"A three-year fling," Liz said.

"Okay, listen. I'm going now," Jo said. She grabbed her bra off the bed then turned to Rachel. "Give me a call if you want to get together again." She winked and left the bedroom.

What the hell did I tell her last night? Rachel gritted her teeth against the silence. She looked at Liz, but Liz refused eye contact.

"You know I love you," Liz said.

"I know," Rachel mumbled, angry at the petulance seeping out in her voice.

Liz sat on the bed. "Mike's migraines knock him out. You have to be less sensitive. I can't always dance around your needs. My sponsor keeps telling me—"

"Why don't you just have an affair with your sponsor?" Ever since Liz had started going to her Al-Anon meetings for adult children of alcoholics, she pulled the sponsor out every time Rachel wanted a little more from her. "My sponsor thinks I'm codependent. My sponsor says you act like an addict."

Liz shook her head. She retrieved the gift and thrust it at Rachel. Coffee dribbled onto a previously unstained part of the comforter.

"Listen, I just wanted to give you your birthday present. That's why I came by. I felt bad I missed your birthday. I didn't expect to find someone else here. You need to tell me. I mean, I don't suppose I have any rights, but it's embarrassing, you know, to walk in on this."

Rachel refused to look at the gift, which smelled like coffee. "I want more," she said quietly, hearing her uncertainty weaving under the words. "I want something real."

Sometimes, Rachel comforted herself with memories from that first year, and in particular, the day Liz had shimmered onto the set of *My Fair Lady* and offered to choreograph the dance scenes. She and Rachel had looked at each other, and it was as if they had always known they would meet and it would mean something. They both felt it. They talked about it later that night, after the kids had left. Rachel remembered all those late nights after rehearsal, kissing in Liz's car with the smell of her musky perfume and that way she gently took Rachel's lip between her teeth, placed a hand on her thigh, then pulled back and said, "Let's go to your house."

Every time Rachel decided to end it, she returned to those early days, and she just couldn't let go. That Liz from the early days was somewhere, and she might come back, and Rachel wanted to be there when she did.

Liz dropped the gift on Rachel's lap and scooched up next to her. She wrapped Rachel in her arms and kissed her. "This is real," she murmured into Rachel's neck. "I love you. You know I do."

Rachel allowed it for a second then closed her mouth, forcing Liz's tongue out. "It isn't real. Real is you and me celebrating birthdays together. Not me alone at Prism on my birthday and you out to dinner at fucking Denny's with hubby and the twins on your birthday, because it's where hubby proposed to you and it's romantic. Real is shopping together and making meals together and going to bed and waking up next to you in the morning." The words came out in a rush and left her deflated.

She leaned across Liz and grabbed the coffee. The warmth against her palms was almost as soothing as the coffee with just the right amount of half-and-half, the way Liz knew Rachel liked it, on her tongue. It was so hard to explain even to herself why she had stayed so long and would probably continue, but the coffee was part of it. Her only other serious girlfriend had never stopped putting sugar in Rachel's coffee when she made it for them. She knew it would sound silly if she said it out loud: "I stay with Liz because she knows how I like my coffee." But she didn't know how else to explain the feeling of being seen and why it mattered.

Light from the window haloed Liz's hair, and Rachel couldn't help noticing, as she always did, how even during a fight, Liz seemed to shimmer, as if any second she would pirouette off the bed and lift Rachel into the air. Outside, a dog barked, and a woman yelled at someone to shut it up.

Liz took Rachel's free hand. "Let me take you out tonight. We'll celebrate your birthday properly. We'll go to Rhonda's and get a table in the back corner." She reached forward and slid a finger across Rachel's cheek, and Rachel couldn't help but lean into the gesture, allowing Liz to caress her lips and taking the finger into her mouth.

"Okay," she finally said. *Is that all I have?*

"Okay." Liz smiled and kissed her again.

After Liz left, Rachel imagined a different outcome. In her new version of events, Rachel insisted on a timeline, a decision, a plan. But she kept seeing Liz's face when the cop walked in, the impassive blankness of her eyes that Rachel suspected meant she was really hurting. Rachel was not good at being the one to hurt people. Then there was the thought of the school year starting—Liz would turn distant, unreachable, and untouchable, like she did when they were in a fight, and Rachel wondered how long she would stay that way and what would happen if she never warmed up to Rachel again. Rachel knew Liz might even hook up with someone else, and Rachel would have to see them sneaking out to the parking lot or lingering in the teacher's lounge after school got out. She knew what she needed to do, but she needed time to work up to it.

She turned on the television and logged into Facebook. It was her morning habit to manage her public profile and respond to posts from people who had seen her perform. It was what an actor did if she wanted to promote herself.

But with everything else that had happened, she had forgotten about the posts on her feed from the night before. And the new comments were not the usual positive reviews of her performance. Deplorable2 wrote, *So we have decided to share the bitch's address with you all. It's 25 Meadow St., Pineville, NY. She is in this super left-wing play written by a faggot. The play is pure baby-killing propaganda. Also, she's a Jew dyke. She deserves everything you throw at her.*

She sat for a long time, trying to reassure herself that there was nothing to fear. It was just a bunch of people at their computers. They probably didn't live anywhere near her. But she didn't quite believe her own reassurances. She blocked Deplorable2 and concentrated on making her mind blank. Then she found the bottle of Vicodin she'd saved after some dental work, took one, went to bed, closed her eyes, and did what she always did when things got to be too much.

She'd started doing it as a kid after her grandmother had moved in and after everything that had happened with Stephen, and it always worked. It involved locking an experience or a memory into a magic vanishing box deep inside her mind. She unhappened everything and went back to sleep.

Chapter 4
Rachel
1991

Grandma Gladys brought black suitcases heavy with kitchen supplies enshrouded in Bubble Wrap and newspaper. Her first full day there, she insisted on "Koshering the kitchen."

Rachel's mother, taut shouldered, chapped her hands in the sink while Grandma Gladys purged the cupboards, dumping plates, bowls, and silverware into black garbage bags, and Rachel organized the *new* forks and spoons in their separate kosher drawers with masking tape labels for meat and dairy.

"You must never use a dairy knife to cut meat," Grandma Gladys lectured. "You must never eat pizza with the same fork you used for steak." Rachel tried to spot the bald patch her mother insisted was on top of Grandma Gladys's head, but instead, she noticed the small eyes and sharp chin and thought that her grandmother resembled the birds of prey she'd seen at the zoo.

Rachel didn't understand why anybody would eat pizza with a fork, but she nodded and kept putting the dairy forks in the dairy drawer. Her father retreated to his study, where he was surrounded by magic books and boxes full of hidden compartments. He didn't invite Rachel to join him. He didn't say anything about how she'd be performing on real stages soon.

Finally, Grandma Gladys carried a large white serving platter painted with roses to the discard pile, and Rachel's mother flung her arms out, spraying water from the sink all over the floor and surrounding countertops. She snatched the plate out of Grandma

Gladys's hands. "I'll keep this," she said. "It was a wedding gift from my mother."

Grandma Gladys squeezed her lips and crossed her arms. "Well, I won't have it in a kosher kitchen. It's probably had meat and cheese on it at the same time." Her tone implied that Rachel's mother must have murdered somebody and served the body parts on that platter.

Rachel's mother hugged the platter to her chest and crept out of the room like Lucky did when he was caught in the garbage. Grandma Gladys patted Rachel's head and said, "No, Rachel, that fork goes in the meat drawer. See, it was on the right side of the tablecloth." She pointed at the shiny array of silverware on the floor, carefully organized on the right and left of their picnic tablecloth, glinting like treasure against the faded yellow flowers.

After the kitchen had been koshered to her satisfaction, Grandma Gladys sat at the kitchen table with Rachel and her mother, inhaling curls of steam from decaffeinated Lipton tea and explaining exactly why the kosher rules must be honored.

"Do you understand, Rose? We are in a covenant with God. The Jews were chosen by God to be pioneers of religion and morality, and that is our purpose. You must understand this, and you must raise your daughter as a religious Jew."

Rachel sipped hot chocolate, squirmed in her chair, and tried to think of the words that would release her to go play. Her mother nodded and stared fixedly into her tea as if also trying to divine the response that would send Grandma Gladys away.

She craned to see out the window in case the kids might have gathered for a game of tag. The drone of Grandma Gladys's voice echoed through her mind without registering actual meaning. Stephen appeared at the window. She could see his chapped knees, the bruise on his arm when he lifted it to wave, the grin that beckoned her to freedom. She lurched to her feet with enough force that the chair clattered onto its back. The room went silent, and Rachel held her breath.

Grandma Gladys squinted at Rachel. "Where are you going, young lady? You haven't finished your hot chocolate."

Rachel focused on righting the chair, so she wouldn't have to look at her grandma's pinched lips or her mother's hunched posture. "Outside to play," she mumbled.

Grandma Gladys turned her stringent gaze on Rachel's mother and held it until she sighed and said, "Why don't you just finish your hot chocolate first?"

Rachel wasn't released to play for another thirty minutes, not until Grandma Gladys finally yawned and said she needed to lie down. Even then, as Rachel headed for the back door, Grandma Gladys said, "You should really wear dresses, Rachel, not those tomboy clothes."

Rachel tried to catch her mother's eye, but her mother was still at the table, her eyes focused on her full teacup.

"I'm so happy to get to be involved in your life," Grandma Gladys continued and clasped her hands together the way Rachel's kindergarten teacher used to when it was time to clean up. "Tomorrow, we'll do a Hebrew lesson together." Rachel nodded in agreement but felt grim inside and wished she could put Grandma Gladys in her fist and make her disappear like one of her father's foam balls.

Rachel's friends usually played tag, raced bikes up and down the hill, or became explorers discovering the canyon in the empty lot for the very first time. But today, Stephen, who was almost seven and older than Rachel and Tina, wanted to play war.

"You be the Jew," he said. "You and Tina. I'm the Nazi."

"But Tina's Catholic," Rachel reminded Stephen.

Tina nodded in vigorous agreement.

"Pretend," Stephen said. "Just pretend you're both the Jews."

Tina and Rachel hugged the edge of the canyon, digging rocks out of the caked mud. "Pretend they're bombs," Rachel said, handing a palm-sized rock to Tina. Tina threw it, and her rock landed a foot away from Stephen.

"Kaboom!" she yelled.

But Stephen jumped back and said, "Ha! I got away before it exploded."

Rachel found another good throwing rock, turned it sideways for the best leverage, and heaved. It nailed Stephen in the stomach. He grunted and grabbed the spot where she'd hit him.

"I got you," she yelled. "You can't say I didn't get you."

Stephen advanced, still holding his stomach with one hand. Rachel and Tina bolted. They ran hard, panting and clutching their sides. They found a bush near the back wall of the canyon and ducked behind it in a last-ditch effort. "Hold the fort," Rachel urged Tina.

"What fort?" Tina had always been more timid and was already moving to step out from behind the bush.

"You know," Rachel said. "The fort."

But there wasn't any fort, and then Stephen threw a dirt clod, which exploded around them. Tina coughed and stepped forward.

"Pretend I just blew you up! You're injured!" he shouted.

Rachel stayed where she was, but Tina collapsed to the ground, moaning and clutching her legs and stomach.

"You, too, Rachel," Stephen ordered, and there was a serious note she hadn't heard before. He rubbed his stomach where her rock had hit.

She dropped, yelping when her knee connected with a sharp pebble. But she pretended she was a prisoner being tortured and she had to bear it. She stayed there even as the pain climbed her leg.

"Now you're my prisoners, Jews," Stephen said in his *Hogan's Heroes* accent.

Rachel bowed her head in the way a good prisoner who had lost the war and been captured by the enemy always did.

"You're the real Jew," Stephen said to her. "You're the real one." He lifted his shirt so she could see the beginnings of a bruise from where her rock had hit him.

In her mind, she felt the rock in her hand and her arm throwing it. She saw Stephen double over with the initial impact. She felt like she had when she'd screamed at a spider and her father killed it, like the time she'd said, "I hate you" to her mother. She knelt in the dirt and stared at the dust as it settled around her knees.

Chapter 5
Stephen
2016

When Stephen's mother wrote that she was getting married again, he hadn't expected it to last. He hadn't expected to come home from Iraq and find her gone and that he had the old house to himself. He prowled from room to room, sniffing, hunting for the familiar odors—his grandfather's cigarettes, his mother's perfume, the smell of booze and pot—telling himself to move on, get a job, get a life. Sometimes, he sat in the attic and cradled his grandfather's World War II guns and tried to picture himself as a child with his grandfather, with Rachel.

He thought about Rachel and Gladys, about the Goldbergs, all the time. Sometimes, in spite of everything, he decided that was the happiest time of his childhood.

He watched *Dr. Phil* and wondered if therapy could help him. He longed for someone, anyone, to talk to. He couldn't go to the VA because of his dishonorable discharge, so he found a sliding-scale clinic in downtown Carlsbad.

A beautiful spring day marked his first appointment. Kids loitered on street corners, eating ice cream cones, walking to the beach. School was done for the summer, he realized. He hated driving past all those kids on his way to the clinic.

The psychologist who came to get him from the clinic waiting room introduced herself as Natalie. She covered her slightly chunky body with a multicolored blouse that hung below her hips. She had curly blond hair and glasses. When he surveyed the barren-walled office, which was not much bigger than a closet, she admitted she was still in school. "I'm a psychology intern," she explained. "But I get supervision. Is that going to be a problem?"

He shook his head because she looked so earnest, leaning forward in her chair with her fingers woven together, her flat-heeled shoes planted on the beige carpet. An alarm clock and a picture of a ponytailed blond kid sat on her desk. He inched his chair toward the wall and turned slightly, so he could face the door.

She took a pad of paper and a pen off her desk. "So, you were in Iraq," she said, writing. "When did you get out?"

"A year ago." He heard the defensiveness in his voice. Technically, he'd gotten out of the army six months before, but that was because they held him, evaluating, deciding on the whole dishonorable discharge thing.

Natalie just nodded and wrote and asked him what he did when he served.

"Infantry." It was true. But the real answer was "glorified delivery boy." They were always sending him off to run MREs to the front line.

"Infantry," Natalie repeated. "So you were in combat?" She sounded eager, like a kid trying to earn a candy treat. "Is that why you got out? Too much trauma?"

"I got out 'cause it was time." He saw no point in telling her how he never quite figured out how to do it in Iraq—how to fling his arm over a buddy's shoulder, share pictures of a girlfriend, a little brother, or a son's puppy, how to trust a battle buddy to have his back, risk his life for him, all that shit. The guys in his troop were polite and worked with him when they had to. Otherwise, they left him alone, at least until he shot that Iraqi man. Then they wouldn't leave him alone.

Natalie's pen worked the paper. He could see large loopy letters. "What made you enlist?"

"Seemed like a good idea." He'd managed okay in boot camp, even if he just missed passing the entrance exam to be a combat engineer, where he would have learned to make bombs like his skinhead friends wanted. But there was no shame in being infantry, on the front line. His grandfather had always said he was frontline.

Stephen liked the drills and knowing how to shoot and the extra bucks. September 11 had happened when he was a senior in high school, and even though that wasn't why he enlisted, he'd been happy enough to ride the wave of patriotism. He'd fantasized about going off to kill the Haji then being greeted with cheers at airports when he came home.

Natalie nodded a lot, almost like a nervous tic. Even though she was only asking a bunch of stupid questions about his family, his GED, his old job, why he still lived in his grandfather's house, why he wasn't working, and whether or not he drank alcohol, he started to think maybe he could talk to her. She seemed awkward, and he liked that. He even imagined telling her about his grandfather and how he had wanted to make him proud. But Iraq had been nothing like being brave in a uniform the way his grandfather had been.

He had known it wouldn't, of course, that such thoughts were all childhood fantasy stuff he'd grown out of years before, garbage that had nothing to do with the present day and Iraq. But somehow—and no one could have predicted it—he hadn't really *known*. He had not been prepared for MREs and long, rolling drives through the desert while the asshole sergeant major in the vehicle with him barely spoke except to say things like, "How'd a fucker like you get in the army, anyway?" then turned away and stared out the window. Stephen had to drive hour after hour in oppressive silence with nothing to think about except the IED that might be right around the next corner.

Natalie consulted her notes. "Do you have nightmares, sleep problems?"

"I can't sleep. I don't sleep or, if I do, I have a dream, usually just when I'm falling asleep."

She kept still, the tip of her pen pressed to her pad.

The silence stretched until he realized she wanted more. "Um, I see children."

"Okay, and does something happen to the children?" Her syrupy voice might as well have been saying "There, there" or "You'll be okay. I'll take care of you."

She probably expected some trauma—the kids got blown up or there was a ten-year-old with a suicide bomb. Everyone saw those stories on *Sixty Minutes*. He clenched his fists. "Nothing happens. They're children, and they want candy, and I don't have any."

They would line the side of the road, staring dark-eyed out of pointy, smudged faces. He saw them with their hands out and palms up. He'd reach into an ammo bag, thinking he would find a rainbow of plastic-wrapped treats to toss at them, but the ammo bag was always empty—no ammunition and no candy. That was it. He was rolling through the streets of Tikrit, and the kids wanted candy.

"What about nightmares? Do you have nightmares?"

He could see she didn't get how his dream was a nightmare. She couldn't imagine why he woke up in a sweat every time. He shifted and glanced at the door then at her.

She nodded at him, her pen poised. The corners of her mouth twitched as if she wanted to smile but thought it was maybe a bad idea.

He stared at his feet and realized he had put his heavy hiking shoes on, which was stupid. It was beach weather, and most people were probably in shorts and sandals. He didn't even remember deciding to dress that morning. "Well," he said. "It isn't a nightmare, exactly. More like a waking dream, I guess. You know?" He felt like he was inventing new words, making them up as he went along, so each one came slow and hard. He glanced up to see her nod, which might or might not have meant a damn thing.

He looked at the towheaded girl in the picture and saw Natalie follow his gaze. There was a dime-shaped stain in the carpet a few inches away from his feet. "Sometimes, when the kids come, I beat them to death. They're maybe five or six years old. I turn them into pulp. People are just meat, you know. Animals. The kids are better off." The same impulse that had produced the words he had never intended to say and wasn't sure he meant drove him to look at her face.

Her pen was still. Her face had moved into a half smile—not the smile she had fought back earlier, more a parody of what that smile had wanted to be. Stephen recognized the look. He had seen it on the first sergeant's face after Stephen shot that Iraqi and the little girl came running up, screaming. He saw it again on one of the other guys when they turned the body over and found only a wallet that contained a few American dollars and a picture of three smiling kids in front of a house.

"But he had a gun," Stephen had insisted when they examined the Iraqi man's body. "I saw it." He hadn't been certain that was true. He would never tell Natalie about any of that, about the wet spot that had appeared in the man's crotch just before Stephen pulled the trigger, or about the feeling of power, shame, and disgust blending together in one nauseating bundle in his stomach. When he pulled the trigger, it had been to wipe the look of fear off the man's face. To relieve the unbearable intensity in his own body.

He puked that day. And the first sergeant told the story to everyone—Stephen had killed some poor man who didn't even have a gun, orphaning that poor kid, then lost his lunch after he did it. "Whacko," they'd said. "We don't trust you," they'd said.

He could never tell Natalie any of that, because she already had that same look on her face, the one that said, "You are one sick fucker." On Natalie, the expression lasted a second and was gone. She nodded again, and he wondered if she was picturing puppies and kittens to get that carefully smooth, everything-is-fine-here expression in her eyes.

He turned his chair the rest of the way toward the door. "You don't have to like me," he said.

"What makes you think I don't like you?" she asked, her voice a pitch higher than it had been. "What about friends? Who do you spend your time with?"

Stephen stared at the floor. There were his skin friends, but they had disappeared right after his deployment, and he couldn't seem to find them. He'd scoured the Internet. No joy. *The Goldbergs? Rachel? Does someone you haven't seen since you were eighteen count as a friend?* "I've got friends." He left it at that. "I do stuff with them."

She nodded, wrote something down, and looked at the clock.

He followed her gaze: 2:45. *Have I really been here forty-five minutes?*

"How about when you were a kid? Did you have friends? Things you liked to do? Any sports, interests?"

As a kid, he'd had Rachel and Gladys. He'd played war, which was different than actual war, of course. "I trained a dog with my grandpa," he said. "My grandpa taught me. He was a great dog." Until the day his grandpa went in the hospital for good, and the dog disappeared.

"Sometimes, it's helpful to pick up old hobbies," she said. "After trauma, people sometimes stop doing things they used to enjoy." She sounded like she was quoting from a book, and maybe that should have bothered him, but her insecurity was as appealing as her earlier awkwardness.

"Anyway," she said, "we're about out of time today."

Was the sigh at the end of the sentence relief?

She put the pad on her desk and wrote something on a sheet of paper. "Hand this to the clerks on your way out, and they'll schedule you for another appointment." She stood and offered her hand. He shook it and held on a few seconds too long, wondering if it made her uncomfortable. Her hand was dry. His was sweaty. She opened the office door, and after he walked out, she shut it behind him.

Chapter 6
Stephen
1989

Stevie and his mother were evicted from their apartment after his mother's big fight with the landlord at two in the morning. They left with only his mother's purse and went to his grandpa's house to sleep. Stevie had seen his grandpa just once before, and he barely remembered the visit. For the whole taxi ride, his mother kept saying, "Just until I get a job. We won't stay long. Don't worry, Stevie."

He dozed, lulled by a spicy cigar smell and the erratic crackle of the radio from the front of the car. The driver let them out at a two-story stucco house that loomed like a yellow castle in the shadows of streetlight and moon. Stephen followed his mother through a wrought-iron gate that opened to a sidewalk made of pink stone slabs. He lurked behind her when she knocked, looking around at the rock garden, a few lemon trees, and a big white wall that surrounded the front yard, blocking any view except for bits of road.

Nobody answered, so his mother dropped her purse and slammed the heel of her hand into the doorbell over and over. Then she turned away from the door, picked up her purse, grabbed Stephen's arm, and dragged him toward the gate and the street, and the door finally opened. His grandpa stood on the threshold, silhouetted by a glow from the living room. Stephen would always remember that glimpse of his grandpa, the faded gray robe held closed at the chest, the gnarled toenails and bushy white hair, how big he was. He wasn't fat, just big and as shaggy as the mountains he could see from Carlsbad, even though it took eight hours to reach them.

His grandpa stared at Stephen's mother with bloodshot eyes. Then he looked down at Stephen and twisted his mouth into a closed-lipped grimace. Later, Stephen learned that his grandpa didn't like to show his mouth when he wasn't wearing his dentures, but at the time, the vampire smile frightened Stevie.

"Well, you might as well come in, then." His grandpa's voice was harsh and phlegmy. After he finished talking, he coughed until his face turned red, and he lit up a cigarette. Stevie's mother propelled him through the front door and into the house, where they stayed much longer than she had promised.

Two weeks later, they were still there. Stevie's mother stayed in her room nearly all the time, leaving Stevie to eat Hungry-Man frozen dinners and watch *The Price is Right* with his grandpa. When she did come downstairs, she pulled a kitchen chair into the living room and sat on that, far away from Stevie and Grandpa on the sofa.

———————◉———————

WHEN STEVIE HAD HIS sixth birthday, his mother didn't come down to sing "Happy Birthday," buy him a cake at the grocery store, or tell him she was sorry she couldn't afford a present but that she loved him. But his grandpa made sure he had a special day. He took Stevie up to the attic and showed him the guns gleaming on their racks inside a tall wooden case with a glass front. His grandpa opened a cardboard box next to the gun case and dug beneath a bunch of magazines until he produced a silver key. He inserted the key into the lock very precisely, as if opening that case was a more delicate task than shaving the whiskers around his throat. Then he removed the guns one by one and showed them to Stevie.

He had six guns in six different shapes and sizes—three thick-handled guns with narrow noses that his grandpa said were Lugers, a smaller-nosed pistol called a Walther, a rifle called a Mauser, and one MG 34 machine gun. Stevie liked the rifle best because its long brown nose seemed sleek and dangerous.

His grandpa cradled it. "With this Mauser, I killed a Jew resistance fighter who thought he could get away. I shot him right in the chest. He screamed and fell back, dead. He thought he could get away. He thought he could fight us." Then he said something in German and chuckled until his laughter turned into a long, hacking cough. Meanwhile, he had handed the rifle to Stevie.

The gun was heavier than he expected, nothing like the plastic ones he played with sometimes. He lifted the gun over his head, feeling his muscles work, then settled it on his lap, running his hand over the long nose and the coarse handle, inserting his finger into the slot where the trigger was. He felt grown up, holding the gun and picturing that Jewish resistance fighter falling over backwards and dying with a single scream.

His grandpa chuckled again. "We nearly got rid of all the Jews," he said. "We nearly did it." Then he laughed and shoved the box of magazines at Stephen. "Someday, when you're ready, all those guns will be yours. And this too—these are magazines for when we couldn't catch any Jewish girls to fuck."

He learned all sorts of things from the pictures in those magazines and from his grandpa's stories.

Every Sunday after dinner, Stephen would follow his grandpa up to the attic and watch him polish those guns with his big gnarled hands. Then he would be given a gun for story time. And sitting in the bright glow of the naked bulb, cradling the gun, surrounded by boxes of junk, mothball smell, and dust, he would drift into the world of his grandpa's rambling tales of killing Jews and American soldiers, raiding houses, fighting for Hitler. And he would forget that his father didn't show up for visitation, that his mother didn't love him anymore, and that he sometimes wished for an older brother or even just a friend who never said anything that made fire explode in his chest and blackness overwhelm him so he lost control and punched and punched until his knuckles hurt and the friend wasn't his friend anymore.

Chapter 7

Rachel

2016

Rachel awoke sweaty and too hot. Her bedroom curtains were open, the late-afternoon sun baking her bed. She squeezed her eyes closed just a few seconds more, willing herself back to sleep, willing the headache away.

Liz. Deplorable1. The cop.

She flushed with the memory of everything, feeling tears press against her eyes and telling herself it was just the hangover making her brittle. She'd get over it. She and Liz would have dinner at Rhonda's. They would talk. It would all be normal. She would make the summer work, wait till school started, then pull the plug.

Finally unable to bear the heat, she crawled out of bed and put on some shorts. She brought Liz's gift into the kitchen and unwrapped it while coffee brewed. The bright-red wrapping paper crinkled loudly when she tore it and felt like an assault on her head. She knew she had to have a bottle of Advil somewhere in the house. It had been years since Rachel had gotten that drunk, and the fuzzy throb of the hangover made everything vague, as if she was locked in a nightmare.

The oak frame was simple but expensive. Liz never skimped on a gift. The photograph was of Rachel in Pete's last play, the one that had earned her reviews that proclaimed, "Goldberg's light is far too bright to stay hidden in Pineville. This reviewer expects to see her on Broadway someday." In the photo, Rachel posed in a spotlight, hands folded in front of her, face tilted toward the ceiling. Her curls hung loosely around her shoulders. She appeared taller than her five three, thanks to the angle of the camera. She was smiling, her face alive with the raw emotion she reserved for the stage. Pete had once commented, "You realize you only smile with half your face in real life?" She hadn't realized but was not surprised. She put the photo facedown on the counter then poured her coffee.

The light on her home answering machine had been accusing her with its insistent red blink for days. The only people who still used that number were her parents and people she knew from years before. She took a deep breath and hit Play.

The first message was her mother wishing her an early happy birthday. "I'm sure you'll be busy with friends on the day, so I wanted to try to reach you earlier. Give us a call. We miss you." The second was an old college friend. The third, her mother again.

"Rachel, dear. We wanted you to know that Gladys has had another stroke. They're keeping her in the nursing home, but she can't walk at all anymore. The doctors don't think she'll live too much longer. Your father and I thought you might want to come and say goodbye. We'd love to see you. It's been such a long time since you've visited. Call us."

"Like hell," she informed the answering machine. "I'm not flying all the way to California just to say goodbye to Gladys." She had taken to calling her grandmother and parents by their first names sometime in eighth grade. She couldn't remember exactly when, but she remembered how Gladys had hated it, which had been the initial motivation to continue through high school. Liz had recently suggested that it helped her feel less enmeshed in her family.

"You know," Liz had said. "You would probably be happier if you felt less need to keep them at arm's length all the time."

Rachel had been driving, which made it easy to not look at Liz when she answered. "I'm really getting sick of all that Al-Anon and therapy BS," she had said. "How can you be enmeshed with people you mostly avoid seeing?"

"The fact that you're so mad about it just proves my point," Liz had said. "You even do it with me."

Rachel had been trying to parallel park in front of the diner, so it took a minute for her to make sense of what Liz had said.

"Do what?" she'd asked as she tried for the second time to back into a spot between an SUV and a very new-looking Subaru.

"Keep me at a distance," Liz had said.

"*I'm* keeping *you* at a distance?" Rachel had said, pulling forward for a third try.

"Yes," Liz had said. "You're always protecting something. I don't even know what you feel half the time. You pretend you're fine when I know you're angry. You won't look at me when you say you love me. Now get out and let me park the damn car."

The conversation had left them both tense and careful with each other, ruining their last traditional Wednesday lunch of the school year. But there was probably something to Liz's theory. For one thing, as Liz had helpfully pointed out later, people didn't tend to avoid seeing family members they were comfortable around. Also, Rachel did sometimes insist that everything was great when inside she just wanted to punch something or someone.

Rachel hadn't been home since that painful visit when they had first put Gladys in the nursing home five years before. She still remembered the devastated look on her father's face when they said goodbye to Gladys that day, the moment when he didn't want to leave her there and Rachel had to remind him that they couldn't take care of her anymore. He'd stopped just before the open door of her room and turned to look at his mother. His entire body seemed to buckle, his crushed expression reminding Rachel of photos she'd seen from when he was a young boy. She'd taken his elbow and walked him to the elevator, repeating that it was okay, Gladys was okay there. He kept nodding as if he agreed, but they had to recall the elevator because he wouldn't get on at first. *Was I the only one who felt relief at the idea that Gladys would no longer consume every corner of my childhood home?*

Then there was Stephen. She shivered, even though Stephen hadn't been to her parents' house in years. At least, they'd never mentioned him, never said, "By the way, honey, we saw that friend of yours last week. Remember Stephen, who you used to play war with?"

Of course, while some kids played war, for Rachel and Stephen, it had been something else. She didn't want to be anywhere near him. She didn't like to think about him. It was those Facebook posts that had put him in her head. And Gladys. *Damn her.*

She deleted her mother's messages. Then, coffee in hand, she settled onto her couch to wait for Liz to text a time for dinner.

She would not look at Facebook.

———◆———

THEY WENT TO MARIA'S Taqueria.

"I know you're always looking for good Mexican like you had growing up," Liz said. "And turns out I'm not needed for summer school this year, and with Michael's job being so iffy... Rhonda's is just so pricey. Is that okay?"

"No problem," Rachel said. "I'm always up for good tacos."

But the bad pictures of parrots and men in sombreros and the menu on the wall behind the counter suggested she would not find what she wanted at Maria's.

After getting their food, which involved ordering then carrying it to the plastic booths themselves, they ate in silence. Rachel's taco shell crumbled when she picked it up, bleeding taco sauce onto her hand.

Yep, that's about right, Rachel thought. *Liz starts off looking like gourmet tapas, but it turns out that she's mediocre fast food.* She got up and visited the plastic-silverware dispenser for a fork.

"I'm really sorry," Liz said when Rachel sat down and began picking at the under-spiced beef. That taco sauce probably came out of a bottle. "I heard really good things about this place. It got a good write-up in the paper, and some of the women in my Jazzercise class were raving about it. They probably just don't know what good Mexican tastes like. I promise I'll take you to Rhonda's next week, after Michael gets paid. Or how about going into Syracuse for Erad Evans like we originally planned? You could get one of those chocolate towers where they write 'happy birthday' in chocolate." Liz used that husky bedroom voice that always got to Rachel.

On the drive to the restaurant, they had discussed the weather, politics, the new principal—"A woman," Liz gushed. "It's about time"—and the weather again—"I think that weather report was wrong. It's definitely going to rain later."

"So, my mother called," Rachel tried. Her head ached from the binge the night before, and her attempts to fill in the gaps—*how much did I drink before I took Jo home? What did I tell Jo? Did we actually have sex or just sleep together?*—had come up empty.

"Yeah?" Liz seemed fine with direct eye contact. Rachel stared at her plate.

"Apparently, Gladys is dying."

"Wasn't she dying last year?"

"Apparently this time, it's for real."

The year before, Rachel had gotten a similar call from her mother and decided that seeing Gladys one more time would give her closure. "I have to go see her," she'd told Liz. She'd had that nervous-energy feeling, like being backstage, waiting for a performance to start. She'd been drinking coffee and talking fast. Ever since her parents had called, she'd caught herself checking the mirror repeatedly, though she couldn't say what she was hunting for. She'd booked an early flight, and Liz had agreed to go with her to the hotel the night before, "Just to make sure you don't dive out of some tenth-floor window."

They'd had the hot tub in the pool area to themselves that night, and they kissed, and in the end, Rachel overslept and missed her flight. That was a good night. A fun night. They laughed together. They were always laughing together back then.

"Will you go?" Liz asked, keeping her gaze on Rachel and snapping her back to the present.

"No." Rachel watched a young woman drag a toddler into the restaurant. "Yes. Maybe." The smell of spiced beef was suddenly too much. She put her fork down. "Anyway," she said.

"Anyway," Liz agreed.

"Thank you for the picture."

"I thought you'd like it," Liz said, nodding as if in agreement with herself. "You don't have many pictures of yourself performing."

"It isn't like dancing," Rachel pointed out. Liz had photos of herself mid-pirouette or flying through the air all over the wall behind her desk in her classroom. Rachel couldn't say whether her house was similarly adorned, since she'd never been there. "But it's nice. Thank you."

"I know," Liz said. "But you're so good. You're such an amazing actor. You should celebrate that." She paused. "Do you understand why I was upset this morning? I know I don't have a right to expect monogamy, considering... But finding you like that, with someone else. You have to know it was upsetting."

Rachel nodded, though part of her enjoyed the hurt look in Liz's eyes. "It isn't as if you're monogamous with me."

Liz reached a hand across the table, palm up, but Rachel folded hers in her lap. *No, I'm not just going to let you hold my hand and everything is better. You have to decide.*

"I'll make it right," Liz proclaimed as though it was an idea that had only just come to her. "I'll end it with Michael. I'll tell him I'm leaving. Just let me get through this summer. He's applied for that promotion at work, and everything's kind of uncertain and stressful."

A blush of hope welled in Rachel. *Is there something different in how Liz said it this time? Maybe this morning had been a good thing, just what she needed to realize I meant it when I said I can't do this anymore.* "Right after the summer break?" God, she sounded like a four-year-old who'd been told she could have ice cream in just five more minutes.

"Right after. I promise."

"Promise-promise?" Rachel let a smile play across her face. A half smile maybe, but still.

"Promise-promise," Liz agreed. "This food really is awful, isn't it?"

They both laughed.

That was the thing with Liz. They might have been having an unexpectedly lousy meal a day late for Rachel's birthday, but they could look at each other in just that way, Liz could say it out loud, and they could laugh, and everything would feel... just... correct. Sympatico. That was hard to find. At least Rachel had never found it before. Pete could keep telling her all the reasons she needed to leave Liz, but it wasn't that simple.

They held hands as they walked out, and Liz rolled her eyes and pulled Rachel into a full-on, tongue-in kiss when the harried mother gave them a dirty look and moved her chair to block her toddler's view of them.

"As if that baby is going to have an opinion about gay marriage," she whispered in Rachel's ear.

The woman stayed hunched in front of her child and did not turn to look at them again, and Rachel noticed that her social-media nightmare had receded to a muted place in her thoughts, like the final twinge of a mostly healed injury.

On the drive home, Liz held Rachel's hand across the gearshift. Rachel let her and tried to ignore Pete's voice in her head, reminding her that Liz had made such promises before.

Liz dropped Rachel at the corner two houses down from her house. She'd done that the last few times she drove, saying it was too much of a pain to turn around in Rachel's driveway with the neighbor's cars parked on the road. "I nearly hit that SUV last week," she'd claimed the first time. Rachel was afraid to wonder if Liz missed the lengthy goodbye kisses they used to share in her driveway.

A car pulled up behind them, and the driver honked. Rachel accepted Liz's peck on her lips and got out of the car. She waited for the taillights of Liz's car to disappear around the corner before crossing the street. *Was I so hungover that I forgot to turn the outside light on?* Her house looked abandoned in the dark—the nearest streetlight was on the next block.

But she must have turned on the porch light. She always remembered. It was such a habit, so automatic that she sometimes even turned it on on Saturday morning when she was just going to the gym for an hour.

She stopped in the dark in the middle of the empty road and looked around her. One neighbor never used a porch light, but the one to the right of her house was lit up in front and back. The lone streetlight flickered on the corner, so it was not a power failure.

It was fine. She just forgot. She was hungover and distracted and forgot. But still, her heart raced, and she dug her phone out of her purse, just in case. All the brutal words she'd read on Facebook came rushing back. They had her address. She finished crossing the street slowly, watching for anything out of place.

By the time she got to the first of three steps leading up to her front porch, she knew she had not forgotten. The place where the lightbulb was supposed to be was empty, except for a few shards of broken glass. She used the flashlight app on her phone and aimed it at the porch floor. Slivers of broken glass glinted at her in the beam. She scrolled the flashlight around her yard and into the bushes on either side then aimed it at the door.

Someone had painted a glaring red swastika on her front door. It covered most of the door, bright against the forest green she had chosen when she bought the house four years before. It seemed alive, like the arms of the symbol could leap from the door, wrap themselves around her neck, and squeeze the life out of her. She choked on her breath.

She bolted up the block, not stopping until she hit the corner. Headlights approached. She doubled over, panting and trembling while a gray station wagon slowed for the stop sign at the end of her block. *Is it them? Should I run the other way?* Whoever had done that to her door had to have been long gone, but she stayed crouched in the shadows until the car's rear lights receded.

Most of the houses were asleep, and Rachel wanted the safety of a door to knock on if the vandals returned. She kept walking past dark houses, activating the occasional motion-sensor light. Finally, she found a brightly lit corner and a house with downstairs lights on and visible through the bay window.

She stared into the stranger's living room, sending deep breaths through her shaking body. The television inside flickered, creating shadows on beige walls. A car revved past her, radio blaring, and her vision faded to a point of light.

Her hands shook so she could barely push the numbers on her phone. The 911 operator sounded young and wooden, as though reading from a script. "Stay where you are," the woman said. "I'll keep you on the phone until the police arrive." Rachel hung up and called Liz.

But Liz didn't answer. Rachel left a shaky message. *Who else can I call?*

Pete's phone went to voicemail. Then she remembered his Provincetown trip. He and Stan were probably drunk at the Crown and Anchor or Boat Slip by now. She imagined them there, hanging out at the bar, dancing, flirting. She hung up without leaving a message.

She scrolled through other numbers, more to distract herself and calm the shaking than because she thought there might be someone else to call. *Ronnie. Who is Ronnie?* She kept going, working backwards from R.

And there, in the J's, was a phone number she had not expected to find. Only a first name. She must have entered it last night, or maybe Jo the cop had put it in for her. *Did I leave Jo alone with my phone?*

Well. Jo is a cop, right?

Hands still shaking, she pushed Send to dial the number. It was a bad idea, but it was Jo's job, and she would know what to do. The phone rang in Rachel's ear. Through the window of the strangers' house, the television turned off, and she could almost hear the happy couple inside the warm room, discussing their day and preparing for bed.

"Hello?" Jo's tone was kind, and Rachel felt a little bit calmer.

Chapter 8
Gladys

The nursing home was full of glaring lights and people in and out of Gladys's room and commotion, and she had a roommate. One morning, though, she woke up, and the roommate was an immobile lump on the bed and had stopped yelling that she'd been kidnapped and calling her sons to come rescue her. Finally, the staff came and took the roommate away, and Gladys was alone.

Her son, Aaron, visited sometimes, and sometimes he brought his wife, Rose, who stared at the clock and wouldn't look at Gladys during the whole visit. Heathen. Rose was a heathen. She was not a good Jew.

Her granddaughter, Rachel, never came. Rachel was far away, Aaron said. Too far to visit. Gladys wrote Rachel letters, but she never heard back—or if she did, she didn't remember.

Gladys thought she could hear coyotes from out in the desert sometimes, or maybe she dreamed them. Her memory wasn't always right. Aaron told her she had dementia, but she forgot that was why she was sometimes in the nursing home and sometimes back in Illinois and sometimes in Aaron's house in Carlsbad when Rachel was still young.

In the Carlsbad house, where Gladys had lived before the nursing home, coyotes often startled her awake with high-pitched screams. She would sit up, pressing her hands to her pounding chest. The first night it happened, she woke Aaron, insisting there were terrified children somewhere, that they needed saving. He told her go back to bed, but she couldn't until she checked on Rachel, who slept through the howls, peaceful and still like she never was when awake.

Even once Gladys understood what the coyotes were, the yips and howls set her heart racing, and she could never return to sleep. When they started, she would climb out of bed, pull the top part of her nightgown away from her breasts to air out the damp, sticky feeling, and walk barefoot to the window, where she pulled aside the curtain.

———◉———

"WHY DO YOU NEED THEM?" Rose had asked the day she hung those curtains on Gladys's window. "We're far from the street. Someone would have to walk down the driveway to the front of the house and want to look in before they would see into your room. Let in some sunlight." She let out a brittle laugh that reminded Gladys of herself, right after Joseph died. It made her want to smack Rose.

Gladys would tolerate the brightness of the California days, but the nights were dark with coyotes and who knew what else. The days were full of Rachel, a granddaughter who alternately enraged her and crushed her heart. Full of Aaron and Rose, who refused to raise their daughter properly. Gladys felt needed in the daytime. But at night, Gladys wanted thick brown curtains to blot out the night.

———◉———

ON THIS NIGHT, SHE pulled a corner of the curtain aside and stared through the glass. Everything wore a dusky glow there at night, like the aftermath of an explosion, as if the air had been poisoned. Standing in the dark, she could make out a little of her own reflection. Her eyes appeared flat, like finger painted smears across the glass. The dog was nowhere to be seen.

For five nights in a row, the dog had come, but only occasionally before that, to knock the garbage over and sniff around inside. Four nights before, Gladys had left it food, taking a scoopful from Lucky's bag of Purina. She had taken food out for the dog every night since, and finally, it had seemed to look for the food, just as Gladys stood, looking for the dog.

The family dog, Lucky, was always climbing in her lap, all forty pounds of him, and she was always pushing him off. Rachel laughed when this happened.

"Lucky, you know Grandma doesn't like you. C'mere, Lucky. C'mon."

Lucky had been annoying, driveling, drooling, shedding, panting, licking. "But against any of the children of Israel, a dog shall not whet his tongue," Gladys would say to Lucky. The Pasuk was meant to protect, but it was Rachel who'd dragged him away.

The stray dog was not like Lucky at all. The night before, she had remained on the porch after putting the food down. The dog stood back, ears perked, watching, and when she stepped forward, it scuttled out into the road, eyeing her. Something about that drew Gladys to it, making her think of the dogs that held their tongues in Egypt so that Jews could escape. That dog could have been one of those, silent and timid.

Gladys stayed on the porch, suspending her breath and compressing every muscle for stillness. The dog waited, twitched its ears, waited, sniffed air, then crept forward, shy and watchful. Like a beaten child, it crawled onto the porch, and like a thief, it grabbed one nugget of food then bolted across the street. She experienced it in her body, a heat in her belly at winning that moment, the dog so close she could have touched its head.

The dog's ribs showed, its hip bones jutted, and she remembered old news stories about concentration camp survivors dying after liberation from eating food their bodies could not absorb. She would be careful not to overfeed the dog.

Gladys pressed her face against the window and tried to shut out the coyotes. The Torah forbade keeping an animal that would scare others, she'd once told Rose, such as barking dogs or dogs like Lucky, who was all over everyone.

But the dog on the porch tingled her scalp, flushed her skin. Taming the dog drove her through the empty night. There was a chamber deep inside where her sister, Esther, danced and laughed, where her father kissed her goodbye before school, where Joseph, so beautiful, bent over his Hebrew lesson—Joseph, her youngest son, who looked like his father and gave her hope. Aaron was like nobody she had ever met, with his scrawny body and already balding head. He could never even throw a ball unless it was those silly foam balls he was always hiding up his shirt sleeves.

"Who is the father?" Ira had asked when he came in to see her cuddling the new baby.

"You are," she'd told him. "You're the father."

He'd stayed for a minute, gazing down at Gladys and the infant. Then he turned away and left.

Aaron sometimes looked a certain way or said a certain thing, and the pit was there. "We could track down what happened, Mother. Don't you want to find out what happened to your family in Germany? Don't you wonder?"

She skirted the edges of the pit, but sometimes she stumbled and sank. When that happened, the chest pain started, her jaw clenched and hurt, and the spinning pressure of grief attacked her.

But when that dog appeared in the night, poised to run away but hungry and longing, the fact that she had something to give it, something it needed, seemed to fill the pit. The thought of caressing its fur somehow obliterated the pit for a second or two, long enough that she could find the prayer, the ritual, the words that made God hear.

Jews should not keep dogs, she thought. People treated dogs like they were God. She'd once seen a bumper sticker on a red Volkswagen, a *German* Volkswagen. She had been riding to temple with Rose, her knees aching, folded tight in the cramped passenger seat. Rose chewed gum with her mouth open, tapping a rhythm on the steering wheel with the heel of her hand and smacking away with her mouth, and ahead, creeping like a death march, was the red Volkswagen with a sticker on the bumper: "God spelled backwards is Dog." Disgusting.

But the dog was not God. It was something she watched for at night and desired to win like a prize in the fair. Desire was a part of the pit she usually avoided. Sometimes, that was impossible. Sometimes, she squeezed her body, holding everything inside like she was putting her thumb on the end of the hose, bracing like she had when they practiced with bombs at Camp Pendleton and the windows rattled, stiffening like she did when she didn't shout as Rachel went too far into the waves. The night, the dark, the coyote howls, and the dog awakened her desire, and she could not suppress it.

She stood at the window and watched for the dog, thinking about how she would feed it and touch it and win it.

Finally, there it was, yellow eyes in the dark, a barely visible movement dipping into a wash of moonlight then fading into shadow, and she experienced a sudden, unexpected impulse to open her window, lean out, shout, and frighten it away. *How dare you expect from me! I have nothing to give you! Nothing!* But she put on her slippers and retrieved the bowl.

A muted nightlight in a hall outlet guided her feet to the kitchen. The kitchen table, counters, and breakfast bar lurked like predators with their sharp corners. In the dark, the kitchen seemed abandoned and sad to her. An erratic drip-drip in the porcelain sink distracted her, and she put the bowl on the counter to squeeze the cold-water faucet tight. The sponge smelled of mold and rotten food, and she grabbed it from the sink, sniffed it, then carried it to the trash, dangling it away from her body, clutching it with two fingers.

The smell transported her to the basement of the Michigan house, where no amount of bleach would erase the creeping black slime that invaded the walls. When it rained, she would taste the mold. It made her sweat and cramp until everything spun and she fled upstairs to the bathroom, where she crouched in the shower, gasping for air.

She stiffened under the burden of the memory of the rocking chair creaking in an irritating rhythm she couldn't bring herself to stop, the basement odor wafting through with the heat, then sitting in the dark in another house at another time, waiting for Aaron to come through the front door. Ira had been somewhere alone and locked inside, and she'd felt the weight of the mold on her chest. She remembered how she had imagined Aaron's face would have looked when he realized they weren't there at his magic show, watching him perform for the first time those magic tricks he'd worked so hard on. She'd imagined him bewildered then determined then closed. There had been no way to explain at that age—he had only been fourteen.

She'd sat in the dark, rocking, but when the front door creaked open and Aaron was home, she went silently to her room and never mentioned that she had waited. There was nothing to say. When Joseph had come to them with his despair and told them he wished he was dead, there had been no question. They had stayed with him and done everything to make sure he was safe.

Aaron looked so much like his father.

The dog was a German shepherd, which disturbed Gladys. Ira never would have understood. *How do you feed a dog that might have been used against your family?* He wouldn't have said that, of course. But his face, his shoulders turning away, and the mumbling prayers said for God but really for her all would have amounted to an accusation.

She accused herself: *How can you feed this dog?* But still, she opened the cupboard, thrust her hand into the bag, and dropped nuggets of dog food into the cracked bowl. Maybe feeding dogs earned their silence, so they didn't announce the fleeing Jews. Maybe they fought for instead of against. Maybe one won them over, and that was how one survived. That was what she told herself, though it seemed a poor excuse. But it was better than the truth, which was that she *wanted* to feed the dog.

Sometimes, she studied Rose's friends, the women from the reading group, drinking coffee and laughing in the living room on Thursday nights, the playdate mothers honking their station wagons' horns for Rachel then stopping later to share a glass of wine. Gladys assessed, studied, evaluated their eyes, mannerisms, expressions. Shifty eyed, false, genuine. *Would this one turn us in? Would that one hide us? Does she have an attic? A hidden room in the garage?* Rose did not seem to notice, and some of her friends had German names.

Gladys carried the food to the front door. On the other side was the dog. She would open the door, and it would run across the street then stop and wait, watching. She would crouch and place the bowl on the porch. She would watch the dog. The dog would watch her. She would feel the moment of watching, the heat in her body. The moment would feel like winning something, and the weight on her chest would recede, and the dark would not be so full of sharp edges.

Chapter 9
Rachel
2016

Rachel sat hunched on the curb and waited for her pulse to slow, waited to breathe, waited for the cops or Jo or the people who had painted a swastika on her door. She ached with the waiting.

Jo pulled up in blue car and parked. She rolled the passenger window down. "Why don't you get in the car?" she offered, and Rachel did.

In the car, she pressed her feet firmly against the floor to stop the shakes. She remembered the soft feeling of Jo's arms around her, a slow dance somewhere before the blackout hit her. She remembered the taste of wine on Jo's lips and the minty smell of her hair.

Jo kept her hands firmly on the steering wheel. "So, why did someone put a swastika on your door? Do you have a secret life riling up the white supremacists?"

The patrol car arrived before Rachel could finish the whole long story about Pete's play and the posts on social media. Jo nodded and seemed very cop-like, but still, Rachel felt relieved at the arrival of the rotating lights, the man with a gun on his hip.

Jo seemed less relieved when the officer knocked on her window. "Greg," she said for Rachel's ears before she opened the car door. "Fucking Greg." Then she and Rachel got in the back seat of the patrol car.

"Sounds like kids to me," Greg said when Rachel had finished with the formal statement. "Probably not anything to worry about. Most of those people harassing you online are gonna stay at their computers." He turned his palms up in a dismissive gesture. "They don't escalate beyond harassment. You probably aren't in danger."

Rachel looked at Jo's set jaw. "That isn't true," Jo said. "These people could really escalate. This was a hate crime. We're supposed to call the FBI."

Greg had turned forward in the front seat to write some notes, and when he looked back, Rachel caught the flicker of condescension that shadowed his eyes. "Or it was some kids and a bucket of paint. No need to blow things out of proportion," he said, his tone chiding. "No need to get hysterical about a little paint on a door."

Jo's mouth opened, but she didn't say anything. Rachel sent her a questioning look, and she shrugged. "He's probably right," she mumbled.

Rachel swallowed her fear. *It's probably fine,* she repeated in her mind. *It's probably just kids.*

"I'll drive you home and check out the house," the officer said in a voice that sounded more like he was talking to an annoying younger brother than to someone who had just had her house vandalized.

Rachel turned to Jo. "Can you?"

Jo nodded at Greg, who looked at her then at Rachel. "Whatever," he said. "I got plenty to do."

Jo and Rachel stood on the side of the road until car was gone. Then they both climbed back into Jo's car.

When Jo turned the engine, the radio came on, and Rachel heard a snippet of Garrison Keilor playing "Guy Noir" before Jo turned it off. "Greg is a racist asshole." Her voice was tight, her fists clenched around the steering wheel.

Rachel wondered whether it had only been the night before when Jo had held her on the dance floor, gone home with her, and touched her with those same hands.

"I've done patrol with him. Nonstop right-wing radio all frigging night."

Rachel stared out at the passing night, the dark houses with people sleeping in them.

"The FBI should be called in on this case," Jo said. "I can do it. I can take you to the station to make a second report."

But the numbness was setting in, and it would have taken a whole lot of energy to go to the station to file a report and talk to the FBI. They would probably blow it off just like Greg had. *What really happened? Nothing. Just some paint on the door. What did you do to make it happen? Nothing. Nothing. Nothing.*

Rachel was not a baby. She could handle it. "No thanks," Rachel said. "I just want to go home." She stared hard at the phone in her lap, willing it to ring.

"Are you sure?" Jo sounded angry. "This is a pretty big deal. Hate crimes shouldn't be ignored."

"I'm sure," Rachel said. Her phone rang just as they pulled into her driveway, blasting the familiar opening notes to "I Could Have Danced All Night." She felt Jo's body tense beside her when she answered.

Rachel cupped the phone to her mouth. "Liz." She felt pressure in her eyes. "You wouldn't believe what happened." Jo cut the engine but kept the headlights on. "When can you come? I really need you."

Liz said something, but it sounded vague and far away. Rachel heard a TV in the background, a kid calling "Mommy." The headlight beam highlighted the red paint on her door. The paint still looked wet, red droplets seeping from the swastika's corners.

"I need a house key," Jo said. Rachel put the phone against her shoulder and dug in her purse, hunting for the keys she hadn't gotten far enough to pull out before. She tried to extract the house key from the ring, but her hand shook, making her drop the phone. She could hear Liz's tinny voice saying something to one of the kids. *Is Liz even listening?* Rachel handed the whole key ring to Jo and picked up her phone.

"Stay in the car," Jo told Rachel. "I'll check things out."

Rachel nodded and turned, startled when Jo opened the back door and pulled two rubber gloves out of a box on the back seat. Of course. Fingerprints.

"Can you come? I really need you." She watched Jo's long, purposeful strides through the dusty glow of headlights as she walked toward the front door.

"What's going on?" Liz asked. "Not now. Mommy's on the phone."

Rachel tried to slow her breathing, tried to find the words. "My door. They painted my door."

"Who painted your door? What are you talking about? Not now, Franky."

In the headlight beam, Jo climbed the porch steps. She stooped to pick something up.

"Swastika. They painted a swastika on my door. Can you come?" Jo disappeared into the house.

"I can't come right away," Liz said. "I need a few hours."

"Just come when you can. Please." Rachel pressed End and got out of the car.

She approached slowly. Jo wouldn't find anything. It was fine. Just some kids and paint. She took the first step. The front door hung slightly open, as if the house were grimacing. She could see that Jo had turned most of the downstairs lights on. She went up the next step, feeling the crunch of the broken lightbulb beneath her feet. She looked at the swastika, the slashes of red marking her house. She noticed some smaller writing on the bottom half of the door and squatted for a closer look. It had been done with a red marker rather than paint. Some of the letters were faded, as if the marker had been running out of ink. It was hard to make out at first: "Jew dykes go to the ovens."

Rachel pressed her hands against her stomach and breathed into her abdomen. Her heart skittered at the sound of footsteps behind her. She gave herself a second for her brain to absorb that it was Jo coming down from upstairs before she straightened and turned away from the image.

"Liz is going to come over," Rachel said.

"Soon, I hope?" Jo asked. Her eyes glinted red in the flare of a passing taillight, and Rachel felt herself sway.

"As soon as she can."

"I could wait with you, if you want." Jo's face looked warm, even concerned, and part of Rachel wanted that, someone who would hug her and hold her and worry that she was okay.

But she shook her head. "No, you've already done too much. You shouldn't have to wait. Liz'll be here really soon." She drew her shoulders back, straightening her posture, finding the role. *Strong-woman part. You can do this.*

"Well, okay. Call me if you need to. And can you use the back door? I'll try to get someone to come check for fingerprints. It may already be too late, but..."

Rachel nodded.

"Oh," Jo said, "I found this." She put her hand out, open palmed, and Rachel saw her mezuzah, old silver that needed polishing. She took it from Jo.

"I don't even remember hanging this," she said. "It isn't like I'm religious." She felt a bitter laugh gush out before she could stop it.

Jo smiled at her. She had a nice smile, and Rachel was a fool not to let her stay. "Lock your doors," Jo said. "Call if you need me or if you reconsider coming to the station or if you want me to bring in the FBI. I don't think Greg is going to follow up." Then she walked toward her car.

Rachel studied the mezuzah the vandals had apparently yanked off her doorjamb, vaguely wondering why she had lied to Jo. She remembered exactly when she had hung it. It was the one time she had let her parents visit her in Pineville after she first bought the house. She and her father hung it together while her mother looked on and offered commentary. "Too tilted. Too high. Too low. There. Perfect." Her father had touched it and then his lips on the way in, but Rachel never did. Not once. She saw no reason.

Rachel entered the house through the front door because strong women didn't worry about fingerprints or follow up. They fought their own battles.

Chapter 10
Stephen
2016

Stephen nearly left the SPCA without looking at the dogs. The sound of barking and howling and the smell of the place—bleach with a hint of urine and dog shit underneath—reminded him of Iraq and all those feral dogs they had to shoot. One never knew what diseases they might have carried.

He followed a fat Mexican woman to the back, where the kennels were. In the first cage, a poodle mix yipped and pawed at the bars. Stephen studied the woman's frizzy ponytail so he wouldn't see the dog's needy eyes. After that, they walked past pit bulls and pit bulls and pit bulls. Then, at the end, in a separate room, he saw it: a German shepherd.

"This girl is a little shy," the woman said. Her tone was affectionate, and she looked at the dog like she wanted to take it home herself.

She let him take her for a walk. Outside, the dog skulked with her tail between legs, ears down, and an embarrassed expression on her face. She didn't pull. A brief look of pleasure flashed in her eyes when he stroked the coarse fur on her head. Then, as if she suddenly remembered she was afraid, she jerked away and dropped her belly closer to the ground. Part of him wanted to yell at her, "You're a German shepherd. Act like one!" But there was something about his brief ability to make something else happy, even for just a second, that felt good, so he stroked her head again.

The dog Stephen trained with his grandpa when he was a kid had been a German shepherd. His grandpa had been patient and kind with the dog and had only yelled at Stephen once, when Stephen lost his patience and swatted the dog on the butt. "Hitting won't work," his grandfather said. "The dog has to want to sit for you. Ask him again."

Stephen did. The dog never sat for him that day. But for his grandpa, every time.

When his grandpa was dying in the hospital, and Stephen was there so much of the time, his mother got rid of the dog. He still remembered the day Dieter disappeared. His grandfather had just gone back in the hospital, and he overheard his mother talking on the phone to his Aunt Margaret.

"Looks like the old bastard is finally going to kick." Then she laughed a strange, bitter laugh that Stephen had only heard one other time, the day his real father had shown up, driving a shiny red Chevy convertible, and his mother asked how he could afford the car when he couldn't afford child support then laughed in that same way.

Stephen still didn't understand how his mother could have lived in his grandpa's house for free and still talk about him that way. Even she admitted her father had saved them.

That day on the phone, she said, "I guess I shouldn't complain. I mean with Mom dead, Stevie and I would probably be on the streets if he didn't take us in. But I'll sure be glad to have him gone. And I worry about him with Stevie. I mean, I don't think he'd touch a boy, but geez. I'll just be glad when it's over."

Later that day, she dropped Stephen at the hospital, and when he got back home, Dieter was gone. He asked what happened, and she just said, "That was your grandfather's dog. I can't be taking care of him."

He never found out what she had done with the dog. He had his suspicions, though. That stray Gladys was feeding looked exactly like Dieter. He figured his mother threw Dieter out of the house to fend for itself, and Gladys wound up feeding him. She wouldn't have bothered to drive it to the SPCA or try to find it a new home.

"I want the dog," he told the Mexican woman, whose name tag said Vanessa.

She thrust a clipboard at him and offered a sad smile. "She needs a good home. She needs to be loved."

He had to leave a lot blank. He didn't have a veterinarian or any other pets. Fenced yard? When he was a kid, dogs went wherever they wanted. Nobody had fenced yards. Under references, he put his mother's name. He had to consult his phone contacts to find her latest address at the trailer park. And he couldn't find a phone number for her. Then there was the cost: three hundred and fifty bucks to rescue a dog from euthanasia.

Vanessa studied his application, frowning. "We'll see," she said doubtfully. "You've really never owned any pets? Not even a fish?" He and his friends used to call people like her "beaners." This beaner had no right to tell him whether or not he could have a dog. But he shook his head. He considered mentioning Dieter, but Dieter had been his grandfather's dog, and he didn't know if that counted. He had expected to leave with the dog, but he would have to see his mother. He would need money to pay for the dog, and she had to give him a reference. The thought of seeing her and her new husband made him tired and angry, but he couldn't think of anybody else who would give him a reference.

He said goodbye to the dog in her cage before leaving. She pressed her body against the bars in the back of the cage and gave him a furtive look with her sad brown eyes.

———◦———

STEPHEN FOUND THE TRAILER park with only one incident, an asshole standing on the side of the road with a sign that read Support Our Troops. Bring Them Home.

Stephen rolled down his window and hollered at the guy, "You don't know a goddamn thing about it! You don't have a fucking clue!" Then he slammed his foot down in a tire-squealing escape before he could yield to the impulse to attack the guy. He leaned toward the passenger seat and reached under so he could brush the cool metal of his grandfather's Mauser. The feel of it always evoked his grandfather, the smell of cigarettes and whiskey, the calm feeling of being loved, sitting in the attic, listening to stories. He breathed.

He navigated through a rat's maze of endless, identical tin houses that dead-ended in neat little circles edged with avocado trees, streets with names like Cypress and Garland, veering off in all directions, mutts that ran out barking, backyard trash cans, and sad-looking shrubs carefully placed to hide the shiny metal bottoms of the trailers. By the time he found 57 Pine Street, he was vibrating with frustration. He gripped the steering wheel hard so he wouldn't lose control and crash the Volkswagen into the stupid pink-flamingo lawn ornaments in front of his mother's new home.

He parked in the road behind an ancient black Volvo, lit up in the car, and sat for another twenty minutes, staring at the picture window that jutted from the front of the trailer like an afterthought stuck on a child's dollhouse. He stayed there until his heart stopped exploding in his chest and the pot had dulled the sharp edges of his thoughts.

The man who answered the door did not resemble any man Stephen's mother had previously married or lived with. He was beardless, short-haired, clear of any tattoos, and dressed, at three o'clock on Sunday afternoon, as if he was about to attend a business meeting. Plus, he smelled like aftershave instead of cigarettes or whisky.

"Can I help you?"

Stephen made a point of looking the man in the eyes and not blinking. Dressing in a suit didn't mean he wasn't just another asshole like all the other assholes. "I'm looking for my mother."

"Oh." The man stepped back then forward and offered a hand. "You must be Stephen. I'm Jeff."

Stephen nodded but did not accept the offer to shake on it. "Is my mother here?"

The man stepped into the trailer and called, "Heidi, Stephen's here!" as if they were all living in a trailer-park version of *The Brady Bunch*. He stepped aside, gesturing into the neatly carpeted, clean living room.

Stephen crossed the space between the front door and the cheap blue colonial sofa with his eyes down, remembering crushed beer bottles, old Del Taco food wrappers, and smoldering cigarette butts from his childhood years. His feet flattened a trail from front door to sofa in the green shag. The man disappeared into a yellow-lit kitchen, and Stephen perched on the edge of the sofa, listening to the clattering sounds of something happening in the kitchen. The trailer smelled like one of those plug-ins that tried to make it seem that cookies were baking. Stephen fought down nausea.

Jeff, hubby number whatever, finally emerged with a tray of cheese and crackers. He asked what Stephen wanted to drink and frowned when Stephen said beer. There was a sound of drawers slamming in a back room and water running. Everything echoed in the trailer.

"We don't have beer," he explained. "Will juice be okay?"

"Coffee," Stephen tried, and the man shook his head.

"How about some black tea?"

Stephen accepted the tea in a fragile white cup that he could break with one hand if he wanted. He sipped, curling his fingers around the thin handle and studying the asshole, who stood in the open doorway between the living room and hall.

Finally, his mother emerged, swirling into the room in a long yellow skirt and flat sandals, her gray hair in a ponytail behind. She seemed china-doll thin. Her face looked naked and old without the overdone rouge and lipstick that used to make him think she was a movie star. When she squeezed past the husband, she went on tiptoes to kiss him on the cheek then smiled at Stephen, revealing a row of perfect white teeth. No gaps and chips, no flashes of silver, no closed-mouth smile to hide the fact that some uncle had recently knocked another tooth on the floor. Dentures, he decided, although it was hard to be sure.

She sat on a rocker adjacent to the sofa and examined Stephen as if he were a fossil she had discovered on an archeology dig. "You look okay," she finally announced. "I've been reading about Iraq and the soldiers and what's happening to them. You don't look that different."

An explosive impulse to break something surged through his body. Stephen wanted to scream at her that she had never really seen him before, and she certainly didn't see him now, but his anger made him incoherent.

"I'll go buy some coffee," Jeff said and stepped toward the front door.

Stephen's mother jumped out of her chair like a teenager to kiss him goodbye before he left. Then she sat across from Stephen. "I'm so glad you came," she said. "I've been worrying about you." Outside, a car, probably the old Volvo, started with a whining shriek.

Stephen didn't know what to do with this worrying mother, this stranger who looked into his eyes instead of studying the floor, who walked a straight line, who couldn't give him a beer or even a cup of coffee, and who might very well kick him out of this metal-box home if he asked for a joint. She stood again and disappeared into the kitchen, where he heard water running. He knew how to handle a drunken mother, a drugged mother, a get-out-of-my-face-I'm-busy mother.

She returned with a glass of water, sat, sipped, crossed her legs, and giggled. At least she still giggled, that stupid you're-so-powerful-and-I'm-so-weak giggle that used to hook the uncles when he was a kid.

Finally, she said, "So, tell me what you've been doing since you got back. And what was Iraq like? You never answered my emails."

Stephen remembered the nearly daily emails, which he'd deleted immediately. He had stopped reading them after her final drunken essay on why he should come home and take care of her—the message had triggered such an intense feeling of helplessness that he had to sit on his hands all night so he wouldn't take his weapon to the nearest village and start shooting people. The last email she had sent was her wedding announcement. He had found her change of address and put it in his phone and ignored the rest.

"Yeah, well, it wasn't like I could come to your wedding—what was it anyway, number six?" The need to use words as if they were weapons was more powerful than the guilt that surfed along the edges of his thoughts. He wanted to draw blood and was happy to see the wince that soured her fake serene smile.

"This one is different. Jeff is special. He helped me get off booze and drugs."

Stephen laughed. "Whatever, Mom. I think I liked you better on booze."

She drained the water out of the glass and stood. "I've been reading about post-traumatic stress disorder. Is that what's wrong with you?"

No, Mother. You're what's wrong with me.

She returned to the kitchen with her water glass and came back holding a magazine, which she handed to him. *The Watchtower*, the cover said. A white bird soared through puffy clouds. "Instinct Guides Birds," it said next to the picture. "What Guides Man?"

When she reached across his lap to open the magazine and point at the table of contents, he noticed her clipped, unpainted fingernails, which would have been unheard of in his childhood. He remembered long hours spent in hotel rooms before they moved in with his grandfather, him on the bed watching cartoons, her leaning against the headboard, filing and painting her nails. He'd always ended up turning the volume off and watching the Road Runner silently escape his pursuers, because the combination of nail polish smell and noise overwhelmed his senses.

She tapped at the page impatiently: "Coping With Post-Traumatic Stress Disorder." He read the other titles: "Does God Really Care About Us?" and "How Can You Benefit from Godly Principles?" He pushed her hand and the magazine away. *The Watchtower* drifted and landed softly on the shag carpet. He imagined throwing himself off the couch and storming out the door, but the couch had wrapped tight arms around his body and would not let go.

He used words instead, keeping his voice soft, pushing down the rage. "Come on, Mom. When did you get religious? You finally found God? You gave up booze and drugs and moved in with some new asshole? Did he beat you up with God instead of fists?"

A distant part of him saw the twist of his mother's mouth, the tears in her watery blue eyes, the way she reached down and retrieved *The Watchtower* then rolled it into a cone in her lap.

When he lunged to free himself from the couch, he lost his balance, nearly tripped over the coffee table, and nearly landed in his mother's lap.

She screamed once. "No," she said. Then, "Stephen." And she was up out of the rocker, wrapping her arms around him, holding and rocking her body against him. Against his will, he felt his body relax in her arms like he was five years old and she was comforting him after her fight with an uncle. Her hair smelled like strawberries, and he fought the urge to bury his nose in it, regained his balance, and jerked away.

"I am not going to cry in your arms or any of that bullshit," he said. "This is not a fucking movie." He sidestepped away from her, avoiding the couch, the coffee table. Everything about the visit seemed artificial—there was probably a plastic sink, a Betty Crocker cake machine in the kitchen. The need to escape competed with a need to break his mother open, crack her like an egg to expose the rot under the surface of her shiny new life. He did neither but instead stayed, focusing on her pale face.

Her arms slowly descended to hang brokenly at her side. His body swirled with need he couldn't contain, thoughts he couldn't grab hold of, everything building toward explosion. When his mother collapsed into her chair, as if she thought he was done, he grabbed the white teacup off the coffee table and threw it hard at the bay window, where it detonated with a brief dissatisfying powder of amber liquid and paper-thin white shards. Tears streaked his mother's cheeks, and the gnawing in his gut reminded him of the stomachaches he used to get when an uncle was beating her up and Stephen cowered in his room instead of protecting her.

He sat down, panting. "I'm sorry," he said, though he wasn't. He felt nothing in response to her tears except an empty knowledge that he *should* have felt something, that a normal person would have felt guilty. Hell, a normal person would have felt happy to see that she'd gotten her shit together, found a nice man, stopped the booze and drugs. "I'm sorry," he said a second time, hoping the repetition would make it true.

When she just kept crying and avoided looking at him, he decided on the truth. "Look, I came here to tell you I used your name as a reference at the SPCA. And I need a phone number that works so I can give it to them. Also, I need help to pay for it. It costs money to get it from the pound. Do you have money? Can you give me some money for the dog? Then I'll leave and you can go to church or whatever it is you do now."

She shook her head, sniffled, then wiped the back of her arm across her nose. "I was so lonely after you left. I just drank and drank. I wound up in the hospital from internal bleeding. It was bad. These people. They helped me. I don't drink anymore. Or do drugs." She sounded as proud as if she had won an award.

After Grandpa died, Stephen remembered, she'd had a bout of drinking too much, more than usual even for her, out with a different man every night. After she came home, he would go up to the attic and sit, cradling one of his grandfather's guns, listening to the bed frame pound rhythmically against the wall in his mother's room, the grunts and occasional shouts of the men. That was when he started jerking off.

Her story came out in a rush. Stephen deployed to Iraq, and she had been so worried. She told him how every day she woke up wondering if he was going to die that day. She was alone in the big old house. Ghosts. The Jehovah's Witnesses came knocking on her door. The first one was "the nicest young man. He could have been you, Stephen, if you got dressed up in a suit." The next day, the young man came with a pretty girl, maybe nineteen, with long red hair and a summer dress. They brought her literature, they brought her conversation, they even brought her groceries. They took her to church. "Not church. We don't call it church. It's Kingdom Hall." They helped her get off the drugs. They stayed with her while she flushed the Valium, Xanax, speed, and marijuana down the toilet. Stephen listened because the alternative was to go home and sit in the darkened house. Because he would have to drive past the man holding the sign. Because she was his mother, and there was nobody else.

Somewhere in the middle of her rambling story of salvation or whatever it was, the husband returned. While Stephen's mother talked, Jeff blotted the spilled tea off the carpet with a dampened paper towel, picked up shards with his fingers, and then ran a handheld Dustbuster thing. When he had finished, he stood behind his wife, hands on her shoulders, rubbing. He never did make coffee. Stephen wondered if they even owned a coffee maker.

Finally, the asshole looked at his watch and interrupted Stephen's mother in the middle of a description of her baptism, some ritual involving a large tub of water, and said, "It's time to go, hon."

She explained that they were off to a meeting at the Kingdom Hall and invited Stephen. He declined. She offered dinner next Saturday. He said he would consider it. All genteel, like the teacups.

When he was sitting in the car with the engine running, working up his courage to leave, she ran out of the house, brandishing the magazine with the PTSD article like it was a million-dollar check he had accidentally left behind. He reached across and rolled down the passenger window.

"Here." She panted, peering in, all concerned, the mother she had never been. "Just take it. Maybe it will help." She dropped the magazine, which fluttered onto the seat beside him.

Driving away, out of nowhere, he remembered his mother's frequently repeated words the year he was nine and his grandfather taught him to shoot, the year before his grandfather got too sick to shoot anymore. "You think your grandfather is such a special guy," she'd said, glaring at her father while he calmly cleaned the hunting rifles with Stephen on his knees, learning technique. "But he's nothing like what you think he is. Nothing. You'll see. Someday, you'll figure it out." Stephen's grandfather always ignored her, so Stephen did too.

Chapter 11
Rachel
2016

Rachel sat on her couch, propped against pillows, half watching reruns, drinking wine and reading her Twitter feed in case somebody claimed credit for her door. Someone had threatened to incinerate her "just like Planned Parenthood does to the poor babies."

"You're gonna be sent to the Jew showers, bitch."

She read the stuff, flashed to the swastika on her door, drank, unhappened it, then started over. Finally, her phone battery died.

She dropped the phone on the floor, burrowed under a blanket, and concentrated on fantasizing about that time next year, on vacation with Liz, celebrating her birthday at that resort in Mexico she and Pete had stayed at once. In the fantasies, Liz was always so present, listening to Rachel, wanting to know what she thought and felt, and Rachel was open and trusting, as she had been when they first met.

By the time Liz finally let herself in, Rachel had convinced herself the non-fantasy Liz was never coming, so she had tried to drink herself to a point where she didn't care. Jo had offered to stay. She should have let her.

But when Liz rushed in, Rachel jumped to her feet and let Liz wrap her in a hug. She immediately broke into sobs.

"I'm so sorry," Liz said over and over, patting Rachel's back. "I'd never have just dropped you at your house if I'd known."

Rachel pulled out of Liz's embrace and turned the television off. "What took you so long?" *Am I slurring? Am I swaying on my feet? Two days in a row, getting drunk enough to slur my words.*

"Danny had a stomachache and wouldn't stay asleep. When Michael tries to calm him, he just gets more upset. I had to get him down. I got here as fast as I could." Liz plopped on the couch and patted the spot beside her. "I'm sorry you had to deal with the police alone. I'd never have left in the first place, if I'd known."

"I wasn't alone," Rachel said in an out-of-body moment—or maybe just a drunken one. She should stay drunk. She was beginning to like that version of herself.

"Did Pete come?" Liz asked and patted the sofa again.

Rachel lost her balance on her way to the couch and sat down too quickly. Maybe she could sleep now that Liz was there. The room only spun a little. "Pete's out of town, remember? I called Jo."

"Jo? Oh, that cop. That's who you called?" Liz laughed, which was not the reaction Rachel had expected. "She's the cop they send to the school. Right? I mean, I really doubt it's her job to investigate the kind of stuff you're dealing with. You need, like, cyber experts or something." She laughed again, but her voice cracked, and Rachel experienced a rush with the realization that she had succeeded in unsettling Liz.

"I called her for emotional support, not to be a police officer," Rachel retorted.

A wounded look briefly crossed Liz's face, and Rachel watched her struggle to cover it with something else. She landed on an impassive expression Rachel had never seen before on Liz.

"I mean," Rachel rushed to add, "I just figured she'd know the police and could help make sure they take me seriously. That's all."

"I get it." Liz's voice was infused with sadness. "You were scared, and I wasn't there for you. I'm just... I'm sad because I want to be the one who comforts you. I want to be there for you."

"I know." Rachel wondered whether that was true.

"I don't understand, though," Liz said. "Who are these people? How did they find you?"

"Through my social media." Rachel pointed at her computer on the coffee table. "I don't know if it's the interview where I said I was pro-choice or the play being sort of anti-religion, but for whatever reason, I caught someone's attention."

"But I'm the one who urged you to put more stuff online." Liz sounded less confident than usual. "I built your website for you. Is that how they found you?"

Rachel stroked Liz's cheek, enjoying the feeling of power instilled in her by Liz's guilt. "I don't know. It probably isn't that hard to find someone's address online." But Liz was right that Rachel hadn't bothered that much with her online presence before they'd started dating. She had even resisted at first. Liz pointed out the way her dance videos helped her get work in other cities, suggesting that more social media presence was all Rachel needed for her career to take off and she could stop teaching. But Rachel had spent years avoiding that kind of publicity.

"It could risk my job," she would say, leaving the rest—that Rachel didn't have a husband to help out if she were to lose her job—unspoken. "You never know what some parent is going to make a stink about. The plays I'm in aren't always family-friendly."

But Liz had been relentless, and Rachel had agreed to give it a try, and there they were. Liz was right to blame herself.

"I want to help," Liz said. "There has to be something we can do. Should we take down your profiles and webpage?"

"I think it's too late for that."

Liz winced.

Rachel knew she was being silly. She could already hear Liz's sponsor telling Liz to knock it off. After all, Rachel was an adult. She made her own choices. But something familiar welled up in her, a feeling that seemed to justify Liz's guilt. Rachel had been victimized, and Liz should have been there. Liz should have helped her see it coming. Rachel had done what Liz suggested, and the result had been horrible. She thought it should make her want to push Liz away, help her end things once and for all. But for some reason, the feeling bonded her more closely to Liz, as if she were in fact a child who had been hurt and it was Liz's job to help make it right.

"It's okay," she told Liz. She would leave Liz. She would. As soon as these stalkers were caught and she was safe.

And it was okay. Liz stayed, and they made love, and it didn't matter that Rachel couldn't let go and couldn't manage an orgasm, because of course she couldn't. It was all too upsetting, and for once it wasn't about those subterranean desires that Liz recoiled from when Rachel rarely dared suggest they experiment. Liz kissed her and held her until she fell asleep. And it was all okay until she woke herself up a few hours later, shouting Stephen's name.

Liz sat up. "What? Who's Stephen?"

"Nobody," Rachel said. "It was just a dream. Go back to sleep." But she lay with her eyes open the rest of the night, trying to calm the inside shaking and turn her mind back off.

How many times did we play the attic games? How many times did I let him? She'd let him. And for that reason, she would never tell anybody about Stephen. Or think about it. Ever.

Chapter 12
Rachel
2016

On Sunday afternoon, Rachel got herself together and bought some lightbulbs and paint for her door. She chose a deep barn-yard red so it would cover the red swastika. She swept shattered glass into a garbage bag. She swept until she had eliminated every foot-print, every shard of evidence on her porch.

Then she dragged a footstool out to the porch and went to work on the door. She had expected to feel satisfied, drawing her brush over the sharp corners of the red hate symbol, but instead, she was hit with a conviction that she was being watched, that they were com-ing for her, and that she didn't have a right to cover the symbol. A car swept past, and she intensified her speed. She painted frantically, wiping away her shame and fear. But the fresh paint could not oblit-erate the sound of her grandmother's voice in her head: *They watched and did nothing. People died, and they watched and did nothing.*

A white truck sporting several bumper stickers that she couldn't make out slowed in front of her house. Her heart slammed against her rib cage for several seconds after it had passed. *Up to the attic, Jew Girl.* The thin red paint didn't cover the hate underneath. She was certain she could still see the words bubbling through. She would need another coat—maybe two or three or as many as it took. She heard Stephen's childhood voice in her head and was overcome with a mix of shame paired with arousal paired with despair, and she un-derstood none of it.

After she had finished painting the door, she sat on her couch, trying to not think, to distract herself somehow. Liz had left early that morning. She always spent Sundays with the family. Pete was still in Provincetown. Other friends, acquaintances, people she went to a movie with now and then, wouldn't do. Some company intensified instead of easing her loneliness.

She went to Facebook and read the comments that had infested her feed. She blocked them then checked her Twitter feed. People with handles involving words like Nazi, Deplorable, and BabyAvenger had tweeted threats and attacks. She read every single tweet. She didn't even block them.

She had students who cut themselves when they were overwhelmed or numb or needed to make a statement. She had spoken to more than one parent about their confessions, usually made in essays or in a lingering after-drama-class can-I-talk-to-you-for-a-minute disclosure. She prided herself on being a teacher the kids could trust. Rachel had enough insight to understand that reading the words telling her to die, bitch, telling her she was a dirty Jew dyke baby killer, telling her she was worthless and ugly and shameful—reading those words and not doing anything about it was a way of cutting herself. When she had reached the end of the updated tweets, she turned to her vibrator and used a shameful, ugly fantasy involving Stephen or men who could be grown-up Stephen to make it all go away.

She stood in the shower and repeatedly scrubbed her parched skin with grainy exfoliating soap. *Time for your shower, Jew Girl.*

She couldn't get warm, so she put on a pair of winter sweats and a sweater Liz forgot to take then wrapped herself in a robe that was too heavy for spring and sat on her couch, scrolling through Sunday afternoon movies, news shows, and sports.

She broke down and called Liz to hear her voice on the voicemail, even though Liz never answered on Sundays. She didn't leave a message. She scrolled through her contacts over and over. There was Jo's number. Still there. Finally, she muted the television and hit Call, and Jo answered on the third ring. "Rachel?"

Rachel was so surprised, she couldn't think what to say. "Hi."

"Hi." On TV, a car drove off a cliff and silently crashed into the water below. Pursuers swerved and screeched to a silent stop. She knew they screeched by the dust storm the tires kicked up.

"Did you want something?" Jo asked. Rachel hadn't noticed before that Jo's voice was smooth and rich like red wine.

"I guess I just felt like saying hi." Lame.

"Okay." Jo sounded hesitant. "Then, hi. Again."

"I painted over the swastika. That was okay, right?"

"Fine." She heard Jo sigh. "It's probably too late for fingerprints, anyway."

The silent pursuers on TV drove away. A man climbed out of the sinking car and swam toward shore.

"But if you have the mezuzah that was on the door, it might be worth putting that in evidence."

Rachel remembered Jo's touch on her skin, the husky voice she used to whisper in Rachel's ear. Today, Jo sounded tired, but still, Rachel shivered and felt a throb of want. Jo even knew what a mezuzah was. She wondered why that mattered. "Okay. Thanks," Rachel said. "I just thought I should make sure I didn't screw up the investigation or anything."

"Nope."

"Okay. Thanks." She shouldn't have called. She had no idea how to keep Jo on the phone. "Anyway, have a good day."

"You too," Jo replied but didn't hang up.

"So, um, bye." Rachel waited to hear Jo say bye then pressed End. She was immediately consumed with grief. She felt empty, as if Jo had been withholding something Rachel needed to be whole.

She turned the volume up on the television, lay down on her couch, and closed her eyes. Her landline rang, and she listened in silence while her mother again asked her to visit. "Gladys is really dying," Rose said. "You should come. She'd want to see you, before she goes. Your father and I want to see you too. You should come."

Gladys.

Rachel slept dreamlessly. She woke in the dark, groggy and sweat soaked. The television had moved on to a zombie movie. The clock on her cable box said it was nearly midnight. She sat, watching the silent zombies lurch across the screen and trying to understand what had woken her. A sound. Something outside. Maybe a car passing. Maybe something else. She should check.

In her bedroom, she dumped the robe and changed into a T-shirt. She hung Liz's sweater over the back of the couch. She left a message for Liz: *You left your sweater here. You can come by and get it any time. I'm home.*

Then she called Pete. She heard crowd sounds in the background when he answered—laughter, music, the hum of nightlife.

"Where are you?" she asked.

"Shipwreck Lounge. One more hour of the party life before they close. Let me step out."

She stayed quiet and listened to bits of conversation, the drumbeat of a dance song, then brief silence.

"How's it going?" he asked. "It isn't like you to call this late at night. You're missing your beauty sleep."

She told him everything. When she had finished, he stayed quiet for several seconds before responding.

"Seriously. All that from one little radio interview? And it's my fault. That play. Maybe it was too much for Pineville."

She heard laughter and shouting and imagined him sitting on the curb somewhere, groups of drunk people stumbling to their hotel rooms. "It isn't your fault," she said. "Who knows if those people even live in Pineville?"

"What are you going to do?"

"Call you," she said, and it felt good to laugh.

"You should do what that Jo person said. Go in and report it. Let them bring in the FBI or whatever happens next."

"Sure." She wasn't going to do that. She kept seeing that cop who took her report about the swastika, the one who had looked at her like she was dirt, like it was her fault. *What if they ask questions about me? What if my whole life ends up out there on display?*

"Well, you have to do something," Pete insisted. "Fight. You have to fight them. Don't be passive Rachel. Be fighting Rachel. Be the Rachel who goes out onstage and kicks ass."

"I think I'll go to bed now," she said. "Thanks for listening. I just needed to know I had a friend out there."

"You've always got me," Pete said.

She knew it was true. Since his first play, since the first late-night post-rehearsal confessional breakfast, he had been there.

"I'll check back in tomorrow," he promised.

They said their good nights, and she sat again on the couch in front of the silenced television. She scrolled through a new influx of hate posts on her Twitter feed. *Be fighting Rachel. Be the Rachel who goes out onstage and kicks ass.* She could block them all, but she couldn't block the feelings in her body, the confusing mix of arousal and shame. The part of her that wanted to... she couldn't figure it out. *Do I want to see them?*

On your knees, Jew Girl.

Let them...? What?

They were probably all just kids in their parents' basements. She googled white supremacists in Pineville to prove it to herself.

"White supremacist messages found hidden in boxes of diapers sold in local Pineville store."

"Black man attacked at white nationalist rally in Pineville."

"47 hate groups are active in New York State."

"Hate crime expert decries new white supremacist bar opening in Pineville less than a block away from LGBT bar."

Rachel clicked through. She knew where that bar was. She walked past it every time she went to Prism.

She went to bed but couldn't sleep. She had to fight these people. They were attacking her. She had to do something. *Be fighting Rachel.* She should call Jo again. Let the feds handle it. When she finally slept, she dreamed she was in an attic. Deplorable1 was there. He looked like a grown-up Stephen. *On your knees, Jew Girl.* She awoke sweating and overwhelmed with disgust at herself. She wanted to die. She wanted to do something. Maybe she could be fighting Rachel. Maybe she could make it stop without help from anybody.

She finally fell asleep in the middle of a fantasy in which she went to that white supremacist bar, found the people who had painted that swastika, and confronted them. Rachel was empowered. Rachel was *doing* something about it.

IN THE MORNING, SHE studied the white supremacist Internet in the same way she would have to prepare for any role. She read blogs and comments and Twitter conversations. She read articles and essays. She memorized the names of right-wing websites. She educated herself about their speech patterns and their core beliefs.

"Kill yourself, you Jew Rat."

"Women are stupid and not worth defending."

"Faggots suck dick. Ha ha."

"Race traitors will be just as culpable, if not more, on the day of the rope."

She googled "race traitors" and "the day of the rope." It was from a white supremacist novel, something to do with a day in which all supposed race traitors were dragged out and hanged. Race traitors were anybody who cared about anybody who wasn't white and presumably anyone who wasn't Christian.

She sat and waited, letting Netflix show her one movie after another. She couldn't have told anybody what the movies were about.

Finally, the clock said 8:30 pm. She figured that would do.

Thirty minutes later, she stood outside the bar, called That Place. She had her hair tucked behind her ears and slathered with greasy gel and wore a denim jacket, upon which she had placed a Celtic cross pin, and leather boots she had dug from the back of her closet. The cross pin was from some play—she couldn't remember what, but Google said it had become a white supremacist symbol. She always kept the costumes and props she bought for plays. She never knew when she might need something.

The bar was quiet and occupied mostly by men, though she noticed a couple of women in the back near a pool table. Every now and then, an anemic cheer broke out in the corner where the TV played a muted football game. Rachel ordered a draft and found a spot near the pool table. She preferred wine, but her character drank beer.

A man about Rachel's age with a shaved head and a tattoo of a rope coiled around his scalp appeared to be winning the pool game, beating a bearded guy in a Rangers cap. Two women at a table nearby alternated between cheers and moans as the men shot. Watching them, Rachel grew uncomfortably suspicious that her idea of how to dress for the night had more to do with an outdated image of a biker bar than anything like reality for a neo-Nazi hangout. The women, sleek-haired, well-dressed, and not overly made up, were people she would have offered a ride to if she passed them with the hood of their car up. They looked like ladies who lunched, whom Rachel sometimes overheard in the gym locker room, discussing their personal trainers, the best day care, and their trips to Italy.

Rachel wandered closer, choosing a single chair at a small table nearby. The blond woman erupted in a cheer and offered a high five to her brunette friend, who reluctantly returned it. "I knew J.T.'d win. He's the best damn pool player ever," the blonde exclaimed. "Beer's on you."

Rachel caught the blonde's eye and smiled. She could do it. She knew how to play a role. She glanced at the rope guy's tattoo, the muscles on his arm. The woman eyed her skeptically. "Do we know you?"

Rachel shook her head and took a long draw on her beer. "No. I'm new in town. Liz." The name came to her tongue without thought or premeditation. "I heard about this place from someone at work. Wanted to check it out."

They all studied her. "Where do you work?" the rope tattoo guy—J.T., she guessed—asked.

She looked down at his shoes, which were leather and expensive looking. He was her darkest fantasy. His grey T-shirt read White Pride.

"My old job, in Chicago." She hedged and was relieved that her voice did not quiver. "Government employee. Haven't started working here yet." She took a long sip of her beer and coughed when some went down wrong.

"Huh," the blonde said. "Government jobs are the worst. Mind-numbing. Stupid. I worked for the state once. Damn child protective. Half those people we investigated should have been sterilized at birth."

They all chuckled, and Rachel joined in, acting. It was a role.

"I'm Leanne," the blonde offered.

Rachel nodded a greeting.

"J.T." the tattooed guy said, and Rachel nodded again.

The brunette was Moira, and the Rangers cap guy was Alec.

"Anyway," Rachel said, "I was home, browsing through Storm-front but feeling kind of lonely. No friends here yet. So I thought I'd check the place out. I heard it has good beer. Good company." She made brief eye contact with J.T. He had pale eyes, blue or maybe hazel. She fought the urge to turn away. *Steady.* She drank. The glass was more than half gone already.

The group exchanged glances. "That isn't a bad site," J.T. said. "But it's always better to hang with your friends than read a bunch of junk on a computer." He smiled.

She returned it and edged close enough to smell the cigarette smoke on his shirt. Leanne offered Rachel a close-lipped grimace and took J.T.'s arm.

"So what do you guys do for fun?" Rachel asked, trying to walk an edge somewhere between farce and melodrama, finishing off her beer.

"Pool," J.T. said, gesturing at the pool table. "Beer." He pointed at the bar. "Grab me and Liz here another, would you, Leanne?"

Leanne glared at Rachel then stalked in the direction of the bar, teetering a little on her heels.

"I'm not so good at pool," Rachel said. She felt nauseous. It wasn't like being onstage, and it wasn't some Lifetime movie with a guaranteed happy ending. But when J.T. took her arm and led her to the pool table, she let him. Every nerve in her body flared at his touch and the look of interest in his eyes. It felt as if revulsion and desire had knotted together in her belly. If she tried to unravel them, she doubted anything would be left of her.

J.T. handed her a pool cue and leaned into her back, taking her arm. He pressed into her more closely than was necessary, almost pinning her against the table.

"Like this?" she asked, struggling to keep the tremor out of her voice. She tapped the white ball with the stick. It bounced off the ball in front of the triangle and sent a few behind it skittering.

"You have to hit a little harder than that," J.T. said and laughed, his mouth brushing her ear. His laugh was kind, even charming. Rachel didn't want to notice that. She focused on the trapped feeling, the way he had pushed through any reasonable boundary, the tattoo, the T-shirt. He was a monster, a white supremacist monster. She despised him.

"I have your beer," Leanne said, and Rachel inhaled as he stepped back from her.

"Thanks," he mumbled and offered Rachel a lopsided grin.

She turned away from the pool table, taking the beer from Leanne. Alec and Moira also held replenished beers, and they all clustered around Rachel. Some part of her insisted she should leave immediately, but years of improv had taught her that committing to a role meant saying "Yes." For all she knew, J.T. had been the one to paint her door. Maybe they all had. She could find out if she hung in there. She could figure it out without going to the station and facing that cop's condescending look and dismissive tone.

"You guys don't hang out in this bar every night, though, right?" she asked. "Where else is fun to go around here?" *Sip beer. Shuffle feet a little. Lean into J.T. as if you return his interest.* She did not. No, she did not.

He kept a possessive hand on her arm. *If only this were Prism, if it were Liz's hand, Liz flirting possessively, catching her eye with interest.*

"Well, yeah, sometimes we have dinner and watch *Game of Thrones* together," J.T. said.

"Oh." Rachel felt relieved at a topic she knew something about. "I'm totally into *GOT*. Do you think Arya is going to be okay?"

"I don't know," Moira said. "That stab wound seemed pretty fatal."

"Maybe you could join us. We're at my place next week," J.T. offered.

"You don't even know her." Leanne spoke loudly enough that the football-watching group glanced in their direction.

In improv, you never say no. Someone makes an offer, you say yes and then up the ante. But it was not improv, and Rachel hedged. "Yeah, maybe. I'll see if I'm free."

"You should come." J.T. pulled her against him, squeezing her ribs so she felt smothered.

"So," Leanne said, "you lived in Chicago?"

"Yeah." Rachel swigged beer, letting the buzz blanket her thoughts. Her body loosened. She felt reckless.

"Where in Chicago? Cause I know people there. Lived there for five years myself."

"Really, Leanne?" Moira said. "I didn't know you lived in Chicago."

Leanne shushed Moira. "I'm trying to find out who she is," she said.

J.T. draped his arm over Rachel's shoulder. "Leave her be, Leanne. She's new. Let's make her feel welcome."

"Don't you want to make sure she's for real?" Leanne's voice cracked, and her eyes welled.

"Let's take a walk," Moira said, tugging Leanne away. The two women headed toward the bar, leaning into one another. After a quick glance at J.T., Alec followed them.

"We used to date," J.T. said.

"Oh." Rachel took another long drink.

"It's over, though," he added. He had not removed his arm from her shoulders, and her mind swirled with drunken ideas of how she could extricate herself, but her body stayed put. *Say you need the bathroom. Say you have a sick friend you need to check on. Just step away.* She let J.T. lead her back to the pool table. "I remember how hard it was when I first moved here," he said as he reset the balls into a triangle. "You don't know anybody, no social life. You can only play so many computer games." He chuckled.

"Yeah," she agreed.

He handed her the pool cue and guided her into position.

"It's been hard. I had the flu this spring, and I had to do my own shopping and stuff." The flu part was at least true. But she'd had all the help she needed between Liz, Pete, and a few other friends.

"If you need anything, I'll help you out." His lips brushed her neck.

She couldn't stop the cringe, and she held her breath. But he did not seem to notice. Maybe she wished he had. "Great," she managed. "I'm glad to finally have a friend here." She hit again, and one of the balls rolled into a corner hole. J.T. cheered, and she let out a startled gasp. She'd been too distracted to pay attention to what she was doing.

She hit a few more balls, relaxing into her role, discussing TV shows, movies they'd both seen, food they liked. She struggled for an opening to initiate a conversation about her play, social media, or swastikas on doors. The conversation was too normal, and she wondered how she had imagined she could walk into the bar and find a bunch of rabid swastika painters.

J.T. bought her another beer. He smelled like cigarettes and cologne. The rolling beat of country music mingled with the ongoing cheers of the football watchers, and maybe J.T. lacked boundaries, but he hadn't tried to hurt her. In fact, he'd been kind. It was better than hiding in her house.

"Hey, Liz," Rachel heard, and J.T. stepped back, releasing her arm. She dropped the pool stick and turned toward Leanne, who stood with her legs slightly spread, hands on her hips.

"So, tell me who you knew in Chicago," Leanne said, her voice harsh and confrontational.

"I had a whole group of friends," Rachel answered.

"Yeah? Who? Where did you hang?"

"Let it go, Leanne." J.T. offered Rachel an encouraging nod.

She focused on the words on J.T.'s T-shirt and thought again of that knot in her belly—revulsion, arousal, shame. Then she did what J.T. had asked of Leanne and let it all go. "Well"— she wondered if she was drunk enough, stupid enough to do it—"we'd get together regularly and go out and, you know, slap something on a synagogue or someone's house." She heaved a breath, hearing how foolish and put-on her words sounded. "What a rush," she finished, puncturing any credibility that might have remained. She laughed, though even she recognized the panic in her voice.

Nobody responded, and the sound of a louder cheer erupted near the TV. Everyone turned toward the sound. Then J.T. stepped back so he could look at Rachel with those pale eyes. She felt his anger and suspicion envelop her, like the dusty attic in her recurring nightmare, enshrouding her like every fantasy she fought to deny.

"Well, we don't do that sort of thing," JT said, drawling out his words as if each were a nail he must hammer exactly on the head. "We here are law-abiding citizens. We just like to get together and have a good time. Have a drink." His voice sounded wooden, accusatory. He held Rachel's gaze, and she looked down. *Don't. Don't look down.* She raised her head and focused on projecting power and confidence, pushing away the onslaught of panic insisting she get out of there. The others watched the exchange, and Leanne smiled triumphantly.

"What are you, a cop or something?" Moira asked. Rachel's ears grew hot and itched, a sure sign a blush had colored her face.

"Nope," Leanne said. "She's no cop. Looks like a wannabe biker chick. Bet she's never even ridden a motorcycle." She brought her phone to J.T., who glanced at it then at Rachel. "I image searched you," Leanne said. She showed Rachel her phone, which was open to Rachel's Facebook page.

Leanne laughed, took J.T.'s arm, and led him toward the other end of the bar. Moira shook her head, shot a look of disgust at Rachel, and followed, leaving Rachel alone with her half-drunk beer and the stupid outfit she had hoped would help her blend in.

Goddamn, Rachel, can't you do anything right? Part of her wanted to follow them and insist that she really did belong. *Why care if you don't belong with a bunch of Nazis?*

More people thronged into the bar, and her breath quickened. She brushed a damp lock of gel-slicked hair off her forehead then sat long enough to finish off her beer, more for medicinal purposes than for taste. But nobody approached her. Nobody talked loudly enough that she could hear.

It had been a stupid idea. Dumb, dumb, dumb. She was an actress, not an undercover cop. She'd figured it would be like playing a role. Wear the clothes. Play the part. She did it every day. She couldn't believe she had imagined she could walk in, find the actual people who painted the graffiti, and confront them. She'd seen too many movies. Too much fantasy.

She carried her empty mug to the bar. Maybe one more beer, just to prove she wasn't intimidated. She signaled the bartender and offered her credit card. When the beer arrived, she sipped. She didn't have to finish it. She would not be chased out. She spotted an empty table well away from the pool group and headed in that direction.

Leanne stepped into her path. Her eyes, Rachel noticed, were green, made more vivid by expertly applied eyeliner. Rachel experienced a moment of disgust that this neo-Nazi in a dive bar could make her feel in any way inadequate.

"You should just leave us alone," Leanne said. "We aren't hurting nobody. We're entitled to our First Amendment rights, same as anybody else."

"You aren't entitled to paint swastikas on peoples' front doors," Rachel said, feeling the bitterness from an old, dark place, usually buried too deep to be inaccessible. "You aren't entitled to harass people on Facebook or whatever else you get your jollies doing." *Get your jollies? Did I really just say that?*

J.T. appeared behind Leanne. "Who says we've ever done anything like that?" he said. "I bet you're just some bitch who thinks she can be some kind of superhero or something. Defend the poor Muslims or Jews. Defend the stupid illegals. You don't even get what they're doing to our country. You should be fighting to evict them, not defending them."

Rachel felt Gladys rise up in her, lecturing her mother and reminding Rachel that she was a Jew, and she would always be a Jew. Gladys uncoiled in her brain and stood beside Stephen. *Nobody fought back. They just let it happen.* Gladys stood with Leanne and J.T., accusing, judging. The sound disappeared. She sensed an audience, people turning to stare. She recognized the feeling. It was older and bigger than she had ever understood. It was everything she had swallowed to stay calm, to get through her day.

Only this time, it grabbed hold of her, and she went helpless in the pulsing rage. Before she could stop herself, before she knew what she was doing, she threw what was left of her beer at J.T.'s face.

Then the sound kicked back on. J.T. stood in front of her, beer dripping off his face, soaking his shirt, and puddling on the floor around his expensive leather boots.

"Bitch," he said, and there was nothing charming about it. "Fucking bitch."

Rachel fled the bar and left that other self, the Rachel who had dared to flirt with her nightmares and her fantasies, had dared to step into something dangerous and take a risk, there. *What did I think I could prove?* She left and unhappened everything.

Chapter 13
Stephen
2016

At a red light, Stephen checked the Jehovah's Witness pamphlet, in case his mother had written her phone number on it or slipped in some cash, but there was nothing. He tossed it out the car window.

He couldn't stop picturing her neatly clipped, unpainted fingernails and her pale cheeks. No matter how deeply his mother had descended into the booze-and-drug haze, she had never neglected to file and paint her nails or slather her face with makeup. Drugs and men were all she had ever focused her energy on. Getting and using drugs. Getting and fucking men. With the religion crap, it was as if she'd transformed herself, like she was a poor Iraqi woman who couldn't afford to do her nails. Maybe that was what it took to please the new man. Maybe Jehovah's Witness women spent their days on their hands and knees, scrubbing the fucking kitchen floor.

She was still the same mother, as far as he could tell, but with religion and men instead of drugs and men. Whatever. But some part of him felt furious that she had sobered up, when he needed her guilty and drunk enough to give him money for the dog.

Back home, Stephen wandered the house, searching his bedroom for any shreds of pot or money then turning the TV on then immediately off, shutting down the Prudential ad with the happy family moving in to their happy new house.

He popped a Swanson's turkey dinner into the microwave and fired up his computer. Maybe he would find his old skin friends. If he could remember any detail—a real name or the name of that store Rick owned—he would find them. They had stopped writing him shortly after he deployed. He'd checked his Facebook page regularly from Iraq, so he knew exactly when they stopped posting or at least when they all set their pages so he couldn't see what they posted. He wondered whether they hated him and why they'd purposely cut him off.

He dug into *The Daily Stormer,* reading comments and looking for Frank's name, or even just something that sounded like Frank. A headline informed him that evidence suggested Hitler used were-wolves to exterminate Jews. He laughed and clicked through. He couldn't tell whether the author was being serious or if it was satire. He liked the idea of werewolves. As a child, he had wanted to be one for a while, especially when he helped his grandpa train Dieter.

He googled the bar, Surf Me, even though he'd done that regu-larly when he was deployed, and it never turned up. No website. No nothing. But one never knew. He searched his own name now and then, but the only things that came up there were old Facebook posts Frank and some of the others from Surf Me had responded to. He'd written, "Getting ready to deploy to Iraq," and Frank had comment-ed, "You're a great soldier for the cause."

He stared at Frank's meaningless status yet again. It said, "On my way to the bar. You know which one. White Pride Worldwide." But according to Facebook, Frank hadn't logged on for three years, so Stephen doubted that status update was accurate.

If he had more courage, he would find a new tribe. They were out there more and more. He'd seen videos of actual here-and-now peo-ple with their arms up, doing the *Sieg heil.* But they looked young and clean-shaven and had expensive haircuts. They would see him, with his male-pattern balding and bulging gut, and probably close their circle with him on the outside. He just wanted to find Frank.

He wanted his old friends. They had sent him off to the military, and he was back. They were supposed to have waited for him.

He considered investing in one of those sites that said it could find people, but he couldn't afford to get high or get a dog out of the pound, and those sites were expensive. There was also the chance that even if he found them, they didn't want him anymore. He googled Sally Featherwood, but of course that wasn't really her name, and there was nothing except Google asking if he meant Leatherwood and a bunch of random street names. Frank was AdolfFrank. He should have asked his mother what Frank's last name was. She'd dated him. She had to have known.

He'd almost googled Rachel plenty of times before, but something had always stopped him. It was like the difference between thinking about having an ice-cream sundae and actually having one. He could think about it, want it, and imagine how it would taste. Then he could eat it, and it was over. The wanting it and knowing he was going to have it was better and lasted longer than the getting. He liked imagining Rachel's life and what she looked like and where she was. Maybe he would run into her at the grocery store. Maybe she would show up at his door someday. *What if she's ugly now? What if she doesn't recognize me? What if she thinks I'm ugly?* He placed a hand on his pale stomach and promised himself he would start running again. He'd enjoyed running when he was in the military and had to pass his fitness test.

He hadn't always felt so needy, as if something was missing. It was that Natalie, that damned therapist—she had made him want things. The dog. Rachel.

He googled Rachel Goldberg.

There were hundreds of hits. Apparently, there was a filmmaker named Rachel Goldberg. She had pages of Google hits devoted just to her. Further in, he found a psychiatrist. There was a doctor in Philly with the name, a university professor in Boston, and a movie with a character named Rachel Goldberg that also had full pages of links. Finally, he found a photo of Rachel in a play review. He changed his search terms and tried "Rachel Goldberg, Actress." After scrolling through several more links about the filmmaker and the movie character, he got one of those Rachel-Goldberg-is-on-Facebook links. His heart pounded against his chest. It felt like he was about to see her for real and like he was doing something forbidden.

Rachel Goldberg's Facebook page... there were several—the one in Boston, another in England, and one in Pineville, NY. He tried that, since it was New York and she was apparently an actress.

Her dark curls haloed her face in exactly the way he remembered. He wanted to touch it, run his fingers through it. Her mournful brown eyes made it seem as if she was trapped in the photo, silently begging him to rescue her. He was the knight, and she was the fairy-tale princess. *I'm coming, Rachel,* he thought. She was half smiling in most of the photos, a secret smile as if saying, "You don't really know me." Under the photos, he found links to play reviews. He read a few of the reviews. There were likes and shares of the photos of her performing.

Then came the comments: "Rachel Goldberg is a baby killing Jew dyke." "Rachel Goldberg should be sent to the showers and gassed." He sat for a long time, reading those comments. They made his body quiver. He pictured the sixteen-year-old version of Rachel, the last time he had seen her in that canyon. "Abortion Rachel should get the same fate as the babies she thinks it's okay to kill. Incinerate her."

He read comments until his eyes ached. His shoulders ached. Everything about him ached. The light had gone dusky, which made the house seem abandoned. In the evening, he usually turned the TV on to blot out the emptiness, but the only sound was the blurry whine of his overheated computer. He wanted to be little and in the attic with his grandfather and the guns and magazines. He wanted to eat dinner at Rachel's house and doze in Gladys's study and have Aaron show him a magic trick and see his shoes in the row next to the door with everyone else's shoes. He studied Rachel's photos and that not-quite-a-smile smile. He wanted his skin friends. He wanted to see Rachel, talk to her or something.

He found Rachel's profile picture again and studied it. Then he opened Messenger. *Hi, Rachel. It's Stephen. Remember me?* The words looked foreign, like a bunch of letters that didn't mean anything. He highlighted then deleted. *Rachel, this is Stephen. Can we talk?* He read and reread, wondering whether she would reply or even see it. He hit Send.

It didn't matter, anyway. If she ignored him, nothing would be different. He would be fine. The next day, he would drive to San Diego and check out Surf Me. Even if he couldn't find Frank and the crowd, at least it would be company. He needed people, people like him. Hell, he was ex-military. Surely, they would welcome him. Maybe someone would help him get that dog. Frank would have done it. Frank loved Stephen like a son. He could just about pay for the gas if he broke into the rolled-up change in his sock drawer. It was the best plan he could come up with.

———◆———

THE NEXT MORNING, STEPHEN was on the freeway toward San Diego and Surf Me. It was the first time since coming home from Iraq that he'd driven that far.

The VW's radio had died years before, but there was a sort of music—the clang of something under the car, the roar of other vehicles pulling left and rushing past, the whistle of wind through the windows that kept sliding open, too heavy for the faded rubber meant to hold them in place. The faster he went, which wasn't all that fast in the old Bug, the louder the music got, a rhythm to match his thoughts, disjointed, too intense, rattling toward something. The ride took over an hour.

First, he stopped at Mission Bay, just to see if it was still there. He parked in one of two lots and walked to the beach near where people could rent paddleboats. It looked about the same as he remembered from childhood summers with Rachel's family, with women sunbathing, kids splashing in the edge of the water and digging holes, teenagers drinking soda and flirting, smoke from a barbeque, the smell of meat watering his mouth, and seagulls, everything still languorous.

A man tossed a ball into the water for his dog, and Stephen watched for several minutes, contemplating how he could take his dog there, when he got her. He would take her for walks and throw balls for her, and she would stop being so afraid. She would know she was loved. The man's dog emerged from the water and shook. Droplets sprayed the man when he dropped to his knees and hugged the dog.

Stephen swallowed his longing, his wish to be that man standing at the water with his own dog. He thought about other times he'd been there with Rachel's family: a vivid day, sun glinting off the water in white-and-green squiggles of light, the ache of his legs pushing the pedals to keep the boat going. Rachel beside him, giggling. She brushed aside the curls that had blown into her face and looked at him. He smiled back. And it probably never happened this way because they were probably all doing their own thing, but he pictured it like this: Dad, Mom, and Grandma stood at the water's edge as if he and Rachel were giving a performance. They smiled and nodded, like that damn Natalie at the clinic had smiled and nodded. *You're all right. You're just fine.* It looked like they were giving Rachel and him a fucking standing ovation.

He didn't even know why he kept thinking about Rachel, why she had entered his fantasies so vividly all of a sudden, after so many years. It wasn't as if he'd never had a real girlfriend. He should think about Theresa, not Rachel. Anyway, Rachel had turned out to be a dyke and her grandmother a bitch, and Stephen couldn't afford the dog. That was the truth, and Surf Me was the only real home for Stephen.

Rachel was nothing to him, yet she was everywhere.

Time to go find my real friends.

———————●———————

STEPHEN SAT IN HIS car in the Surf Me parking lot for several minutes. The bar was still nestled in the middle of a few palm trees, a couple of faded surfboards marking the entrance. There had never been a sign on the building, and that hadn't changed. People just knew it was there from word of mouth. The dented metal door and the narrow, too-high windows were cleaner than he remembered. The owner used to leave them murky with grime, so people couldn't see in. But really, they were too high to see in, anyway.

He couldn't hear the music through his car window, but he re-membered it well and had been playing it in his head since he left Mission Bay. In the early days, the DJ had alternated rock with punk. First, it had been plain old punk, like Sex Pistols and Dead Kennedys. Then later, just before he joined the army, someone from England brought in a Skrewdriver album, and for the first time, he heard lyrics about the superiority of the white race, patriotism, and belonging. The DJ turned up the volume, and guys started singing along, even though nobody knew the words. They learned fast. Oth-er people left. It emptied everyone but the other skins, guys like him, out of the bar. After that, people mostly knew to stay away if they didn't belong. The music said everything.

Stephen had never stayed away. Ever since his Uncle Frank first took him there, the bar had been his safe haven. When Gladys finally kicked him out of the house for good, that cemented it. He knew by then that Rachel's house wasn't his real home, and Gladys wasn't his grandmother. His grandfather was dead, but that place, the bar... his grandfather would have approved.

"You're a good soldier," Frank had always said. And he was. He was never great—he never got to be a designated marksman as he had always wanted and didn't get promoted as quickly as he should have. But he had managed until September 11 and Iraq and his first and only real deployment.

He sat in his car and wondered what it was like in there. *Will they be happy to see me? Disgusted by my failure? Will they even be there?* He was a fuckup. They had barely acknowledged his deployment or offered any advice. They had been too busy planning a rally he was going to miss. He had half hoped they would encourage him to get himself kicked out, tell him he already knew what they needed for the race war and they wanted him back home. But all they did was send stupid emails saying to do them proud and wishing him luck. It had been as if all the skinheads, his real family, were mad at him. They were avoiding him. So he went to Iraq and fucked up, and they would see it on him as soon as he walked in.

He told himself it wouldn't be that way, picturing how it would go. He would walk in. Frank would be at his usual table. He would look up and see Stephen then shout at the bartender to turn off the music, and the bartender would. "Stephen is here," he would say. "Everyone, Stephen is here." Even though he and Theresa had broken up ages ago, back when he met Crazy Jamie, she would run toward him, laughing, having lost weight and looking sexy. She would wrap her legs around him and kiss him. Everyone would surround him, touching him. "Did you kill any terrorists?" they would ask, and he would tell them he did. He would tell them how he shot that man in the heat of battle, saving the life of his battle buddy.

Finally, he got out of the car and walked toward the bar. That was when he noticed the sign: Maria's Taco Place. He opened the door anyway, just to be sure.

First, he noticed the smells—not the sweet marijuana haze, not good American beer, Coors or Bud. Something different—spices or grease, maybe. A sizzling meat smell. Then noise. A crazy alien rhythm and lyrics not in English. He listened for familiar voices and heard laughter then a woman talking in loud Spanish. There were too many people, too many voices. The people had brown and white and black skin. The crowd should have been enough for him to know it wasn't his bar, not the Surf Me where he had found his family. It was filled with Mexicans blasting crazy alien beaner lyrics he couldn't even figure out. *Fucking illegals everywhere.*

He spun a tight circle right there in front of the door and covered his ears, maybe getting a few stares, but he didn't care. Everyone was talking too loud, the music was too loud, the stinking greasy smells were too strong, and bright, glaring plates of Mexican food on the tables hurt his eyes. The pressure built.

He pushed out through the door and ran back to the car. *Where the hell is Frank? Where is Teresa? Where did they go?*

He sat in his car, panting. "You're fucking weird," they'd said. "You fucking killed some poor kid's father. Get away from me."

The Mauser rested on the passenger seat, sun-warmed from the car. He grabbed it and pressed it to his cheek. "Make him sit now," his grandpa had said. "That's good. Yes, like that. See, you're a great dog trainer."

Stephen put the gun away and pulled out of the parking lot. He fought tears the entire drive back to Carlsbad. *Fuck them. Fuck the crooks and rapists in that damn bar and my mother and my old friends. Fuck the SPCA and the bitch who wouldn't let me take my dog home, the dog that was meant for me.*

The sun was setting by the time he reached the SPCA. He should have gone home to prepare, should have gotten some stuff and made a plan, but he sat in the parking lot with his window cracked and watched people test drive dogs on the lawn. A family emerged from the building, the mother carrying a small, curly dog. He could hear the boy wailing that he wanted ice cream. The mother cradled the dog against her chest and told the boy he couldn't have ice cream until after dinner, but come pet Lancelot.

Stephen sat in his grandfather's car and thought about what he would name the shepherd. Something noble. Something strong. He needed to look up German names when he got home.

Stephen sat in his grandfather's car and watched people come and go, some leaving with dogs, some empty-handed. He sat while the sun went down and the lights in the parking lot blinked on. He would train the dog with the Schutzhund method from Germany, like his grandfather had taught him. He would let her sleep on his bed and feed her treats. He would walk her every day, maybe at the beach, and throw sticks for her. He would get a job, maybe back at the oil-change place, maybe washing dishes. Whatever. He didn't care. He needed to pay for dog food.

Stephen sat in his grandfather's car until that fat Mexican—an illegal, no doubt—locked the doors and drove away. She glanced at his car, but he had purposely parked under some trees in the back of the parking lot. He wasn't prepared the way he should have been, but he knew a little about camouflage. He ducked down, and she must have decided he wasn't a concern, because she got in her car and left.

Stephen sat until his military watch said it was midnight.

Finally.

He should have worn black, should have brought a ladder, maybe. He didn't have a way to pick the lock. He should have gone home, made a plan ahead, come back another night. He cased out the kennel. The building was L shaped, with the front door at the bottom part of the L. He tried the door, but he'd seen the illegal pull out a big ring of keys and lock it. He crept around to the back of the shelter, ducking once when a car drove by.

He walked toward the back of the kennel, where the shepherd lived, and studied the high, narrow windows back there. They were too small for him to fit through, even if he had a way to climb up to them. Also, he would have to get the dog out, but she was big to carry. He knocked on the wall, eliciting a faint volley of multi-pitched barks from inside. He had no idea what was under the white stucco, but it felt thick and solid, the dogs' barks distant on the other side.

He traversed the entire building, ending where he'd started, at the front door. It wouldn't budge. The dead bolt below the doorknob was secure.

Okay. It's okay. Just think. But his mind was racing, and he couldn't think. *I have to do this. Have to do it now. Tonight.* He paced around the kennel several more times, increasingly hopeless, increasingly aimless, just walking without intent.

Finally, he returned to his car and dozed then slept. He dreamed of dogs and Rachel and Gladys, a jumble of images without story lines. Later, the sound of a car in the parking lot startled him awake. He twisted in his seat and watched it turn around in the lot and pull back out onto the mostly empty street. The night was yellow-tinted, and when he consulted his watch, he discovered it was four a.m.—nearly morning, and he hadn't found a way into the building.

Okay. Regroup. She'll be here soon, the Mexican woman. The illegal. He drove to a gas station parking lot across the street, parked behind the attached convenience store, and walked back to the SP-CA, cradling the Mauser against his chest. He thought about his boot camp days and his nights in Iraq, but in truth, he felt more like the six-year-old boy playing war. When he crouched under the same tree he'd parked under and trained his eyes on the road, when he breathed and waited and watched, he was the sharpshooter he'd always wanted to be, the Ranger, the Nazi. His legs cramped, but he did not move. His back ached, but he did not move. He waited. He was still. He breathed.

Finally, a white station wagon rolled slowly into the lot and parked in front of the building. The beaner emerged from the car, large key ring in one hand and a bulging grocery bag in the other. Stephen watched her drop the grocery bag and fiddle with the keys. *Should I move now? Should I wait? She might lock the door behind her once she entered. She'll have to go back to the kennel to feed the dogs, won't she?* She unlocked one of the locks, and he crept forward. By the time she had unlocked the second, he was so close he could hear her heavy breathing. Sweat trickled down his neck. His heart pounded hard against his ribs.

He stepped forward and trained the Mauser on her chest. She screamed and flung the keys away. "Okay," he said. "Let's go inside together." He edged around her and squatted to retrieve the keys. She didn't move, and her ugly beaner face turned nearly white. A laugh welled inside his chest, and he fought to repress it. Nothing was funny, but the laugh gurgled up in him. It threatened everything. He focused on the sound of hungry dogs. A mournful howl carried over the other dogs. That had to be her, his shepherd. She heard him coming, wanted to be rescued.

He jabbed the beaner with his gun. "Come on," he ordered, and she turned and stumbled inside. Her harsh breathing grated his nerves. "Shut up!" he yelled. She breathed louder and turned her face toward him. She was crying. The bitch was crying. *To the attic, Jew Girl. You're my prisoner.* "Shut up!" he screamed again. The barking sounded like Iraq on the day he'd shot that man. The dogs were hungry. They were all so hungry. They were desperately, urgently hungry and loud and barking and screaming in the back cages. They pulverized his thoughts until everything was black and spinning.

He herded the woman in then shut the door and tried several keys in the dead bolt. His hand wouldn't stop shaking. The woman was watching him, her tears drying up. The keys clanged, and he dropped them. *Fuck it. Who else would show up this early?*

"We're going to get the shepherd," he told the beaner, his voice guttural with panic. "We're going to go back to the kennel, and you're going to open her cage and put a leash on her, and I'm going to leave with her. Understand?"

She nodded, and suddenly, her silence unnerved him. "Answer me," he ordered.

"Yes." Something about the quaver in her voice made him afraid, opened darkness in his core. *"I don't like this game anymore,"* Rachel said. *"I don't want to play anymore."* He followed the beaner back through the kennel, past the other dogs, and to the corner where she was. His dog. His girl.

The woman's hands trembled, and that made him feel stronger, less shaky. He waited. The dog cowered in a back corner and looked at him with eyes that made him feel guilty, as if he was harming her instead of rescuing her. He jabbed the beaner's back hard with his grandfather's gun. "Faster."

She finally got the cage open. "You first. Get the leash on." He nodded at a leash hanging next to the dog's cage. The beaner snapped a leash on the dog's collar. The dog whined when the beaner handed the leash to Stephen. She wasn't supposed to whine. She was supposed to greet him with joy, to see that he was saving her. His grandfather said it took time. Training a dog was slow. They didn't bond overnight.

He grabbed the leash out of the beaner's hand, accidentally jerking it a little. The dog yelped, and the beaner flinched. Stephen jabbed the Mauser into her back hard enough to bruise. "Let's go."

The three of them shuffled back to the office, the woman crying loudly. The dog hung back, so he had to drag her by the leash. Finally, she turned and aimed back toward her kennel. He tugged. She planted her paws. He tugged again. She whined.

He turned and crouched so he could coax the dog. "Come on, girl," he urged. "It's fine."

She turned back to look at him and sat down.

That was when the sirens came. Stephen heard the howls first, all the dogs joining in with the high-pitched wail of the sirens outside. He spun around, gripping the leash hard in his fist. The beaner wasn't crying anymore. He realized she had a hand in the pocket of her jacket, the same one she'd pulled the keys out of.

Cell phones. How did I forget about cell phones? Because he couldn't afford one. Everyone had them. Everyone. Rage consumed him, and he pushed the tip of the Mauser into her back. She screamed, one short yelp, and he just wanted to make her shut up and make the approaching sirens shut up and make the howling dogs shut up. Stephen pulled the trigger. The beaner flinched. The empty weapon clicked. He pulled the trigger again and again. She flinched every time, and every time his body jerked. His dick jerked. He inflated with the power of her flinches and the panicked look in her black eyes.

Finally, he dropped the gun and collapsed to the floor, still gripping the leash. The dog crept closer and gazed down at him. Tears burned his eyes, and he fought to push them back. Just before the police came in, the dog sighed, lay down, and rested her head in his lap. It was what he'd been waiting for. He touched her head with his palm and felt the soft warmth of her fur.

He didn't resist the handcuffing. When he got in the car, he saw Vanessa standing in front of the SPCA, watching. He met her eyes and wondered if he was sorry, and if so, what exactly he was sorry for.

Chapter 14
Stephen
1990

Stephen jabbed his trigger finger into Rachel's back, driving her through the front door of his house. His mother laughed in the living room with that husky, wild, come-and-sit-on-my-lap hilarity she reserved for company. He drove Rachel slowly through the hall toward the sound of his mother's laugh, which was also the direction for the stairs to the attic. His finger pressed into the rough fabric of Rachel's blue T-shirt, and he could see she was dragging her feet a little, scuffing up dust bunnies as she walked.

"Move," he whispered, poking her. The lace on his right shoe had come undone, and he kept his legs wide to avoid tripping himself and making his gun go off by mistake. He kept looking for Dieter, but Dieter was gone. His mother or the new uncle had sent him somewhere.

"We can't take care of him right now," his mother had said.

Stephen would have fed him, walked him, kept his training going. He imagined shooting the new uncle until he was bloody on the floor. The shades were down in the living room, and everything looked like the ocean through a dirty car window. The smell of cigarettes made him cough. *It's smoke from a bomb.* He must duck, aim, and shoot but also keep an eye on his war prisoner.

His mother poked her head up over the back of the couch. "Stevie, come in and say hi to your mother. Come and give me a kiss." Her giggles were muffled under the laugh of the unfortunately alive man beside her.

Stephen could see the back of the man's head and his brown hair, wound like a bandanna to hide the obvious bald spot. His mother ducked and disappeared behind the back of the couch. Stephen eyed the empty carton of Swanson's vanilla ice cream and the usual overturned ashtray and pushed Rachel toward the attic stairs, but his mother called again. "Come on, Stevie. Come say hi." Rachel stopped moving, forcing Stephen to stop too.

He could see over the couch that his mother's head was on the man's lap, her legs crossed at the ankles, propped on the arm of the couch. He saw one high-heeled sandal, but the other foot was bare except for chipped red nail polish. She wiggled her toes on the shoeless foot, as if she was playing piano notes in the air. Her sundress was bunched high on her hips, revealing skin and the edges of lacy black underwear. She laughed again and tugged the dress down.

"This is Stevie's friend, Rachel," she told the man. The man played with his mother's hair, his beefy fingers twisting and tugging at the bleached-white strands.

Stephen's mother stretched a lazy arm in Stephen and Rachel's direction. "Come on and give your poor mother a kiss," she said. "Come on, Stevie. Come and tell me about your day."

"I'm busy," Stephen said and grabbed Rachel's arm to hurry her up. He could tell his mother wouldn't be taking him to the hospital to see his grandpa that night. He had been counting on going earlier, even though he hated the bleachy medicine odor, how white and clean everything was, and the nurses bending forward to say, "Hi, Stevie, how are you today?" as if he were three years old. His grandpa was supposed to come home that week, but now they wanted to keep him for another week. "To stabilize him on the oxygen," his mother had said.

The man turned swollen eyes in Stephen's direction. "When your mother tells you to do something, you should do it. What are you, some kind of ingrate kid who can't give his own mother a kiss hello?"

"Now, Brett, you leave the discipline to me. Nobody touches my kid but me." Stephen's mother sat up and swung her legs around so her feet touched the floor. Her dress rode up farther, and Uncle Brett slid a hand underneath the hem and glared at Stephen with a look in his eyes that made Stephen want to punch him in the face and run away all at the same time. Stephen's mother giggled and swatted Brett's hand away, tugging the dress down. "Come *on,* Stevie. Give me a kiss."

"It's *Stephen,*" he wanted to shout, but instead he barely whispered.

"What?" she asked, and the man threw him a hostile look.

"Nothing." Stephen dropped Rachel's arm and moved cautiously toward his mother. He leaned forward and pecked her on the cheek, trying not to gag at her breath. She tousled his hair the way the nurses at the hospital sometimes did, and he jerked back and speed walked away.

"Did you do your homework?" she called after him.

"It's Saturday," he mumbled.

"What?" she asked again, but he ignored her and shoved his finger back against Rachel's back.

"Go," he ordered her.

Uncle Brett called after him, "Your mother said to do your homework, kid. Better do it."

Stephen's mother scolded him. "I *told* you. I'll worry about my son. You just take care of me." Her laughter followed Rachel and him up the attic stairs.

While he and Rachel climbed to the attic, he imagined his grandpa waiting for them up there, waiting to tell them one of his war stories: how they'd rounded up and killed the ugly Jews, how he saw Hitler talk and knew he would do anything that man wanted, how the world would be different if only they'd won.

His mother always got mad when his grandpa told those stories, saying they were full of shit and that her father sure as hell never fought for Hitler because she would know it if he had. She was just embarrassed because in America, being a Nazi wasn't good. But not Grandpa. Grandpa was proud, and he would tell anyone as much.

Chapter 15
Gladys

Gladys prowled the kitchen and urged the kettle to whistle already. She sorted tea in the cupboards and opened a Lipton bag. Most of the mugs were in the dishwasher, so she was forced to use Rose's mug, with its pithy little prompt to Embrace the Day.

She could see Rachel and *that boy* through the open doorway that separated the kitchen from the living room. There was something familiar about that boy. He was like nobody she knew, yet whenever she saw him, she was filled with longing and grief.

Rachel's blue quilt, the quilt Gladys had made her, was forted between the sofa and coffee table. Rachel sat cross-legged just outside the fort, a deck of cards scattered around her. She looked up at the boy, and Gladys could see her pinched face and quivering jaw. Whiny Rachel, who didn't understand how good her life was, how safe she was, how she had nothing to whine about.

"C'mon. We're playing war," the boy announced. He stood above Rachel, his legs slightly spread, aiming a toy rifle at her head.

Gladys shuddered. She didn't like toy guns in the house, and she wanted to march in there and order him to leave. But Rose and Aaron had a soft spot for the boy. "His family life isn't good," Rose had said. "And Rachel doesn't have that many friends. Let them be."

"I don't feel like it. I wanna do a magic show." Rachel turned a few cards over. "Pick a card, any card."

"Come on," the boy insisted. He climbed onto the easy chair, briefly wobbled, and transferred the weapon to his left arm so he could thrust his right arm into the air. He leapt, thumping to the floor inches away from Rachel's hand. "Ha!"

Gladys stiffened. *Was that a Nazi salute?* He could have broken Rachel's hand.

Rachel scattered the cards and destroyed the fort. She draped the quilt over her shoulders to make a cape. Gladys had done a good job on that quilt. The Magen Davids were just right and formed a pattern of a bigger Magen David that covered the quilt. But it belonged on a bed, not on Rachel's back like some kind of Superman cape.

Rachel climbed onto the easy chair, clutching the cape around her shoulders. "I am a great and famous magician," she announced. "I'm going to amaze you." She imitated the boy, thrusting her right arm forward and up, holding onto the cape with her left hand. Then she jumped into the air. "Hi ho, Hitler!" Her childish voice echoed into the kitchen.

Behind Gladys, the tea water began to boil, knocking against the inside of the kettle like a danger sign, like footsteps approaching the door. Her muscles turned to stone.

The boy laughed and pointed his gun at Rachel again. "It isn't 'hi ho, Hitler,' stupid. It's Heil Hitler. Anyway, you can't be the Nazi. You're the Jew. I'm the Nazi."

"I don't wanna be the Jew," Rachel whined, collapsing to the floor and spreading the quilt around her. "I'm tired of being the Jew."

Gladys forced movement. One foot forward. Another. She gained speed and hurtled forward. The boy saw her first, his pale eyes widening as she approached. She strode toward them, erupting with everything she had just seen.

"You," she said, jabbing a finger in his face. "You leave. Now." He stared up at her. His face was pale, and his small frame shook, but he met her gaze with defiance, and she wanted to hit him, shake him, hurt him. "Out!" she shouted. "Out, out, out!"

Lucky, whom she hadn't noticed on his bed in the corner of the room, wriggled toward Rachel's bedroom with his ears down and tail tucked. The boy stood erect and met her eyes.

She channeled her fury into her gaze and straightened to her full height. She held her breath until finally, he turned away, and she heaved out a relieved sigh. He stumbled toward the door and stooped to slip his feet into a pair of leather boots at least three sizes too big. She would not let herself see the way his ragged shirt hung too low against spindly legs or the hand-shaped bruise on his arm. She saw instead the man he would become, white haired, blue eyed, and dangerous. She glared until he slipped out the door and shut it behind him.

Gladys turned to Rachel, who had not moved from her position on the floor. "You." Gladys kept her voice low. "In the chair."

Rachel skulked to the chair and sat. Her feet dangled off the floor. Gladys moved in until she could smell peanut butter on Rachel's breath. "If I ever hear the word Hitler out of your mouth again, you will not eat for a week. If I ever hear you say you don't want to be a Jew, you will not eat for a month. Maybe your mother lets you get away with this, but I will not. You are a Jew. That is the most important thing about you. Do you understand?"

Rachel turned her head.

Gladys grabbed her shoulders and shook, gently enough. Far more gently than she wanted to. "Do you understand?"

"Yes," Rachel said, so softly that her voice was obliterated by a sudden high-pitched shrieking, like a warning of approaching bombs.

Gladys gripped Rachel's arm and felt the bones so small, so fragile in her hands. "Something is happening. We have to leave. We have to go." She tugged and dragged Rachel out of the chair and toward the door. The alarm, louder and louder, was both out in the room and in Gladys's head. *Is it a bomb? A fire?* Rachel had said she didn't want to be a Jew, but they would go anyway. It didn't matter if they went to synagogue, if they were observant, or if they ate treyf.

"Gladys." A hand on her shoulder stiffened her and made her drop Rachel's arm. "Gladys, what are you doing?" She unclenched and spun around with fisted hands. Maybe she was just an old lady, but she would have fought if need be.

Rose, holding a brown grocery bag in one hand, stared into Gladys's face with inflamed cheeks and frightened eyes. "What are you doing? The kettle…" She glanced toward the kitchen, where the alarm—no, the teakettle—shrieked and shrieked. "Rachel? Are you okay?"

Gladys turned back to see Rachel staring into the air, unblinking. "This child said she doesn't want to be a Jew," Gladys explained, making no effort to hide the bitter taste of her words. "That's what a heathen for a mother gets you." Then she walked away, through the kitchen, where the teakettle settled into a long wail like coyotes, like the night, like death.

Chapter 16
Rachel
2016

Rachel wondered how many movies existed about women fighting back against violent, child-abusing men and how long it
would be before she got bored. She took a break for the locksmith on
Tuesday afternoon, standing under a throbbing sun, noting the swirl
lines on her freshly painted door while he fiddled and drilled and
gave her a dead bolt. Then she returned to the television. She closed
her curtains when the glare affected her TV screen. She slept on the
couch, waking to mute the sound at some point. She wasn't afraid.
She wasn't angry. She didn't feel violated or any of those other things
one was probably supposed to feel when being Twitter stalked and
having it bleed into real life. She just didn't want to get off her couch.

Pete came home and stopped by on Wednesday morning. She
heard him trying to let himself in as he usually would, but she didn't
get up until he rang the bell. She knew it was Pete and had known the
minute she heard the loud rattle of his car that had somehow passed
its last inspection. She almost didn't get off the couch to let him in.
But it was Pete.

He stood behind her couch, and she followed his gaze around
her living room, watching while he crouched to collect some Kleenex
she'd crumbled and dropped on the floor. There were several—some
of those Lifetime movies were tearjerkers—and he retrieved them all
without saying a word. Then he started on her mail, which he piled
on her dining room table.

A good thing about Pete was that they didn't need small talk. That was what she told herself as she silently followed him into the kitchen, where he skidded to a halt and let his jaw hang open in exaggerated surprise.

"Sweetie. What on earth?"

She laughed, though it sounded forced even to her. "Being stalked really throws a person out of whack," she said.

"You're living in a hazardous-waste dump."

Rachel didn't know what to say, so she said nothing.

"You could stay with me," he offered. He wandered back to the living room and went to sit on her couch but then obviously noticed the wet place where she had spilled coffee that morning and remained standing. "You need some taking care of. Clearly."

"They could go after you too," she pointed out. "You wrote the play."

"But they don't have my address, and I don't have Facebook or a Twitter account." For years, Rachel had harassed him about maintaining an online presence to help promote his writing, but she knew his refusal was a gift.

"I won't let them drive me out of my own house." Gladys's voice echoed in her head: *They stayed because they didn't want to leave their things behind. They died for things. And in the end, no things anyway. The Nazis got it all in the end.* "Anyway, they haven't come back."

"You ought to just cancel that Twitter account. It isn't that important to be all over the web, you know."

Rachel's jaw tightened. Her teeth ached from grinding them. "It isn't just Twitter. It's Facebook. It's all over the Internet. Anyway, I won't let them win."

He spun in a circle, pointing out the piles of mess in her house. "I hate to tell you, but I think they're winning."

Rachel's landline saved her from answering, and they listened in silence while her mother left another message about Gladys and unreturned phone calls.

Rachel deleted the message.

Pete gathered the rest of the garbage around her couch and carried it all to the trash in her kitchen. "Maybe visiting your family right now isn't such a bad idea."

"I know," she said. "I should go. But it isn't like Gladys is there to say goodbye to. She hasn't really been present in years."

"You should go for your parents, then. And to get the hell out of here."

Pete started on the dishes, and Rachel felt heat rise in her face. "You don't have to do that. I'm perfectly capable of cleaning up my own mess."

"Are you?" Pete turned the garbage disposal on before she could answer.

Rachel dried the pot he had washed, focusing on the grainy texture of the towel, the sound of water running.

"So, anyway," he said over the water, "what's up with the *Titanic*? Why isn't she here, helping out?"

"Her name is Liz," Rachel mumbled, feeling about twelve years old. "She's got the kids." Her voice sounded small, even to her.

He stayed quiet for a good long time, rinsing dishes and loading her dishwasher. Then he turned off the sink and closed the dishwasher. He turned to face her. "We're getting out of here. We're gonna take a walk."

"No," she said. "No way. I'm not going out. I'm happy here. I'm fine. I don't need to take a walk."

"Sweetie."

"Don't fucking call me that. You only do it when you're being patronizing." She was surprised at the surge of anger, the impulse to lash out and hurt him. It passed in a wave of shame that left her staring at the cracked yellow linoleum on her kitchen floor.

Pete raised his hands in a gesture of helplessness. Rachel put the pot away and slammed the cupboard door harder than necessary.

"I thought about it while I was in P-Town," he finally said. "I'm gonna stop the show early. I want to rewrite that second act. I want to make it better. Just one more week then done. You could go to California. See your family. Take some time."

"Sure." Rachel met his eyes so he would think she meant it.

"Sure," Pete agreed as he brushed past her and headed toward the door.

"Pete," she called when he had his hand on the doorknob.

He turned.

"I'm sorry. I'm a bitch."

He smiled. "You could do with a little more bitchiness now and then. You're too nice most of the time. Come hug me goodbye."

Rachel did.

After he left, she returned to her sofa and unmuted Lifetime. A police car on the show wailed down the highway in pursuit of something or someone, and the sound hurt her ears. She muted it again. She kept seeing the wounded look on Pete's face and hearing herself, harsh and distant, pushing him away. She doubled over and stayed curled into herself. But she couldn't cry.

HOURS LATER, LIZ WAS at her door. "You've been sitting around your house in the dark long enough. It's gorgeous out. We're taking a walk." She was dressed in a cheery red tank top and over-sized sunglasses, and her hair was pulled back into a ponytail that showed brown roots under the red.

"What happened to the kids?" Rachel asked.

"Peter called me," Liz replied. "I found a babysitter."

"I'm perfectly fine. You can leave. Go be with your kids." Rachel's body felt coiled as if she was in her corner, ready for a fight.

Liz studied her. "He was really worried about you. And rightly so, methinks. You look like a caged animal."

They walked at Pineville Lake Park. It was the first time Rachel had seen Liz since the night of the swastika. A man Rollerbladed past, wearing a T-shirt with something on it. She couldn't see what, but after he was gone, she decided it had been a swastika. Two women glanced at her, and she glared back until they looked away because more than anything, she wanted to run. The sun felt too bright, and her bones vibrated with anxiety.

"Talk to me," Liz chided. "Seems like days since we've really talked."

"That isn't my fault," Rachel said. "Sorry. I'm just... I'm not myself." The park was full of dog walkers, Rollerbladers, people picnicking. Half of Pineville must have called in sick. The lake glinted with sunlight. But Rachel shivered and zipped her long-sleeved jacket up to her chin.

"Well, you can't just keep everything locked up inside. Tell me what you've been doing with your free time." Liz rested a casual arm over Rachel's shoulder. Rachel had always basked in Liz's energy, the way she popped with static electricity, but it burned.

"Just relaxing. That's what summer is for, right? Downtime?" She made no effort to purge her voice of hostility.

"You can't just spend your whole summer sitting around your house, though." Liz squeezed Rachel's shoulder then took her hand, gently swinging their arms between them. A young couple passed, and the man stared pointedly at Rachel and Liz's linked hands.

Rachel jerked her hand away. She despised the skittish version of herself. Briefly, she reveled in an explosion of rage toward the people who had made her their special project. Trouble was, there was nothing to do with the rage. Twitter told her to block them, and they eventually pulled the really disgusting tweets, but more came. She could get off social media altogether, but that would have been letting them win. It would have been allowing them to erase her. She felt so helpless.

"Yeah, I know," Rachel said. She spotted a bench and headed for it, trusting Liz to follow. "Anyway, I've got the play starting back up tomorrow night." No need to tell Liz that Pete was stopping it early.

Liz glided down onto the bench beside her. There was a hint of that patchouli perfume, mixed with the smell of cut grass and someone's nearby barbeque. "Then what? How shall we spend our summer?"

Rachel shrugged. "How shall we spend our summer? Maybe a week in the Cape? How about a trip to Italy or Paris? Or we could hibernate in my house together and make love every day."

A group of teenagers passed, giggling. "She's such a disgusting slut," one of them said, and she flinched, because for a second, even though she knew it was paranoid and crazy, she thought they meant her.

"You know I can't..." Liz trailed off. "Next year we will, though. We'll plan a trip to Paris."

"And we'll stay in that little hotel I stayed in the time I went with Pete. The one in the Latin district, with the bakery and café right outside the door. And we'll sleep late and linger over fresh croissants and coffee and kiss in the alley." Rachel couldn't quite keep the edge of sarcasm out of her voice, but Liz proceeded as if she didn't notice.

"We'll walk all over town, or just spend entire days in the hotel." She winked.

"But this time, it isn't just a fantasy, right? It's real this time?" She felt soothed, fantasizing about future time with Liz.

Liz cupped Rachel's face and tilted it up so Rachel could stare into those vivid blue eyes that had first captured her. "It is real. By next summer, I'll be all yours."

"Sooner than that, right?" Rachel asked.

"Well," Liz replied, and Rachel felt it coming. "Michael didn't get his promotion. He found out yesterday."

"So? What does that have to do with us?"

"We have all those medical bills from the twins' asthma, and we can't... financially, we need to be stable. I might not be able to afford to separate right at the end of summer. It might need to wait until after Christmas. After we've paid off those bills."

Rachel felt herself shut down. She thought of Jo and how she'd sent her away the other night. Jo had been willing to stay. She looked at Liz, who had carried her for three years on a roller coaster of passion and fantasy—not reality.

The teenagers clustered around a tree nearby. They burst into laughter, and she felt it again. They were laughing at her. Her naïveté. Her shame.

"It's gonna happen," Liz said. "I promise. I want you. I want to be with you. You're my love. But I have to prioritize the kids' welfare. That's what being a mother means. It means putting them first, even when I can't have what I want."

"Do you really want to be with me, or do you just like the excitement? Do you like that it's forbidden?" The words, things she often thought but never said, surprised Rachel.

"How can you say that?" Liz sounded genuinely distressed. "I love you."

Rachel should have been done. Enough was enough. It was something she could control. She was sick of Liz playing the mother card. Liz's facade of being so put together and emotionally healthy was bullshit. She was just as scared as Rachel. But Rachel didn't say any of those things, because she suddenly felt so very drowsy—drowsy the way people who froze to death got drowsy, heavy limbed and lethargic, as if she could sleep and sleep and never wake up. She shrugged. "Okay," she said calmly. "I guess it will be what it will be."

They finished the walk, talking about everything but the relationship that wasn't or the way Rachel felt—the paranoia, the sense that the comments she had been reading on social media were somehow visible, tattooed onto her skin. A young man wearing black jeans and combat boots glanced at her and slowed, lingering with his gaze on her, and she actually checked the inside of her arm in case the words "Dirty Jew Girl" had sprouted there for him to see.

Then he smiled and said, "Hey, you're that actress, right? I've seen all your plays. You're awesome."

She almost couldn't smile back or absorb the words because for a second, what she heard was, "To the showers, Jew Girl. Time for your shower."

When Liz drove Rachel home, she pulled into the driveway instead of parking across the street. Rachel opened her door, but before she could get out of the car, Liz touched her arm then leaned across the gearshift for a kiss. Rachel kissed back, her body heating in response.

Liz ended the kiss. "I have to get home." Her face was flushed, lips swollen. "I wish I could stay."

Rachel touched her own lips, feeling the ghost of Liz's mouth there. "I know," she said.

"I'm here for you." Liz straightened but kept her unblinking eyes on Rachel. "You know that, right?"

"I know," Rachel agreed, but she was the one to break the eye contact as she exited the car. When she reached her porch and heard Liz backing out of the driveway, she could not stop herself from turning to watch Liz leave.

In the house, Rachel slipped out of her shoes and back into sweats, turned the television on, and curled up on the couch with her laptop. She stared at the blank screen for a long time before yielding, first to Facebook, where she had several Messenger alerts. *Were they from one person or hundreds? Thousands?*

The written attacks merged and blended together. They felt more personal on Messenger. At least on her timeline and Twitter were public, and anybody could see. There, it felt like they were posting to the world, not just to her. But Messenger was like email. They might as well have been calling her. She deleted several messages then closed the app, leaving more unread.

In her mind, Jo and Liz stood side by side with Liz offering a small seductive smile and Jo with those warm brown eyes. Rachel wanted to turn away from both of them. She couldn't. Maybe she preferred the safety of Liz. If Liz was the *Titanic*, all orchestra and gourmet food but headed for an iceberg, at least Rachel would know she needed a life jacket.

What if I let someone like Jo know me? What if Jo is repulsed by what she saw? What if I gave up Liz and then Jo doesn't want me? Rachel had been there before, in a triangle of possibility, what Pete called being "addicted to someone's potential." The excuses were familiar: *I've decided to commit to my girlfriend. I've come to realize I'm not really over her. If I wasn't about to move out of state, I'd totally commit to you...* She was Facebook friends with all of them, though she never understood the lesbian obsession with hanging onto friendships after a breakup.

She opened Twitter. The comments seemed endless. It should have been satisfying to block them, but it wasn't. She had to read them—she couldn't avoid the revulsion, the feeling she deserved them and that deleting them, trying to unhappen them, was the wrong thing.

Then, all of a sudden, as if she'd been looking for it, she found it. JT51 wrote *I think we saw the bitch at That Place last night. I'm sure it was her. Bitch came on to me then threw her beer at me. She deserves whatever she gets.*

Below that, Deplorable34: *Bitch's address is 25 Meadow St., Pineville, NY. Go get her.*

Rachel couldn't breathe or make her mind slow down. She couldn't grab a thought and make sense of it. She gasped for air. The walls of her living room pressed in, squeezing the breath out of her.

She went outside and stood on the warm planks of her porch, trying to slow her breathing and get out from under the weight of it all. Going to that bar had made things worse, not better. If she'd thought about it for five minutes instead of plunging in, she probably would have figured that out ahead of time. She shuddered at the memory of J.T. pressing her into that pool table and the way she had let him. Now, he knew where she lived.

Dusk was settling in, and the lone streetlight flickered on. A loud car radio grew closer until a white truck appeared and idled in front of her house. A man in the passenger seat stared out the window at her. The cab light was on, illuminating the clean-shaven face and bald head of the driver. *Is it J.T.?* The truck had several bumper stickers. She could see the dim, meaningless writing in the night, pasted to the back. The man pointed a finger at her then pulled a pretend trigger. He mouthed something. Then the truck revved and sped away.

First, she froze. Then she couldn't move fast enough. She fumbled with the door to get inside, her heart racing and sweat drenching her shirt. She slammed the door behind her, locked the doorknob, then pushed the dead bolt into place. She should get a chain. *Why didn't I buy a chain?* "They came for them in their houses," Gladys said. "They came right in the house and took them to the camps."

Her body trembled. She sobbed once then wrapped her arms around herself to push it all back in. She knew she should leave. *But where?* What if they broke in and wrecked her stuff? She should stay. She should hide. She needed a weapon, some way to fight back. She went to the kitchen, opened drawers, opened cupboards, and grabbed the first thing that seemed solid and heavy enough.

She sank to the floor and curled around the large clay serving platter. She stayed huddled against the wall, listening as hard as she could to cars as they passed her house. *Did it have a radio on?* She couldn't remember. *Was it loud or quiet? Did it rattle?* Finally, unable to stand another second, she found her phone.

Jo answered right away. "Hi, Rachel."

Rachel focused on breathing, getting her words out. "They're here," she said. "They're here. They're here. They're here. They're out there." She needed a paper bag. She couldn't remember the last time she had hyperventilated like that.

"Okay," Jo said. "I'm on my way."

Rachel pressed End. The serving platter felt solid like a shield, something between her and whoever was out there.

She let the doorbell ring three times before she could bring herself to leave the safety of her wall. *What if it isn't Jo? What if it's him?* Finally, she pulled the door open a crack and stepped sideways, hoisting the platter over her head, just in case.

The door opened.

Rachel held her breath.

Jo walked in. She tucked her head and put her arms up. "Sheesh. Put that thing down." She stepped back until Rachel slowly lowered the platter. But she didn't put it down. She hugged it against herself, backing into the room until she was pressed into the far corner.

"What do you have there?" Jo asked.

Rachel tried to back up more. "A weapon." Her voice emerged whisper thin.

"I see that. Maybe you should put it down."

Rachel tried to focus on Jo's face. *Is that warmth in her eyes? Caution?* Rachel's hands shook hard.

"Take a deep breath," Jo said. "Breathe with me."

Rachel tried to suck in air.

Jo stepped forward and took the platter from her. "Man," Jo said. "This thing would have knocked me out if you'd used it." She set it on the floor, and Rachel slid down next to it. "Where'd you get it? I like the roses."

"My mother." Rachel tried to breathe.

"That was nice of her. Can you breathe now? Can you talk?"

Rachel sucked air. "There was a truck. They were looking at me. They're after me. They're watching me."

"Okay," Jo said. "Did you get a license plate off the truck?"

Rachel shook her head. "I didn't think of it. I just ran back inside. What if they come after me? What if they can get in the house?" She grabbed the platter and locked her arms around it. She could fight back. She could hurt them if she needed to.

"Looks like you have yourself a weapon if they do," Jo said.

Rachel heard herself laugh, though Jo's voice had an edge of anger. Well, she had nearly whacked her with a serving platter.

"You really ought to just get off the Internet," Jo said. "Just cancel your account. They'll forget about you and move on to someone else."

"I know," Rachel whispered. She leaned back. "I can't let them win." Outside, a loud car roared past, and Rachel folded in around the platter.

"Then come down to the station and file a fucking report. Let me call the FBI."

Rachel shook her head. "It's just kids. Right? Just kids." If she believed it hard enough, maybe she could make that be true. She could will it. She could unhappen everything.

Jo stayed quiet long enough for Rachel to count several heartbeats. "Listen," Jo finally said, her voice sounding resigned, "do you want me to call Liz for you? Or some other friend?"

Rachel shook her head. "I was just with Liz. She had to get the kids to an appointment."

"Someone else? I can't stay here." There was definitely a harsh tone in her voice. "You keep calling me. I don't know what you want from me." Jo backed in the direction of the door, and Rachel felt everything start up—the panic welled. She was going to die. Jo would walk out, and then they would kill her, the truck-driving, swastika-painting white supremacists. She had let J.T. think she was one of them. She had flirted back. She was an idiot. They would kill her. They wanted to kill her.

Rachel tried to slow her breathing. The air sucked in but wouldn't expel. The room spun. She swallowed thick air. She dropped the platter, hearing the crack, the clap like a gunshot. Her vision blurred.

"Rachel."

Jo's voice drifted into her consciousness from far away. Rachel felt like she was being yanked backwards down a tunnel.

"Rachel. You have to breathe."

Breathe. It's fine. I'm fine.

"You'll be okay. This will get better. We'll find the guys." But there was something false in Jo's voice.

Rachel didn't believe the platitude. There were no happy endings. Rachel breathed. She felt her mind spinning, and everything was dark, and there was nothing, and then she felt a hard sting on her left cheek.

She startled and glanced up in time to see the second slap coming.

When it connected with her cheek, she stopped breathing. She looked at Jo and felt a surge of something else, something unexpected. She felt her lips part, and her body leaned in. Warmth spread through her.

Jo took a step back.

Rachel leaned against the wall, eyeing Jo, feeling the burn on her cheek and a sudden, brutal desire to erase everything in the best way she knew. Jo glared back, and Rachel absorbed her anger like the flare of a match, warming her body in spite of—or more likely because of—the sense of danger, drawing heat to her center. A brief fantasy of Jo pouncing on her and pinning her arms against the wall engaged her. *I'll make you talk, Jew Girl.*

She pictured Jo the other morning, wet from the shower, her nipples prominent beneath her shirt. She pressed back against the wall, digging her hands into her stomach, trying to hold everything inside, but instead the awareness of her own fingers so close to her crotch only increased her arousal. She focused everything on that desire.

"I need to go," Jo said. But she didn't. Instead, she moved toward Rachel. They both looked at Rachel's hands, so close to the button of her jeans. Rachel's heart seemed louder than the traffic passing outside or the movie playing in the background.

"I don't understand you," Jo said, focusing on Rachel's hands. "Nothing about you makes sense to me." She tugged Rachel's hand away from her stomach and turned it palm up, studying it as if she was a fortune-teller.

Her hot touch and the sensation of skin on skin overwhelmed Rachel.

"You *like* that I'm pissed, don't you?" Jo took Rachel's other hand and held both of them, locking them together and leaning in to look directly into Rachel's eyes. "You like that I slapped you."

Rachel shifted a little, unable to turn away, powerless to stop the desire that made her inch forward until her breasts brushed Jo's. She pressed in. For a moment, there was the enveloping warmth of lips and bodies merging.

But Jo jerked away. "You keep calling me, but you're with someone else. Someone married. You want me, but you don't want to dump her."

A familiar empty feeling wiped her brain of words. She stared at a gouge in the hardwood floor. A flaw. A broken place.

"You don't know what you want." Jo sounded more matter-of-fact than angry.

Rachel bit the inside of her mouth until it hurt.

"I'm attracted to you," Jo said. "I don't know why. You seem like you're kind of a fucked-up mess of a drama queen." Then she laughed, though the laugh had a bitter edge. "Maybe that's why I like you."

Rachel hugged herself and tried to think. "I do want you," she whispered, wondering how to stop being a drama queen when she was scared to death.

"But you're still with Liz. Right?"

Rachel searched for a response that would keep Jo from leaving, but there was nothing to say.

"Okay," Jo said and turned her palms up in a gesture of surrender. "I get it. I need to go. You should call 911 if that truck comes back." She turned and headed toward the door.

"No, wait." Rachel would not cry. She wouldn't. She felt the memory of Liz, of abandonment. Everybody was gone. "Please stay?"

The phone rang. They both froze until the answering machine picked up.

"Rachel, honey. We're wondering if we should call the police. We've seen what people are saying on your Facebook page. We really need you to call and tell us if you're okay." There was a long silence before Rachel's mother hung up.

Jo stood by the door. "Your mother?"

Rachel nodded and felt herself flush.

"I guess you should let her know she doesn't need to call the cops." Jo laughed, and it seemed more genuine to Rachel. A rush of hope welled up.

Jo moved toward Rachel, reached out, and touched the stinging place on her cheek. She stroked it gently.

"I could get my shit together," Rachel said. "I can do it." The words poured out while another part of her brain hunted for the ones that would appease Jo and make her stay. "I'll go to therapy. I'll break up with Liz. I-I'll figure it out."

But Jo backed away. "Call me if that happens." She turned and opened the door.

Rachel followed and peered over her shoulder, breaking out in an instant sweat. "Please don't go," she whispered.

"There's nothing there," Jo said. "It's fine."

But there was something there. The white truck sat in the road in front of her house. Its engine revved. It was close enough that Rachel could see inside, see the jut of chin, the shaved head. The window rolled down. The arm moved. She caught a glint of metal. He mouthed something. "Pow." The truck squealed away. Her mind replayed it. The pow. The metallic glint. *Did he have a gun?*

Jo bolted toward the truck. It spun around the corner, and Jo stumbled then pointed her cell phone at the back of the truck. *What is she doing? You can't shoot the truck with a phone.* Rachel crept out onto her porch and felt her hands clenched into fists, her shoulders tense. *Breathe,* she told herself, and she pushed air out then sucked air in. *Again. Just breathe.* She made herself unclench her fists.

Jo came back, panting and red faced. She pushed Rachel inside then followed, shutting the door and staring at her phone. "Damn," she said. "I was hoping to catch the license plate, but he took off too fast." She turned to Rachel. "I half thought you were imagining it."

Rachel nodded. She wanted to crawl in her closet or under her bed. She made herself stay put. *Jo is here. You're safe.*

"I need to call this in. At least I got a photo of the truck. You can make out some of the bumper stickers." She fidgeted with her screen while Rachel watched and felt the horror rise up. *Did he point a gun at me?* She couldn't tell beyond the glint of metal. She sucked in air and studied her hands. They only shook a little. *What if it was a gun, and he fires it next time?*

"Are you going to lose it again?" Jo finally glanced up.

Rachel surprised herself by managing a jittery smile. At least Jo knew she wasn't going crazy. There really was a truck. "I don't know," she said. "I think I'm going to get the hell out of here."

"Good," Jo said. "I think you should. But what say I drive you to the station so you can give a statement first."

Rachel shook her head. "No. No statements."

"Why not?" Jo's voice had that angry edge again, but Rachel didn't feel turned on by it anymore.

"You were here. You give the statement." She imagined the news reports, the story leaking out into her school district. They would hear how she went to the bar, how she flirted with J.T., acting like she was fine with everything he stood for. Half the parents would hate her for that. The other half would hate her for being a lesbian and for Pete's play. She commuted more than ninety minutes to teach for a reason. It mostly worked. But she hadn't missed the NRA and Abortion Causes Cancer signs in front of houses she drove past as she wound her way through the residential areas to her high school. A friend in the English department had quit last year after some of the school board campaigned against him when they discovered he was transgender. He wasn't fired for it, but the constant harassment, threatening emails, and inevitable rock through his window meant that he might as well have been.

"I don't understand why it's a problem. I'll drive you there. I'll be with you."

"I don't know." She tried to steady her voice. "I just... I can't. Can't you do it for me?"

Jo stayed quiet a long time. "Do you have somewhere to go?"

Rachel had to admit the concern in Jo's voice was gratifying. "I'm going to California. My grandmother is dying." Her voice felt small and tentative in her own ears. She breathed and still felt the tremors.

Jo nodded. "Okay. Will you be okay if I leave?" She looked hesitant, like maybe she wanted to stay or maybe she wanted Rachel to release her.

The panic welled up again. Rachel could collapse, and Jo would step in, and she would stay, and maybe they would go to the bedroom. She could get Jo to stay. Instead, she pressed her fists into her thighs. "Can I call you if the truck comes back?"

"Please," Jo said. "Please call me." She stepped out onto the porch for the second time but stopped. "Buy your plane tickets, okay? Get out of here. And in the meantime, lock your door."

Then she was gone. Rachel locked and dead bolted her door then stood in the silence of her house. Sounds of traffic passed outside. A horn blare. A radio blasting rap.

Finally, she retrieved the platter. She traced a large crack with her fingers then put it back in the kitchen cupboard. She went into the bathroom and stared in the mirror. She touched the red mark on her cheek. She unfocused her eyes, but when she looked again, the mark was still there. She glared into the mirror, concentrating on the burning place on her cheek and the empty place deep in her gut that Jo could have eradicated if only she'd stayed. A real man with a real gun was harassing her, but at least one person knew she wasn't crazy.

Then Rachel got online and looked up plane tickets to San Diego.

Chapter 17
Rachel
1992

Grandma Gladys stood in front of the mirror in her room, brushing her hair with a round black brush. Rachel sat on the floor, walking a model horse back and forth, waiting to start her Hebrew lesson. Then she made the dappled mare gallop and stop in front of a dust bunny that she pretended was a bale of hay.

"Did you study the words I gave you last night?" Gladys asked, and Rachel nodded, focusing on the magic foam balls in her other hand. She opened her hand, and two shot under the bed. She got on her knees and arced her hand across the floor. Her hand bumped something else, something harder than the squishy balls. She sank to her stomach so she could peer under the bed. The balls were there, nestled against a box of some sort. She grabbed the balls then dragged the box out. It was white with a yellow top.

Her grandmother swooped down and yanked the box away in an action so violent that it sprained Rachel's finger. Her grandmother slapped her cheek so hard that her ears rang. The shock of it felt like the time she was in a car accident with her mother. The jolt came first, then the sound, then her heart going so fast she could hardly breathe.

"You don't ever, ever touch that box. It's private. Do you understand? Private."

Rachel nodded because she couldn't talk. She wanted to leave the room and go anywhere else, but she stayed.

"Now," Gladys said as she slid the box back under the bed and straightened with a grunt. "What is the word for 'book' in Hebrew?"

Later, her mother asked, "What happened to your cheek?" Rachel turned away so her mother wouldn't see it anymore. Already, the slap on her cheek had merged with the box and become "private," which meant "not to be discussed."

At dinner that night, it hurt to grip a fork, and everybody was quiet, and Rachel's father wouldn't look at her. Later, he and her grandmother went in the library and closed the door, and there was a long, muted conversation. Rachel hovered outside the door, wondering what her father and her grandmother were saying, wondering how bad she had been for her father to refuse to look at her.

"She's only seven." Her father's voice was suddenly loud enough that she could hear with no trouble.

Her grandmother mumbled something she couldn't make out.

"She's a child!" her father yelled. Then the voices got low again, and she heard only the urgent rise and fall of their fight.

Still, she lingered by the door for several minutes, hoping to hear something that would help her know how to be good, how to make sure her father never refused to look at her again.

That night, when she took her bath, she saw the mark on her cheek, a bright-red bruise just below her right eye. She stood in front of the mirror and practiced focusing and unfocusing her eyes until the bruise disappeared from her reflection. By the time she got in the bath, the water was cold, but the bruise had never happened. She had unhappened it.

———— ◉ ————

THE NEXT DAY, SHE SQUATTED under an overhang in the canyon. She tried to pretend she was dead by holding her breath and not moving. Dead people didn't breathe. A rock gouged her back, and she pressed into it, letting the pain flood her body until it was everywhere and nowhere. *I'm dead. I'm dead. I'm dead.*

Stephen yelled, "I'm gonna find you, Rachel. I'm gonna find you and Tina too." His footsteps were close. A fly buzzed, tickling her face. She fought the urge to swat it away and waited. She had to breathe. She sucked air. She shifted. The motion dislodged a clump of hardened dirt nearby, which landed on the ground with a soft thud. She held her breath, but he was already standing there. "Told you I'd find you." Their agreed-upon white flag of defeat involved dropping to their knees and bowing their heads. But he didn't leave her there long.

"You're my prisoner now." With a dirt-smudged hand, he dragged her to her feet and out of the shallow cave. She followed with no resistance. There wasn't a cloud in the sky, and down in the canyon, there was no ocean breeze. She couldn't even hear a bird, except the finches. The wind was dry and hot and smelled faintly of smoke, probably from a wildfire somewhere, a California Santa Ana. Rachel tugged her sweat-soaked shirt away from her skin with her free hand and pushed a strand of wet hair out of her right eye, accidentally brushing her cheek. She did not allow herself a flinch. The pain was there but not there.

"Hurry up." Steven squeezed her arm harder, and she realized she had slowed, focused on cooling herself.

"Sorry," she mumbled.

"You're my prisoner, and you must do as I say." He released her arm and faced her, thrusting his bony shoulders back. She studied his torn brown shorts and the large purple bruise that darkened the spot just above his right knee.

"I know," she said. "It's just so hot."

"Come on," he ordered then turned to walk.

She followed.

"So, where is Tina? I bet you know."

"No, I don't." Tina was hiding behind a shrub, in a small dip in the canyon wall.

"If you tell, I'll let you go."

Rachel considered it then shook her head.

"I'm the oldest. You have to tell me."

Rachel shook her head again. "Only by a year."

"If you don't tell me where she is, I'm gonna send you to the showers. I'll torture you first then send you to the showers." He was imitating his grandfather's German accent, and she shivered, even though she was boiling hot.

That accent always reminded her of her grandmother. Her grandmother spoke with a Yiddish accent, and it was supposedly nothing like German, but they sounded the same to Rachel. When Stephen's grandpa looked at her, she felt like garbage, which was what Stephen said his grandpa called her behind her back. But there was nothing *bad* about showers.

"So, you gonna tell or not?"

One of her sneakers had come untied, and she stopped so she could squat and tie it.

He kept going for a second then spun around. "I *told* you to follow me. You are definitely going to the showers, Jew Girl."

Her fingers fumbled the laces. Too loose, and the bow instantly released. She straightened and studied an anthill near her foot, avoiding his eyes.

"Come on, Jew Girl. This is your last chance to lead me to Tina."

"Jew Girl" was a dirty phrase, and Rachel was supposed to tell Stephen not to call her that. But she was a little afraid to tell him not to. Anyway, maybe she was a Jew girl. Maybe she was a dirty Jew girl. She was mean and bad, and bad girls did bad things.

She met his eyes. "I'll take you to Tina."

He nodded and gestured for her to lead the way. She moved toward Tina's hiding place, keeping her legs wide to avoid stepping on the shoelaces.

Tina must have seen them coming, because she ducked out from behind the shrub and took off running. Stephen sprinted after her. Rachel lagged behind, half running. There was no point in escaping. He would just catch her again.

Then, just as Rachel was slowing, Tina suddenly fell forward and immediately began shrieking. Stephen threw himself on top of her. Her shrill scream was barely muffled under Stephen's scarecrowed body. He rolled off and stumbled to his feet.

"My arm! My arm!" The high-pitched shouts drowned everything, echoing in Rachel's head and roiling her stomach. It was not the usual white flag of surrender.

"Let me see." Stephen squatted to look, but she jerked her body away from him, using her good arm for support to crawl onto her knees.

Rachel edged closer to see the arm.

Tina rocked forward and back, snot pouring from her nose. "You hurt me," she whined, focusing on Stephen or Rachel—it was hard to tell which.

My fault. I gave her up. The Jew Girl ratted her out. "We should get help," Rachel offered but stayed frozen in her spot a few feet away, clutching her stomach to keep the nausea in. The arm looked funny, like a useless doll arm dangling from Tina's elbow.

It was hard to make out words through Tina's sobs, but she seemed to be screaming for her mommy. Rachel often forgot that Tina was a whole year younger than she was, practically a baby. *I shouldn't have ratted her out.*

"Let me help you up, and we'll take you home," Stephen ordered in his you're-my-prisoner voice. But he'd forgotten to use the German accent, and his face was too pale, his eyes dark and frightened.

His fear twisted through Rachel's body, intensifying her own. She swallowed. Tina sniffed, seemingly unaware of the stream of thick snot that hung from her nose, and allowed Stephen to slip his hand under her good arm and drag her to her feet.

Rachel remembered that they were in the bottom of the canyon and had to climb out, using the path they figured out long ago, grabbing bits of shrub first, then dents in the canyon wall, then the big jutting rock near the top. The climb was easy. She'd done it at least ten times already that day. But nobody moved toward the path.

"You stay with her, and I'll get help." Stephen began to walk away. Tina gulped a sob.

"No, Stephen stays," she whimpered.

"Okay. Go, Jew Girl." Rachel felt as if the Santa Ana heat had melted her shoes into the canyon floor. She couldn't stop staring at Tina's dangling arm. "Now, Jew Girl. Go," Stephen ordered again. She forced herself to turn away, stared instead at a gray rock embedded in the canyon wall, then moved toward it, movement growing easier with every step away from the sobbing Tina.

The climb only took less than a minute. Then, Rachel was running down the road toward the first house, a walled-off, squat yellow stucco a little bit away from the road. The tall gate didn't budge, but once she started, she couldn't stop pounding on the door. She barely noticed the tears streaking down her own face. The sound of Tina's screams in the canyon ricocheted in her mind. If the Jew girl hadn't given her up, she would have been okay.

Her mother would frown and walk away. Her father would look sad, because Rachel was a disappointment. Grandma Gladys would sit her on a chair and talk in her face about what it meant to be a Jew.

Her fists hurt, but she didn't stop pounding—couldn't stop until a man came from behind and grabbed her arms.

"What's the matter, kid?"

It took forever for the man to drive Rachel back to the canyon, see what had happened, carry Tina out of the canyon, take them all to his house, offer Rachel water and a towel to wash her face, call Tina's mother, explain his version of what had happened, which didn't include *the Jew girl ratted her out,* and send Tina and her mother off to the hospital. Forever and seconds later, Stephen and Rachel were alone in front of the man's house in the hazy July afternoon sun.

"You're still my prisoner." Stephen remembered the accent, and she shivered a little, but not in a bad way.

She sort of liked being his prisoner. She liked the feeling of not having to worry about what she was going to do next or whose fault it was.

"And you need to be punished." Stephen sidled behind her and pressed a finger into her back. "To the prison camp, Jew Girl."

Rachel knew just what he was punishing her for—for ratting out Tina, being a Jew girl, being dirty.

Chapter 18
Stephen
2016

The psych hospital seemed determined not to let anyone kill themselves. They'd put him in a room with an old man who kept losing his dentures and complaining that he couldn't eat the tough Salisbury steak or even chew the overcooked broccoli. They had confiscated Stephen's belt, his shoelaces, and his pocketknife. The cops had his grandfather's Mauser, and he was scared to death he wouldn't get it back. The bed had a railing on it, like for babies, so he didn't fall out. There weren't even any pictures on the walls. Maybe they were afraid he would hang himself from the hook they put the pictures on.

The whole handoff thing had been surprising. One minute, Stephen was sitting on a cot in a jail cell, and the next, the cops—not the same cops who'd arrested him, but other cops—were taking him into the emergency room at UC San Diego Hospital and handing him off to a doctor. He was pretty sure they hadn't left until they saw the doc lead him back to one of the rooms.

There he was, a nutcase, a psych patient locked up and not free to leave. Not for seventy-two hours, anyway, and maybe longer if the docs decided he needed it. They'd explained his rights. He had talked to psychiatrists and nurses and social workers, and some psychologist had given him a giant three-hundred-page questionnaire asking him to answer true or false to stuff like, "My soul sometimes leaves my body" and "Evil spirits possess me at times." He had thought about marking that one true.

The nurse who came on at three was a bitch. All the patients in the rec room said it, and she had already frowned at Stephen and said, "You're new. Have to read your chart yet," in a voice one might reserve for a bug found in the shower.

Stephen didn't care. The night before, he'd slept better than he had since coming home from Iraq. Maybe better than he ever had. Something about the barrenness of it all rebooted his brain and let him start clean.

And there was his mother, clutching her pamphlets in the same way the old man's wife had clutched her box of Kleenex when she said, "You'll be coming home soon, Larry."

Larry stayed on his bed, watching Stephen and his mother with cataract-glazed eyes. Night before, when Larry couldn't find his dentures, Stephen had tried to tell him they were in the bathroom in their case, right where they were supposed to be, and he'd had to shout before the guy even looked at him. Weird to have someone sitting there who couldn't hear and could probably barely see. But still, Stephen led his mom to the rec room and found an empty corner with a couple of chairs.

"I'm glad you decided to come for help," she said. "I'm glad you called me."

He didn't explain his involuntary status and didn't tell her he liked it there, where there were no childhood trains on the walls. He was lucky not to be in jail. He didn't tell her they'd insisted he call someone, and she was the only person he could think of. He hadn't wanted to call her.

"I thought you might like to learn more about God. About my new life," she offered.

"Maybe later," he mumbled. Then they sat side by side on the rec room couch, watching *NCIS* with a bunch of other mentals until his mother finally set the pamphlets on his bed and left with a promise to come back the next day.

FOR HIS FIRST PASS, Stephen agreed to let his mother take him to dinner at the house of "The Elders," which was how she referred to Josh and Maria. They didn't seem old to Stephen, maybe early forties at the most, but he pictured it in his head with quotation marks and capital letters—"The Elders." She meant they were elders in the church, he understood, and their job was to help him or teach him or convert him or something.

"Are you sure you're ready to go on a pass?" Natalie had asked him earlier that day. The doctors had set up phone sessions for him, and he had talked to her a couple of times. Once they found out he had seen a shrink at the outpatient clinic, they'd started arranging the calls.

"Yes," he'd answered. "I have plans to get my grandfather's other rifles, load them, and go on a real shooting spree in the mall. Is that an acceptable use of my pass?" He loved the momentary silence then her husky laugh as she realized he was joking. He might have been just a little bit in love with Natalie but knew she would never go for it. He was a nutcase, a whack job in the loony bin. Besides, there were those therapist boundaries she kept talking about.

She would lose her job if she went on a date with him, but that didn't stop him from fantasizing, alone in the shower with Denture Guy still asleep in the room. Sometimes, her face lost shape. Sometimes, his eyes glazed over. Sometimes, it was Rachel's name he imagined yelling as he wrapped his body around her and forced all his anger into her.

He hadn't told Natalie about Rachel or Gladys yet, and he wondered what she would say. "Well, of course you think about her. She was your first sexual experience, after all." Or maybe just "You creep—dirty rapist" and getting up to turn that picture of her kid over. He wouldn't see her do it on the phone. But Rachel had been into it too. It was just a game.

—————◦◦———

JOSH AND MARIA HAD two kids, aged twelve and ten, and they both looked like their mother—slightly exotic, maybe Spanish, maybe Italian. Stephen was too embarrassed to ask. The kids were Natasha, ten, and Philip, twelve. Their last name was Baker. *Patty-cake, patty-cake, Baker's man.* Funny how bits and pieces of his childhood kept popping up like that, like the image of his mother sitting on the edge of the tub, playing with him during one of her rare uncle-less interludes. He had to have been about four.

They all sat nicely at the table, which was spread with white linen and lit candles, and they ate chicken and vegetables and salad. Grace was said, mumbled words for which he closed his eyes but tuned out the God stuff. Funny how much it reminded him of dinners at the Goldbergs' house. He was almost surprised when Josh didn't invite him into the study for a magic lesson the way Rachel's father used to.

He'd been hanging out with Gladys for years when those magic lessons started. He'd been, what, maybe thirteen that day, when Aaron invited him to learn a magic trick. Though he'd been old enough that it had seemed silly, he agreed to it anyway. There was something about that time in Aaron's study, learning to manipulate the cards, to use the hidden boxes, to hide coins between his fingers.

"Rachel, come help me teach Stephen some magic," Aaron said that first time. But Rachel shook her head and said she'd rather read, so Stephen got Aaron to himself.

There was a family picture on the desk, one without Gladys in it. Everyone was smiling. Novels and journals and books with names like *The Diagnostic and Statistical Manual* and *Abnormal Psychology* were jumbled on the oak bookcase.

"Now, the most important thing about magic," Aaron said, "is that you have to distract people from what you're really doing. You make them think you're doing one thing and get their attention on that, and then you really do something else. Here, I'll show you what

I mean." Then he told a dumb joke that Stephen never forgot. He said, "Doctor, I have a problem. Every time I say 'abracadabra,' someone disappears. Doctor? Doctor, are you there?"

"So, you were in Iraq?"

The question startled Stephen back to the present. Josh was so clean-shaven, it made Stephen reach up to trace the sandpaper scrape of three days of whiskers on his own face. It wasn't as if they let him keep a razor at the shrink lockup. He nodded and broke a piece of chicken off the bone with his fingers, ignoring his mother's scolding look.

"That must have been tough."

"Did you kill anyone?" Phillip had stopped eating and was leaning on his elbows, staring right at Stephen.

Yes, I killed a nosy kid who asked too many questions. That was the kind of thing he would have said before, but he was trying to listen to Natalie, who told him to surf his urges like they were waves that built and built and then receded. "Suuuurf your urges," she would say when he vented about Denture Guy going on and on and not even noticing that Stephen didn't respond, since he couldn't hear anyway.

"That's an inappropriate question," Josh informed his son. "We want our home to be a welcoming place for Stephen."

"Everybody in Iraq kills somebody," Stephen said, more loudly than he intended. "It's a rite of passage, practically. You don't get out without killing someone." *So much for urge surfing.* He tossed a piece of meat into his mouth and deliberately chewed slowly, watching the boy watch him.

"Did you get a chance to read the pamphlets I left you?" His mother's shrillness broke the silence. *Gong.* He waited for someone to come out and usher him offstage. *I'm out. Bad act. And how the hell does husband Jeff put up with this chirpy version of her?* One of the patients was always putting the cooking channel on in the rec room at the hospital. The new incarnation of his mother reminded him of one of those cooking-show hosts. *Say something bright, force a laugh, then pour sugar in the pie filling.* But Jeff held her hand under the table and acted gaga. Stephen had never dreamed he would miss the whacko drug-addict version of his mother.

"Yes, I looked them over." The truth was, he hadn't read a word.

"That's great!" Josh said. "Listen, we really love your mother, and we want to help you. We've been reading about PTSD. Maria and I have discussed it, and we don't think you should be home alone when you leave the hospital. We've got an extra room. We'd like you to stay with us for a while."

He studied them a minute but couldn't find the trick. He'd never been good at seeing underneath the illusion, really. He'd tried and tried before, but look at what happened with his skinhead buddies, who'd sent him off to the hellhole desert and walked away without turning back. Look at Gladys, who'd turned on him one day for no reason he could understand. *Nazi.* Well, that was true. He was a Nazi. At least he wanted to be. Not even Natalie knew that, not really. Nobody really knew how deep and how strong it still was. He couldn't live up to his grandfather's pride.

"I'll have to talk to my therapist," he finally replied. "See if she thinks it's a good idea." *My therapist.* Natalie would probably accuse him of using PTSD to get sympathy.

"I'm not even sure you have PTSD," she'd said when they'd talked that morning. It was frustrating not to be able to read her body cues on the phone. "Regardless, people with PTSD don't take unloaded weapons into animal shelters and terrorize people. They don't try to steal dogs. You're lucky the judge let you go to the hospital instead of giving you jail time." Her voice had sounded harsh, maybe even angry, and he'd been surprised that it bothered him.

He was lucky that his mother's friends were offering him a place to stay, but he wasn't sure if he cared. He just wanted a dog, but he would have been arrested if he went anywhere near the SPCA.

That night, he dreamed of Rachel in her living room. The dog was there. In the dream, she was seven, and he was an adult. "I'm going to show you a magic trick," he told her. "Watch my mouth, not my hands."

Chapter 19
Stephen
1990

The night that Stephen broke Tina's arm, he opened his eyes later, alone in his room, to see trains slithering across the wallpaper in the glow through his window. He woke up frightened, hearing the sound of Tina's arm snapping, a dry sound like crunching a snail. He saw the bone poke against her skin. He tried hard to be fine, told himself it wasn't on purpose, told himself the trains weren't demons coming to get him. He said, "I'm good, I'm good," over and over, just like his mom taught him when he was little and woke up in the middle of the night to her screaming fights with the old uncle. Finally, he gave up and crept to the door of his mother's room.

She was asleep with the new uncle. He peered in through the cracked door, staring into the darkened room, where he could see only two huddles under the blanket, a giant fat lump and somewhere on the other side, a smaller lump that sometimes had warm arms to hold him.

He moved down the hall to his grandfather's room and stood by the bed in the flicker of a silenced television set, listening to the wheeze and gasp of his grandfather's breathing until finally there was a release of air, a rolling over, and pale eyes opening, glinting in the television's flickers. At first, his grandfather put up a defensive arm, as if he expected Stephen would harm him. Then he sat against his headboard and sucked in several painful-sounding breaths.

"What?" he asked, gruff and whispery through his panting.

"I hurt a girl today," Stephen said, a confession he had swallowed all night. "I hurt her bad." His heart sped up, and the sick feeling gripped him, again hearing the sound. He had blamed Rachel, but he was the one who'd jumped on Tina, landed on her. *Snap.* "I was scared," he wanted to say. "I didn't know what to do." But the words didn't come.

"Well?" His grandfather wheezed. "Was it the Jew girl?"

Stephen shook his head. Tina was Irish Catholic and went to church every Sunday.

"Well, come here," his grandfather said, patting the mattress.

Bedsprings squeaked, Grandfather rasped, and Stephen searched for the quiet place inside where he was not afraid. *I'm good. I'm good. I'm good.* He climbed onto the bed and leaned into his grandfather, absorbing the familiar smell of whiskey, a smell he had hated at first but had come to love, because it meant special time with his grandpa, stories, and a feeling that he mattered.

"Were you a man?" his grandfather asked in a half whisper. "Did you do what had to be done?"

I was afraid, Stephen thought, but he nodded. *I made Rachel go for help. It was my fault.*

"That's good, then," his grandfather said. "If you were a man, then you were a soldier. That's all that matters. People get hurt. Sometimes it's necessary to hurt people for the greater good. If you hurt a girl, and you were a soldier, then you did good. Next time, break the Jew girl's arm instead."

It was an accident. I didn't mean it. Snap. But his grandfather's hand rested on his shoulder, and he thought of Rachel and how to make his grandfather proud. "Maybe it was the Jew girl," Stephen said. "Maybe I mixed things up in my memory."

His grandfather nodded and squeezed his shoulder.

Stephen's grandfather went in the hospital for the last time a few days later, and Stephen forgot the details of Tina's arm, forgot the snapping sound.

But he remembered the story he had told his grandfather. The story had morphed until, by the time he told it to his skinhead buddies in the bar years later, he remembered that he had raped a Jew girl then broken her arm when he was done, all at eight or nine years old.

But no, he was a man, a soldier, and his grandfather was proud.

THE LAST TIME HE WENT to the hospital, his grandfather couldn't even whisper. Stephen kept talking to him, jabbering about school, the damn math teacher who made him sit in the front row, the kid he beat up after school. "He was a beaner," Stephen assured him. "You'd have been proud."

The ventilator wheezed in and out, billowing his grandfather's chest.

"I hit him real hard. I punched his face and gave him a nosebleed."

His grandfather's closed eyes twitched, and Stephen thought maybe he'd heard. Maybe he was proud. He touched the sheets where his grandfather's heart was but felt coarse fabric and raised bumps that he knew contained the wires that stretched to machines that beeped and flashed numbers.

Stephen's mother came in the room and perched on the chair next to his grandfather's bed. She wouldn't look at Stephen. "You're going to have to wait outside," she told him. "You're too young. I don't want you here."

Too young for what? Stephen was old enough to go to a different classroom for math—he was in third grade. He was old enough to punch a beaner.

But more people crowded into the room—nurses, a doctor. The doctor brushed past Stephen and went to the machines. He smelled like a swimming pool, like the bathroom on days when Stephen's mother got fed up with the black stuff around the edges of the tub. The nice nurse who brought Stephen sodas and called him "honey" came and put her hands on Stephen's shoulders. She was pretty, with white curls and bright lipstick, and Stephen thought for a minute that she might hug him and tell him everything was going to be okay.

"You need to go out to the hall now," she said.

He didn't want to, but his mother turned to him, and he was shocked that her eyes were red and wet. "I'll be glad when the old bastard is gone," she'd said to the latest uncle just the week before.

Stephen had heard her. He was getting a drink, and they were in the living room.

"I hate him," she said.

But she was sitting where Stephen wanted to be, by his grandfather's head, and she was crying. The nurse took his hand, led him out to the hall, then went back in and shut the door.

He hovered right outside the door, trying to see in through the crack by the floor, but there was only a splinter of light and hushed voices. He ran away from the room, from the dark feeling of not knowing. *What are they doing?* He dashed down the hall then back again. He pressed his hands against the cool wood then ran again.

Then he sat, leaning against the door, trying to hear something, anything. But it was quiet. Stephen's mother got to stay, while he was stuck out there in that stupid long hallway with nothing but white walls, doors, rushing people, and bright lights.

Finally, his mother opened the door and let him back in. He went straight to his grandfather, but something was different. The ventilator wasn't wheezing or billowing anymore.

His mother pressed her hands to her face, and her shoulders heaved just like they did that time an uncle broke her leg and Stephen had to call 911. The white blanket covered his grandfather's face. Stephen wasn't stupid. He knew exactly what that meant. But he ripped the blanket off, because it was smothering his grandfather. His grandfather's closed eyes didn't twitch or do anything. His face looked different, flatter. The room smelled of absence. His grandfather wasn't his grandfather anymore.

The nurse tried to hug him. "Are you okay, honey?"

But he jerked away. He skidded through shiny halls, past white-coated doctors doing late rounds, through the semi-dark lobby and out into the night.

He kept going. He ran all the way to Rachel's house.

That was when he saw the stray. It looked just like Dieter. It could have been Dieter, only skinny.

The thin dog who might have been Dieter had eyes that glinted yellow in Rachel's porch light. Stephen crept forward, calling Dieter's name. The dog didn't respond. It stood on Rachel's porch and stared at the door.

Rachel's front door opened. Stephen quickly crouched behind a bush. He watched while Gladys stepped out. She set down a bowl of food then stood silently while the dog that might have been Dieter hunched over the bowl and began to eat. Stephen crawled closer.

Gladys squatted and put out a hand, palm up. The dog barely glanced up, stayed focused on the food, muscles bunched like it would bolt any second. Just as Gladys straightened her knees, the dog scampered away, heading straight toward Stephen's hedge. Its eyes gleamed with moonlit fear, and its tongue hung out of its mouth. He could hear it pant. It sounded like his own breath, in and out too quickly.

He saw the dog see him. It swerved sideways and ran up the road toward the Murphy house. Stephen held his breath and froze, but it was too late.

"Who's there?" Gladys's thick accent slammed the air out of him. It wasn't quite the same accent as his grandfather's but so close. For a moment, he lost where he was and smelled his grandfather's whiskey, the arid dust of the attic. *We nearly won the world.* He forced himself up onto shaky legs and waited there, behind the hedge.

"Who is it? Come to the light, where I can see you."

Later, he would learn that her accent thickened when she was upset, and he would realize she must have been afraid that night. Later, he sometimes provoked her fear so he could hear that accent and think of his grandfather. But at the time, all he knew was his own grief, and it was strong enough to overwhelm anything else. He stepped into the light.

"Who is it?" she asked again, and he cautiously approached, stopping at the bottom of the porch steps.

"You're that boy, Rachel's friend. The *Aryan*." Illuminated under the porch light, she was nothing but sharp chin, jutting tufts of gray hair, and shards of light glinting off thick glasses.

Stephen stayed quiet. *What is an Aryan?* He thought he should know. But his thoughts were too jumbled with grief and fear.

"Well. What are you doing here? You should be home in bed."

The full knowledge of his grandfather dead emerged in that moment. It buckled his knees, and he collapsed into sobs.

"What?" she asked again and took a step toward the edge of the porch.

But he couldn't answer, couldn't stop the tears, the pain in his stomach, or the desperate, lonely ache of the loss. He looked up at her porch-lit face, and his ears buzzed with panic. His grandfather was dead.

She watched him for ages before she took him in and sat him at the table. She gave him a damp towel to wipe his face.

That night, she was kind in a way she had never been before. She gave him warm milk and told him God loved him even though his grandfather had been a Nazi. She sat at the table with him and talked on and on about God, but he didn't listen to the words, just the drift of her voice. Listening that night, holding the warm mug in his hands in the dimly lit kitchen, he could almost smell his grandfather's cigarette smoke and hear his grandfather's voice weaving stories, carrying him away in imagination to Germany and killing the Jews. Her voice rose and fell with a slight hint of accent, and Stephen felt comforted. She might even have mentioned Germany and Jews at some point. At the time, it didn't matter that she was on the other side of it all. The stories and the accent felt familiar, and that was enough.

That night in the kitchen, after he had drained the warm milk even though he hated warm milk, after he had been lulled into a doze by her almost-but-not-quite grandfather's accent, she put him on the living room couch with a blanket and pillow. He woke the next morning to find Rachel staring down at him, that stuffed dog she called Guarder dangling from her right hand. He always remembered the shock in her voice when he explained.

"My *grandmother* let you in?" she kept saying. "My *grandmother*?"

Chapter 20
Rachel
2016

Rachel's mother had already opened the front door by the time Rachel parked in the driveway of her childhood home. Rachel sat in the white rental Ford for a second, noting her father's manicured flower garden, the new swimming pool, and the garage door—*has it always been the same red I chose for my door, or had they painted it?* When she finally turned to look at the house, her mother was still there, a diminutive, sun-blurred form, framed by the L-shaped California ranch. Rachel lagged, retrieving her suitcase from the trunk then walking the few feet to the front door.

She dropped her suitcase and let her mother hug her. Rose's face was etched with anxiety, and she monologued while she led Rachel to her childhood room. "I'm so happy you came. I wish you'd told us ahead of time. How long are you staying? Do you need anything? Do you still prefer soy milk? Are you eating meat? We've cut back to practically a vegan diet since your father had the high cholesterol diagnosis, but I picked up a roast for you. I can ask your father to stop on his way home from work if you want soy milk. Did you know it increases your risk of breast cancer? Can you believe he's still seeing patients every day? He just won't slow down. I tell him enough is enough."

Rachel grunted, offering "I don't know" and "no" in response to the questions, but it wasn't clear that her mother wanted answers. Rose had streaked her hair with red highlights and was wearing a blue sundress, displaying varicose veins and unpolished toenails. Her bare arms were spotted with freckles. Rachel had seen the Facebook pictures and updates about personal trainers, yoga, and healthy eating, but it hadn't prepared her for this new version of Rose. One would never have known she was creeping up on seventy, except for the varicose veins.

"Here we are. I've made the bed. It's a guest room now, of course, but it's the same bed you had when you were a teenager. Some of your stuff is still in the closet. You should really go through it while you're here and take what you want." Rose patted the bed then went to the closet and opened the door as if Rachel otherwise wouldn't have been able to find it. She paused for a breath, leaning against the wall by the closet.

Rachel looked around. The room was nothing like her teenage haven. The green walls had been painted sky blue, and gauzy brown curtains framed the windows instead of the simple shades Rachel remembered. An antique bureau she'd never seen had replaced her childhood dresser.

"So, you finally decided to come," Rose said in the same noncommittal manner she had applied to everything else she had said, but Rachel's practiced ear caught the edge of curiosity. "Is it because of those posts on your Facebook page? Are you in trouble?"

Rachel glanced at her mother and responded with a teenage shrug. "I don't know. It just seemed like a good time. You're right. I should visit Gladys. You know, before she dies." Rose stared at her with a bemused expression, and she knew she had not really answered the question, but she wasn't prepared to get into all that. Not yet. She realized that she had imagined that her childhood room might somehow provoke cathartic memories leading to an outcome in which she would be immediately whole and able to right her life. Stupid. "You wanted me to come, right? I mean, you kept asking."

"Yes." Her mother was mercifully quiet for a few seconds, her jaw working as if she was chewing on her words before spitting them out.

"Of course we wanted you. I'm just surprised you finally came. It's been five years since we've seen you. We asked and asked, and you ignored us. We could hardly get a return phone call out of you, and then suddenly, here you are."

Rachel carried her suitcase to the bed, turning away from the anger in her mother's voice. "I'm sorry," she said, keeping her back to Rose.

"We've been worried..."

She felt relieved when Rose's voice softened. *Was I really only twenty-five the last time I was here?* Rose moved to stand beside Rachel. She reached out a hand as if she was going to touch Rachel's arm but let it drop without making contact. Rachel imagined she could feel the impression of Rose's almost-touch just above her wrist, and she didn't know why that aborted contact seemed more intimate and somehow more unwanted than the earlier hug had been. She opened her suitcase and stared at the top layer of summer T-shirts. Maybe she could just live out of her suitcase. She wasn't going to stay that long.

"Well, you came at a good time," Rose said.

Rachel began unpacking shirts and shorts so she wouldn't have to look at Rose.

"We don't know how much longer Gladys is going to last," Rose added. Rachel felt her shoulders relax when Rose moved away, stopping just inside the doorway. "Also, I plan to clean out her room this week and see what we want to keep and what we can donate. Maybe you can help. Do you know she has suitcases buried in the back of that closet that are covered with, I swear, a good two or three inches of dust? I picked one up, and it was heavy. There's stuff in that one. It isn't as if she unpacked and just kept the empty suitcase. I haven't really dealt with it yet, but who knows. Maybe there will be something you want to keep in there. You should help me."

Rachel removed her toiletry bag. She could at least hang that in the bathroom. "Why haven't you opened them yet?" Even as she asked, she could feel the sting of a long-ago slap on her cheek.

"I don't know." Rose offered a nervous laugh. "I guess, since she's still alive, it seemed like a violation."

It was easy to imagine her mother opening those suitcases and Gladys leaping out, inflated with rage. *Gladys the Golem. Ha.* Maybe some things were better left alone.

"Anyway," Rose said again. "I'm going to open them. It's silly not to. Your grandmother probably doesn't even remember they exist. You should help me. It could be interesting."

"Yeah," Rachel said, finally turning to look at her mother. "I will. I can't believe you didn't do it right away." Part of her wanted to desecrate Gladys's room. Part of her wanted to avoid that room the same way she avoided the plague of memories in her head. "Definitely. Let's clear out Gladys's room this week."

Her mother nodded. "I'll leave you to unpack. You father should be home in a couple hours. I'm going to start dinner. I'll do the roast I got. We'll eat at six."

She left, giving Rachel just enough time to dump her shirts back into the suitcase before she reappeared, lingering in the doorway with her new perfect posture. "You know, we don't keep kosher anymore," she said. "Now that Gladys isn't here." *Kosher,* Rachel thought, *is code for so many things.* Rose might as well have said, "We aren't prisoners anymore."

Finally, she was gone. Rachel dumped her suitcase on the floor and tugged her phone out of her pocket. Two messages. Liz: *Hey. I got your message. How could you leave without even saying goodbye? How long are you planning to be there? Call me.*

Rachel deleted it.

The second was from Pete, who had driven her to the airport and wanted to make sure she'd landed on the other end. *When you're back, I expect your help on the rewrite of the play. Now go see Gladys. And be safe. Also, get Liz out of your system once and for all.*

Rachel sent him a text: *I'm here. Mother driving me crazy already...*

Then she climbed onto the bed and fell asleep instantly, lulled like a child by the clatter of her mother working in the kitchen.

When she woke up, Twitter alerted her that she had messages. Heart racing, she opened the app.

Imadeplorable: *Hey, bitch, we know you checked in at the San Diego Airport on Facebook and then at a gas station in Carlsbad. We know you're in California. You're going to regret you ever did that fucking play.*

She clicked through to Imadeplorable's feed, finding a creepy tweet from an hour before: *I think her parents live in Carlsbad. I found her Dad's business address. He's a Jew shrink.*

Rachel didn't remember checking in anywhere. But she had logged in to Facebook in the airport. When she stopped for a cup of coffee in one of the restaurants and wanted to access their Wi-Fi, they had routed her through Facebook. She hadn't even thought about it.

She googled "disabling automatic check-ins on Facebook." Okay, she had to find the privacy icon. The notification and messenger icons in Facebook accused her with glaring red numbers—she had more than two hundred alerts and messages. She clicked through. *What are a few more threats and attacks? They can't really find me here. Can they?* The familiar nausea that accompanied every recent social media foray made her feel right at home in her childhood bedroom.

She nearly missed the message from Stephen, nestled between a promise to find her and kill her slowly and a photoshopped picture of her knifing a baby. She stared at the message for a full minute, forgetting that she was supposed to be trying to disable automatic check-ins, forgetting the stalkers. She realized she was holding her breath and concentrated on slowly releasing it. She wanted to believe she kept anything Stephen related locked away where not even a tendril could reach her. But recent experiences had put the lie to that. Anyway, she'd gone to California to deal with her childhood—no, she'd gone there to pretend to deal with her childhood while avoiding crazy stalkers. But still. She closed Messenger but did not delete his message.

She walked through the process for disabling automatic check-ins. Then she lay on the bed and tried to go back to sleep until her mother called her for dinner.

Rachel longed for a very large glass of wine to wash away the dry taste of fear in her throat. *Did I bring the stalkers to my parents' house? Should I stay in a hotel?* She could no longer reassure herself that they would remain at their computers.

"Did I tell you the pot roast isn't kosher?" Rose asked for the third time. "I bought it at Vons. Just went to the store and bought regular old packaged pot roast from the meat section."

"Vons? Is that a grocery store?" Growing up, it had been Safeway and Thrifty's. Rachel could still taste the banana split ice cream she used to get at the Thrifty's counter after a day at the beach.

"Yes, that's the main one now, honey. But I used to have to drive to Laguna Hills to get the kosher meat that made Gladys happy. She wouldn't trust that the meat you get at Vons was really kosher."

Rachel chewed another piece of the dry meat. She didn't remember the kosher meat being so chewy, but maybe Gladys had done the cooking.

"So, Rachel, what is going on with this play you're in?" Her father's voice seemed older, with that rasp men got as they aged. His hair was thin but still more blond than gray. His cheeks were sunken, and the bones in his wrists and narrow shoulders jutted. The lenses in his glasses seemed thicker to her, too, and she could remember him always losing them, back when he only needed them for reading.

She reminded herself that he was twelve years older than her mother. He must have been over eighty. Her parents had always been older than her friends' parents. It wasn't unusual anymore, but in those days, people in their forties didn't have kids. "You were a late baby," her mother had always said. "Wanted but unexpected. We didn't think we could. We'd stopped trying."

"It's nothing," Rachel said, but she knew the tremor in her voice was audible. "Sometimes when you do provocative plays, you get some unwanted attention." She laughed. "You know what they say. Any publicity is good, even if it's negative."

She thought about that day Gladys moved in, how they had stopped at a restaurant after the airport and she wanted to order the Monte Cristo.

"That has ham in it," Gladys had said. "You can't eat ham. It's treyf."

"We don't keep kosher," her father replied. "She can eat what she wants."

But Gladys had pursed her lips and folded her hands on the table, and Aaron's face had collapsed into an impotent scowl. In the end, Rachel had ordered a grilled cheese sandwich and hated every bite of it. Something about that look on his face that night had frightened her. It had diminished him, as if instead of picking the right card in a magic show, he'd messed up, and the audience had laughed at him. She'd always known he could carry her if she got tired, but she suddenly realized he might stumble and drop her.

She couldn't bear that she might have put Aaron in danger, but more than that, she couldn't bear that he might be helpless to protect himself or her—that she might have to see that expression again.

"Maybe I should stay in a hotel," she offered and pushed some meat around on her plate. She could check in there and lure the stalkers away from her parents.

Rose offered a tentative smile. "No, of course you shouldn't stay in a hotel. We're very happy to have you. I'm sure Gladys will be glad to see you, though you do realize she probably won't recognize you or understand who you are?"

"Yes, I know. She already had dementia last time I was here." She couldn't quite choke back the peevishness in her voice.

The kitchen was sunny and cheerful. Outside, a hummingbird hovered around a feeder full of pink liquid. They could have been in a Glade commercial. Or maybe something about an antidepressant. But the atmosphere between them reminded Rachel of her freshman English class reading plays out of the book—stiff, rehearsed, and trying too hard.

"It would be hard to get used to that kind of negative attention." Aaron offered a faraway smile.

Rachel felt anger bubble up at the shrink words. "I'm fine." She avoided looking at either parent. "But, Dad, they might have your office address. You should maybe stay away from work for a few days." The words came in a rush before she could censor them. *There, I said it. I've put you in danger.* She felt the shame of it color her cheeks.

"I'll be okay," Aaron said. "They're probably just a bunch of fat kids in their parents' basements, right?" He laughed, and Rachel laughed with him, and there wasn't any point in telling them about the swastika on her door or J.T. "Anyway, I just rent hours in a friend's office nowadays, since I'm only working part time. I don't use that office anymore."

"What about this address, though? What if they find you? Us?"

She could feel Aaron's eyes dissecting her as if she were a patient. Finally, he sighed. "You probably don't remember this, but early in my career, I treated someone who became very fixated on me. She wasn't dangerous, but she did track me down and kept ringing the doorbell and calling in the middle of the night. I learned from that. We are unlisted, and I google my name regularly to make sure it stays that way. There's nothing online that will provide them with this address."

"Oh." Rachel should have gotten advice from him before letting her life spread all over the Internet. But she wasn't a mental health professional with potentially unstable patients. She was an actress trying to get her name out into the world.

The silence expanded, and Rachel forced down a couple chewy pieces of pot roast.

"Well," Rose finally said. "What do you want to do while you're here?" Leave it to her mother to seek out the most neutral topic she could find.

"Just see Gladys, I guess. And I was thinking of seeing Stephen. Do you guys see him at all?" *When had she decided that?* The words had popped out without her permission.

"Oh, we haven't seen Stephen in years," Rose said.

"You were still a teenager the last time we saw him." Aaron smiled his first genuine smile. "I always wondered what happened. Sometimes, it seemed like he practically lived here. Then all of a sudden, he stopped coming around. You were what, fifteen or sixteen? His family was pretty messed up, but he was a good kid."

"Well, maybe I'll meet up with him while I'm here." *Could seeing Stephen put an end to whatever it was from those attic days that has haunted me all these years?*

"You could invite him to dinner," Rose said, and Aaron nodded vigorously.

"Okay," Rachel said. "Sure."

Rachel's fork clicked loudly against her plate in the ensuing silence. Her mother watched her. Rose's face was full of questions Rachel didn't want to answer. Something tugged at her, something old and young and hungry. That small part of her that wanted to crawl in her mother's lap and bury her face in her mother's hair.

She put her fork down, acknowledging to herself that she was not going to eat any more. Maybe her mother's cooking was why she had turned vegetarian for those last couple of years in high school after Gladys became dangerous in the kitchen.

"Okay. I've got some work to do," Aaron said, pushing his chair back and standing.

Rose turned to him. "Not tonight," she said, and the words repeated in Rachel's ears with echoes of multiple childhood dinners.

Aaron sat back down but stayed perched on the end of his chair. "What really brings you?" he asked. "I can't believe it's to see my mother, who won't even remember you. You've avoided visiting her since the day you moved out. I know those people have your address. Are you in danger? Has something happened?" He didn't sound like he used to when he wanted to know why she'd come home past curfew. He sounded like later, when she stopped coming home at all most nights and the anger and "consequences" turned to a hesitant tremble, as though he was afraid of her answer.

The earlier nostalgia for a childhood that she had mostly manufactured in fantasy dissipated. She shook her head. "I just needed a break, I guess." That dance with her parents was like putting on one of those childhood dresses Gladys had always made her wear to temple. She had grown to appreciate the discomfort of the ways they chafed against her skin, how the too-tight shiny black shoes squeezed her toes. She couldn't stand those dresses with their frills and bows, but wearing them had felt powerful, as if wearing them and hating them and suffering silently from the discomfort meant that she won something. If she found one of those dresses and could still fit into it, if she put it on, it would feel exactly the same. "Anyway," she finally said. "Is there dessert?"

"Oh, we're off sugar," Rose said. "But I could make you some tea. I'll buy cookies or something tomorrow if you want them."

She was startled by an impulse to cry. "It's okay. I shouldn't eat that stuff anyway." Her silenced phone vibrated, and she jerked to her feet, pushing her chair back. "I have to take a call. I'm pretty wiped out. I think I'll just take a bath and go to bed. Is that okay?"

"Of course, honey," Rose said.

Rachel retreated to her room before checking the phone. Liz again. She let it go to voicemail. She would not check Twitter. She would delete that account and get off Facebook. Cut all social media out of her life. Pete had the right idea. She promised herself she'd do it tomorrow.

She looked at her closet. It was exactly the same, two accordion doors that opened to a long, narrow space. She was always finding things she'd forgotten about in the back corners. "Why not?" she said out loud and opened the doors.

She got on her knees, crawled into the narrow part of the closet, and dug under several long winter coats she remembered from childhood visits to Yosemite for sledding. Cloaked by an old wool coat and some long dresses that must have belonged to her mother, she discovered a crate full of high school yearbooks and playbills from local theater and school musicals. She located her senior yearbook. The spine was hardly broken, the cover purple. Her graduation year, 2003, was splayed across the top.

She leafed through pages until she found the drama club. There she was, standing next to her best friend and brief first girlfriend, Bridget. Bridget looked sunny, with ocean bleached long hair, a sharp contrast to the goth look Rachel had sported back then. She smiled at her younger self with the black lipstick, black-shaded eyes, and stringy brown hair that just frayed more if she washed it too much. Further in, she found herself with the cast of *Guys and Dolls,* wearing Adelaide's hip-hugging, thigh-high red dress. A few pages later, the last football game of the season, the one where everybody drank and cheered when the Carlsbad Lancers finally scored a touchdown. Forget winning.

She put the yearbook and crate aside and dragged out a large cardboard box. The box wasn't closed, and she could see a few pictures and homemade cards on top. "Dear Mommy, Happy Mother's Day. Love Rachel." She didn't remember writing that, but it seemed young, maybe pre-Gladys. Pre-everything. The picture was a pair of stick parents and a little girl with brown hair. It was hard to imagine why her mother had saved such a thing, but the card provoked that longing again, a desire to go back out to her parents and tell them something—maybe that she didn't feel well. Then her mother would make her Campbell's chicken soup and bring it to her room on a tray with Ritz crackers and ginger ale. She would place a cool hand on Rachel's forehead.

Rachel pressed the heel of her hand against her eyes, pushing back the tears. Her phone vibrated on the bed and she looked at it. Liz again.

Underneath the childhood pictures, she could see the edges of the quilt her grandmother had made for her when she was seven, with all the Stars of David on it. *Did she ever do anything that didn't scream "Jewish" at the world?* She let the card drift onto the top of the other cards and pictures and pushed the box back in the closet. She returned the crate after grabbing her junior yearbook.

She called Liz.

Liz answered quickly, as if she'd been watching her phone and waiting for it to ring. "Finally. Are you in California?"

"Yes."

"Why didn't you call me first? Just a text... I don't understand."

The question made Rachel feel tired. Everything made her tired. She suddenly wanted to go to sleep and not wake up for days or weeks. "We've been at this a long time, Liz," she said. "And I guess

I've been feeling like I want something real. Like I don't know why I can't let myself have someone who's available."

"But I am available," Liz said.

Rachel talked quickly, wanting to interrupt before the familiar path was tread. "I know you want to be. But I'm thirty. I'm tired of waiting. And I think, I just wonder..."

"You think I'm stringing you along. I know. But I'm not. I love you, Rachel. I really do." Rachel could hear a choking sound and was surprised that Liz might have been crying. "I don't want to lose what we have."

Six, maybe even three months before, the obvious fear and pain in Liz's voice would have been enough to keep Rachel going for days. She would have fed on it like a gourmet meal, cuddled with it at night when she couldn't sleep. But it just made her sad and maybe a little angry. "What do we have, Liz? Sneaking little flirtations in the teacher's lounge? Squeezing in dates in between your dates with Michael? I think you forget that your life is full with me and Michael and the twins. But I'm the one sitting at home, turning down invitations because I don't know when you're going to be available or when you're going to show up. I'm lonely."

She felt gratified by Liz's silence.

"It's that cop, isn't it?" Liz finally asked. "The cop you slept with."

Rachel's ear felt hot from the phone. Her body felt loose and young and frightened and hopeful all at once. "I've wanted something more for a long time. Maybe Jo made me realize it's possible."

"Should I come? I could come to California. Get a babysitter for when Michael is working."

"No, Liz. Don't come. I need to do this alone."

"Do what alone?"

Was that fear in Liz's voice? "I need to go. I'm really tired. I just want to sleep now. We'll talk later, okay." She hung up.

She opened a different yearbook to the juniors' pictures and found herself. That had been the year of the awkward perm. Her smile was crooked, and she didn't think she was imagining the hint of sadness in her eyes. She touched the photo, feeling something tender well up.

She flipped the pages past the football team, the speech club, the band, and found the seniors. There he was, Stephen Drescher. His sun-bleached hair hung too long over his pale forehead, just brushing his scowling eyes. She shivered and wondered whether he had grown up to be the kind of man who would paint a swastika on her door. It seemed entirely possible.

She opened Messenger on her phone, found his message, and replied. *I'm in town, and I'd like to see you. When is good?*

Chapter 21
Gladys

"Rachel's Sunday school teacher has agreed to tell his Holocaust story to congregation members before he leaves for Israel," Rose said at breakfast, sipping coffee and spooning that sweet cereal she loved into her mouth. Rachel giggled and threw her toast on the floor. Lucky, hovering always under Rachel's chair, gobbled it. "Do you want to go?"

Gladys watched Lucky frantically wolf the toast, grunting and scraping his teeth against the pale-blue tiles, and didn't answer. The way Rose said "He's telling his Holocaust story" made it sound as if there would be Manischewitz wine and maybe some rugelach, and everyone would politely nod as if he were sharing an only slightly melancholy story about his trip abroad. For a man to get on the pulpit and talk—it was obscene. Yet, she knew she would go, and she would listen and pay careful attention as always to each description of others in the camps, in case she might hear about a girl with curly hair and buckteeth, a balding father with reddened, watery eyes, or a mother clinging to the blue plate that had once belonged to her great-grandmother.

For all of these, O God of forgiveness,
Forgive us, pardon us, grant us atonement.

She dreamed about the stories she heard and read. Sometimes, she could not tell whether she was awake or asleep. The stories burrowed inside like maggots, devouring her. She imagined them so vividly that they began to feel personal, as if she had lived them herself.

If Rachel's teacher told his story in synagogue, Gladys would listen, and the pictures in her mind would become memories in her body, and she would be unable to stop remembering. If she read about somebody's experience, she would feel as if she had been there, living it as if it were her memory, and she would be unable to stop remembering.

She kept old issues of *The New Yorker* under her bed next to the dog bowl. They contained Hanna Arendt's reporting on the Eichmann trial. She read and reread the stories. The prosecutor asked witnesses, "Why did you not protest?" "Why did you board the train?" "Fifteen thousand people were standing there and hundreds of guards facing you—why didn't you revolt and charge and attack?"

Hanna Arendt's articles become Gladys's memories. Gladys had been there. She'd watched the trial. She'd told her story on the witness stand. She was Eichmann when he hanged.

For the sin which we have committed in Your sight through arrogance of our will,

And for the sin which we have committed before You by breach of trust.

Sometimes, reading those stories sent her stumbling through the house in the dark. She would imagine she could hear the pounding on the door, rush to find a hole in the attic, and hide from the men barreling in with rifles and violence and murder, gutting the house, stealing the things that belonged to her family.

If Gladys had been there, she would have found a gun. She would have shot back. She would have killed them all. She would have rushed through the house and killed, killed, killed. *Why did you not protest? Why didn't you revolt?* More would have come, but she would have died fighting back.

Sometimes, she ran to Rachel's room and leaned over the bed so she could watch her chest rise and fall. Seeing Rachel breathe reassured Gladys. She fought the urge to shake her—*she's alive. It's okay.*

She's alive. In her imagination, or maybe it was a memory, she was the man with a gun, and she stomped through the house and killed the family, making noise with her big boots and crushing things beneath her heel. But she was also the baby in the crib, and the pain seared her chest when the man with the boots fired his weapon, and then she was the German, and she wanted to kill the Jews—she wanted to solve the Jewish problem. She felt like she contained all of it, and all of it consumed her.

For the sin which we have committed in Your sight by casting off responsibility,

And for the sin which we have committed before You by denying and lying.

I am not going crazy. She repeated the words like a prayer, chanting them as if they would save her from the crushing grief and rage at all the stories she heard. She sat on her bed. She breathed. Soon, she would put on her bathrobe. She would remove the cracked blue bowl from under the bed. She would go outside. She would feed the dog. *I am not going crazy.*

She was a child hiding in an attic, waiting to die, waiting to live, dreaming about a boy. She was buried under piles of corpses, one of six million, smothered under the weight of them. She struggled to breathe and fought, clawing, buried alive, but nobody heard the screams as she scratched at the earth to dig her way out.

Sometimes, they were dreams, and she woke, gasping and sweat drenched, her blankets flung to the floor.

A few nights after they'd buried Joseph, she had dreamed of him clawing at the wood casket, screaming for someone to free him. Still asleep, she got out of bed, found the shovel in the garage, and went to the backyard. She began digging as if she could heave and punch earth and move dirt and he would be there, pounding on the wood of his casket, screaming, "I can't breathe! Please let me out. I'm suffocating." She dug and dug.

Aaron woke her. He stood before her in his bathrobe and grabbed her shoulders. "Mother, Mother, what are you doing? Wake up, Mother." He shook her until she dropped the shovel and gazed down at the dark chasm of earth and the pile of dirt beside it.

"Joseph was calling for me," she explained. But Joseph wasn't in the backyard. He was buried in Detroit in the Orthodox cemetery, next to Ira and an empty plot reserved for Gladys. Aaron gazed at her with that screwed-up monkey face, and if she had not dropped the shovel, she might have whacked him. The horror in his eyes numbed her, and her shoulders trembled with fatigue. She tried to imagine Joseph quieting in his box underground.

"Go inside. There is nothing for you to worry about here," she told Aaron.

And he did—he turned and walked away without a question. Joseph would have stayed, would have helped her dig or at least offered comfort. But Aaron simply obeyed his mother and left her in the cold night.

For the sin which we have committed in Your sight by evil thoughts.

She peered out the window, seeking movement, wondering whether the dog was there. Something crouched in the bushes outside her window. She dropped to her knees, reached under the bed to find the bowl, and went down to the kitchen. The dog would not starve. The dog would live. The dog would be her friend. She would tame the dog.

But in her thoughts, she dragged her feet not down the steps but along in a snowy death march, stumbling forward, leaning, and falling into strangers as the frozen silence was punctuated by occasional gunshots. She longed to sleep on the side of the road. She was also a marching soldier. She pointed her gun at a child, a girl with curly black hair, buckteeth, and exhausted brown eyes. It was Esther. She pulled the trigger, the child tumbled back into a ditch, and blood spattered across the white snow. She was Mother, and she stumbled forward, too numb and cold and hungry to weep for the child who was no longer at her side.

Ira died in the hospital while Gladys slept at home with the boys, who were still teenagers at the time. When they called her in, she refused to look but saw anyway, his uncut fingernails and curls of black hair in his ears. When they first married, she had teased him for being so meticulous.

"You groom like a lady," she'd said, and he'd laughed and leaned in to kiss her.

"They didn't clip his nails in the hospital," she told the boys over and over at the funeral. "Why didn't they clip his nails?"

It had been Aaron, not her Joseph, who'd dropped his eyes and taken her hands between his damp palms. "It'll be okay, Mom. We'll be okay." Joseph was already somewhere else, lost in his own mind by then.

And for the sin which we have committed before You by passing judgment.

And for the sin which we have committed before You by resisting those in authority.

The kitchen windows were open, and she heard a sound of movement outside. The dog seemed louder that night, more aggressive, rattling the bushes.

She closed her eyes, lost in the image of herself stumbling through snow, her feet bloody and frozen. She tripped, she fell, and a dog jumped on top of her, growling and moaning its hunger, scraping and digging at her face, pinning her down in the snow.

I must feed the dog.

She placed a hand on the cupboard where the dog food was kept. She would open it, though she feared she would find a child hiding from stomping Nazi boots, Joseph scraping the lid of his coffin, Esther and Mother and Father, or herself, carefully scrubbing the corners and praying.

In Your abundant mercy, cleanse us of our guilt before You.

Avinu Malkeinu, bring us back to You in perfect repentance.

Our Father, our King, be gracious unto us and answer us although we have no merits of our own. Deal with us in righteousness and loving Kindness, and save us.

Gladys opened the cupboard door. Outside, the bushes rustled and spoke, and the nightly ritual of coyote screams began. The dog waited.

But when she opened the front door, it was not the dog she noticed. It was the shock of white hair on the boy who crouched behind a bush.

Chapter 22

Rachel

2016

Every time Rachel's father brought a forkful of food to his mouth, he tilted his head forward to meet it. It crushed her. She had never expected to feel toward her father the sadness that frail older men provoked in her. He might as well have already been hiding out in his study. He seemed to spend as much time locked in that study as he had when Gladys had lived with them. The ghost of Gladys lingered in the seat at the other head of the table.

Even Rose had shut up, for once. It was the third family dinner, her third day there, and it already felt as if she'd been living with them for her entire life. She heard nothing but forks against plates. Rose seemed to have given up trying to initiate conversations that would make it feel as if Rachel was five again and Gladys hadn't ruined everything. Rose wound down, her battery dead.

Rachel had told Pete the night before that it seemed like everything they weren't saying was in the do-not-use-this silverware drawer, some kind of new kosher rule. He had laughed, but she hadn't meant it to be funny. Somehow, Rachel hadn't considered that coming home to say goodbye to Gladys and escape the stalker would also involve her parents. When she thought about everything wrong with her life, it always came down to Stephen and Gladys, not awkward dinners in a silent house with Gladys nowhere in sight. When she remembered her parents as they were in her childhood, Aaron was already behind the closed door of his study and Rose an annoying gnat to be ignored.

Rachel's phone vibrated in her pocket, and she resisted the urge to look. She was eating non-kosher meat loaf with mashed potatoes and butter in her childhood kitchen. Her mother claimed to be vegan but kept feeding her meat. That was so very Rose. Rachel didn't like milk, but she had poured herself a glass, just so she could be absolutely certain she was mixing dairy and meat, murdering Gladys with every bite.

"So," Rose said. "Did you set up a meeting with Stephen? Are there any other old friends you want to find? That girl you were always hanging out with—what was her name?"

"Bridget." Sexy Bridget, Rachel's first. First to leave her for a man too. Her phone vibrated again, and she jumped.

Aaron looked at her, and then Aaron and Rose looked at each other in the same way they used to when they wanted to have a discussion about something or were upset that she'd sneaked in through her bedroom window the night before.

Could it feel more like being sixteen?

"Yes, Bridget," Rose said, her voice gaining volume. "We didn't know then, did we, Aaron? You spent so much time with that girl for a while. Then she was just gone from your life. We didn't know you were gay. I just couldn't understand why you were so broken up when you stopped spending time together."

"Yeah, well, she wasn't gay in the end." Rachel sipped water to avoid saying more about Bridget. "I think I'll just stick with seeing Stephen," she said in what she hoped was a tone that would end the conversation.

Aaron smiled. "He really was a good kid. I felt bad for him. That grandfather of his—"

"Not just his grandfather. Do you remember that time he spent the night?" Rose beamed. "His mother hadn't come home. Grandfather was dying in the hospital. When his mother's boyfriend came to get him the next day, do you know, I heard him tell Stephen he

wasn't to spend the night with those Jews again. I couldn't believe it."
Rose shivered, but the note in her voice was cheerful, as if she was
enjoying the fact that Stephen's family had hated them.

"I believe it," Rachel said. She was halfway to her mouth with a
spoonful of mashed potatoes, but her cell phone would not shut up,
rattling on the wooden chair.

Rose asked, "So, what's the deal with that thing?"

Rachel made herself smile. "My phone?"

"Yes. Seems to be constantly going off, but half the time, you
don't answer it, and when you do, you disappear."

"It's rude to take phone calls at dinner," Rachel said.

"Then maybe you shouldn't bring your phone to the dinner
table."

If Gladys had been there, she would have chimed in with something that escalated the tension. There must have been a prayer that
reminded people that "thou shalt not bring thy phone to the dinner
table." Gladys would have recited it, and Rose would have tried to
catch Aaron's eye with that help-I'm-drowning look that he always
ignored. When Gladys was done, everyone would shut up until
Aaron excused himself and hid in his study and Rose retreated to the
sink, where she took an inordinately long time doing the dishes. The
drama echoed in Rachel's memory, and she played her part, scooting
out of the chair. "I think I need to check my messages."

She retreated to her room and made herself look at her phone.
Even reading her text messages had become panic inducing. A text
from Liz: *Call me please. I'm looking at plane tickets.* One from Pete
checking in. A voicemail from Jo and another from a strange number. *Why is Jo calling me? Would it be a bad idea to call her back? To
even listen to the message? What would I say? "I'm done with Liz, and
I want to jump right into something new with you?"* Part of her wanted
to say exactly that, but then she'd have to call Liz and tell her not to
come. The thought made her gut clench with irrational panic.

Maybe she would stop listening to the messages or checking her phone at all. With the phone silenced, the vibrate alert was the same, whether it was a message from Jo calling to say she was blowing Rachel's world up or a Facebook or Twitter alert informing Rachel that she was a dirty Jew bitch. Maybe she would throw the phone into the ocean.

But she pressed Play to hear the voicemail from the unknown number. "Hello, this is Sergeant Robbins from the Pineville Police Department. Can you please call me at 315-559-4200, extension 92058."

Her shaking hand contradicted the thought she soothed herself with, that it was probably just an update on the graffiti. It couldn't have been anything else, unless something had happened to Pete or Liz, but Liz had texted her five minutes before.

The phone vibrated in her hand. Pete.

"Hey," she said. "Are you okay?"

"Hey, sweetie," he said. "I'm fine, but your house..."

"What? Did they paint my door again?"

"Well"—Pete hesitated as if he was trying to slow down the telling—"not exactly. Listen, I drove by to check your house, and your door was standing wide open. I called the cops. It's okay. Nothing was taken."

"But?"

"Well, you know that picture, the one above your fireplace with the two women? Someone pulled it off the wall and slashed it all to shit."

Through the rest of the conversation with Pete, they reassured each other. Pete promised that the cops were on it, and she reiterated that she was fine and not upset. But a part of her that felt split from the rest was thinking that she had always played the shock of upsetting news wrong when she performed it. One didn't throw up, she realized, or faint, drop the phone, or scream. No. Maybe the fear of learning one had terminal cancer was actually worse than finding out it was real. Maybe there was relief when the doctor finally called with the news—the horrible thing had happened.

That was what she thought, because she felt a sudden, relieved calm, as if she had just been told she was going to die and didn't have to wonder anymore. *Okay, they broke into my house. They slashed my picture. They know where I live. I already knew that. Is this really that much worse than graffiti on my door or the truck driving by? I'm fine.* That was how she would play it from then on, she thought. She'd play the relief instead of the fear. She wondered if she could ever go home again, but she couldn't stay in California either. *How long before they found my parents' house? How far will they go?*

"They're cowards, right?" she asked Pete. "I mean, they only seem to do stuff when I'm not around. Or they stay in the truck. They wouldn't actually come after me? Right?"

"I don't know," Pete replied. "I hope not."

"They know I'm here. I accidentally checked in on Facebook at the airport." She felt numb.

"I'm sorry," Pete said. "It's all my fault. That stupid play. I wish I'd never written it."

"It isn't your fault." She sounded unreasonably calm. "I gave that interview. Liz posted it online. That's really what caught their attention." She'd always thought it was dangerous to express strong opinions, but she was an actor. They were supposed to do that sort of thing.

After they said goodbye, she considered calling Sergeant Robbins back, but she already knew what he was going to say. She scrolled to Liz's contact, but any potential words constricted her throat, and she hung up without finishing the call. She should tell her not to come, of course. There were no more chances.

Maybe it was habit or a feeling that she needed to say goodbye in person, or maybe she just wanted to remind herself that she was making the right decision. Those were the excuses she ran through as she replied to the text: *Okay. Let me know when to pick you up at the airport.*

She listened to Jo's voicemail. "I've just been to your house. You need to call me. This is beyond a few kids. We're going to pursue this as a hate crime. Call me."

Rachel returned to the dinner table, where her parents looked as if they had been frozen in place, waiting for her.

"I've got a friend coming sometime this week. I assume it's okay for her to stay here?"

Rose smiled the first genuine smile since Rachel had arrived. "A *friend* friend?"

"Sort of," Rachel replied and watched her parents do that non-verbal glance-at-each-other thing. "Also, I'm going to go see Gladys tomorrow." She looked at her father. It was what she had come for, after all.

Her father nodded but didn't smile. He studied her the way he used to when she was little and trying to learn a new magic trick, when he wanted to see every tiny flick of her fingers and every tell on her face.

Rachel forced a smile and couldn't decide whether she was relieved or dismayed when her mother started in: "So, are you going to tell us what's going on with you? Is everything okay? Aren't you going to eat anything, Rachel? You're too skinny. Do you want to come to lunch with me to see Louise and Joanna from the book group tomorrow? They still remember you. They ask about you all the time. Do you want to go to the beach tomorrow? You're in California. You should go to the beach, get some sun. You're so pale. Do you want more potatoes?"

If she didn't respond, her mother filled in the blank with another question. All the unanswered questions piled up on the dinner table. She could almost see them, like leftovers nobody wanted to dump in the trash. Aaron left the table, his familiar hunched shoulders disappearing into the hall.

After helping with the dishes, just as Rachel started in on her escape to her room, her mother asked, "What time do you plan to visit Gladys, Rachel? I'll go with you, if it's after the book club. I promised Louise and Joanna. It's our weekly lunch."

"I'd rather go by myself." Rachel flinched inwardly at the hurt look that shadowed her mother's face before the sunny "Okay, dear."

For a second, she swore she could smell perfume, something flowery and too strong. The masking tape was off the cabinets, and the dishes were haphazardly piled together with no concern for meat or dairy. But the imprint of Gladys lingered like the desolation in a forest after a wildfire.

She retreated to her bedroom, and the shakes finally hit her. She stood in front of the bureau, her elbows on the stack of clean sheets and towels where there should have been high school playbills, pictures of friends, and a journal she never wrote in.

Everything was pressing down on her, and the fatigue was like freezing to death. All she wanted to do was sleep, but instead, she opened her laptop and read the things her stalkers had written to her, twisted love notes and dark promises.

Chapter 23
Rachel
1999

Rachel scanned the faces of people who were already seated or talking in groups as she trailed her father and Grandma Gladys into the junior high school cafeteria. The room smelled like the meat loaf they had served at lunch that day. She spotted a cluster of kids she knew from music class, sitting together in the front two rows, and she dipped a toe in the idea of it.

"I see some friends." She looked up at her father.

He smiled. "Go sit with them if you want." But the bruised look in his eyes didn't match the smile, and he turned quickly toward the door, probably looking for her mother, who was parking the car. She thought about how he had come home on time every night for the last two weeks so they could practice in his study. Even away from home, he smelled like that study—pipe tobacco, spiced aftershave, starch from the white shirts he always wore. They had woven a spell together with their practice, divined an island that belonged only to them. When they worked on tricks together, it was like being five years old, before Grandma Gladys moved in, before the women at synagogue started whispering about how "Rose has been struggling with depression," as if depression were contagious, more so when named out loud.

"That's okay." She followed him and her grandmother to an empty row. She had been too nervous to eat much for dinner, and as she perched on the edge of the folding chair between her father and Grandma Gladys, she couldn't tell whether the pang in her stomach was hunger or nerves. Maybe it was nausea from the excess lavender perfume Grandma Gladys wore.

She fidgeted with the top hat on her lap and checked that she still had her wand and the bag of props. Onstage, Ms. Westcott rambled on about her role as junior high principal and the school year so far. She earned applause when she announced a plan to hire more teachers and shrink classroom sizes. Then she said, "But tonight is about the traditional Carlsbad Junior High holiday talent show. We have some great acts and some great teachers who helped make it all happen."

Rachel tuned out the litany of teachers, donors, and kids who had made the talent show possible and wondered if it was too late to change her mind about sitting with the kids. That group of kids in front were all in the orchestra or chorus, and Rachel wasn't part of that. They'd had to choose just one thing, and she'd chosen magic. Other kids who had gone their own way weren't sitting with that group either. But a survey of the audience confirmed her suspicion that nobody else was with their parents. They were bunched in groups of two or three, sitting on the floor against the wall or in aisle seats where they could easily get out when their turn to climb onstage arrived.

Maybe the kids wouldn't notice. Maybe they wouldn't care. Maybe on Monday no one would call her "Daddy's Girl" or some other name. The last few months, she'd been surrounded daily by a group of girls from her social studies class who appeared just as the end-of-lunch bell rang and taunted her with things she couldn't quite grasp how to change. She was too thin, too good in school. She didn't know how to wear makeup or do her hair right or... It had started after the High Holy Days, when their social studies teacher had explained that Rachel would be missing class and told them why.

There was only one other Jewish kid in Rachel's class, and his family wasn't religious. Rachel's family hadn't been, either, until

Grandma Gladys moved in. Rachel was pretty sure the problem was something she couldn't change: she was too Jewish. They made her late to her science class every single day.

Rachel's mother appeared, walking toward their seats with her new, slow walk that always embarrassed Rachel and made her stay a couple of feet behind when they were in public together. Her green skirt hugged hips that had expanded since the last time she'd worn it a year before, when Rachel had played violin in the sixth-grade spring concert. At least her hair was done, and Rachel had seen her go into the master bathroom for a shower before they left. The couple in the aisle seats stood up to let her pass, but Grandma Gladys didn't move as she struggled in an awkward crab step toward the seat on the other side of Rachel's father. Rachel stood and felt grateful to catch a whiff of strawberry shampoo when her mother sidled by.

Ms. Westcott introduced Mrs. Alvarez and the Holiday Singers, and half the group in the front row clambered out of their chairs and climbed the three steps up to the stage. Rachel sang along quietly with the girls' part of "Baby It's Cold Outside." She had heard them practicing in the room next to her homeroom class, and she knew every song. She could have joined the chorus. She could have proven she knew the songs, Mrs. Alvarez would have let her in, and she wouldn't have been sitting there, squeezed between her father and grandmother. She would have been up on the stage, singing with the other kids, part of a group, one of many.

Grandma Gladys coughed, and a kid in front of them turned around then nudged the girl she was sitting with, who turned as well. Rachel stopped singing and stared down at her Mary Janes. Her father touched her shoulder, and she glanced up at his encouraging smile.

"You're going to do great," he whispered.

She nodded. Grandma Gladys sighed loudly and went rigid in the chair beside Rachel when the chorus launched into "Silent

Night." The kids in front turned again then whispered to each other. When the chorus began singing "Away in a Manger," Rachel's grandmother squeezed past the people in their row and left the cafeteria. *Good,* Rachel thought. *Maybe she'll stay away.* But the chorus finished with "Stopping by Woods on a Snowy Evening," and Grandma Gladys returned with a hint of the disinfectant smell Rachel associated with the school bathrooms clinging to her.

The principal spoke again, telling them all about the junior high orchestra and the outstanding director, who had turned down a chance to direct the San Diego Symphony because he loved working with the kids. While she talked, the chorus kids returned to their seats, grinning and whispering to one another, and the orchestra kids ascended the steps and found their seats in the semicircle of chairs, where their instruments had been left earlier that day. The sound of last-minute tuning drowned out Ms. Westcott's final words, and she returned to her chair on the side of the stage, making way for Mr. Yaeger.

When the band moved on to its second song, a compilation of Christmas TV show songs, Rachel breathed then stood. "I have to go get ready," she whispered to her father.

"Break a leg," he told her, and she edged out to the aisle, ignoring her mother, who leaned forward to smile around her father, her grandmother's whispered "good luck," and especially the two girls in front, whose eyes she felt follow her all the way to the foot of the stage.

She stopped at the foot of the three steps while the final off-key notes of "Rudolph" assaulted her ears. She saw Mr. Yaeger's bony shoulders rise to his ears and wondered if he was reconsidering the offer to direct a famous orchestra.

He turned to face the audience. "It's still early in the year," he said, and a few people laughed. "This is just a taste. They've only been rehearsing for a month, but I do hope you'll all come back and see this wonderful, talented orchestra in the spring concert. Now, for our final number, to give you a taste of the kind of music you'll be hearing in that spring concert, I give you Richard Wagner's 'Ride of the Valkyries.'"

He turned and lifted his arms. The room flooded with the first notes, which sounded to Rachel exactly like a call to battle. That was it. The song would end, and she would carry her props up to the stage, produce her magic wand, and begin her schtick. She found her father in the audience, but he wasn't watching the performance. He had bent his head toward Grandma Gladys, who looked agitated and half stood in front of her chair. Rachel's mother touched her father's wrist, and he turned but then faced Grandma Gladys again.

"Excuse me," Grandma Gladys said in her hoarse, accented voice.

Several people twisted in their seats, and even Mr. Yaeger turned and frowned into the audience, his long face wrinkling between the eyes, his arms still going. The two girls in front of Rachel's family giggled.

"Excuse me," Grandma Gladys said again and pushed her way in front of the couple next to her. Her movement seemed discordant, like a ballet that was out of step from the orchestra music. Rachel's parents followed, and soon the three of them were in the aisle, bunched together and whispering loudly.

Rachel took a step toward them, still clutching her bag and wand. "But the man is an anti-Semite," Grandma Gladys said, not bothering to whisper. The musicians faltered, and someone's violin screeched. Mr. Yaeger put his arms down and turned fully toward the audience.

Rachel's father coughed. "I'm sorry," he said. "I apologize."

"Richard Wagner is an anti-Semite, and I won't sit here and listen to that music," Gladys announced.

Mr. Yaeger's shoulders hunched forward, but he turned and gestured at the orchestra again. They resumed playing the notes they had played just before the commotion. Rachel retreated toward the steps and studied her prop bag, pretending she was checking to be sure she had what she needed. When she looked at her family again, Grandma Gladys had retreated to the door and stood there, rigid in her yellow dress and black jacket.

She caught her father's eye. His face seemed scrunched and sad. He shrugged and mouthed something that might have been "I'm sorry." The orchestra concluded their song, and the audience clapped, though several people kept turning to stare at Rachel's grandmother, who had not left but clearly had no intention of staying. Ms. Westcott returned to the front of the stage.

"Now," she announced as if everything were normal, "we'd like to welcome Rachel Goldberg to the stage for a performance of magic that will dazzle and amaze you. Everyone, please welcome Rachel the Great."

The clapping sounded half-hearted, distracted, and almost pitying. She climbed the steps and set up the folding table and disappearing box she'd left on the stage that afternoon.

"Ladies and gentlemen," she began while her father followed her grandmother toward the back door. Most people had their heads turned, openly staring at the small drama. Rachel knew they saw her father's hunched form slip through the cafeteria door behind her grandmother, heard the door slam shut, and saw her mother—fat, embarrassing, and alone—return to one of the three empty chairs. The girls in front giggled loudly.

"Ladies and gentlemen," Rachel repeated, the words feeling like mud in her mouth. "Watch while I amaze you. Maybe you've seen a quarter disappear. Maybe you've even seen a rabbit disappear. But have you ever seen a person disappear? I'm going to need a volunteer for this one. Who is willing to come up onstage and risk disappearing, maybe never to be seen again?"

The audience laughed, and she couldn't remember if that line was supposed to be funny. *Are they laughing because everybody, every single one of them, knows that my father has just disappeared, and he was supposed to be my volunteer?*

After a long moment of silence, her mother stood once again. "I volunteer." Her voice quivered.

"Okay." Rachel found some deep, composed place inside, where she had maybe sung with the chorus instead of doing the magic show, where her voice had blended with the others and she had been one of many, belonging. "Okay. Please tell the audience your name."

"Rose," her mother said in a little girl's voice.

"Come on up, Rose." She gazed at the back door, but it stayed shut. She scanned the audience. The smirking girls from the row in front of her family would tell the entire school that Rose was Rachel's mother. The chorus kids' faces wore bored expressions. Ms. Westcott flashed a look of pity. "Prepare yourselves," she told them all as Rose made a steady path to the stage. "I will now make my mother disappear."

The audience laughed again, and at least that time, she knew she'd been funny intentionally. *Right?*

Chapter 24
Stephen
2016

Stephen's room at the Elders' house was not the sunny cinnamon room he had imagined. It was a finished room in their basement and smelled moldy in spite of the dehumidifier that ran twenty-four hours a day. The first night, he was bothered by the sound and couldn't sleep at all. He tried to trace the source, but that proved impossible until daylight, which was when he discovered that it was way on the other end of the basement, by the furnace. All the lights in the part of the basement that weren't his room involved bulbs hanging from the ceiling with short chains he could barely reach. Even in daylight, it wasn't that easy to find the thing. He slept better once he knew what it was. He appreciated the white noise that drowned out everything else.

He ate most of his meals with the Bakers, and he let them talk to him about religion, but he refused to go to their church, their Kingdom Hall. Even Natalie seemed to think it would be a good idea. "You have to believe in something," she said.

He did believe in something. He believed in white power. If he'd had enough money, he would have bought an iPod and downloaded some of the old music he used to listen to. But the idea felt immediately hollow. *I already failed. I'm sorry, Grandpa.* He still hadn't told Natalie about any of that. He wasn't ashamed of it, but he didn't think she would understand. Plus, it was private, something that was his and not to be shared with just anyone.

Philip let Stephen use his computer when he wasn't around. The family spent a lot of time at Kingdom Hall, and the kids went to some kind of summer camp. The kid's room was disgustingly clean. No joint hidden in his sock drawer, under his bed, in the toe of a shoe or anywhere. No porn shoved under the mattress. No lingering cigarette odor on his jacket, which he hung neatly over the back of his desk chair on days he didn't take it to school. His bedside reading was the latest *Watchtower*.

Stephen had followed Philip to his summer camp once, just to find out if the kid was as clean as he seemed. Stephen hung back a good distance, doing recon, feeling more like he was back playing war in the canyon than anything. The kid joined up with a couple of other boys, and they walked together. Stephen could only catch bits of their conversation, but it seemed to involve Pokémon. *Isn't Pokémon for little kids?* Once they got to Kingdom Hall, Stephen turned back to the house. There was probably something creepy about doing recon on a twelve-year-old. Another thing on the do-not-tell-Natalie list. Maybe Philip was a really young twelve with no hormones yet.

Beth, the ten-year-old, showed more promise. She had painted sex parts on some of the pictures in her copy of *The Watchtower*. The penis on the cherubic blond boy wasn't very realistic, but still. She kept it in the drawer in her bedside table. He wondered where she'd even gotten the idea. It was something he would have done at her age.

Maria taught Bible study or whatever the hell they called it at someone's house on Tuesday and Thursday afternoons, and Josh went off every day in his suit and tie to sell beds at Marco Mattress. Stephen could never have sold beds. He would have started imagining the couples who came to buy them fucking, and then he would just crack up and lose his train of thought. He would have suggested beds with brass headboards so mister could tie the little lady up then stepped back to see how they reacted. But he supposed Josh's mind stayed clean and pure. Then again, they had to have done something to get two kids.

He googled Rachel again, but half the links didn't show up, because the kids weren't allowed social media. Facebook was blocked. Twitter was blocked. He did turn up a phone number for her at Cortland High School, but of course, it was summer. There probably wouldn't have been anybody there. There wouldn't be any connecting with Rachel that way.

He went to the SPCA site to see if the dog was still there. Her picture was gone. *Did that mean she was adopted? Did they euthanize her?* He had failed her. If she died, it was on him.

He checked the time. Camp was just about out. He decided to go wait for Phillip.

———◉———

FOLLOWING PHILLIP BECAME part of Stephen's ritual. Phillip had hinted that there was some girl he liked when they were fooling around on the Wii over the weekend, but he wouldn't cough the rest of it up. That first day, it hadn't been planned. Simple curiosity drove Stephen to sidle out a few minutes after Philip and head in the direction of the Kingdom Hall as if he was taking a walk. But he'd gotten more intentional about it, choosing a gray sweatshirt and green army fatigues to blend in with the bushes and road. He even took a water bottle, strapped to his waist. He wore sneakers for stealth.

Philip always met up with the same two kids about halfway there. They seemed nerdy to Stephen. One had glasses, which he knew didn't really mean anything, but when he was a kid, it had definitely meant smart and nerd. Now, he thought it probably meant the kid's parents noticed that he couldn't see. He had gotten reading glasses when he had his free eye exam when he enlisted. It had been the first time in his life he could read a whole magazine without getting terrible headaches and eye pain.

He told himself he wanted to be sure the kid was okay, that whoever the girl was wouldn't break his heart. He knew it was creepy and that if Josh found out, he would probably lose his basement room, but he didn't care enough to stop. He could always say it was PTSD. Another vet who'd been in the hospital with him had complained that ever since Iraq, he couldn't stop worrying about his kids being safe.

Sometimes, Stephen pictured what would happen if he accidentally killed Josh and Maria, how the kids would scream and cry and how they would feel after, completely alone in the world with nobody to love them. Sometimes imagining that made him feel like crying, but he didn't. He pictured them curled up on the floor in their bedrooms, or maybe both kids together in Phillip's bedroom. He pictured them just lying there, staring at the ceiling with glazed eyes. Some things were too sad to cry about.

Philip met up with his two buddies, the kid with the glasses and the too-tall kid with lots of T-shirts that said things like, "My parents went to the Grand Canyon, and all I got was this lousy T-shirt." They met in front of Glasses Kid's house, the shabby one on the street with a rusty fence around the front lawn. The house next door always had a red SUV parked out front, and sometimes, Stephen left early and hung out behind it until the boys gathered. He followed, keeping his distance. Kids were so absorbed in themselves, it was amazing what they didn't notice.

The boys had given up talking about soccer. It had turned to *Avatar* and whether Bethany, which Stephen gathered was the girl's name, would like Philip better if he were a vampire. Friday, the other kids had urged Philip to "just ask her out, man, just go for it." But Philip wouldn't. Not because he was a chicken, but because his parents would never let him. They had boundaries about stuff like that.

The girl wasn't a Jehovah's Witness. Phillip didn't say that, though. "Maybe next week," he'd said instead.

That afternoon, Stephen returned around the end of the day and hung out in a front yard next to the church, where he could watch the kids walk up the hill.

Phillip walked ahead of his friends and approached a girl who was loitering across the street. She was taller than Phillip but chunky and looked like she was trying to hide it, wearing an ankle-length skirt with a baggy top that covered her entire ass. Disappointment choked in Stephen's throat. He didn't know what he had expected. Something exotic. Someone dark-haired and intimidating. She just looked like any other twelve-year-old kid. He walked away quickly, before Phillip could notice him.

Back at the house, he sat on the bed in his basement and leafed through the *Watchtower* magazine he'd taken from Beth's room. She had colored in the hair and drawn breasts on every girl in the magazine, but she hadn't put another penis on any of the men or boys. Just the two on the cover. He wondered if it would freak her out to find it missing. He wondered why he had taken it.

When he was finished looking, he hid it under his mattress and headed out to the library. At dinner the night before, Josh had commented that he heard one of the congregation members say they'd seen Stephen at the library. "That's great, Stephen. Any leads on jobs?"

Stephen shook his head. "Not much. The job market sucks."

Josh nodded and spooned some mashed potatoes into his mouth. "If you like, I can ask my manager if there are any openings at Marco's Mattress."

Stephen hunched his shoulders forward and studied his overcooked spinach. "I guess it couldn't hurt." He couldn't get used to those family dinners, where everybody sat around at the table and acted like they were happy to be there. Even his memories of dinners at Rachel's house were shadowed by Gladys's constant attacks on Rachel's mother. The kids hardly talked, and they didn't even ask to be excused until everyone was done. One time, Beth wouldn't eat her broccoli, and she had to sit there at the table with the over-cooked broccoli straight through *American Idol.* Stephen thought that might have been a little extreme, but she wasn't his kid. When he was her age, he ate alone in his bedroom half the time, while his mother flirted with some uncle in the living room. He always made sure he ate everything Maria put on the table, although he doubted they would try to punish him if he didn't.

THE LIBRARY HAD TAKEN getting used to, but once he was comfortable, he could walk right in and get the little card with a computer number on it, sit down, and log in without breaking a sweat. Sure, if someone had come up behind him, he would still have jumped, and that one time, some kid wouldn't stop crying and Stephen'd had to leave, but other than that, he'd been good. He made a mental note to tell Natalie that exposure stuff worked.

He got the number six computer, the one near the front by the window. When he looked out, he could see the tops of some palm trees and cars. He watched a car with two surfboards strapped to the roof stop at a light while he waited for Windows to boot. Finally, the light changed, the surfboards took off, and he turned to the comput-er. Lately, he'd been doing some weird stuff in his head, telling him-self he couldn't look away from the surfboards until they moved and counting all the spots on the basement ceiling before he got out of bed in the morning, as if maybe a new one had appeared. It was stu-pid, but he couldn't stop himself.

He opened the browser and navigated to Google. First, he did the ritual: google Frank. Google Rick. Google Sally. Google Theresa. None of their fake names came up. Then it was on to the pawn shops.

He had searched pawn shops all around Carlsbad and San Diego. *Where else?* He tried Del Mar. He typed, "pawn shop and Rick."

There it was, Rick's Pawnshop. All those weeks of hunting, and he'd found it just like that. The bit of narrative underneath said, "Rick Lindstrom opened this pawn shop in..." He clicked on it to see the rest, but the link was dead. He googled Rick Lindstrom. There were three hits, so he clicked on the first link. Rick Lindstrom was one of three men arrested for the murder of a Mexican clerk at a convenience store. As soon as he saw the article, he knew he didn't need to bother googling the others. The article said it was believed to be a drug-related crime, but Stephen doubted that. At least they got shorter sentences if it wasn't hate related. He wondered if it bugged them, the truth not being reported.

"Check in with yourself," Natalie was always saying. "What's in your body?" He checked in with himself and felt nothing. His body was numb, and his mind didn't care.

He hadn't really been thinking about it so much lately. He'd been thinking about Rachel, Phillip's girlfriend, Natalie, and getting his shit together. Maybe he would even take that job selling beds. Natalie would smile and nod if he did. He liked to see her smile and nod.

He logged into Facebook and found a message from Rachel. He bit his lip so hard he tasted blood as he clicked to open it. She had said yes. She would talk to him. Hell, she would see him. She was in California, and she would see him. He suggested his grandfather's home. He wasn't going to bring her to Josh and Maria's house. No fucking way did he want her thinking he was one of those Witnesses.

After he had responded, he read the comments on her wall. He had a feeling she had a personal page, too, but he couldn't access that. There was a link to an announcement that the play she was in was on hiatus. But the comments hadn't slowed down at all.

We're coming for you, Jew bitch.
We're going to incinerate you.

He thrummed with the words. They were after Rachel. They were his people, but so was she. He wanted to protect her. He wanted to join them. He didn't know what he wanted, but the words filled him with dread and provoked an urge to burn himself and allow the pain to obliterate all other emotion, leaving only numbness. He clicked on one of them, ImaNazi. He followed the responses to ImaNazi and clicked through, following comment threads and reading bios. Then he found a link to a private Reddit group called "Get Rachel Goldberg." He clicked through.

Clintman: *I'm gonna rape that girl before I kill her.*

ImaNazi: *We have to find her first.*

Deploarble2: *So, we know she's in California, but that father clue was a dead end. Someone must have gone to school with her. Address?*

Proud Boy: *I know someone who works at Old Oaks Nursing home. He says there's a Gladys Goldberg there. Says he's seen Aaron Goldberg on the sign-in. Isn't that her father's name?*

Deploarble2: *I think we have a winner. Now what's your friend doing working in a kike nursing home?*

Proud Boy: *Gotta make a living, man.*

JT51: *I'm already in California. I'm on it. I have a personal grudge with that bitch.*

The rest were plans for staking out the nursing home to keep an eye out for Rachel. Stephen read every single comment then googled the Old Oaks Nursing Home and wrote down the address. Gladys was there.

Chapter 25
Stephen
2001

H e'd gotten the invite from some of his skinhead buddies. "It's a high school party," they said. Kid's parents vacationing, left the kid alone in the house. Rumor was a black family lived next door. For a while, it had seemed like the skins would accept the story that he'd raped a Jew girl as a kid and let that be enough for his admission to the club. But they wanted an initiation they could see. "Something to prove you're one of us," they told him.

The party was going to be his chance. Most of them had dropped out of high school junior year. Stephen was barely hanging in through senior year, and he wasn't one with contacts to find out about hot parties. He spent lunches crouched behind the band room, getting stoned. Stephen thought Rick kept tabs on things. He'd even managed to get elected to school government, treasurer or something. "It's about playing the game," he said.

Frank didn't go, since he was too old to fit in with the crowd. But he gave Stephen his best knife, the one with White Power engraved on the handle, and said he would be waiting to celebrate when they came back. The party was two hours away in Los Angeles, so Stephen didn't expect Carlsbad kids to be there. But it turned out the host was a big drama kid at one of the neighboring LA high schools. The whole reason anyone from Carlsbad even knew about the party was because the LA kids and the Carlsbad kids had met at a drama competition or convention or something. When Rick mentioned it was a drama party, Stephen put the cap back on his gin bottle and shoved

199

it under the car seat. He even turned down the next toke and stopped singing along with the radio. He started imagining Rachel there and thinking how it would go. He planned how he would say hi, how she would respond. He hoped maybe they could take a walk or find a corner and talk.

THE HOUSE WAS A TYPICAL LA house with stucco, lots of windows, and sliding glass doors that looked out onto a gated land-scaped paradise. The porch light was on, but other rooms glowed with dim half-light, as if the kids were hoping the lack of light would make up for the noise if the neighbors complained or maybe to make it better for kissing in dark corners. The house next door looked iso-lated and dark, with a half-dead lawn in front and a stray cat lurking on the sagging front porch. Stephen doubted he would get a chance to beat up anyone in that house. *Am I relieved or annoyed?* He prac-ticed being annoyed, so he could tell the story to Frank correctly when they got back. *That damn nigger house was empty.*

Someone had put on the *Rocky Horror Picture Show* album, and kids were doing the Time Warp in the oversized living room. They all seemed young to Stephen, sophomores maybe. But they were already staggering and slurring their words. Stephen couldn't see Rachel any-where. He wandered through the living room, nearly tripping over a couple of kids making out on the floor, and found the kitchen, where someone had filled several plastic cups with beer. He pushed through a crowd of girls who were passing around a joint and stopped for a toke when a girl with frizzy red hair and too much makeup offered it to him. Then he took his beer back out to the living room, where he found his buddies in a corner watching the Time Warp kids.

"Fucking fags." Rick poked Stephen in the side.

"Fucking fags," he agreed. Theresa came over, put a Coors in his hand, then leaned against him. He tilted the bottle to his mouth and let his hand roam across her ass.

"Getting a little too chunky," he told her and pinched.

She squealed and giggled.

He'd once asked Frank why the fuck she did that all the time, and he said it was because she wasn't all that bright and tried to do what she thought would turn him on. It didn't, though. It made him want to smack her in the face so she would squeal for real. *That* would turn him on. At least it did in the shower. He pinched again, harder. She giggled and pressed her ass back against his hand. The music changed to "Sweet Transvestite," and one of the guys started a wobbly strip tease. The other kids cleared a space. He was wearing makeup and a wig and heels that could double as weapons.

"Can't get the Jews, you'll nail that guy," Rick whispered to Stephen. "Can't get a Jew, go for a fucking fag."

The kids in the circle started clapping in rhythm while the guy played around, rubbing a belt against his ass and wiggling. That was when Stephen finally saw Rachel. She looked the same as the time he'd found her down in the canyon with that girl, only her hair was longer, and she wasn't half naked. In fact, she had a dress on, a sleeveless blue dress that hugged her hips and stopped just above her knees. She'd probably had to change into that after she left the house, if Gladys was still around. She was swaying awkwardly on a pair of those corky-looking platform shoes and what was sexy wasn't so much the swaying as the danger that she might fall off the shoes and hit the ground if she kept it up, her dress riding up her hips when she landed.

He felt the familiar tug of wanting rush straight to his balls. He smacked Theresa's ass hard, and instead of giggling or squealing, she grunted in surprise. "Ouch," she said. "You really hurt me," which made his dick jerk, and he pulled his hands away from Theresa to cover it.

Rachel turned and saw him. Lots of kids turned. Theresa had a loud, high-pitched voice, and she'd made no effort to keep it quiet. But what was important was that Rachel turned. Rachel saw him. He lifted a hand to her. A little wave. A little salute. A little Heil Hitler. He wanted her to blush. He wanted her to smile. She did not approach him. In fact, she turned away, presenting her ass, which was a hell of a lot shapelier than Theresa's. *Why did she turn away? Isn't she just a little happy to see me?* He was wearing his skinhead clothes—leather and probably a cap with a swastika symbol on it.

The idea might have burst in suddenly, just like that, or it could have grown slowly, while he watched her ass. Maybe he was already working on the idea when he heard it was a drama party and realized she would probably be there, even before he saw her. He leaned over and whispered in Rick's ear, "You know that Jew dyke I raped? The one I'm always talking about? Well, she's here. Right here at this party."

Rick grinned and punched his arm. "No way," he said. "That would be too perfect. You're making that shit up."

"I'm not." He tried to point Rachel out, but the group had closed around her again. Then the song ended, and people drifted apart.

"There. Wait, no, she's moved. Over there." He dragged Rick with him and followed her from the living room to the kitchen, where she grabbed one of the plastic cups. He followed her up the stairs, where she entered a pink room with posters of unicorns and the smell of pot. A couple was making out on the bed. Rachel joined a group of kids who sat in a circle on the floor, passing a joint. He held his breath while she lowered herself to the floor, waiting to see if she would lose her balance. But she somehow managed it, not even taking off the platform shoes. He stood outside the open door and watched her accept the joint. She either didn't see him or was pointedly ignoring him. He stared hard. She shifted her position, and her hips touched with a long-haired blonde. *Are they a thing?*

He stepped back to find Rick and Theresa behind him. "Go for it, man," Rick said. "That's too good to be true. Rape the Jew for a second time." He was already slurring his words, but Stephen was still nursing his first beer. If he'd known, he wouldn't have smoked the pot either. A good soldier didn't let himself get impaired. Theresa pouted and clutched at his arm, but he pushed her away.

"This is for the cause, baby," he told her. But it was much more personal than that.

"Man, oh man, could it get any better? You've got to brutalize her, man. That will be a perfect initiation." Rick's voice was getting too loud, and Rachel glanced in the direction of the open door. She had to have seen him.

Rick's initiation had involved beating up an old drunk on the beach. Every time he told the story, the drunk got younger and fought back harder. Stephen figured pretty soon, he would be going on about how he beat up a gay Navy SEAL. Frank had a ring made for Rick after he beat up the drunk. It had an eagle on it with the word "skins" etched into the gold plating in all capital letters. Rick also got a new tattoo of the same thing. Stephen wanted that ring the same way he used to want his grandfather to touch his shoulder and say, "You're a real soldier."

Sometimes, when Rick didn't think anyone was watching, Stephen would see him staring at that ring, turning it round and round on his finger, and he would wonder what it felt like, the moment of his fist hitting the nose of the old drunk. *Was it intoxicating? Did he get a rush every time?* He never understood why Rick's expression often went dark and sad when he twisted that ring. Rick should have been smiling. Stephen would have been smiling.

So Stephen walked into the pink room and stood by the bed, right above where Rachel sat on the floor. Rick followed, and Theresa lagged behind. "Hey, Rachel," he said and squatted to tap her on the shoulder. She twisted her head to look at him, and he leaned close enough to get a whiff of the booze on her breath. She stuck out her lower lip and squinted like she couldn't quite believe who she was looking at.

"Hi, Stephen." Perfectly natural.

"Where's your girlfriend?" He twisted the word "girlfriend" into an ugly thing, so she would know exactly what he meant.

Theresa giggled. "That's a good one, Stevie."

He whirled to face her. "I told you never to fucking call me that." She dropped her head and blushed.

Rachel turned back to her friends. "So, as I was telling you..." she said, babbling about something involving a play she'd seen. He could hear from downstairs that they'd started the damn song over again, and kids were chanting something. "Take it off," he thought they were saying.

He glanced at Rick, who raised an eyebrow and mouthed something that might have been, "Get the fucking Jew girl, man." Stephen poked Rachel on the head. "I was talking to you, Jew Girl." It tasted funny to say the words, almost as an adult and at a weird party. He hadn't addressed her as "Jew Girl" since he was ten years old, that last time they played the shower game. She'd said, "I don't like this game anymore," and that was that. It had never felt right to call her Jew Girl after she didn't like the game and after Gladys made friends with him. That was back when he still hated Jews but not Rachel's family. He said it again, just to get used to the feel of it. "Jew Girl."

Rachel's lips curled off her upper teeth like an angry dog. She squinted up at him, glanced at her friends, then scrambled to her feet. "What the fuck did you just call me?" She slurred on "just."

"I said I was talking to you, Jew Girl." God. He felt sick, powerful, disgusted, aroused. He could taste the buzz, a sour feeling that curled his toes and hyped his whole body. He barely recognized himself. Rick and Theresa were both behind him somewhere, laughing, and the rest of the room had gone quiet. The kid holding the toke froze, and the couple on the bed sat up, the girl yanking her shirt down. Stephen took in the laughter of his friends like a drug, pushed his chest out, spread his legs a little.

Rachel was almost as tall as he was. She stared into his eyes. "You're pitiful, *Stevie.*" Then, she brushed past him, out of the room, and down the stairs. Part of Stephen wanted to make her pay for what she had said, and part of him wanted to give up and leave the damn party.

Rick and Theresa dragged him into a football huddle. "Go after her, man," Rick said. "Don't let her disrespect you like that."

"She's a bitch," Theresa said, sidling up to him.

Rick puffed up. "Want me to do it for you? We can always tell Frank it was you."

Stephen pictured Rick's brawny body on top of Rachel, pinning her to the ground. He wanted to puke. "No," he told Rick. "She's mine. I'll come find you when it's done." Then he went down the stairs after Rachel.

Later, he would never quite remember how he got Rachel to the beach that day of the party. He didn't drag her there. She must have gone willingly, but he didn't know why. He didn't know what he'd said to make her go with him. They walked past Rick and Theresa on their way to the beach. He knew this because Rick yelled, "Bring proof," as they walked by. But on the beach, they were alone. The beach was dark and fishy smelling. The waves crashed, and it probably could have been romantic, walking on the beach together, but he was too fucking scared of what he was supposed to do. He was always scared when he was supposed to be the bravest.

They walked barefoot, the water tickling his ankles. At first, she wouldn't take off those stupid platform shoes she was too drunk to walk in, but after she fell into him and nearly dragged both of them into the water, she did. He stared at her ass when she bent and lifted her right leg sideways to reach under and remove the shoe. She caught him looking and dropped down onto the sand for the left shoe. When she stood up, there was a wet patch, and grains of sand stuck to her dress and the backs of her thighs.

He looked at her, and he wanted her, not to rape her. He just wanted her. "Are you a dyke?" he asked.

At first, she didn't answer but turned and let the waves wash over her. "I don't know," she finally said, brushing off her ass. "I think so." She glanced at him then quickly looked out at the ocean. "Why do you care, anyway?"

He could—should have said that it was wrong for her to be a dyke, and he was going to show her why she needed a man. He should have pushed her down right there, with the waves sloshing in and out over their legs, and raped her. That was what Rick would have done. It was what he should have done. Instead, with absolutely no warning in his own head that he was going to, he asked, "Why does Gladys hate me all of a sudden?"

"I have no idea," Rachel said and giggled. "But I sure as hell wish she'd stop liking me."

He nodded like he understood, but he truly couldn't imagine ever wishing anybody would stop liking him. Hell, even that time when he was eight or nine and his grandfather took him out to the empty lot to train Dieter, he cried because the puppy wouldn't come when he called. "I'm supposed to rape you," he said out loud. *Did I really say that? What an idiot.*

She laughed too loudly, with an edge of hysteria. She walked away from the water, up to the dry part of the sand. "It will be hard to rape me if I'm willing." She stripped, right there on the beach. Just like that. He must have chickened out if he told her he was supposed to rape her. That wasn't the kind of thing you told someone. She slipped her dress over her head in one swift motion. She was wearing a white lace bra and white underwear. Light from the moon glinting off the ocean speckled her skin. He felt his erection and heard a whooshing in his ears that might have been the ocean and might have been his own blood pounding through his veins. He held his breath.

She lay down on her back in the sand and looked up at him through the inky night. He dropped to his knees beside her and reached out to touch one of her breasts through the bra, feeling the small hardness of her nipple through the thin fabric. It was like being in a movie. Like a fantasy, only when he fantasized, the real him would be hunched over himself in the bathroom, working with his hand. He kneaded her breasts a little, the way he did with Theresa. But Theresa would giggle and moan, and Rachel just lay there, staring up at the sky. She didn't make any noise. She sure as hell didn't fight him. She just said, "Come on, Stevie. You're supposed to rape me."

That was when it happened. He felt a sudden rush, and everything went sideways for a second. It wasn't until he felt the wet, sticky mess at his crotch that he understood. That had happened the first time he'd fucked Theresa, when he was so excited he just couldn't stand it, but it wasn't supposed to happen with Rachel. She just kept lying there, on her back in her underwear, not moving. He climbed on top and pressed his lips to hers, hoping it wouldn't leak through so she could feel it, hoping his hard-on would come back. She opened her mouth to accept his tongue, but she didn't kiss him back.

He pulled away. "Do you like this?"

"I don't know." But she seemed detached, not aroused. She took her bra and underwear off. He turned his back to remove his pants and boxers, so she wouldn't see the wet spot. They were stupid boxers his mother had gotten him for Christmas, with a Santa Claus and reindeer print. Stupid fucking boxers to not rape someone in. If he'd known how the night would turn out, he never would have grabbed the first pair of clean boxers in his drawer. He would have been more careful.

He felt between her legs, the wiry bush of hair. She didn't move when he touched her there. Theresa always thrust up against his hand. Theresa was always shaved and sopping wet down there, leaving a trail of slime on his fingers. Rachel was just hairy. He rubbed up and down, trying to get a reaction out of her, but she was inanimate, like one of those blow-up dolls they sold at sex stores. He could hear her breathing, steadily in and out, no panting the way Theresa did. He got on top of her again and rubbed himself against her, but he couldn't get hard. Usually with Theresa, he could do it two or three times. But there he was, with Rachel lying there and willing, and all he could manage was one stupid time in his own pants. He kept at it, feeling with his hands, trying to guide himself in, pushing a finger inside her dry, unyielding center. She started laughing. Hysterical drunken laughter. He needed an erection to rape someone, and he couldn't get it back.

Finally, he stood up and looked down at her. She put her bra and her dress on and handed him her underwear. "Here. They said you need proof."

He walked her back to the party and left her there and found Rick and Theresa hanging out with the pot-smoking kids.

On the way back to Carlsbad, Rick put Rachel's underwear on his head like a hat and kept bringing them down to sniff the crotch.

Chapter 26
Rachel
2016

At first, Rachel thought Stephen's house looked exactly the same, right down to the yellow Volkswagen Beetle in the driveway. She couldn't be sure, but the dent in the car's bumper even looked familiar. A closer look revealed signs of neglect and a house that was much less gothic than her imagination had painted it over the years.

In Pineville, if people stopped taking care of their yards, lawns sprouted out of control and filled with dandelions, bushes grew high enough to obscure windows, and trees merged together to form balconies of pure shade. Rachel knew this from experience. But in California, a neglected yard turned dusty, overtaken with poison ivy and rattlers scuttling underneath. The flat rocks that paved the walkway to the front door of Stephen's old house were chipped and faded. She remembered them glistening with color as if someone had planted jewels in them. But that might have been her childhood imagination. She remembered the front door as being huge like the door to a cave, to a world of hidden secrets. But really, it was just a normal front door, weathered natural wood set in a little against the decorative gray bricks of the house.

She was starting to wonder if meeting Stephen there was such a good idea. She could have asked to meet anywhere—a Denny's, a McDonald's. It would have been wise to do it in a public place where there wasn't any danger that she would wind up in his cellar or—she choked on an unexpected laugh—his attic.

When she knocked, the sound was hollow, as if she was tapping against a metal trash can. She half expected she was going to have to knock harder, but then she heard footsteps inside, and the door swung open.

Stephen did not look the same. His head was white and bare, but whether from shaving or early balding, it was hard to tell. He'd grown paunchy around his jowls, and while he wasn't fat, he had a beer belly and looked soft and out of shape. His pale-blue eyes still compelled, though. She looked at his eyes, and she felt six again. She felt like dropping to her knees and holding out her hands. *I'm your prisoner.*

"Hi." His middle-aged-man's voice had a bit of a cigarette rasp to it and pulled her back into the present. He was wearing army pants and a sweatshirt, which looked damp under the armpits. She had tried on several outfits before coming—first, her khaki shorts, which had grown too big, or she had grown too small, so they fell down and stuck at her hips, revealing the top of her rose-colored underwear. She'd taken them off and tried her tight jeans, which were a better fit but too hot. Finally, she had settled on her yoga pants, black with a drawstring at the waist. Maybe clingier than she really wanted, but a long T-shirt hanging over the hips helped with that. She kept telling herself she didn't want to dress sexy for him. The last thing she wanted was to dress sexy for Stephen.

He led her through the kitchen too quickly for her to feel comfortable stopping, but she was certain the ribbon from the one year he'd played Little League and his team won second in the series was still tacked to the small white refrigerator. She remembered him telling her how his grandpa put it there, right on the fridge, how proud he was of that bit of yellow fabric.

She sat on the living-room sofa she remembered from childhood, with its brown-and-white fabric, stained here and there, stuffing coming out of the cushions, and cigarette burns forming what appeared to be deliberate patterns on the back. She thought of her own haphazard house in Pineville, with garage sale furniture she never got around to replacing. *Who am I to judge?* she wondered in Gladys's voice and inhaled the musty, closed smell of the room.

Stephen went to the kitchen and came back with two beers. "I wasn't sure I had anything in the fridge," he said, handing her one. She sat back against the overstuffed arm, pulling bits of wispy white stuff out of a hole and taking a sip of the Coors. He settled on the other end, leaning on his knees, his beer on the floor between his feet. "I haven't been here in a few months," he said. "I'm staying with some friends of my mother."

The bitter taste of the beer slid over her tongue and down her throat. "How is your mother?"

He picked up his beer then put it down. "She's discovered religion." His laugh sounded a little like a sob. "She's one of those people who shows up at your door, trying to convert you." He drank several gulps of beer, and for a few seconds, the only sound was him swallowing hard. "She's off drugs, though. That's good, I guess."

Rachel nodded but didn't say anything. *What the hell am I doing here? I should leave immediately.*

"How's Gladys?" he asked casually, but there was an intensity to the way he leaned forward and stared at the lip of his beer bottle.

"She's in a nursing home. She's suffering from dementia." Rachel laughed, hearing the irony in her own voice.

"Yeah." The sound came out with a breath, like a sigh. "But do you think she'd remember me?"

"She calls me Esther," Rachel said. "I doubt she'd remember you." *Did he already know about Gladys?* Something about that prickled her fear, but of course he would have googled. After all, she had googled him. That weird arrest story had nearly changed her mind about meeting up with him.

"Oh." He sighed. "I thought she might remember me."

"She was calling me Esther five years ago," Rachel said. "I don't know why she'd remember you."

"She thinks you're her sister?"

Rachel swallowed too fast and coughed, tasting the beer, feeling it slosh into her sinuses. When she finally stopped coughing, she panted and concentrated on slowing her breath before she asked, "What sister? She doesn't have any sisters."

"Esther. That's the older sister that died in the concentration camps, isn't it?"

Rachel stared at him. "Where did you hear that?"

"Well, she told me. You know, when I used to hang out in her room all the time? She told me stories about her family and stuff. Esther was the older sister. She took care of Gladys. Helped her sneak out a window the night she came to America. You know."

"Honestly," Rachel said, "the last time I saw her was a few years ago. I keep meaning to visit her while I'm here, but I don't know. There's always something else that comes up. I told my parents I'd go see her today." *Why am I surprised that Gladys told Stephen stuff she never told the family? That was so Gladys. Don't tell the people it matters to. Fucking Gladys.*

"I could go with you." Stephen sounded like a little kid hoping to be invited to the party.

Rachel didn't answer. The sharp edge of everything they were not talking about dug into her gut. His eyes kept flitting from her to the ocean picture on the wall to the lace curtains hanging like something dead in front of the closed window. It was a scene that ought to have included a tense drumbeat in the background, a sense of something terrible about to happen. Instead, it felt like every day, as if he was someone she had met doing a show or someone she'd known for years. Worse, everything about him was, well, frumpy. Mundane.

"What I really want," she said, "is to see your attic. Where we used to play. I want..." She clamped her lips and sucked air through her teeth. "I just think about it a lot, you know. We spent so much time up there. I want to see if it's like I remember." The point of the trip was to visit childhood haunts, to remember and work it through or something.

Neither of them said anything for a long time. Several minutes passed, long enough to finish their beers. Long enough for Stephen to silently retrieve two more beers from the refrigerator. Long enough for Rachel to guzzle half of the second, relaxing into the warmth of the alcohol.

Finally, Stephen nodded and stood. She stood, too, leaving the second beer on the floor beside the sofa, and followed him through the living room, to the hall, to the narrow winding steps. She was six years old, using her hands to help herself up the steep parts where the stairs curved around, letting Stephen pull her up the final step into the attic. She was his prisoner. *On your knees, Jew Girl.*

She had to crouch a little to walk in the attic. She didn't remember the ceiling being quite so arched or the space being so small. The wooden floorboards creaked under the weight of their bodies. A thin layer of dust obscured the glass of the gun cabinet, although it looked more recently cleaned than the narrow window, which was thickly coated and hosted several spiderwebs. She scanned the piles of cardboard boxes, wondering which ones contained the magazines, then glanced at the corner where she used to take pretend showers. She could see how it had worked for a shower, the boxes piled high at an angle, creating a square space. Little kids wouldn't have been able to see over them.

Turn you into soap, Jew Girl. She hadn't understood what it meant back then. She wondered if Stephen had. Her eyes found a box near his feet, half open, something familiar about the inked letters in careful block print on the box: "Niklas's Bedroom." She dropped to her knees to look inside. On the top was a magazine with a glossy front cover, the image a half-naked woman eating a banana.

The box smelled like sex to her. The dust, the attic, it all smelled like sex. It triggered arousal, and her body tingled. From Germany, or so Stephen had said. German porn from when his grandpa fought for Hitler. She pulled the magazine out. Underneath, another magazine was still encased in a plain brown envelope. The address tag on the envelope was in English, addressed to Niklas Drescher at 135 Alder Avenue, which was Stephen's address. Under that was another loose magazine but then an empty envelope.

"I always thought these came from Germany, from World War II," she said. "But they're addressed to here. And the dates aren't right." She saw in the top-right corner of the top magazine October, nineteen sixty-one. Well past the end of the war. He squatted beside her to look. Their knees bumped, and neither of them pulled away. She thought she should, but it wasn't the game if she pulled away. *What are you doing, Rachel?* She thought of him touching her leg like he used to. Thought of wrapping her arms around his legs. Thought of kissing his shoes. Army shoes, she saw, glancing at his feet. God, she was twisted.

"That's funny," he said. "Grandpa always told me they were from Germany. From when he fought for Hitler." He dug through the rest of the magazines and envelopes, throwing them into piles on the floor. "Oh well. Maybe he just kept getting them sent here, after he moved to America."

"Must be," she agreed and helped him return everything to the box, handling picture after picture of nude women posing in a variety of obscene or sexy scenes, touching themselves, spread on beds, bent over and gripping their ankles. The images, the heat of his breath, the feeling of being small again, made moisture leak to her crotch in waves of desire. And that disgusted her. *Jew Girl.* She needed another beer. She wondered if he could sense her arousal.

Her cell phone played "I Could Have Danced All Night," buzzing against her right hip. "I should go." She stood and swiped her hands across her knees to get rid of the dust. He lurched to his feet, too, and she backed away a little, sweating with the smell of him, beer, and something spicy and minty—aftershave or maybe cologne. She had to hunch over to get through the low-ceilinged parts of the attic, and she felt him behind her and imagined he was watching her ass.

"Can I see you again?" he asked behind her. "Maybe we could have dinner or go see Gladys together? You shouldn't go alone."

"I don't know. I'll call you." Her heart was beating too fast. "Bye," she added over her shoulder as she speed-walked to her rental.

He called out once more before she reached the car. "Don't go see Gladys alone. Call me." She opened the car door and quickly climbed in, pretending she hadn't heard.

She looked at his house one more time, relieved to see its reality diminished compared to the way it had dominated her memories. She started in the direction of the nursing home, but her phone buzzed, and she couldn't stop herself from looking. It was a Messenger alert.

You think you can escape, you fucking cunt Jew baby killer, but we can find you anywhere. You saw me with that gun in front of your house. Well now I'm in California. It's only a matter of days before I find you.

She threw her phone to the passenger-side floor and gripped the steering wheel hard. Her stomach, her entire body heaved with acid. She pulled to the side of the road several blocks away from Stephen and opened the door, dry heaving. An elderly man with a cane started to approach then turned and crossed the street instead. *Screw Gladys.*

At her parents' house, she brushed past her father, who came at her with hands out. "Did you see Gladys? How was it?"

"Fine," she lied and went straight to the bathroom. She took a long, hot shower, thrusting a finger into herself, panting as images of Stephen, the attic, the magazines, and the stalker raced through her mind, too quickly to grab hold of. She started to orgasm, but something stopped her, turning it into a small shudder of release instead of the knee-bending surge she had expected. The water pounding her face almost convinced her that she was not crying, but her nose had started running. She removed her finger from inside herself and soaped there, hard. Then she dropped down and sat in the bathtub, feeling the hot water pour around her until she was done releasing the sobs that came instead of the orgasm she had wanted.

They knew she was in California, but she'd already realized that. They didn't know her parents' address. They couldn't find her. She would stop, she decided. Stop reading the comments. Stop checking Facebook and Twitter. She'd gone to California to escape all that. She breathed and urged the seductive cloak of avoidance to descend on her.

Chapter 27
Stephen
2016

S tephen knew that if he kept following Phillip, he would eventually get caught. But every time he thought of stopping, his gut clenched, and he wanted pot or booze or something to take the edge off. He'd mostly given up smoking, but he took a walk up the street when he really needed air and had a cigarette. He never smoked anywhere near the house, because it was against Jehovah's Witness rules, and since they'd started dragging him to their services, he had to follow the rules. No booze. No pot. No cigarettes. He would find himself humming one of those songs Gladys used to play on the old turntable in her room. Judy Garland, she'd told him, which didn't mean anything to him until he realized it was the *Wizard of Oz* girl. He couldn't quite remember the lyrics—something about not having fun or love until the baby came home. At one time, he'd thought the person singing must have lost an actual baby, but he later realized that "my baby" meant her boyfriend.

He obsessed about Phillip, wondering whether he would kiss that girl, if he masturbated or had wet dreams, whether he loved his parents, if he was happy, or if he ever wanted to hurt people. The buzz in Stephen's body amped up, vibrating his bones till he thought he would explode into pieces hurled out into the universe. Probably, no one would miss him.

He had the cigarette then held the tip against the inside of his arm. It seared his brain like overloading a circuit, shutting it all down. There was pain. There was numbness. There was relief.

But the next day in his session at the VA, Natalie asked what it was and how he got it and forced him to make up a story about cooking something. By the time the cigarette was finished and he was back at the house, the thoughts were assaulting him again. He had to go and stand outside Phillip's closed door and listen for the sound of sleeping breathing. He told himself it was because he was curious to know what it would have been like to be twelve in a normal family, and he was pretty sure that was all it was. But still. He even creeped himself out. And he was fooling himself if he thought those religious whackos were a normal family. They were just as fucked-up, weird, and crazy as any other family. Even his. Even Rachel's.

<hr>

HE WANTED TO SEE RACHEL again, but he couldn't bring himself to knock on her door, and she hadn't given him her phone number.

He'd been to the library so many times now that the woman manning the computer desk smiled and asked how he was when she saw him. She didn't even ask what he wanted, just handed him a number for one of the computers. He'd let her know he liked the ones by the window best, and she usually gave him one of those.

He went to Rachel's Facebook feed and sent her a message: *How are you? Can I see you again? Can we see Gladys together?* He should warn her about the nursing home. But he'd tried when she was at his house, and he'd said she shouldn't go alone. She'd blown him off. He started to compose a warning anyway, but he didn't hit Send. Instead, he closed his eyes and imagined being the one to rescue her. He imagined the expression on her face, the gratitude—or was it love?—if he saved her.

He sat back in his chair and watched the librarian help an old man with one of the computers. The librarian nearly tripped on the guy's cane when she walked away, and Stephen could see that the old guy still didn't understand how to use the computer. He watched the guy play with the mouse, moving it around and clicking randomly. If Stephen had been a different person, he would have offered to help.

He'd felt something, having Rachel there at his grandfather's—a connection. It was almost as if no time had passed and they were still little kids, so familiar with each other. Of course, she'd had a whole life since then. At least she seemed to have, given all those theater reviews he'd read.

He had no life. There was Rachel and Gladys. There were the skinheads. There was Iraq. They were all gone. All in the past. That was why he had agreed to go to those Jehovah's Witness services. His mother may have been nuts, but she had friends. Loads of them. She was always doing something, going somewhere, staying busy. So he ripped up that *Watchtower* he'd stolen from Beth and told Josh he'd like to go to a service with him. The family was so excited. Maria even made a special meal for him—roast chicken and Stove Top stuffing.

But he couldn't let go of the feeling that getting close to Rachel would fix something in him. Maybe he could see Aaron. They could do some magic together. He would have talked to his grandfather if he could have. In his last session, he had told Natalie a little about his grandfather, and she said it was like he held two grandfathers in his head, the one he could never please and was always apologizing to and the one who made him feel loved. He hadn't said anything about the Nazi stuff, just that his grandpa fought in the war and had wanted Stephen to be a soldier too.

"That's interesting," she'd said, her voice going higher-pitched, like it did when she was super excited. "If you have any letters or things from him from when he was over there, you should save them. People are interested in the experiences of soldiers who helped liberate the camps. It's history."

He didn't correct her. He just looked at his shoes and said there weren't any letters like that. Only porn, but he didn't mention the porn. He rubbed one of the burns through the long-sleeved shirt he'd put on before his session.

STEPHEN WALKED TO HIS grandfather's house. He'd never really been through all those boxes up in the attic—only the porn and one or two others that contained childhood shit like his army toys and the stuffed bear he used to sleep with every night until they moved in with his grandfather when he was seven, when Stephen learned that real men didn't sleep with stuffed animals. He figured maybe somewhere, in one of those boxes, he'd find a treasure, maybe even letters from Hitler.

Most of the boxes were stacked way in the back of the attic. His mother never threw anything away, as far as he could tell. He dragged one of the boxes down to the floor, where it landed with a shattering sound. It was taped shut with packing tape, and he used his army-issue combat knife to slice the edges open. There was a child's crayon drawing of stick figures—a woman, man, child, and dog in front of a house with a chimney. Scrawled across the bottom in careful writing that must have been some teacher's was "Dear Mom. You're the best mom ever. Happy Mother's Day. Love Stephen." How young he must have been when he wrote drivel like that. He'd stopped bothering with Mother's Day by the third uncle. His mother was too distracted to care, or at least he thought she was. Then again, she apparently had saved everything.

He rooted through ratty pillows with no stuffing, worn blankets, and single shoes without matches and found a bunch of cracked white plates with flower patterns in the bottom of the box. He went for the next box and nearly gagged when the smell of mothballs wafted up from the ratty blanket he discovered on top. He yanked out a few blankets, but they only covered more ratty blankets. Three boxes, four, all full of junk most people wouldn't save. More childhood drawings, old plates and utensils, gardening supplies, and school pictures, including a whole pile of those pictures where every kid got their own little square, like *The Brady Bunch*. He studied those but barely recognized himself, let alone any of the other kids.

Finally, he reached a box pushed way into a back corner. It was lighter than the others. He carried it into the dim puddle of light from the window and worked at several layers of tape with the knife. The box popped open to reveal a pile of yellowed pictures and, underneath the pictures, envelopes with ink-scrawled words in loose, chaotic handwriting that he recognized as his grandfather's. His body accelerated into high alert, and he succumbed to the fantasies. *Letters from the German front.*

He scooped a handful of pictures and letters and sat against the wall under the window in the very same spot where he and Rachel used to play sex games. Sitting there with the old black-and-white pictures and letters, he thought he could smell her—not the new salon-shampoo-deodorant Rachel, but the childhood sweat and dirt and hint of the soap he'd swiped from his grandfather's shower.

He studied the top picture. It was a black-and-white picture of a boy, maybe five or six years old, standing ankle-deep in a river, holding a fishing pole. The boy's hair appeared to be blond, though it was hard to tell with those old photos. He was wearing shorts and knee-high rubber boots. Someone had written on the back: *Niklas learns to fish, vacation in Maine.* His grandfather's name was Niklas, but his grandfather had grown up in Germany, so vacation in Maine made no sense. There were more pictures underneath, mostly of the same boy at different ages—*Niklas rides a bike* and *Niklas ready for Boy Scouts*, wearing a uniform that definitely was not Hitler Youth material. There were a few with other people, like the boy standing between a man and a woman, holding their hands.

Stephen wondered if his mother had a brother she had never mentioned, a little boy named after Stephen's grandfather. He felt jealous, holding those pictures with the careful printing from family vacations and imagining the boy who might have been his uncle. *Did the boy die some tragic death? Maybe drowned on a fishing vacation?* No wonder Stephen couldn't please his grandfather. There had been another boy—a real son, not a grandson. Maybe there was a car accident. A terrible sickness. He would ask his mother next time they had breakfast. Maybe she would tell him about the other Niklas in the picture. Niklas junior.

Stephen dug more pictures out and flung them aside until he found a pile of letters, tucked into unsealed envelopes. The top envelope was addressed to a Mrs. Schuster at the very same house Stephen was sitting in. The date was 1945. The return address was from Niklas Drescher in the New York State Penitentiary. The handwriting—printing, really—was familiar from the accounting books he'd found in an old desk in his grandfather's study. He stared at that return address for a long time with no idea what he felt or thought or if he even cared.

So, maybe Niklas came to America and was arrested for being a Nazi sympathizer. He fought alongside Hitler but came here sooner than he remembered. People forgot. They remembered things funny. There were more letters under that, all from the New York State Penitentiary. He opened one and began to read. It didn't take long. His grandfather was not a big writer, and the letters were all short. The early ones all seemed to follow a similar theme:

Dear Mom,

The food here isn't great, but I'm doing okay. I do feel bad about what I did to that girl. You should know it was really Ralph's idea. I just went along. I'll help pay for the baby when I get out. I'm not a bad guy. I hope you haven't stopped loving me.

Your son,

Nick

If someone had told Stephen would have found those letters one day, he would have imagined the moment as a great betrayal. He would have imagined himself sobbing violently, punching holes in the attic wall, or killing himself. But in the end, he felt... he tried to identify it... like the day Gladys kicked him out and told him not to come back. Like the day he found Rachel naked with that girl. Like his mother going back with the uncle who hit her or getting a new uncle who hit her or getting hit himself.

His grandfather never fought for Hitler. His grandfather was in jail during the war. His grandfather was a rapist. It was all a lie, all fake. No real German accent. No Nazis. Nothing to live up to. Maybe some part of him had known all along. Maybe that was why he couldn't try just a little harder to be the man he thought his grandfather wanted him to become. It was his grandfather's fault Stephen was a loser. The truth, the filthy reality of his imposter grandfather, the reason Stephen could never be a real Nazi, had lived buried in boxes for years.

He dumped the letters into the box with the German porn magazines. There was nothing to feel. He was his grandfather's grandson and a disappointment, however anyone looked at it. He lit a cigarette, took a long drag, and pressed the burning tip to the inside of his left arm. He held it there until the pain faded to numbness. He felt so drowsy, as though he had been awake his whole life until that moment, when he could finally sleep.

He finished the cigarette then put his head down on one of the old, ratty blankets and let sleep drag him under. He dreamed about Gladys and her sister, Esther, marched out of a house with a gun in her back and loaded onto a train. He dreamed of people dying naked in fake showers. In his dream, he shot a man in Iraq, but the man morphed into Rachel's father. The arm-flapping child was a six-year-old Rachel. He woke drenched and nauseous and fought back the bile that pushed into his mouth.

He found some clothes in his bedroom and took a shower. There wasn't any soap, but he felt better after inhaling the steam from the shower. Then he drove his car to the Bakers' house and walked the familiar road to the gate outside of the Kingdom Hall. Kids hadn't started coming out yet, and he told himself he ought to leave before they did. He waited a little off to the side, an unlit cigarette dangling from his mouth, leaning against a parked car like it was his, like he was a dad waiting for his kid. He wouldn't have minded being Phillip's dad.

Kids emerged from the building in small groups. Some waited by the front doors for their rides, and others started walking up the hill. Phillip was usually a lagger, which gave Stephen time to cross the street and get behind the orange tree in front of a house on the corner. The kids were so oblivious, so engrossed in their own conversations that they never even looked in his direction.

But that time, he was lost in the fantasy that he could be Phillip's dad. He was thinking how that would be, how they would walk to the Carl's Junior together and get hamburgers, and Phillip would tell him about camp, and then maybe Stephen would take him up to the attic at his grandpa's and tell him stories. He lost track of time. At the last minute, when Phillip came out, it was too late to hide, so instead he stepped forward and smiled at him like he really was a dad surprising his son with a visit. Phillip stopped halfway up the hill and glanced at his two buddies. The one kid wasn't wearing his glasses. Phillip said something to them. They nodded and kept walking, trailing Phillip a little ways up the hill. When Phillip reached Stephen, he didn't smile or act happy to see him. He looked anxious. "What's wrong? Did something happen?"

Stephen shook his head. "No. I just felt like walking you home today. Is that okay?"

Phillip twisted his head to see his friends, still waiting a little ways off. "Really, I was kind of in the middle of something with my friends. Can't we talk later tonight at home?"

The feeling of erasing all the hurt off his face was familiar to Stephen. He had done it with his grandfather when he wasn't strong enough or man enough. He had done it with Gladys the day she kicked him out. He had done it in the army every single day.

"Sure, kid. No problem." He spun and walked quickly in the opposite direction of the house, feeling the eyes of a bunch of twelve-year-olds on his back.

LATER, AT DINNER, MARIA was spooning broccoli onto her plate, and everyone else was waiting for her to pass the bowl, when Phillip said, "So, what made you go by the Kingdom Hall, anyway?" Maria stopped her move to get more broccoli, hovered the spoon halfway between her plate and the bowl, and watched Stephen. He thought she was going to say something, but she didn't. Just returned to spooning broccoli.

"I dunno," Stephen mumbled. "Just felt like walking you home, I guess." No big deal. That night, when Phillip got his Wii time, Stephen said he was taking a walk and went up the hill to where he could look out over the city and see the ocean. He could have walked to Rachel's house, if he'd felt like a long walk. It was maybe two miles away. He lit a cigarette, and after a few puffs, he held the burning tip against his arm. It was almost like being dead—eyes wide open but seeing nothing. But he didn't feel like letting loose his grandfather's Mauser on the family anymore. That night, he put himself to sleep thinking about Rachel and the nursing home. In his fantasy, a gang of men came after her, weapons in hand, but Stephen used every combat skill he'd ever learned. He subdued the men one by one. He kicked and kicked, leaving bloody pulps on the ground. Rachel, filled with gratitude, hugged him and thanked him. They kissed.

The next day, instead of following Phillip, he drove to Rachel's street and parked three houses down. When Rachel pulled out of the driveway in her white rental car, he stayed back but then followed. Once he was sure she was on her way to Old Oaks Nursing Home, he dropped back even farther. The address was already in his GPS.

Chapter 28

Rachel

2016

Fucking California, where the radio station only played songs from the seventies. It was like a time warp. She was seventeen years old, one of three or four drama kids piled into Janet's ancient Camaro, singing "Desperado" at the top of their lungs. California was determined to send her spinning into her past. *Isn't it enough that I'm finally on my way to the Old Oaks Jewish Nursing Home to visit my grandmother, and there are crazy white supremacists stalking me? Isn't that enough? They have to play Barry fucking Manilow and the Temptations?*

A gray van rode her tail, so she swerved into the fast lane and sped up. Then, just to reassure herself, she sidled back to the other lane and pulled into a gas station parking lot. She would stay long enough to let that van get far away. She tried to convince herself there was no reason to think Deplorable1 or J.T. or whoever would be driving a van in Carlsbad and recognize Rachel in her white rental car. But they knew she was there. They knew her dad's old address. And they probably knew a lot more.

The crawl of cars on the road was endless. Friday, she thought, but it might have been Saturday. Summer, travel, and all the craziness had thrown her sense of time all off. A blue Toyota pulled in behind her and stopped at one of the gas pumps. It was probably safe to leave. That van wasn't following her. It was just a van. If it was still there, if she started driving and it pulled behind her again, then she would freak. Then she would lock all her doors and drive and drive and not stop.

She locked her doors anyway.

She could turn around, drive back to her parents', and postpone seeing Gladys just one more day. But her mother kept asking questions: *Did Gladys recognize you? Did she talk to you? Was she awake?* She couldn't keep pretending she'd gone when she hadn't. She was starting to feel more and more like a teenager, always lying about the class she skipped or the study session that was really a pot-smoking session. Time to go.

But just when the traffic cleared enough to pull out onto the road, her phone vibrated on the seat beside her. She lurched the car into reverse and spun back into the parking spot in front of the convenience store. A gray-haired man coming out the door with a hot dog in one hand and a cane in the other stared in at her through the passenger-side window. She smiled at him and waved the vibrating phone before holding it to her ear.

"Hi." Jo's voice was tinny and echoed a little.

"Hi." Rachel's face heated up.

"I saw your house."

Rachel breathed. "Is there anything else, besides the picture?" There was no background noise on Jo's end, and Rachel imagined her sitting in her car somewhere quiet, maybe in front of Rachel's house.

"I don't think so. Your bedroom was a mess, but..." Jo's voice sounded placating, almost apologetic.

Rachel pulled the phone away from her ear and tried for a long, deep breath, but her lungs wouldn't expand. She pushed the air out instead.

"Hey. Are you still there?"

"Sorry. Yes. I think I left my bedroom a mess. I was kind of in a rush."

"Yeah. I get that. Listen, I saw your Twitter feed. Are you aware they know you're in California?" Rachel nodded but didn't answer, and Jo filled the silence. "Do you want us to set up some protection? When are you coming back to Pineville? Can I have someone call to take your statement?" Jo coughed. "Also, how are you?"

"I'm here to visit my grandmother," Rachel said as if that was even an answer. "She's dying. I'm fine. They haven't figured out my parents' address or anything. Just that my dad is a psychiatrist. The work address they found for him is old. He only keeps a small practice now. He uses a colleague's office. I'm fine. Really." And Liz was coming. Liz, willing to leave the twins and Michael and fly to California to prove how much she really cared. She had never done anything like that before. She'd let Rachel go to Women's Week in P-town alone. Maybe it was going to be a goodbye thing, but maybe they would finally get somewhere. Sometimes, walking away was the best way to get someone's attention. She was ready to let go, but she was also ready to see if Liz really meant it.

"Will you at least call me when you get home?" Jo asked.

"Okay," Rachel said and hung up on Jo's silence, shutting down the conversation and her own desolate feeling of desire and emptiness.

Time to go see Gladys. But the gas pedal seemed too heavy to push, the gearshift impossible to get into reverse. Her hand gripped the handle until her knuckles turned white. She stayed and breathed and watched cars speed down the freeway. Finally, after several minutes, she pushed the gearshift into Drive.

RACHEL HAD CALMED HERSELF down a little by the time she got to the nursing home. But that didn't mean she took chances. She passed an open parking spot near the back of the lot and hunted for one nearer the entrance. There was a plaza with a Chinese restaurant and a couple other businesses across the street, and all the available parking in that small plaza looked taken. She wondered how many of those cars didn't even belong there. The lot seemed full for a nursing home in the middle of the day.

She crawled past open spaces, not ready to park and get out but unwilling to yield to panic and leave. She was being stupid. They couldn't find her there. She could just keep driving, turn around and go all the way to the airport, and fly back to Pineville. Fly anywhere. Alaska, maybe. She finally found a spot near the big arched entrance, where a security guard stood near a column, sipping from a Styrofoam cup. She stayed in the car. Her phone alerted her, and she glanced at it. A text from Jo. She turned the phone upside down on the passenger seat without reading the text and sat. Sun seeped through the window, and she yielded to its seductive warmth and closed her eyes, just for a second. She felt calmer than she had in days, sitting there, not yet in the room with Gladys, the comforting security guard nearby.

"Just do it," she said out loud. "Be a Nike." She laughed and made herself get out of the car, ordering her hand to unlock and open the door, her legs to swing out and stand.

And before she could take a step, before she could think or move, she heard her name. "Rachel Goldberg!" A man engulfed her, wrapped her in a bear hug, and pulled her away from the car. The door shut behind her, and she felt the tug of him dragging her where she didn't want to go. She recoiled at the bittersweet smell of him and shrugged out of his arms, stumbling back. Her heart beat an alarm warning, flushing her body with adrenaline.

She glanced toward the nursing home. The security guard was still there but talking to a woman who must have come from inside the home. Some part of her thought to yell, but it might not have been one of the Twitter people. He could have been an old high school friend or something. He had released her from the hug, though he kept a loose grip on her shoulder. *The way you might touch someone you're happy to see?* She wouldn't have recognized most of those kids as adults.

The guard and the woman entered the nursing home together. A flick of her eyes told her the parking lot was empty. She tried to step back toward her car, feeling the pull of the man's hand on her shoulder. He was wearing a black beanie and camouflage pants. He regarded her with pale-blue eyes and scratched his cheek through a wispy red beard.

"Do I know you?" Her voice didn't sound like brave Rachel. It tremored with fear.

He smiled, displaying a row of even white teeth. "Maybe this will help," he said and removed the beanie. She flinched as he revealed a rope tattoo that snaked around his shaved head with all the threat of an actual noose. "I didn't have a beard the last time you saw me."

J.T. A glance toward the nursing home doors told her the guard hadn't returned. Her car was only a few steps behind her, but it seemed unattainable, and J.T.'s grip on her arm was as solid as the bulge of his bicep.

"Howdy, sweetheart," J.T. said.

"Let me go." Her voice sounded pitiful in her own ears, like a helpless little girl. She forced herself to push the air out, to slow her breathing and expand her lungs.

He stepped closer and reached out to stroke her hair almost tenderly. "I just want to talk to you." There was something feral in his voice. "I feel like we have some unfinished business, Miss *Chicago.*"

Nausea surged from her gut to her chest. Her shaking legs, combined with his grip on her shoulder, kept her off-balance enough that he was almost holding her up. She heard her own rasping breaths through the panicked ringing in her ears.

"Let's take a walk. Let's talk. You can tell me all about your life, splashing swastikas on people's doors." She remembered thinking his laugh had been charming, but now she heard only the hint of derision in his chuckle. He slid his hand down her arm and grabbed her hand. She pulled hard, trying to jerk away, but his grip was too strong. It felt as if he was compressing every bone in her hand. She had read stories about women not getting themselves out of dangerous situations quickly enough because they worried too much about being polite. She'd always scoffed at that. If she were in a dangerous situation, she'd insisted she would fight. She would scream. She would jab with her keys. But there she was, and she hadn't even shouted. She was trying to extricate herself without making a scene. She felt her mind trying to shut it all down and unhappen everything, as if she could just space out and everything would be fine again.

Her keys. She had dumped them in her purse before getting out of the car. *Can I get to them?* "I don't think so," she said, stepping back. *Find your inner actress. Make it a scene. Make a scene.*

"I'm not going to hurt you," he said. "I promise." He yanked, dragging her farther from the car. Pain shot from his grip and up her arm, making her gasp. "You owe me a date. At least a kiss."

"Ouch! You're hurting me." She planted her feet, but he pulled her forward. "Let me go," she said, and her voice sounded stronger, closer to an actual yell.

Instead, he slid his hand up to grip her wrist. She imagined a bruise forming under his fingers. She swiveled her head to see the empty space where the security guard was supposed to be.

He started moving again, and she stumbled, unable to jerk away. She could hardly hear through the rushing in her ears. She felt small and passive as she watched the ground, dragging her feet. She tried to slow his pace and felt herself letting go, drifting into that safe place where bad couldn't touch her. But he was leading her back, back, back to the far end of the parking lot, exactly where she'd tried to avoid. She breathed and yanked her arm. A new surge of pain burst in her wrist, and she was grateful, because it shocked her back into reality.

"Help," she said and breathed. *Louder.* "Help." This time she managed an actual shout. She swiveled her head. *Where was that damn security guard?*

Part of her insisted she was being extreme. He just wanted to talk. That was what he said. He'd been kind in the bar. But she ignored that voice and shouted again, this time louder. A car approached. She recognized that car, a yellow VW Bug. *Stephen?*

The car stopped beside them and Stephen—yes, it was Stephen—rolled down the window. "What's up?" he said.

"Just a friendly conversation," J.T. said, not letting go of Rachel's arm.

Stephen stayed quiet, taking in the scene, and she realized it could go either way. He'd seemed happy enough to see her when they'd visited. *But what is he even doing here? Did he follow me here? Is he one of them?*

"Stephen," she said. "I need help."

J.T. put his free hand in his pocket, and when it came back out, he was holding a switchblade. He pressed a button, and the blade popped out. It gleamed, sharp and dangerous. "Maybe you should just mind your own fucking business." Rachel's heart raced with panic, and she feared if she did somehow escape J.T.'s grip, her legs would simply collapse under her.

Stephen opened his car door but didn't get out. Rachel screamed again, relieved at the full force of her voice yelling for help. J.T.'s sweat smelled like fear, cigarettes, and a shadow of that cologne. All the things she associated with that Nazi bar were the last things she would smell before she died.

"Hey, man," Stephen said. "Just so you know, I'm ex-military. I'm trained in hand-to-hand combat."

J.T. laughed, and Rachel screamed again.

"I don't know who you are, *Stephen*," J.T. said in a mocking tone, "but I have a score to settle with this bitch."

Rachel couldn't name the expression she saw on Stephen's face—a complicated mixture of curiosity, dismay, and maybe something like yearning. He lunged forward, grabbing for J.T.'s arm. J.T. easily swung away from Stephen, kicking out to knock him in the leg and dragging Rachel farther away. Stephen went down on one knee.

"What's going on here?" someone yelled, and Rachel thanked God it was the security guard, who had a weapon in his hand. Metal jangled on his uniform as he jogged toward them. J.T. dropped her arm, and she jerked away and ran hard toward the nursing home. She heard scuffling behind her, and when she glanced around, she saw Stephen limping toward her.

"Drop the weapon," someone said from somewhere far away.

The opaque glass doors swung open as she approached, and then she was in the cool, bleached lounge of Gladys's nursing home. She curled into herself, heaving air and reveling in the odors of disinfectant and processed air. She concentrated on slowing her breath until the pounding in her ears quieted and she could hear the Muzak floating through the room.

A young woman behind a mahogany-colored desk stared at them. When Rachel looked, she smiled, revealing braces stained red with lipstick, then focused on a computer screen in front of her. Rachel sank onto one of the vinyl couches in the front lobby. The walls were green with ocean murals. Her arm hurt. Her teeth hurt from clenching. Her chest hurt. *Slow,* she told herself. *Breathe slowly.* Stephen hobbled over and stood beside the sofa. He bent to rub his right knee.

"What are you doing here?" she asked.

"You should be glad I was here."

She thought about how easily J.T. had knocked him to the ground. "I'm glad the security guard was there," she replied and couldn't decide whether she felt guilty or triumphant when a wounded look shadowed his face. "Why were you here, anyway?"

"I wanted to see Gladys. Also, I knew someone might try to hurt you."

So, he is one of them? "How did you know."

"There's a plan on Reddit. Hell, they all know Gladys is here. A whole bunch of them."

She felt sick. "How?" Her voice sounded young. *On your knees, Jew Girl.* Tremors assaulted her legs, and she pressed her hands into her thighs to stop them.

Stephen shrugged. "Someone who works here."

"A Nazi works here?" It sounded incongruous when she said it. There weren't Nazis anymore, not like in Germany in the 1940s. Nobody was going to drag Gladys out of her bed and put her on a train to Auschwitz. But they might put swastikas on the door to her room.

Stephen shrugged. "I guess."

"You could have warned me," she said, staring at the glossy brochure on the table so she wouldn't have to look at him.

He shrugged. "I tried."

"When?" she asked. "When did you warn me?" She noticed the receptionist staring and tried to soften her voice.

"When you came to my house." There was a hint of petulance in his voice. "I told you not to come here alone."

"That was not a warning," Rachel snapped. The brochure on the table in front of her promised to tell its readers how to enjoy the final years with their loved ones. She wished it would tell her how to stop the shaking, the nausea, the constant flashes of J.T. with a knife in hand. *Does this employee have access to records? Can they find my parents' address?* "What does this person do here?"

"I don't know," Stephen said. "I think he said nursing assistant or something."

They descended into a tense silence while Rachel tried to imagine what records a nursing assistant might see and berated herself for not finding the Reddit site. She would have known if she'd paid better attention.

The woman at the desk answered the phone in a cheerful voice that jarred Rachel's nerves. "Old Oaks Nursing Home." Rachel watched her nod and say "okay" and "yes" a few times. She left her spot behind the desk and approached. "Um," she said, "you guys are supposed to wait. The police are on their way."

Rachel considered running. She could get in her car and go back to her parents. J.T. probably wouldn't tell them who she was. But running was a habit, and it hadn't kept her safe.

"Okay." She let her eyes close, blocking out the woman's bright lipstick. She stayed that way until her phone vibrated again.

Opening her eyes felt like emerging from deep under water into a bright summer day. She reinhabited her body against her will. Seconds might have passed. Minutes. Hours. Days. But Stephen remained, perched on the vinyl chair opposite her, leafing through the brochure that promised the best of times with dying loved ones. He did not look up when she shifted, grabbing for her phone. The shakes had stopped. Instead, she felt heavy and exhausted.

She looked at her phone screen, scrolling backwards through the texts. There were several messages from Liz, updating her on her travel plans.

She found the text from Jo that had arrived just before she got out of her car. "Please check your Facebook page. They know about your grandmother. They know where she is. You could be in danger."

The doors swooshed open, and the security guard entered. *Where is J.T.?* Rachel had expected to see him cuffed and subdued, safely contained by the guard. She half stood, but the floor surged beneath her feet, and she fell back onto the couch and waited while he spoke to the woman behind the counter then approached them.

"The police will be in to get statements in a second," he told them. "We'll bring you to an office to wait. Do you need anything?"

Rachel and Stephen followed the guard as he led them past the elevators, down a hall, and into a room with motion-sensor fluorescents illuminating a desk scattered with nursing books, papers, a computer that looked bigger than anything made in the last five years, an antiseptic-looking tile floor, and three straight-backed office chairs. Rachel took the one closest to the wall and scooted it as far away from Stephen as she could. She could hear the whirring of the central air and the occasional ping of incoming email on the computer.

"I saved you." His voice sounded petulant.

"You nearly got yourself killed along with me. You should have warned me." She glanced at him. He looked defeated, hunched in the chair with his hands cupping his knee. *How can a person appear old and frail and childlike all at once?*

"I was watching you," he said. "I wasn't going to let anything happen to you."

"I see." She released herself into the quiet anger that infused her body. "You're always protecting me, aren't you? In your grandfather's attic. That party."

"What party?"

"The one where you nearly raped me." She wished the room had a window or even an interesting piece of art on the wall that she could turn to. She stared at the linoleum tiles under her feet.

"I didn't." His voice had turned shrill. He half stood then sank back into his chair. "I never raped you."

Rachel laughed. "No, I guess you didn't." She'd been drunk that night and sad about the loss of that girlfriend, Bridget. When Stephen said he was supposed to rape her, she had assumed it was a joke. Then, she'd thought it was sweet. Not that he was supposed to rape her, but that he stood there, looking so lost, and told her and then couldn't even manage to fuck her. Rachel still wasn't entirely sure why she had gone along with it. She'd been drunk—so, so drunk and high. Maybe she thought she would get revenge on Bridget, or maybe she wanted to prove she could swing both ways too. Maybe she had decided that if she was ever going to give up her virginity, she might as well do it with the one boy who had already touched her naked body. The school psychologist often referred to the adolescent I'll-show-you, I'll-hurt-me approach to life. Rachel wasn't entirely sure she'd completely grown out of that.

"But why did you want to rape me? What was that even about?"

She found a big crack in the wall in front of her. *Is that a foundation problem? Maybe the whole damn place is about to collapse on us.*

"It was just... like a bet, I guess?"

"Are you asking me?" She barely recognized her voice or the fury that made her rise out of her chair and spin to glare down at him. "Why did you do it?"

He had called her "Jew Girl" at the party. He had called her "Jew Girl," just like when they were kids and did what she couldn't say ever to anyone, write in a journal, or barely let herself acknowledge later. He'd called her that, and she'd gotten instantly wet. Though later, by the time she was naked on the beach, it was gone. By then, the booze was wearing off, and it was just something she had decided to go through with.

She paced the small room. She was asking the wrong question. It didn't matter why he had wanted to rape her that night. It mattered why she would have let him. She understood that was the real question, just as she understood it didn't only apply to that night. It didn't matter, but she couldn't back away. "Why?" she asked again. "Tell the truth. You were one of *them*, right? A Nazi, just like J.T."

Stephen didn't answer.

"You're pitiful," she said.

"I came here to help you," he insisted, and she imagined herself a mean girl, the kind of person who never felt guilty after hurting someone. She laughed then paced around some more and counted pens on the desk, wishing for a window.

Stephen stayed silent until the security guard knocked and entered. He nodded at Stephen. "You first." Stephen rose and limped after him. As he walked past her, she noticed a trickle of blood where he must have bitten his lip.

———◉———

SHE HADN'T BEEN AFRAID of Stephen that night. She had never been afraid of him. She thought he was a creep, but he was a brother-like creep. That night, while she was at the party, her first-ever girlfriend, Bridget, was off on a date with the football quarterback. God, it had all seemed so important at the time. Bridget with her shoulder-length red hair and pale skin—alabaster skin, if that was a thing. Strange how vividly she remembered the day she learned about the quarterback.

"I'm sorry, Rachel. I just can't deal with this anymore. Maybe it's okay for you, but my parents would never handle it. I need to be normal." Bridget had wiped a tear, or at least pretended to. "But I'll always love you."

Rachel hadn't cried. She had unfocused her eyes and turned Bridget invisible. Then, that weekend, she climbed into the back of the van with Mark and Randy and Eileen and shared a joint, and they went to that party in LA.

"I'm supposed to rape you," Stephen said that night, and she wasn't afraid.

When she saw that counselor for a few sessions, the counselor had suggested that she'd been sexually abused after she'd mentioned the things that happened in Stephen's attic. But Rachel had never thought of it that way. Hell, Stephen was only a year or two older than her, and he was young for his age. There was the attic, the magazines, and war. It had all just been part of their war games. It didn't mean anything.

"Did you have any sexual experiences as a child?" the woman asked.

"Well, yes," Rachel said. "My friend and I fooled around in his attic."

The woman literally leaned forward in her chair as if she'd just had her favorite kind of cake set in front of her. A gray curl fell over her glasses, and she pressed the heels of her hands into her floral-print skirt. "How old was your friend?"

"A year older, I think. Maybe two."

"Oh, so you were sexually abused, then." The woman sat back with a satisfied smile and crossed her legs. She could see how the woman meant to link those games with Stephen and Liz and too many Xanax all together, but it wasn't like that. It was much more complicated than that.

Rachel never went back to that therapist.

That night at the party, when Stephen had called her Jew Girl, she couldn't help herself. She got aroused. That was why she mocked him. To make it go away.

"You're pathetic, Stevie," she'd said. But she knew he was still there. Felt him behind her when she climbed the steps to get a hit of pot from Eileen, felt him in the kitchen when she drew more beer out of the keg, heard the screen door close behind him when she went out on the porch alone to look at the night. No, that was a lie. She went out on the porch alone because she knew he would follow, and she wanted him to.

"What are you doing here?" she'd asked, not bothering to turn around, knowing it was him.

"Came with my friends." He didn't elaborate. She didn't ask him to. Her stomach roiled with the beer and the taste of pot, and everything spun. A cat or maybe a skunk crept across the backyard, one of those manicured lawns that could have earned the owners a ticket for using too much water in Southern California. She remembered hearing that the kid's parents were somewhere in Europe.

"But how did you hear about it? You aren't exactly into drama. Hell, you aren't even in high school anymore." It was strange how talking to him seemed so familiar, even though she'd started ignoring him long before her grandmother finally sent him packing. It was like they had always been, the two of them, and she suddenly missed her childhood with an ache that made her double over and hug herself against the warm breeze.

"Someone knew someone." He sounded nonchalant. "Wanna take a walk?"

What she thought was *no way in hell*, but what she said was "sure." After that, neither of them said a word. They just climbed down the porch steps and walked across the lawn, startling the skunk—it was clearly a skunk, its tail pointing at the sky—and he opened the quiet, well-oiled gate latch. The gate didn't creak when he swung it open.

When he said he was supposed to rape her, after she fell into him, she didn't even stop to wonder what that meant. *Who told a person he was supposed to rape her? Why was he supposed to rape her?* None of that mattered. What mattered was unfaithful, I-don't-want-to-be-a-lesbian Bridget with the football player, and more than that, her sudden wish to make everything simple again, the way she thought it had been during the shower games.

After she undressed that night and she saw the way his eyes darted and how he could barely look at her, when he climbed on top of her and kissed her, and she tasted sour beer and bad breath, she lost her arousal. But even then, she didn't stop him. She waited to see what it would feel like.

Chapter 29
Stephen
2000

Gladys kicked Stephen out of the house for good when he was sixteen, during one of those rainy months when everyone was making jokes about building an ark. He was sitting on the floor, leaning against the wall in the same corner he'd been claiming since she first took him in. It was just past dinner, and he was half asleep from the spaghetti Mrs. Goldberg had made or maybe from thinking about the war book he'd been reading earlier or the D&D guys who had made it clear they didn't want to play with him anymore because he supposedly freaked them out.

She was probably already losing her mind. It had probably been happening for a while. She'd call him Frantz sometimes, then Aaron, then Joseph. She'd ruffle his hair like the nurses in the hospital when he was little. That night, he was staring at his stocking feet and stroking the fuzz on his chin that was trying to be a beard. It was growing in darkish, even though his hair was still blond enough to be nearly white.

Gladys was babbling about something. She only had a few themes—what it meant to be a Jew, the six million in Europe, Hitler. But lately, more and more, she kept talking about stuff from her past, the sister, Esther, her family, her childhood memories. Also, she went on and on about Rachel, how Rachel needed protecting, wasn't very good at practical things, needed someone strong to make sure she was okay, needed a man. "You take care of her, Frantz," she said, and he knew she meant Rachel.

Maybe she knew about the girlfriend. Stephen hadn't figured it out yet, but that was probably just because he was dense. There had been plenty of clues—Rachel and the redhead, whatever her name was, going off together all the time, shutting themselves in Rachel's room for hours. Rachel barely talked to Stephen anymore and acted like he was garbage when she encountered him in the house.

"Rachel's just being a teenager," Aaron had told him. "Girls." But Stephen suspected it was something more. Every time he looked at Rachel, he remembered those childhood games in the attic, and it made him want to touch Rachel again. He figured Rachel remembered the same stuff, but it made her not want to look at him anymore. When Gladys said that, about Rachel needing a man, he puffed up inside. At least Gladys thought he was the right person for Rachel, even if Rachel didn't know it yet.

Gladys came close, and she bent over and brushed the hair out of his eyes but kept her hand there, on his cheek. "You'll help my family, too, won't you, Frantz?" she said. She stood there with a hand on his cheek, staring into his eyes, and if it wasn't completely whacko, if it wasn't going too far even for crazy Gladys, he would have sworn she wanted to kiss him. Which, of course, was disgusting as hell. But at the time, he didn't think so. In fact, when he thought she wanted to kiss him, he got a hard-on right there, sitting on the floor. He felt it happen and wondered if he'd let her if she tried. But she didn't, of course. It was probably all his crazy imagination.

She jerked her hand away, looked at him, and said that name again. She slapped him hard in the face. It jerked him out of his reverie, though it only intensified the hard-on. Funny, the things he remembered—the sudden, dark rage in her eyes, the slap, his own crazy arousal, like hearing his mother's headboard as a kid.

"I can't do this anymore," she said then. "I can't love you. You're a Nazi." She turned her back on him and moved toward the door. "You let my family die." When he didn't move, she stopped and looked at him one more time. "Leave," she said. "And don't come back."

On his way through the kitchen, the German shepherd who might have been Dieter thumped its tail against the linoleum tiles and looked at him with stupid, tame eyes. "You were better off a stray," he told it. "This is a nuthouse." And he wondered why he ever helped Gladys tame the dog, luring it with Milk-Bones and bits of kosher steak until finally, it was nothing more than any other family pet, curled up in its bed by the kitchen door.

The rain had let up for once, though the air felt exactly like the inside of the bathroom after he'd taken a very long shower. He went to the canyon, where he always went when he needed a place to be that wasn't home and wasn't Rachel's house.

He knew every ledge, every narrow path to the bottom, every shrub. He could do it with his eyes closed, even in the mud and even with night beginning to settle in. He went in on the north side that evening, the part where he had to grab a shrub here and there to keep from slipping in the mud and falling off the narrow footholds. Even though he was too old for it by then, he still imagined he was in Germany on a mission and had to take the dangerous way in so he wouldn't be seen. He started thinking about going after Gladys and the whole damn family. He kept seeing her pinched face and narrow eyes before she sent him away for no good reason. She deserved to die. He found a stick. It was a weapon, a machine gun. The target waited.

He was about halfway down when he heard a girl laugh. At first, he thought Gladys and the family were really down there, all laughing at him. He eased toward the bottom until he got to the shallow cave a few feet from the floor of the canyon and crouched there, where he heard another laugh. He cupped his hands over his eyes and searched the canyon. At first, all he could make out was hip-length blond hair on someone who appeared to be lying on her stomach.

But then the blonde rolled over and stood up, and there was someone else who had been sprawled on her back under the blonde. Another girl.

The girls were several feet away, near the edge, where an overhang would shield them from the rain and from anybody walking by up above, but not from Stephen. The blonde turned away. The girl sat up. The girl was Rachel. He would have known her anywhere—the way she sat, the length of her hair. Even in the dim night, he knew the shape of Rachel's face, her nose, her posture. It took a minute for him to realize she was not wearing a top. He could just make out the pale curve of her breasts.

The blonde had been on top of Rachel. On top of her.

He stood and shouted Rachel's name, so the blonde turned, and Rachel shot to her feet. The rain started to come down in heavy sheets. The whole world rattled with a sharp, threatening buzz in his ear. Rachel looked at him through the assault of rain. He looked at her. Water flooded his back and hazed his view. The blond girl stood back, arms crossed in front of her. He realized she was topless, too, and was trying to hide her breasts.

Then, because he didn't know what to do—because he wanted to go after Rachel, beat her with the stick, and claw her face until her skin shredded off, because he wanted to kiss her, to be the one on top of her, because Gladys had decided she hated him, Rachel was kissing a girl, and he was a fucking coward—he ran. He booked up out of that canyon faster than he had ever climbed in his life, even slipping a couple times, and ran through pouring rain toward his house. He pounded that road as if he could outrun the image, as if he could outrun time and turn the clock back a week. A week was all he needed. A week when he was eating dinner at the Goldbergs' with Gladys smiling and Rachel right next to him. He ran until the double toot of a horn startled him into an abrupt stop, and he spun to see his latest uncle, Uncle Frank, trolling along beside him in his jacked-up black truck.

"Hey, buddy," Frank called out the passenger window. "You're drenched. Need a lift?"

Stephen slowed to a walk then climbed into the truck, which was when he noticed that Frank had a gold swastika hanging on his rearview mirror.

That was the day Uncle Frank became a real uncle as far as Stephen was concerned.

Stephen's mother dumped Uncle Frank quickly, but Stephen didn't. His mother never liked the whole white-power thing, hated Stephen's grandfather, and cut it off with Frank as soon as she caught on, but he changed Stephen's life. He took Stephen to Surf Me that very day. "You look like you could use a drink," he said then backed the truck into a nearby driveway to turn around and head for the freeway.

Stephen was barely seventeen the day Uncle Frank found him running home and took him there, but nobody seemed to mind. Frank even bought him a beer, sat him down in a quiet corner, talked to him. Had him pegged right away. "You've got a good German name," he told Stephen. "That makes you family." He reached a hand across the table and showed Stephen a small black swastika tattoo on his wrist. "Family," he said again and grinned at Stephen. He showed his other wrist, tattooed with a picture of two dog tags, one colored like an American flag. The other said, My Life, Your Freedom, inked where a name would normally be. "That's where I figured out who my family is," he said, tapping the tattoos with his other hand. "The army. That's where I learned what I'm going to need to fight the war."

"What war?" Stephen asked.

Uncle Frank grinned again, his tongue pushing against the gap in his front teeth. "The war against the beaners and the Jews and the niggers," he said. "You gotta know how to shoot and blow things up if you want to fight in the war." He laughed.

Stephen stared at the tattoos for what felt like a full minute then smiled back. That whole evening was better than a dream. A bald guy with the words "white power" tattooed across his knuckles came to talk to Uncle Frank and shook Stephen's hand. "Welcome to the family," he said. "We'll take care of you." A woman named Teresa danced over to the table.

"Who's the handsome man?" she asked Uncle Frank in a slurred voice. She walked over to Stephen and collapsed right into his lap. She grabbed his hand, and he thought she just wanted to hold it, but she placed it on her bare thigh, just at the point where her shorts ended. It was his first time touching a girl, and the unexpected heat of her skin startled him, so he jerked away, but she laughed and reached for his hand again and kissed it then put it back, this time between her legs where he could feel heat and wet. His erection pressed against her leg. Her bleached hair and excessive makeup weren't pretty, and her fat bulged out of the shorts and too-small red tank top, but he knew right away that she would not say no when he asked her to bed.

He had never dreamed that the white-power movement existed beyond his grandfather's stories from Germany. Uncle Frank's friends opened up their circle for him, and he knew he could finally live up to his grandfather's dreams. It was that easy. That five years after first following Frank into Surf Me and before he joined the military was the only time in his life when he didn't feel like he was behind glass, watching everyone.

He had thought he belonged with Rachel's family, but once he found the skinheads, he knew the difference. He went there every weekend, even when Uncle Frank didn't. He still remembered the first time someone put that Skrewdriver album on. At first, people just went on talking, but then, bit by bit, the lyrics started filtering through, and the talking drifted away. He was sitting with Uncle Frank at their table in the back, and Frank smiled, nodded at him, then started singing along. Stephen listened hard, and when the needle was picked up and the song started over, he sang, too, going quiet when he wasn't sure of the words. Teresa came over and climbed on his lap—*his* girl, right there on his lap. By the third time the song started over, everyone was singing, and it really was family. All the voices blended together. Everything was peaceful, everything right, a thing in his chest he'd never felt before. It was as if his breathing let go, and everything softened in him. He belonged.

That was the day he decided to join the army and be the best soldier he could be. He would learn to fight so he could come back and follow in his grandfather's footsteps. Frank nodded and smiled when Stephen told him. "You're a good soldier, buddy. We need guys like you."

You're a good soldier.

After the bar, he went in the attic and jerked off over a picture in one of those old magazines. The woman was dark-haired, and her hands were bound behind her with thick rope, so her bare breasts thrust forward, inviting a hand to touch them. He kept that picture right on the top of the box. Her hair reminded him of Rachel.

Chapter 30
Rachel
2016

Officer Rhodes had gray hair and a beer belly. Rachel followed him to a white room, where a round table provided a barrier between them. The pile of brochures scattered across the table offered to help the reader in "coping with dementia" and provide a "step-by-step guide to arranging a funeral."

He handed her a glass of water and asked if she was okay before he started in with the questions. Twice, she flinched at the unexpected shrilling of her phone, and he waited in polite silence while she checked the caller ID—her parents both times—and told her he would wait if she wanted to answer. But she silenced her phone the second time.

She described the moment J.T. appeared, the way he grabbed her. She realized for the first time that her hand was throbbing. She glanced down at where it rested in her lap. It was already puffy and swollen.

"Did you know this individual?" Officer Rhodes asked.

She answered without thought. "No."

He wrote something down.

Is it a felony to lie? They'll find out anyway. Of course. Just tell the truth. "Wait," she said. "I did. I did know him. Sort of." And she surprised herself by telling him everything, including her attempt at going undercover in the white supremacist bar.

When she was done, he studied her, wrote a few notes, then sighed. "You really ought to leave the policing to the police." It sounded like a scold, but his voice was gentle enough. He told her not to leave town and that someone would be in touch, and they were done.

She couldn't decide whether his neutral response was reassuring or worrisome. Her actions could have made it harder to prosecute J.T. She hesitated on her way out the door, thinking she might ask him about next steps, but he remained hunched over his paperwork, so she left, easing the door shut behind her. She hesitated briefly outside the room she had waited in with Stephen. But he had spoken to Officer Rhodes first. He was probably long gone. Anyway, she had nothing to say to him.

She continued down the hall and into the lobby, where the security guard offered to escort her to her car.

When she got home, she found her parents sitting in the living room, waiting in tense silence.

"The nursing home called us," Aaron said.

"Are you okay?" Rose couldn't keep her hands still, and Rachel focused on them, imagining little foam magic balls, red like the nail polish that glossed Rose's fingernails, appearing and disappearing.

"I'm okay," Rachel said. Part of her wanted to fling herself onto the couch beside her mother and sob in her arms.

"We were so worried." Rose's voice quavered. "Why didn't you call us?"

Rachel looked down at the checkered pattern of the living-room carpet so she wouldn't have to see the brittle expression in her mother's eyes. "If I'd known they called you, I would have. I didn't want to worry you." Everything about the scene felt deeply familiar. "I'm fine. Really, I'm okay. It's taken care of."

"If you need to talk," Aaron said.

"I have a built-in psychiatrist," Rachel replied and wondered why her father's need to play shrink seemed like code for "please just be okay." She found her best and brightest smile. "Right now, I just need a shower." She turned her back and escaped into the bathroom.

She scrubbed her body as if she could scrape the entire J.T. incident off her skin. Instead, the smell of soap and the pain in her hand transported her to Stephen's attic. In her mind, she was with Stephen in a different childhood shower. He pointed into a corner. "On your knees, Jew Girl." She complied. She could still feel the wooden floor pressed hard on her bare kneecaps, still see the triangle of sun from a narrow open window near the ceiling, and still feel the guilty certainty that she deserved punishment.

She'd undressed for him the day that Tina broke her arm. Always before, she'd undressed behind the curtains, but that day, she stripped right there in the open, where he could see. Whenever shards of memory from that day broke through into her adult consciousness, she asked herself why. She would never understand that. Stripping like a tease, like she knew exactly what she was doing, with the imaginary shower in the corner of the attic and Stephen going on about Jews being sent to the showers and it was what she deserved for ratting out Tina, all while she pretended to soap herself with that flaky green-swirled bar of soap.

She tenderly soaped burgeoning bruises on her wrist with unscented Dove, but in her mind was the dusty smell of attic, the hint of spice in the dried-out bar she scrubbed across her belly. "Turn you into soap," Stephen said while she rubbed the dry bar over her belly. Goose bumps raised under its rough sandpaper texture. *Why did I let him touch me then go back to that attic again and again? Why did I never tell anybody?*

But she knew the answer. She still remembered coming home that evening after Tina's accident. Rose had sat at the kitchen table in her nightgown. Rachel had come to recognize the nightgown and the unbrushed hair as signs that her mother was having a bad day. Gladys stood at the stove, stirring something in a pot. Rose looked up when Rachel entered the kitchen and offered Rachel a thin smile. "How was your day, sweetie?" she asked.

Rachel opened her mouth to answer. For a wild moment, she planned to tell the truth. It was there on her lips, in her head to say something. "I don't like the new game Stephen and I played," maybe, or "I don't want to play with Stephen anymore."

But Gladys turned from the stove and said, "You're late, and you're filthy, and you haven't done your Hebrew lesson yet. It's dinner time. Go take a shower."

Rose had jerked up out of her chair. "I should shower, too, before dinner. So, it was a good day, sweetie? Did you have a good day?" She'd looked so hopeful.

Rachel had nodded. "It was a great day," she said. It was always a great day back then, because it couldn't be anything else.

Rachel turned off the shower and went to bed.

———◉———

THE NEXT MORNING, RACHEL sat by the pool, tracking Liz's drive to the airport, waiting in the security line, boarding. She flipped through pages of a thriller without absorbing the words. She gave up and paced from her room to the kitchen and back to her room.

She discovered Rose in Gladys's room, staring into the closet.

"What are you doing, Mom?" she finally asked.

Rose turned, startled. "Oh good. There you are. Still want to help me clean out this room? I was thinking I could make it into a study for me. Your father has his study. I could have mine." Rose did not seem eager to get started. The room smelled like mothballs, and with the curtains drawn against the bright afternoon sun, Rachel felt more than ever as if she'd walked back in time. Any second, Gladys would appear with that disapproving, tight-lipped, what-are-you-doing-going-through-my-stuff look. But she crossed the threshold and stood beside her mother.

Rose sank to her knees and reached into the closet. She dragged a dusty leather suitcase to the center of the room, wiped a hand across the faded triangle of metal on the cracked leather, then rubbed the dust off on her pants. Rachel leaned closer. The name on the metal was Schwartz. Funny to realize she had never known her grandmother's maiden name. Rose pushed the silver button to release the latch and open the suitcase.

A blue baby gown—the fuzzy kind with feet and a zipper up the front—sat neatly folded on top of a pile of other baby clothes. There was lots of blue, little pajamas, slacks, and white booties too small to fit on a hand.

Rose smiled hopefully at Rachel. "You want to help?" Rachel squatted beside her mother. On top were more little gowns, booties, and even some cloth diapers. Beneath were the toddler clothes, white pajamas with blue Stars of David and the name Aaron stitched on the pocket, and an identical pair with the name Joseph. Rachel unfolded Aaron's pajamas, and they studied them together. Rachel could almost picture her father as a little boy, tucked into his bed. She had seen childhood pictures of Aaron, white-haired and smiling with his hazel eyes.

They once went on a family vacation to the mountains so they could play in the snow in the winter. Rachel was six or seven, and the family next door to them had kids her age. When they were all huddled over hot chocolate after a day of sledding, one of the kids had asked, "How come Rachel's dad has white hair when everyone else is dark?" Actually, Rachel remembered, the kid looked at her father and asked, "Are you adopted?"

The adults all had a good laugh, but Rachel had been in that phase in which she thought maybe she had been left on her parents' porch by some other family that didn't want her, so she perked up as she waited for the answer.

"Must be some relative in Germany, I guess. Nobody I know on my father's side," her father said, and the conversation moved on with no real resolution to the adoption question.

Rachel's father had grown nearly bald, with nothing but tufts of hair above his ears. That must have been from his mother's side. Rachel knew from pictures that her grandfather had a full head of hair until the day he died.

Seeing her father's childhood picture always touched something deep inside her, especially the one of him with his father that sat on the desk in his study. The sight of that little boy in a white shirt and necktie hanging nearly to his crotch, grasping the hand of the man beside him, evoked an inexplicable feeling of loss that tightened her throat. The man, his father, smiled through oversized round glasses, looking awkward in a formal suit that was clearly fitted for a lankier frame than his. There was just something about that image of the boy and his father getting all dressed up for the boy's first day of first grade.

Gladys almost never appeared in pictures, and when she did, Rachel didn't feel moved by the sight of her. Gladys never smiled at the camera for a picture, just stood with the evergreens or the giant waterfall or the ocean behind her, thin lipped and squinting at something behind the photographer. Rachel experienced that same tenderness for her father as she held the pajamas. For a moment, it was as if he were a younger brother or a child she had agreed to care for instead of her father. She pressed the soft cloth of the pajama top against her cheek before her mother could refold it.

"Your hand." Rose reached tentatively to touch it. Rachel's hand was puffy and red, and blue bruises had encircled her wrist.

"It's okay," Rachel said. "Just a little tender."

"Maybe you should get it looked at." Rose stood up, a child's pajama bottom dangling from her hand.

"If it isn't better in a few days, I will. I'm fine."

"Are you sure?" Rose asked.

"Yes," Rachel said, her voice sharper than she had intended. She wiggled her fingers and moved her wrist. "See? I can move it fine." To prove it, she dragged the soft-sided leather suitcase out of the back of the closet, the name on a label attached to the handle instead of sewn into the top of the suitcase. It said the suitcase belonged to Gladys Goldberg. The latches were also more modern—two of them pushed toward each other to get the top to spring open. A bit of dust wafted into her eyes and made her cough when the lid popped open. It smelled like old books, like the very back corner of the library, where hardly anybody went.

"I wish you'd talk to me." Rose sat on the bed.

Rachel wiped a sleeve across her eyes. "We are talking." She knew she sounded like her adolescent self. She knew she was regressing from being in the house with her parents. She briefly wondered why it was so important not to *need* anything from Rose.

In the suitcase was a stack of several black-and-white photos of a family, faded to white in spots and curled at the corners. The top photo was of a woman, a man, and two little girls, maybe seven and ten. The youngest showed off her missing teeth, and the older girl looked down at her sister with a serious expression on her face. The adults' faces were spotted white where the photograph had gotten wet at some point.

Rachel glanced at her mother, who stayed perched on the bed, watching her with a worried look. The Rose of her childhood would have let go and moved on by then. Any question about Rachel's well-being was aimed at soliciting reassurance, not information. Rachel ignored her mother's expression and turned the picture over to reveal the names Gladys and Esther and a date.

"I think this is a picture of Grandma when she was a child."
Rachel took the photo to Rose, who gripped the edges carefully.

They studied the photo together. "Is Esther Grandma's sister?"
Her mother didn't answer.

"I think this is Grandma's sister, and she got killed in a concentration camp. Do you know anything about that?"

"Where did you hear that?" Rose asked.

Rachel turned toward the bed, still made with the heavy blue comforter Gladys had insisted on even when it was eighty degrees outside. "Stephen."

She pulled from the pile another, older picture of two teenage girls standing side by side on some steps in front of a modest-looking house. The younger of the two, with hints of Gladys around the narrow chin and wide-set eyes, looked chunky in a long skirt and heavy blouse. "He said she told him stuff about her family sometimes when he sat with her in her room in the evenings after dinner. He assumed I knew. Didn't you and Dad know?"

Rose shook her head and snatched the photo from Rachel.

The memory of a long-ago burning cheek sent Rachel back to the floor. She reached under the bed and pulled out an old dog bowl. "Lucky." She glanced up at Rose and smiled a little, even though her breath came quicker with anxiety.

"Always wondered what happened to that damn dog dish," Rose muttered, and Rachel couldn't help laughing. Rose laughed too. They looked at each other then fell into awkward silence.

Rachel reached under the bed again and produced a yellow shoebox. It was taped closed. She returned to the bed beside her mother and worked at the ends of the tape, tugging at threads of the stuff, taking yellow cardboard with it. Finally, she got one side off and opened the lid.

At first, she thought there was nothing in there to be all that worked up about and wondered why that box, of all things, was what had earned her that long-ago slap. There was some jewelry—a Star of David necklace and a few heavy silver bracelets, green with age and lack of care. Under the jewelry, there was nothing but a bunch of old yellow newspaper articles about the Holocaust. She could have found the same thing online in seconds. She rifled through them. Then, at the bottom, was a letter. It was tri-folded and yellow with age. She handed it to Rose.

"What's the language, German?"

"No. I think it's Yiddish." Rose studied the letter, mouthing the words.

"Oh, right. Do you mind if I hang on to this box?" Rachel could feel her hands shaking.

"Sure," Rose said, "but I want to keep this letter. I think I know some people at synagogue who can translate it."

The headline on the top article read: Free, 32,000 in Horror Camp. A photograph, cut out of a different article, obliterated the words. The photo was wrinkled and torn in places, but Rachel could still tell that it was of a group of men standing in a semicircle around a pile of corpses, some naked, many still wearing the striped concentration camp clothes they had been murdered in.

As Rachel rose to leave the room, Rose reached out, brushing Rachel's arm with a featherlight touch. "Let me know if you change your mind about the urgent care. I'd be happy to take you."

Rachel studied her mother. It had been a good moment, the shared laugh over the dog dish and desecrating Gladys's room together. Maybe someday, Rachel would find a new way to be with Rose. Maybe, she realized, it wasn't Rose who needed to change.

She nodded. "I am totally fine."

Chapter 31
Gladys

G ladys studied the photo in the newspaper. The people in the pictures were nothing but skeletons and flesh, piled like garbage. Soldiers in hard hats and army uniforms surrounded the skeletons. One stood with a cocked hip, as if he was standing at a baseball game, waiting for a soda or a hot dog. That was what she saw, the soldiers looking at a pile of dead Jews as if they were waiting for a hot dog at a baseball game. Somewhere in that pile might be her father, her mother, Esther. It was impossible to tell.

A naked foot jutted out of the pile. She found a head, the neck obscenely twisted, and the face—it was so hard to see the face. The grainy picture in the newspaper created distance. The photographer only allowed the viewer to get so close. But that face could have been Esther's, her mouth warped in terror, eyes bulging in pain. *What if it was Esther? What if it was Esther's head hanging off her neck like a flower dangling obscenely from its stalk? What if it was Esther's neck?* Esther's hand could have been reaching up from the pile of dead Jews, seeking Gladys as if they were children again, Esther taking her hand to lead her to school, making sure Gladys was safe.

Gladys crumbled the newspaper and deliberately placed it back in the shoebox where it settled, nothing but a white wrinkled ball. Her muscles trembled with the effort of not heaving it against a wall.

If only her mother had come with them when they'd traveled to America the first time instead of staying behind for the china, nobody would have died. *China. Things.* Esther, her father, and her mother were all dead because of *things. It's your fault, Mother. Your fault.*

Gladys remembered her kitchen in Michigan and the dishes with little blue flower patterns Ira had bought for their third anniversary spread on the table. Something had bubbled inside, warm and damp and heavy like dirt piled on corpses, when he gave them to her. She had only been able to think of her grandmother's china, left behind with her mother in Germany. At the time, she felt the loss of that china, the things meant for her on her wedding day. She didn't understand yet the price her family was already paying. They were all dead because her mother would not abandon the house, all for a few plates and bowls etched in red. They were probably shattered, looted, and on someone else's table, bearing German pork sausage.

She remembered the night she told Joseph and Aaron what was happening. She stood outside their bedroom door and looked at her sons in their pajamas, tucked into bed under matching blue-and-white quilts. Aaron had taken the top off, because he got hot so easily, and Joseph had his head buried under a pillow, always wanting to go to sleep earlier than Aaron, who would read those silly comic books until Gladys ordered him to turn the light off. Light filtered under the door like a stream of water colliding with her slippered toes, and she told Aaron to turn it off because some things should not be known in the light.

She could not sit alone in her room with the knowing anymore. Ira stayed away all the time, hiding out in his steel vault at the bank as if that could protect him from the knowing. She entered the room and sat on Joseph's bed.

"Your grandparents are dead," she said, and she told them everything.

Gladys put the box under her bed and went out to the living room to sit. Soon, she would make dinner for the family. That Rose was useless with her *depression*. It was lucky Gladys had come when she did, or Rachel would have no real mother. She closed her eyes, just for a second.

Later, she startled, and there was Rose, staring down with that lip-chewing please-don't-be-mad look on her face, and Rachel, who looked so much like Esther, clutching that silly stuffed dog, staring bubble-eyed as if Gladys was pointing a gun or had threatened to kill her. Gladys looked around slowly, orienting. She was in Aaron's living room, stretched out on the green couch. She saw the beige indoor-slash-outdoor carpet, the blank television staring down from its pedestal like some obscene god, every carpet stain, the dent in the pale-green wall just above the television, and the spider hanging from threads in the corner.

"I can't believe you pay that Mexican girl to clean," she said to Rose, pointing at the spiderweb. "She does a terrible job."

"Are you okay, Grandma?" Rachel hugged that stuffed toy tightly to her chest, and Gladys forces a tight-lipped smile.

"I'm fine. Did you study your Hebrew today? You should study every day, Rachel. It will help you be the best Jew you can be."

Rose had the judgmental look. Sometimes, Gladys could still see Joseph as if he had lived and gone to yeshiva. She could imagine him at the bimah in billowing white Rosh Hashana robes, beaming power from beneath his kippot.

"You fell asleep," Rose explained. "You were dreaming." She pushed stringy black hair behind an ear then set a hand on Rachel's head. Rachel shrugged out from under the hand and sat on the couch by Gladys's feet.

"Why did you tell my mom it's her fault?" Rachel asked, her hand stroking that stuffed dog's fake fur.

"She was dreaming, honey." Rose jumped in before Gladys could answer. "She wasn't really talking to me." Rose's voice sounded as if she knew what it meant to plead for her life.

Gladys twisted herself into a sitting position and rubbed out the blur, stretching, pulling at her eyelids with age-roughened hands. *Was I dreaming? When did I fall asleep?*

"Tonight is Shabbat. What time is it?" Gladys looked at her empty wrist. Her watch had stopped the day before, and Aaron forgot to bring a new battery home. He was always forgetting, so focused on his practice and playing God with people's lives. She sometimes imagined him talking to mothers after their children had cut their wrists or shot themselves with a gun. Curled around a pillow in her bed, she often screamed at his imagined back: *I did not kill your brother.* In her imagination, he would always turn to look at her, his eyes like dark empty rooms, then walk away.

Rachel pulled tufts of fur from her toy. Rose turned to leave. "It won't matter that much if we don't go to temple just this once," she said, her words drifting behind her retreating back.

"We must keep the covenant and honor God," Gladys called. "It is our duty as Jews. It's our duty as the Chosen People." Gladys knew other women at the temple who couldn't stand up without rocking first. They would rock and heave just to leave a chair, but not her. She could still rise from the couch almost gracefully, and she did. Walking carefully to hide a slight limp from the painful callus on her right foot, she went to her room to change for dinner and Shabbat services.

Chapter 32
Rachel
2016

In the dream, Nazis stormed Rachel's childhood bedroom. Liz sat up in bed beside her and said, "See, I told you there were Jews living here." The Nazis were shaved and tattooed. One of them held a rope.

Rachel awoke, damp and shivering in a sunny room that contradicted everything she had just dreamed except that Liz was in fact beside her in bed. She dragged blankets over herself, trying to get warm, and felt Liz press against her back.

"You're wet," Liz said.

"Bad dream." Rachel leaned into Liz, trying not to see the dream Liz grinning at the Nazis, turning Rachel in.

"Kiss me," Liz said.

Rachel rolled over to face her.

"You are sweaty," Liz said and pressed her lips against Rachel's.

Rachel allowed the kiss. "So, you're really here," she said after Liz pulled back. "I was just to the point of deciding you were never really going to leave Michael. But now you're here. So the question is, is this a beginning or an ending?"

"Yep, I'm really here." Liz kissed her again, more a peck. "And it's a beginning. I promise." She seemed to be asking with her lips, "Are you glad?"

Rachel knew her answer was noncommittal.

"Maybe I'll give you a tour of my childhood," Rachel said. "I think I can fill up a few days with that. Then, rest of the week, Disneyland? The beach?"

"Week?" Liz's voice carried a familiar hint of appeasement. "I'm only here for a long weekend. I can't stay a week."

"Why not? You're here. It's ridiculous to only stay for a few days. That's a long flight for just a few days." God, she sounded desperate, even though she'd insisted to herself she was ready to let go. It seemed hard to change old habits.

"Michael's got a work-dinner thing Tuesday night. I have to go. It's a chance to get them to reconsider his promotion."

"So, what would happen if you skipped it?" Rachel leaned in, offering a change-Liz's-mind kiss.

"It would look bad. All the wives go."

"Wait," Rachel said. "So, you can cancel on my birthday with some lame excuse, but you can't blow off a work function with Michael, because all the wives go? Why did you even bother to come here?"

"The kids were sick. That wasn't a lame excuse. And I came because I don't want to lose you," Liz said. "I wanted to prove you're important to me. I wanted to see you. Look how far I was willing to come for such a short time, just to see you. That proves how important you are to me. But Michael needs that promotion. We need the money. It means I could leave him sooner than September if he gets it. This could be good for us." She touched Rachel's cheek, a gesture that used to make her feel cherished. "I'm here," she said. "Be happy. Doesn't this prove I love you?"

"Is it love, or do you just get off on yanking my chain? Stay the week. Come visit Gladys with me." Rachel shivered. She hadn't tried to visit Gladys again. It would help to have Liz with her. "I'll show you my old school. The beach I used to go to. The best Mexican restaurant ever." Rachel sounded whiny, even to herself. *Is this about having Liz here or just about fear of going to see Gladys, going back to that nursing home alone?*

"We could do that over the weekend, can't we? Does that require a week? No matter what I give, you always want more." Liz sounded irritated, and briefly, Rachel wanted to do what she always did—back off, apologize, be grateful for crumbs.

"I'm not a puppy you can appease with a treat," she said instead, surprised at the force in her voice, the surging in her body. Maybe the dream Liz lingered. Liz the betrayer. "Don't get me wrong. I'm glad you came, but what's changed? What's different? There are always limits on how long you can stay and how much you can give. That's what I'm saying."

Liz sighed and used the exasperation-tinged voice that always emerged when Rachel started wanting too much. "Do you even know how selfish you sound sometimes? It isn't all about you. I came all the way here to see you. I've been here one night, and we're already fighting over how long I'm going to stay. Relationships involve compromise. I don't think you always remember that."

"They aren't my kids," Rachel said quietly, more under her breath than not.

Liz sat up and pulled back. "Did you really just say that? Do you even hear yourself?"

Rachel wasn't sure she thought what she'd just said was so terrible, but she responded out of habit, trying to fix it. "No, you're right. I'm sorry. I went too far. Really. I'm just super anxious. I'm here in California. I got attacked by an actual Nazi, and I don't even know how many more there might be still out there... How long before they figure out my parents' address? It's all too much. It's all freaking me out, and I'm taking it out on you." *Too much backing down,* she thought. *Fight for yourself.* "Still."

"Still what?" Liz sat up.

"It's time for coffee," Rachel said and got out of bed, wrapping herself in Rose's old yellow bathrobe.

In the kitchen, they found coffee made and Rose sitting by the pool at the round umbrella table. Rachel poured herself a cup and joined her mother, leaving Liz to help herself.

"I got that letter translated," Rose said. "The one we found in Gladys's box. I got some women at the synagogue to do it."

Rachel sipped coffee. Too bitter for her taste, but she'd slept so poorly that she would have injected it into a vein. "Really? What did it say?"

"I'd rather wait and read it to you and your father together. I'll read it to you all after dinner."

Liz came out and sat across from Rachel.

"You're welcome to be here for that," Rose said. "You're practically family." She winked.

"I don't see wedding bells in our future," Rachel said. She sensed Liz flinch and felt gratified.

"Well, dinner is at six. Your father is going to stop by and pay Gladys a visit after his last client." There was something in Rose's voice that Rachel couldn't place. It triggered memories of surprise birthday parties and presents hidden in the back of the closet. It was Rose with a secret, she realized. Her mother loved secrets and carefully staging their disclosure.

"I am practically family," Liz said, a hint of sadness in her voice. "We could get married someday."

The words should have made Rachel happy, as if she and Liz had a future. She stood. "I'm going to get dressed." She poured the rest of her coffee in the sink.

⸻ ◉ ⸻

RACHEL WAS BRUSHING her teeth, and the sound of a ringing phone over running water meant little. She was focused on imagining Liz's face when she had walked away without any promises. *Was Liz relieved? Upset?* She stepped out of the shower and heard her mother's voice, calling, yelling her father's name. She sounded frightened.

Rachel towel wrapped herself and bolted out of the bathroom.

"Aaron!" Rose yelled again, her voice quavering.

"Is everything okay, Mom?" Rachel called. "Dad's already left for work, hasn't he?" Rose rounded the corner from the living room.

Her eyes were blinking rapidly, a tic Rachel had forgotten about that used to come all the time when Gladys started in on her.

"What's wrong?" Part of her already knew.

"That's right," Rose said. "Aaron is at work. I was so upset, I forgot. It was vile," Rose said. "I've never heard such things. This man, he called me a kike and... other things. He said we were all going to die, and he knew our names."

Rachel clutched her towel to her throat. "It's my fault."

Her mother looked at her, and she felt exactly the way she had felt after the first shower game with Stephen, when she somehow believed they could all see the Jew-girl shame on her. "It isn't your fault that there are terrible people in the world," Rose said.

"We could get a hotel," Rachel said. "Go away for a while."

Rose straightened her spine. "I'm not letting those... those twerps chase me out of my own house. I'll call your father. He has a contact in the police department."

"I've got someone who's already following the case," Rachel said. "I'll call her." She turned to see Liz standing in the bedroom doorway, holding a T shirt over her bared breasts. Rachel brushed past her and grabbed her phone off the bedside table. She didn't even have to look up the number. It was right there in her texts, in her recents. She pressed Call.

She got Jo's voicemail and watched Liz watching her while she left a message: "Hi, Jo." She made sure Liz knew who she was calling. "They've found my parents' home number. What should I do?"

"You're still talking to her?" Liz asked.

Rachel simply nodded and said nothing more about it.

After that, they did not go out. They stayed in the house with the curtains drawn, watching television, drinking bitter coffee, and listening to the landline ring. Jo called Rachel back a couple hours later.

Rachel took the phone to her bedroom, leaving Liz to watch the last episode of whatever season of *Orange Is the New Black* they were on.

"Thank God you're okay," Jo said. "I heard from the police about what happened at the nursing home."

"I'm okay," Rachel said, rubbing her wrist. "But they've found my parents' home phone number. Someone called."

"You need to report it to the local police," Jo said. "I think they would at least have a patrol car swing by more frequently. Also, they'd hopefully file with the FBI that it's a hate crime."

"They can't trace the calls?" Rachel asked, thinking of a million TV shows and movies. The comforting law enforcement people could come into the family living room, set up gadgets, and wait for the next call.

"They might," Jo said. "I've filed a report with the FBI about what happened here. They should be contacting you. They take this stuff seriously."

"Okay." Rachel's voice sounded small to her, so she said it again. *Strong Rachel.* "Okay."

"How are you doing?" Jo asked.

"I'm hanging out with my family," she said. "I'm just taking a break."

Liz appeared in the doorway. Her face was red, and her body, ever her tell, looked taut.

"I'm doing okay," Rachel said. "All things considered, I'm having a good visit with my parents."

"I could come," Jo said. "I have some use-or-lose vacation time I need to use, anyway."

"You'd come?" Rachel watched Liz's hands clench into fists.

"Well, I've never seen Southern California. So it would just be a vacation."

Rachel smiled. Then Liz entered the room and spoke loudly into the phone, "Are you ready yet, Rachel? I want my tour of your childhood."

"Oh," Jo said, and Rachel closed her eyes.

———— ◈ ————

AARON AND ROSE WERE already sitting at the table when Rachel and Liz emerged from Rachel's room for dinner. Liz had wanted to talk, to do something, but Rachel felt heavy with fatigue and dozed much of the day. Aaron looked anxious, perched on the edge of his chair, and Rachel again felt sad and guilty, seeing the stoop in his shoulders. She shouldn't have come. She had brought trouble with her. She glanced at Liz. All sorts of trouble.

"Did you call your person in the department?" Rose asked. She dropped a forkful of salad onto her plate and glared at the salad bowl with an expression Rachel recognized from her sporadic engagements with Weight Watchers throughout Rachel's childhood.

Aaron nodded. "Larry took the info. He said they'd send a patrol by the house. They said I could use star-sixty-nine but that the people were most likely blocking their number. They suggested we change our number." He looked at Rachel. "I had no idea how bad it was. Have they been calling you like this?"

Rachel shook her head. "They haven't called me." That much was true. "I'm just sorry they found me here. You shouldn't have to worry about this."

"We're more worried about you," Rose said. But Rachel knew the call had shaken her. She still looked pale, and she gripped the serving fork as if it were a weapon. When they took their seats, Liz pressed a knee into Rachel's.

"We want to protect you." Aaron put his elbows on the table and tented his hands in a gesture familiar to Rachel from her brief stints in therapy. "You should have told us. We want to help."

"There's nothing you can do," Rachel replied, her voice sharper than she had intended, and her father frowned. *Am I angry that he can't protect me? That he's equally a victim?*

Rose finally released the serving fork and slid the salad bowl toward Rachel. She looked around at all of them.

Liz offered a small, nervous smile back and pressed her knee harder against Rachel's.

"We might as well do what we planned." Rose pushed her chair back and stood up, placing her hands on either side of her plate. "I have news."

Rachel piled salad on her plate then handed the salad bowl to Liz.

"Did you know your mother had an older sister named Esther?" Rose looked at Aaron.

"I could never get her to talk about any of her family." Aaron maintained his calm-therapist stance, but Rachel could see a twitch in the corner of his left eye. "She told Joseph and me about everyone being killed one night. But that's what she said. 'Everyone's been killed.' She never talked about it again. Where did you hear about this sister?"

Rose smiled at Rachel. "From Rachel, first. Then we found these old pictures." Rose sat back down and started talking fast, spewing everything about what Stephen had told Rachel and the day they'd cleaned out Gladys's room and the pictures. She seemed to have forgotten about her earlier scare. That was Rose—give her a story to tell, and everything else disappeared.

Rachel nibbled at her salad but finally gave up and put her fork down. She found Liz's hand beneath the table.

"Stephen was a sweet kid," Aaron said, finally relinquishing the tented hands and reaching across the table for the salad. Rachel choked a little, drawing both sets of parental eyes and a hand squeeze from Liz.

"He was a little Nazi," Rachel said, and Rose nodded.

Liz looked at Rachel. "You've said his name before. In your sleep. How is he a Nazi?"

"Long story," Rachel said.

Rose stopped her story long enough to retrieve the main dishes from the kitchen counter. She piled several forkfuls of chicken and potatoes onto her plate before sitting. *Where are all those vegan dishes she claimed to be making?* Rose passed the chicken and potatoes to Rachel, who passed it to Liz without taking any. Nobody seemed to actually be eating.

"Well, anyway." Aaron picked up his fork then put it down on his plate without taking any food. "That's all in the past. I don't see why it matters now. We have enough worries in the here and now. Rachel's stalkers are far more concerning than any of that."

Rose's face turned bright red, and Rachel laughed, though nothing was funny. She felt giddy, the way she got when things felt out of her control, and she wished Liz wasn't there, watching the family drama play out.

"Anyway," Rose said. "I asked someone at temple to translate the writing on the back of that photo and a letter that was with it. Do you want to hear what it said?" She coughed and produced a wrinkled sheet of lined notebook paper that had apparently been under her napkin.

Aaron glanced at Rachel then turned to Rose. "What were you doing, sharing our private stuff with people from the synagogue without asking me first?"

"I showed it to you last night." Rose's voice got a petulant whine that Rachel recognized in herself, and she vowed to eliminate that particular tone from her repertoire forever. "You barely glanced at it. I told you I was going to get it translated, and you just grunted."

"Oh." Aaron pushed his chair away from the table and crossed his arms.

Rachel experienced a sudden urge to tell her father he needed to eat.

"Okay, okay. What does it say?"

"Are you sure you want me here for this?" Liz released Rachel's hand and pushed her chair back. "I could take a walk."

"No," Rose said. "You're with Rachel. Rachel might need you after she hears this."

What is she doing? Rachel considered sending Liz away. But she couldn't fathom what could have been so upsetting in an old letter to Gladys.

Rose's hands seemed to be trembling as she held the paper. Rachel could see someone's neat cursive scrawled across most of the page. Any number of people could have done the translation—probably one of the older women who baked for Fridays and taught Yiddish on weeknights.

"First," she read, "it says who was in the picture that must have come with it. Mother, Father, Esther, and Gladys. They were posing in front of Gladys's childhood home." She paused and waited as if to be sure everyone was listening. Liz was the only one eating, digging into her chicken as if she could bury her face in her plate and disappear.

Aaron sat up straight, his eyes brightening as Rose continued, "Then it says, 'Dear sister, I thought you might like this picture of the family. Frantz keeps asking about you and the baby. We say you are both fine. He is being sent to fight for Hitler now. He says if he doesn't, they will be suspicious, but he hopes to find a way to join you soon. He says he wants to marry you and be a family. He wants to get us out to join you, but Mother says not yet. She is trying to find a way to hold on to the family heirlooms. She just can't bear to leave that china she inherited from our grandmother.'" Rose put the paper down. "There's more stuff about the town, the way the hairdresser won't cut their hair anymore, the yellow stars everywhere, but this is the important bit. She said the words aren't an exact translation but close enough. It's signed, 'Love, your sister, Esther.'"

It took Rachel several minutes to realize who the baby must have been, and she looked at her father. Rose was also looking at him with something like triumph in her eyes. When it started to sink in, it wasn't like a sudden thing Rachel had never known. It was as if she'd been staring at the pieces of a puzzle for her entire life and suddenly realized which piece went where. It was bits of nonsensical things Gladys said over the years and Aaron's blond hair, which didn't look at all like the photos Rachel had seen of his brother Joseph.

Aaron sat perfectly still for several minutes then started talking, his voice small and not at all like the shrink voice Rachel was used to. "I never told you how I got into magic," he said, looking at Rachel. "There was a man who lived across the street, Mr. Schmidt. Mother hated him because he was German. But it was such a lonely year for me. My brother, Joseph, was the golden child, and I... well, I guess now, I understand... I just always thought my father loved Joseph a little more." He stayed quiet for several seconds. When he finally spoke again, his voice was a whisper. "Mr. Schmidt taught me magic and made me feel special. That's why I wanted to teach it to you. But Mother, when she found out I was spending time over there..." He rubbed his temple and looked at Rose. "I never understood. Mother yelled at me for going in his house, and I thought it was just, you know, don't talk to strangers. But then she said, 'So, you'd rather be a German than a Jew? I should have known.'"

Aaron sat, dabbing his eyes with a stained napkin. Rachel tried to imagine what it must be like for her father to realize his father had not been his father. *But what does it mean about me?*

Liz was the only one who finished her dinner.

———◉———

LATER IN BED, LIZ KISSED her, but Rachel pulled back.

"Not tonight."

Liz looked hurt.

Her parents' phone rang again, and she held her breath until it stopped. Her father had answered once, and Rachel had watched his face flush, watched him close his eyes then slowly hang up. He wouldn't tell them what the caller had said, but after he tried the *69 thing to trace the call, he suggested they stop answering the phone. They were too far from the road to know if the police were in fact driving by the house. Aaron insisted that his friend was on it. He said he'd shown them Rachel's social media pages. They, like Jo, were now working with the FBI.

"I flew all this way to be with you," Liz said. "We only have a couple nights together."

"I know," Rachel said.

"Are you upset about the letter? Or the phone call? The letter doesn't change anything. You're still you."

"That sounds like something your Al-Anon sponsor would say," Rachel said.

"Well, it's true." Liz stroked Rachel's thigh. She knew what worked to change Rachel's mind about sex.

Rachel removed the hand. "Do you understand how this affects me? All my life, I thought I was one thing, and now, it seems I'm something else." Of course, that wasn't really true. Judaism was passed down through the mother. She was still Bat Mitzvahed. But she had an actual Nazi in her family lineage. Maybe it didn't change a thing, but it occurred to her that it wasn't *Stephen's* grandfather who had fought for Hitler. The thought made her laugh out loud, and Liz sat up.

"What?" she asked. "What's funny?"

"It's complicated," Rachel said. But what she thought was that Liz was not the person to tell this story to. Liz might have loved her, but she wouldn't know what to make of that story and all its complicated layers. Even Rachel wasn't sure what, if anything, the new information meant. "I'm going to get some tea."

She put on her robe and left Liz alone in her childhood bedroom. She found the light on in her father's study. She knocked and opened the door.

Her father sat at his desk in front of the computer, typing in his old hunt-and-peck way. His face looked pale in the blue computer light. "Oh, Rachel. Hi." He sounded like a child to her.

She eased into the room. "Hi, Dad. What are you doing?"

"Just some writing. Come on in."

Her mother had filled up most of the empty spaces since Rachel had arrived. She realized that her father had been as absent as he'd become after Gladys moved in. Leaving early, staying late, disappearing into his study. Even when he ate with them, he wasn't present.

She sat in the leather easy chair in the corner.

Her father spun his desk chair to face her. "We haven't really talked since you got here." He had lost weight, she realized. Where he had once been fleshy and bulging, he was gaunt and angular. He'd been shaving what was left of his hair but had grown his completely white beard longer than he used to keep it. He looked at her from behind thick-lensed glasses with his pale eyes. "So, that was quite the revelation from that letter, huh?"

Rachel nodded and waited silently for what came next.

"How do you feel about it? Knowing your grandfather, um, fought for Hitler? Wasn't Jewish." He'd assumed his shrink voice. It had pissed Rachel off when she'd been a teenager. Her mother would be at her and at her, and then, finally, she'd sic Dad on her, and the shrink voice would come out.

"How do *you* feel about it?" she replied. "He was your father, right?"

He studied his hands. "Do you remember when we used to put on those magic shows for your mother? You were, what, maybe five or six? We'd come in here and practice and then Rose would watch? Remember?"

Rachel remembered. She remembered the one time they tried doing a show after Gladys moved in. Gladys and Rose had been settled on the fancy couch in the fancy living room, waiting for "Rachel and Daddy's Great Magic Show," and she and her father were giggling in the study, getting ready. She was preparing for the foam-ball trick again but was struggling keep the extra foam ball tucked between her fingers so she could turn one ball into two. Her hands were too small, and she lacked the dexterity. It had always been hard for her, but usually, her father was patient and helped her until she had them to the point that it would work.

That night, Aaron became impatient, took the balls, and said he'd do that part. What scared her was how much it felt like playing with another kid, like the way Stephen would get if she didn't play a game right. As an adult, she would say it was like a kid taking his marbles and going home. Rachel had cried, and they ended up going out for ice cream instead of doing the magic show.

"Yeah, I remember. It was kind of fun. Maybe it's why I got into drama." She rubbed her hand, which seemed to throb more with the memory. They didn't do any shows after that. They still practiced in his study, but then she turned twelve and had to study for her bat mitzvah and stopped caring about magic.

"I was just thinking about it. How we did that, and how it was maybe a good time—time we spent together." He clasped his hands.

Rachel's mind kept straying to Liz waiting in her bed, J.T. in jail, and other Nazis somewhere out there. It was hard to think clearly, which was maybe why she blurted out what she did. "Seems like you had a lot of fun doing the magic with Stephen too." She instantly regretted it when he looked as if she'd slapped him.

"Honestly," he finally said, "I missed you. By then, you had stopped wanting to practice with me. You had that talent show, and then..." He stopped, rubbed his cheek, and glanced toward the blank computer screen. "You were pretty busy preparing for your Bat Mitzvah. Stephen was interested, and I guess it kind of took on a life of his own, teaching him. I had hoped you might join us. I'm supposed to be this great psychiatrist, you know, helping people. But I didn't know how to relate to my own daughter. I'm sorry."

The silence lingered between them, and Rachel felt grateful that the words had stopped. She had no idea how to respond to a verbal father, a father who wanted to connect with her. "It's okay," she finally said. "It was a long time ago. I guess I just wondered."

"I never meant to hurt you." His eyes welled up, and she looked down at her hands so she wouldn't see. "Are you happy?" he asked. "All I wanted was for my daughter to be happy."

"I'm fine," she told him. "I'm happy. Really." *Just fine. Fucked-up and fine.* She couldn't give him what he wanted, that deep father-daughter talk in which they opened up and expressed their hurt, and everything was healed like the lancing of a wound. Maybe she would, but not yet.

He stood abruptly and walked toward her. She was afraid he was going to hug her, and she tensed a little, but instead, he went to the printer and removed a small sheaf of papers with typed words marching across them.

"I've been writing. About your uncle Joseph and me. And other stuff. After hearing... what we learned tonight... I felt I should write some of my thoughts and memories. I thought it might make things clearer. Explain some things." He proffered the papers, and after more seconds passed than was reasonable for receiving such a gift, Rachel accepted them.

"You don't have to talk about it, but if you ever want to..."

"You never talk about him much." She stared at the papers, where her uncle Joseph's name appeared more than once.

"It was a complicated relationship. He was Mother's favorite, was supposed to be a rabbi. Then he got sick with the bipolar disorder. They didn't know how to treat it in those days, not like we do now."

Rachel knew very little about her uncle, but someone, somewhere must have mentioned that he had killed himself because she did know that. "Is that why he killed himself?"

"Probably," he said. "But the main thing is, what I wrote about is that I have regrets. I let Mother move in with us. I think I was hoping she would love me the way she loved Joseph. Even after he died, I couldn't compete. I think I gave in to her too easily. I was trying to earn her love. I think..." He rummaged in the desk and produced a Kleenex. Rachel tried to remember if she had ever seen her father cry. He blew loudly and returned to his chair. "I think it made your childhood difficult. And I regret that."

It was like an out-of-body experience, as if she was performing a role. An emotional father. A father who talked and expressed regret. *I'm just like him. I don't talk either. I don't let myself feel.* The tears threatened, but she wouldn't cry in front of him. Instead, she turned to a random page and read:

I realize now that Mother and Dad were discovering or confirming what they had already guessed about what had happened in Europe, but I didn't understand then. They spent more and more time reading the newspaper, huddled around the radio. Their faces were always so grim, the house so empty. Dad stayed away at the bank, sometimes not coming home until we were all asleep. Mother kept the curtains closed. Entering the house was like walking into a silent movie late, when the movie is grim and sad and nobody is eating popcorn or whispering. Everything was dark and stale and disorienting. And sometimes, Mother wouldn't say anything all day.

Once, I saw her in the kitchen, crying. I remember the moment—she was standing at the sink, holding one of the blue-patterned plates Dad gave her for their anniversary earlier that year. I ran into the kitchen after a glass of water, and she turned, the plate dangling from her right hand. I saw her red eyes, damp trails on her cheek. Her nose was running. The only sound was water splashing out of the faucet into the white enamel sink. I froze. Then I turned and ran.

I found Joseph. We'd been playing in the backyard. I must have looked upset, because he asked what was wrong. I didn't tell him. It wasn't that I worried about Mother. I remember wishing I hadn't gone in the kitchen. And I kept thinking, she should have wiped her nose, *and balling my hands into fists against the angry feelings I didn't understand.*

She looked up. "Thanks, Dad," she finally said. "I'll read it."

"I'd like to talk again. Maybe get to know you—the adult you—better."

Before she could answer, the phone on his desk rang. They both froze and stared at it, but Aaron didn't pick up.

After Rachel closed the study door, she stood in the hall for a few minutes, her eyes tracing the familiar chip in the wood just under the doorknob and the splash of light under the bottom where it wasn't planed quite right. She had stood outside that door as a child, aware of her father on the other side and longing to enter. But after Gladys moved in, even when he did welcome her, there was always a look of impatience and the way he responded with noncommittal phrases that even six- or seven-year-old Rachel knew meant he wasn't listening. She never stopped wanting to open that door, but only if it would lead to the past, when she and her father practiced magic and Gladys was safely far away in Illinois.

Chapter 33
Stephen
2016

When Stephen was about thirteen, he went through a phase of being scared to death the world was going to end. It started with that movie, *The Day After* or *The Morning After* or something like that. It was about a nuclear bomb hitting and what would happen when it did. That night, he couldn't sleep, thinking about it and worrying. Sometimes, he imagined being killed instantly when it happened—he would see a flash of light, maybe hearing his mother scream, and then *boom*, he was just gone. No more. He knew just what his mother's scream sounded like from the time the uncle broke her arm. Other times, he worried about not dying but losing his hair, getting sores all over his body, and slowly starving to death. He would sit in the attic, holding one of his grandfather's guns and reassuring himself that he had ways to get food and ways to protect his water supply if he needed to.

That old fear had resurfaced, but it was different. He got on Google, typed in "illnesses," read and read, and started freaking out. The funny thing was how one illness could lead to others. It started with Gulf War Syndrome, which he saw a news story about. He wasn't in the Gulf War, but he had been deployed to the Middle East. He had been in Iraq. Whatever was there then was probably still there when he went over for Operation Iraqi Freedom. When he googled Gulf War Syndrome, he read that some people developed kidney or liver problems with it, so he googled kidney problems. One sign of kidney disease was itching. He'd been itching ever since he went to Iraq. Sometimes, he got weird itchy rashes, like scales, all over his legs. He wouldn't ask a doctor about it, but he kept wondering if he would go on dialysis or if he would just let himself die if his kidneys failed.

The fears had started after the nursing home thing. He tried not to think about that, because every time he did, he saw the moment he went down on his knee and the security guard saving the day, when it was supposed to have been him, Stephen, rescuing Rachel.

She wouldn't respond to his messages on Facebook anymore. He'd parked near her house a couple times, but the second time, a police car cruised by, and he panicked and left. He just wanted to see Gladys, and since Josh and Maria had kicked him out of the house, there was nobody to talk to. He felt trapped in his grandfather's house with those letters in the attic, proving everything he'd thought about his family was fake.

In a way, Stephen didn't blame Josh and Maria for kicking him out, but they could have been less humiliating about it. They did it the same day he got fired from the bed store. That day, a man had come in, leaning on a cane and dragging an oxygen tank on wheels.

"I need a new bed," the man had said. "My doctor said I should get a firmer mattress for my back."

Stephen had resisted when Josh pushed him to take the sale.

"Go on, Steve," he had said. "This one is yours." Nobody else ever called him Steve, but Josh had decided it sounded more professional.

"You take this one," Stephen had replied, scanning the store in hopes of finding someone else. "I don't know what kind of bed would be good for an old man with back problems." He preferred working with the young couples. There was something about the man, the way he leaned into his cane, and the raspy sound of his breath that bothered Stephen.

"Go on." Josh gave him a friendly shove. "You have to learn to sell to anyone. That's how you make commissions. You do want to get some money saved up, right?"

"I suppose," Stephen muttered, though he wasn't happy about it. The man stood just inside the doorway, looking around as if he'd come in accidentally.

"Hi." Stephen approached the man, forcing a smile. "I can help you."

"I need a new bed," the man repeated. Stephen dragged his eyes away from the liver spots on the back of the man's hand and the tubes snaking from his nose to the oxygen tank. "I'm Stephen." He offered a hand to shake, but the man did not reciprocate. Stephen counted to three then dropped his arm. "Well, what kind of bed are you looking for?"

"I don't know." The man looked like he should probably sit down. He wobbled a little, and his hand gripping the cane looked bloodless. "My wife usually picked our mattresses. She died." His pale eyes watered when he said this.

Stephen shrugged and started toward the memory foam beds. They were supposed to be the best for backs, though he had tried one out and hated how it molded around his body. When he reached the memory foam room, he turned and saw the old man still back near the entrance, slowly making his way across the store. His left leg dragged a little, and one of the wheels on the oxygen tank squeaked.

Stephen sighed and retraced his steps. "Do you want a king, queen, or full?"

The old man emitted an antiseptic odor, and Stephen noticed a bandage on the inside of the arm not holding the cane, where they usually took blood. *He must have come here straight from his doctor's office.*

The doors swished open, and a young couple with a baby walked in. *Damn.* He should have held his ground with Josh. Instead of trying to help the sad old man with his sad oxygen and his dead wife, he could have been talking to that young couple who probably wanted to upgrade their kid's crib or something.

"I don't know." The man shuffled forward as Stephen baby stepped back toward the memory foam room. "My wife died."

Are those tears? Is this man fucking crying? "Well, these are our best beds for back problems," Stephen mumbled, pointing randomly at one of the queen beds.

The man sighed loudly when he sank onto the bed then scooted to the center of the mattress and lay down, gingerly settling his head onto one of the show pillows. Stephen could hear the rhythmic swish of the oxygen tank working. The man inhaled loudly and spoke in a breathy whisper. "I miss my wife," he said as if Stephen cared. "She always picked the big purchases. I don't know..."

Whatever else the old man said, Stephen didn't hear, because he tasted something acid in his mouth, his body clenched with rage, and without thinking, he yelled, "People fucking die! You don't have to cry about it." There was a feeling of detachment, almost as if he was standing somewhere else. Maybe he was in Iraq. Maybe he was in Gladys's room, and she was kicking him out for no reason. Maybe he was in the attic with Rachel. Maybe he was in a long-ago hospital room, and his grandfather was dying. "People die, and they go away, and they stop loving you, and they aren't who you thought they were, and who even gives a fuck."

The old man started weeping. Stephen saw Josh nearby, his face clenched in an expression that reminded him of the guys in Iraq. *You sick fuck,* they said. *We don't trust you.*

Stephen clenched his fists and wanted to beat the tears out of that man, but the security guard, a potbellied retired cop, grabbed Stephen and propelled him toward the door, breathing so quickly that Stephen thought he would have a heart attack and fall, taking Stephen along, crashing to the hard linoleum.

They hadn't called the cops. If they had, he would have gotten another stay in the psych ward for sure. And he didn't blame Josh and Maria for kicking him out either. It was just that they could have said it in passing, like, "You know, Stephen, it just isn't working out. You're going to have to move back into your grandfather's house." They didn't have to sit there in the living room, the two of them on the sofa, so earnest, holding hands, smiling at him.

Josh didn't have to say, "It isn't just about what happened today. We've been thinking about it for a while. It's also about Phillip. We think you're spending too much time with him. It isn't good for him."

Maria didn't have to nod and look sympathetic. She didn't have to tell him she had asked around in the congregation and found another couple, a couple without kids who would take him so he didn't have to go back to living alone. That was the worst of it. Now he couldn't even go to the damn Kingdom Hall, because they all thought he was crazy. And he missed it. It was stupid, and he didn't believe a word of it, but he missed feeling like people gave a shit.

He hadn't tried to talk to them about it. He let them finish what they had to say, went down to his basement room to collect his stuff, and left through the sliding door down there. He never even said goodbye to Phillip or Beth.

———◈———

MAYBE HE WOULD SKIP the dialysis and just die. It wasn't a bad way to go. He would just get more and more tired then fall asleep and not wake up, according to the websites. Other times, he thought dialysis might not be so bad. He imagined it occurred in a big room with cushy chairs, and everyone got their own personal television set, and the nurses would watch over him and joke with him and bring him box lunches. It might be a little like having a family, all those hours spent connected to a machine with other people around.

And kidney failure would probably kill his sex drive. It might stop him from going back to the attic and playing out imagined scenes with Rachel, scenes in which they were adults but innocent and sweet like he remembered them as children. Though he knew Rachel would laugh if he told her he thought those childhood attic games were innocent.

His mother still took him to dinner every once in a while, when she could fit him into her busy schedule. He'd been thinking that next time they went out, he would tell her he wanted to go back to the Jehovah's Witnesses. But those people didn't want to see him. They thought he was dangerous.

He hadn't told Natalie the truth about which side his grandfather had claimed to fight for or about the letters he'd discovered in the attic. But some things must have slipped out, because in his session the week before, she had asked him if he ever wondered whether his grandfather was lying and hadn't fought in the war at all. He would have thought he would have gotten so angry that he walked out of her office and never went back. But the moment passed, and instead, he just asked her if her husband ever took her for walks in the woods.

"We're talking about you, Stephen," she said. But she didn't ask the question again.

He hadn't told his mother about the letters either. He was pretty sure he already knew what she would say. "You always thought your grandfather was so special. You finally figured him out." Something like that.

———— ◉ ————

HE WENT TO A NAZI RALLY in San Diego. Things were different than when he met his friends in the bar and they had been constrained to their small, safe places, like Surf Me. That had changed, and there were rallies that he learned about easily, just by going on the right social media sites—4chan, Twitter, even Facebook.

He went to the rally and marched with other men. He brought one of his grandfather's German guns. The police had taken most of them after his arrest, but they hadn't known about the Astra 900 that Stephen had been keeping under his bed. He didn't have ammunition, and who knew if it even shot, but he loved the feel of it in his hands. Someone gave him a torch, and he carried both, one in each hand. He hid the weapon in his coat when they passed police. He marched and chanted, "Jews will not replace us."

It felt good, chanting, being part of something bigger than him. "Jews will not replace us." Other voices blended together, the sun was hot, and it smelled like Iraq, but his feet hit the pavement, and it nearly erased the humiliation of the nursing home incident, of Josh and Maria sending him away, of the pity on his own mother's face.

The press came with their cameras and a leggy blond reporter, and the guys around Stephen cheered when he pointed the Astra at the woman. "*Lügenpresse!*" he shouted. Someone put an arm around Stephen's shoulder. His finger twitched on the trigger. *What if the woman was Rachel? What if the gun was loaded?* They marched on. "Jews will not replace us."

Counter-protesters stood on the sidewalk, holding signs. A little girl, maybe seven, held a sign that read Make Nazis Afraid Again. Stephen pointed the empty weapon at her and felt a little sick when she shrank back against her mother. The mother's sign read No KKK, and she glared at Stephen. He made himself smile back.

"Jews will not replace us. KKK." His throat was parched from chanting, but he kept going.

After the rally, some guys gathered in the parking lot, and Stephen stayed, hovering on the outside of the group. But they were all much younger than he was, and his moment of glory, when owning his grandfather's weapon had meant something, had passed.

More counter-protesters stood nearby, holding signs. Kill All Nazis. Love Trumps Hate. Stephen aimed the gun in their direction, but they didn't even look frightened, and the people he'd followed were getting into their cars. Nobody invited him to join them.

Later, when he went on Facebook to look for pictures from the march, he saw himself. Someone had posted him pointing the Astra at that kid. They had linked the photo to Twitter as well. He clicked through and read some of the comments:

Let's make this asshole famous.

Nazis get off on scaring small children.

Someone out there must know this guy. Don't let him get away with terrifying that little kid.

The sad thing was, nobody named him. Not one person, even to punish him, even to call him out.

He got into the Volkswagen, drove to the dog pound, and parked as far away from the entrance as he could get. He sat there, listening to the old Skrewdriver music on the tape deck and watching people leave with their new pets. Maybe the dog was still there. There had to be a way to get her. He just thought if he could get a dog, he wouldn't feel so lonely.

———◉———

STEPHEN NEVER FOUND out where his grandfather got Dieter. The dog just appeared a few weeks after the first time they went to the attic together. He came home from school, and his grandfather greeted him, wearing the closed-mouth smile that had once frightened Stephen and holding a leash with a wriggling German shepherd puppy at the end of it.

Stephen named the puppy Dieter. His grandfather said it meant warrior. Dieter played tug with splayed legs, a wagging tail, and happy barks. But he grew quickly, and his grandfather took Stephen to the empty lot every day and taught Stephen and the dog Schutzhund.

"Sit," Stephen said, and Dieter wagged his tail and barked. Stephen laughed, but his grandfather yelled. Stephen had learned that most people got stronger accents when they were angry, but his grandfather usually sounded more American the angrier he got.

"It's *sitz*, and stop encouraging him. He must learn to behave. Again." Stephen's grandfather doubled over in a coughing fit then spit a glob onto the ground, which was usually what happened when he raised his voice. Once, Stephen was close enough to his grandfather to see flecks of blood in the gunk he spit out.

"It won't be long now," his mother had told Stephen not long before. She'd smiled. "Don't get too attached. He isn't gonna be around much longer."

Stephen forced a stern frown in Dieter's direction and tried again. "Sitz."

The dog wagged its tail and strained at the leash in the direction of the tennis ball they'd brought for after-training reward play.

"Again."

"Sitz."

Dieter sprang off the ground and tried to lick Stephen's face. Stephen's frustration surged, and he grabbed Dieter's collar. "I said sit." He shook the collar a little.

"No. No. No." Grandfather's face was red. "Shaking teaches nothing. Again."

Stephen waited through the coughing fit then tried again.

Stephen's grandfather was patient but stern with Dieter. He said he had learned to train dogs in Germany. They used them to chase down the Jews. Hitler had a German shepherd. Hitler loved dogs. Stephen's grandfather loved dogs.

The first time Dieter sat for Stephen was one of the best moments of Stephen's life. His grandfather's face cracked into a smile, and he set a hand on Stephen's head. "Very good," he said. "That was very good."

———◉———

STEPHEN SAT OUTSIDE the pound for several hours, watching people go in alone or in small groups and leave with cats in cardboard carriers and dogs on leashes. The German shepherd never appeared. He knew he had to accept that she had been either euthanized or adopted, but he didn't want to let go. But as the afternoon waned, he sighed and drove away. He went to the library and sent Rachel another message. "Please answer. I just want to see Gladys before she dies. They won't let me in without you."

Chapter 34
Rachel
2016

In the sanctuary of Rachel's childhood synagogue, she said, "I guess I still belong. I mean I guess I'm still Jewish. It's passed down from your mother, not your father, but still. It's weird." The place was mostly empty, although Sunday school classes were in session in the back classrooms and they had found the synagogue door open. They sat in a front pew.

Liz obviously didn't get it. "You never go to synagogue, anyway. Why would it matter to you whether you still belong in a synagogue you haven't set foot in in years?"

"Because," Rachel said, but she couldn't think how to explain. They had visited the beach where Rachel used to sunbathe; the high school, which was disappointing because of the locked gate surrounding everything and cutting off the swatch of grass Rachel used to eat lunch on; and the elementary school, where they sat on the swings Rachel used to swing on and peered in the windows of the cafeteria.

Rachel had even left her cell phone at home for the tour of her childhood. No checking Twitter. Rachel's father had drawn them an old-fashioned pen-and-paper map to the synagogue. The only place they hadn't visited was Stephen's house, of course. She didn't want to share that with Liz. And the canyon she had once played war in was a major road.

Liz stood. "Nothing is different. Your dad is still your dad. You still had your bat mitzvah. You still belong as much as you ever did. If

290

anything, with everything going on with those people stalking you, I'd think you'd be relieved to be able to say you aren't Jewish. Not that it's even true. I mean your mother is as Jewish as ever, right? Anyway, it isn't as if you ever went around advertising your religious beliefs, such as they are."

Liz sounded cranky and impatient. It was their last day together, and the whole idea of spending it on a tour of Rachel's childhood had started to seem foolish. It was one of those things she had always imagined doing—taking a girlfriend to her childhood home and showing her around, like opening a door into herself. *Here. Know me just a little better.* But Liz seemed bored.

Rachel climbed up on the dais and stared into the ark, where the Torah was kept. "You're right," she said softly, keeping her back to Liz. "I've always been too ambivalent about my heritage to own it." She turned to find that Liz had moved to the door and was scrolling through something on her phone. "But that's the old me," she said with more force.

Liz didn't look up.

Rachel looked down at Liz from up on the dais. She'd stood right there and gazed out at the audience when she'd chanted her Haftorah for her bat mitzvah. She couldn't remember her reading, but she remembered the feeling of the audience nodding and listening, the way they were with her and she was with them. Gladys sat in the front row and smiled the whole time, but Rachel wasn't sure whether that had pleased her or if she had wished Gladys would just leave. She still had the too-big gold Star of David necklace Gladys had given her that day. She still remembered the note Gladys had written in the card: "Always remember that being Jewish is the most important thing about you." And, Rachel realized, she had convoluted that message, the attic games, Rose's depression, and even the recent stalking into something dark and shameful.

Liz was just looking at her phone and tapping away.

"What are you looking at?" Rachel asked.

"It's Michael," Liz said. "He wanted my opinion on what to wear to the thing Tuesday night. He's sending photos of options."

Rachel considered all the times she might have decided she'd had enough. The canceled dates, missed dinners, her birthday. All the times she might have said, clearly and definitively, "I'm through." But she never had. She was always waiting for the old Liz, the Liz from those early days, to return. The little text exchange with Michael was nothing. There had been so many things that were bigger and more meaningful, so many times when she should have taken a stand. She should have shouted, fought, pushed back.

"I need you to listen to me," Rachel said. "I need to know you can listen."

"Okay." Liz put her phone facedown. "What?"

But the moment was past, and Rachel wasn't sure what she wanted to say or if she wanted to say it to Liz. "I need to do something," she said. "I need to visit Gladys."

"Okay," Liz said, looking at her phone again as Rachel climbed down off the dais. "We can do that."

"No," Rachel replied. "I'll drop you home. I need to do this without you."

AN HOUR LATER, RACHEL pulled into driveway at Stephen's house and left her car idling behind the Volkswagen. If she hadn't seen it in the nursing home parking lot, she would have assumed it couldn't possibly run. Stephen had opened the door by the time she got to his walkway. He stood in the doorway, scratching at an unkempt beard. They faced each other in silence. He tugged his sweats up.

"Okay," she said. "Let's go visit Gladys."

"Really?" His smile brought back different, happy memories of bike riding, playing house, and just being kids.

"Yes," she said. "You can follow me there."

At the nursing home, she ignored the parking lot and pulled off the road beside the guard's station. Stephen parked behind her. The guard stepped out from his hut and looked ready to direct them, but she lifted a hand in greeting, and he nodded.

"You doing okay?" he asked.

"Yes," she said, though her heart wouldn't stop racing.

"You just leave your car right here," he said. "But you'll be fine. They fired the aide who gave out your grandmother's address. I investigated until I found him."

She smiled at the pride in the guard's voice and said, "Thank you." Then she followed Stephen through the sliding doors and past the couches and brochures and fake palm trees. She approached the front desk, where a man had replaced the young woman from before.

"Can I help you?" he asked.

"We're here to see Gladys Goldberg?" Stephen scratched the top of his head with jagged fingernails, and Rachel was grateful because the anxiety about being there was choking off her voice.

"Are you family?" the man asked.

Stephen nodded and jabbed a finger toward Rachel. "That's her granddaughter."

"Sure." The man spun his chair to face a computer and pushed a few keys. "She's in room two-oh-four. That's on the second floor. Elevators that way." He pointed toward two more fake palm trees, and Rachel could see the small hallway and elevator buttons on the wall in between the trees.

"Come on," Stephen said.

Her heart raced out of beat with the drowsy version of "Memory" that accompanied them on the elevator. Stephen stood close enough so she could hear his breathing, and she noticed that his hands were clenched, his jaw thrust forward. Realizing he was also anxious calmed her, so she was able to push out a slow exhale. They were safe in there. She was safe. J.T. was locked up. The staff member who had posted the address had been fired. They were safe. The elevator door pinged open.

They exited into a long, well-lit hallway with neutral black-framed paintings placed on the wall in strategically situated nooks above leather chairs and sofas. There was even a white piano in one area, a few doors down from Gladys's room. When they passed the silent piano, she thought that she could live there and wondered how old or disabled one had to be to move into such a place, a place with pianos and everything hushed and calm and smelling of Pine-Sol. Hell, maybe she could stay—just never leave. She would be safe. She could sleep for a year.

But a harsh alarm shattered the fantasy, and any calm she'd achieved fled with the renewed pounding in her ears. She stopped to focus and try to regain her calmness. Two middle-aged men emerged from around the corner to escort a shriveled naked man away from the open elevator door and toward one of the rooms on the other end of the hall.

Gladys's room was done in the same maroon and green of the lobby. There were two beds but no roommate, and the bed was bigger than Rachel remembered. *Had there always been railings and bars hanging from the ceiling like that?* Rachel noticed the open bathroom door, the large-screen TV, and the window with heavy blinds drawn tightly. She noticed all of those things instead of the woman on the bed. She stared at the closed blinds, trying to picture her car outside the room. *You can leave. You don't have to do this. But then what would I be saying? That Gladys is as terrifying, as powerful, as dangerous as I've been telling myself for all these years?* She made herself look at the woman on the bed.

Gladys was asleep, her eyelids loosely fluttering, one darkly splotched hand twitching against the white blanket. There were no tubes or needles or buttons. Thin gray hair, which appeared to have been recently washed, curled against her forehead. *There was a little girl, who had a little curl, smack in the middle of her forehead.* Rachel was surprised by the sudden memory, in a bath, sliding the bar of soap through the water as Gladys sat on the toilet, teaching her that rhyme. *When she was good, she was very good, and when she was bad, she was horrid.* With the last bit, the hands splashed into the water to tickle, and Rachel curled around them, giggling. *Again, Grandma, again.* Gladys smiled, even giggled a little, right along with Rachel.

She dropped into the leather chair in the corner of the room and folded her body against everything. Gladys scolding, Gladys thrusting Hebrew books in her lap insisting she study before dinner, Gladys yelling about Rachel not wearing a dress to temple. Gladys playing with her in the bathtub. Stephen and J.T. and all the people tweeting and posting filthy rage at her.

Stephen approached the bed. She saw a wet patch on the back of his shirt. His neck was red. He reached out to touch Gladys's arm with a hand that might have been shaking. Gladys opened her eyes and seemed to focus on him. Rachel hugged her legs tighter.

"Hi, Gladys," Stephen said. He glanced back at Rachel then bent over her grandmother. "Do you remember me?"

Gladys squinted up at him. She had never worn glasses, as far as Rachel could remember, although it wasn't clear whether that was vanity or if she didn't need them. It was hard to tell what Gladys was seeing or who she thought she was seeing. She was strangely beautiful, not toothless and withered in the way one might imagine old people looking. Her eyes were clear, which seemed odd to Rachel, since her mind was not. They ought to have been cloudy with confusion, not bright and busy, flickering from Rachel to Stephen and back to Rachel. She propped herself up and lifted her head off the pillows toward Stephen.

"Frantz?" Her voice pitched high, almost childlike. "I've changed my mind," she said. "I don't want to go. I want to stay with my family."

Stephen shook his head. "No, Gladys, it's Stephen. You left Frantz a long time ago, remember?"

At first, Rachel didn't absorb what she'd just heard. *Did Stephen just respond as if he knows who Frantz was? Has he known the story all these years?*

Gladys studied him with her brown eyes. "You have your grandmother's eyes," the women lining up to talk to her grandmother after Friday night services used to tell Rachel. "You're going to be a beauty someday, just like your grandmother," they would say, winking.

"No, Frantz," Gladys said. "I can't go to America. My family needs me."

Stephen clenched his fists, his shoulders grew rigid, and Rachel wondered if she should stop him if he were to hit her. She wondered if she would want to. She moved to stand, but then Stephen visibly released the tension.

"It's okay, Gladys," he said. "I'm not Frantz. I'm Stephen."

"Stephen?" She frowned.

"I want to know why you kicked me out that day, Gladys. Can you tell me?" He sounded like a little boy imploring his best friend. "Why did you send me away?" He glanced at Rachel. "She was always confusing me with her first lover in Germany that last year," he said. "I didn't get it then, but I guess she was already losing her mind."

My grandfather, Rachel thought. *He's so gentle with her.*

"I can't love a German," Gladys said. "It isn't right."

Stephen's voice sounded young and hungry. "Why did you kick me out, Gladys? Why did you stop caring about me all of a sudden like that?" He choked a little and glanced at Rachel again, his eyes red.

Is he crying? Rachel pushed out of the chair and moved to stand beside him.

"Hi, Grandma," she said. Her voice sounded different, as if she was hearing a recording of herself. "How are you?"

Gladys looked at her. "Do I know you?"

"It's Rachel, Grandma." The pine odor cloyed, and the overheated room made her dizzy.

"I don't know you. You don't belong here. You and your Nazi blood. Leave." Gladys said it emphatically and reached for her call button. Stephen put a hand out to stop her, grabbing her arm. Rachel noticed smudges of dirt under his broken fingernails and several scars on the inside of his arm.

"Stephen, don't hurt her."

His shoulders twitched, but he let go.

Gladys turned to him with a flash of accusation. "I can't love a Nazi," she said again, and he stepped back.

"I'm not a Nazi," Rachel said, her voice shaking. "I'm your granddaughter."

"Esther?" Gladys asked Rachel then turned toward Stephen. "Frantz, did you watch out for her? Did you keep her safe?"

"No," Rachel said and felt frustration well in her. "I'm Rachel, not Esther." Nothing about what was happening was healing or cathartic or anything like it would have been if she'd written the scene in a play.

"Gladys," Stephen said, and again his voice seemed patient, almost soothing. "I'm not Frantz, and Rachel is your and Frantz's granddaughter, not your sister." He laughed. "She always said you looked like her sister. Then she started getting confused. Kept telling me to look after you. I thought she meant I, Stephen, was supposed to look after you, Rachel. But I just realized she meant for Frantz to look after Esther."

"You knew?" Rachel said. "I didn't even know. My family just found out, and all this time, you knew about Frantz?" She looked at Gladys, the woman who had come into her house all those years before and ruined her life.

Driving there, she had imagined herself standing at Gladys's bedside, letting everything fly. She'd run the monologue in her head: *You made my mother so sick she could barely get out of bed. You made my father avoid coming home. You made me wear those awful scratchy clothes and sit in that synagogue through entire Yom Kippur services while the other kids played and didn't have to fast. You wrecked my whole entire family and my whole entire childhood.*

She wondered what she thought would happen if she said all those things at Gladys's bedside. She supposed she'd imagined they would make her feel whole. Then she would turn on Stephen and do the same.

But all she saw was a sad old woman, and she thought about the picture she and her mother had found—not the letter on the back but the actual picture—of the family Gladys had left behind, people Gladys had loved and presumably had loved her back.

"She talked to me," Stephen said. "When I was a kid, listening to Gladys... I mean, she and my grandfather were on opposite sides of the war, but they reminded me of each other." He laughed again, but it had a bitter edge. "Or I thought my grandfather fought for Hitler. Turns out he was just a sex offender."

"Oh," Rachel said. Then, as easily as if she were asking about the weather, she added, "So were you."

Stephen stepped back, his eyes streaming, his face pale. "I... we were kids. I was a kid too. I was only a year older than you."

"I know." Rachel thought about that therapist all those years before and the way she had insisted that Rachel was a victim of sexual abuse. "But it hurt me. It really fucked me up."

Again, she had imagined some confrontation in which she told him off, let him know how he'd messed her up, messed up her sexuality, confused her, and left her filled with shame. But he was the one crying. She felt calm and in control.

"It's okay," she offered and tried to think if it was the same thing she always did with her parents and with Liz—pretend she was fine to keep their love. But she didn't need Stephen's love. She didn't need anything from him. She could give him something, she realized. Maybe there was power in that. "Whatever it was, it's okay. I forgive you."

She had always imagined forgiveness as something that would cost her, as if she would then have to carry the weight of the other person's shame along with her own. But Stephen nodded and wiped his nose with his sleeve, and she did not feel any different. She thought about his mother, who was always drunk, the parade of uncles, the bruises Stephen wore so often that they seemed like just a part of his skin, like freckles or a mole.

He sniffed, and she turned toward Gladys. She had closed her eyes again, so Rachel placed a hand on her forehead the way a mother did with a child, checking for fever. Gladys's eyes snapped open.

"Esther," Gladys said. "I'm coming soon. I love you."

"I love you, too, Gladys," Rachel said. She wasn't sure she meant it, and maybe she had given something to Gladys that Gladys hadn't really earned, but she felt peaceful as she let the words hang in the air.

Gladys closed her eyes.

"It's going to be okay," Rachel said to herself, to Gladys, to Stephen.

Chapter 35
Gladys

Gladys let the little Nazi in the house but didn't know why. She was always afraid. She forgot what year it was, forgot Ira was dead. She opened her eyes and saw Joseph in front of her, glowing on the bimah, chanting the kaddish, and she knew she was dying. The nurses scuttled in and out with the tides of wake and sleep. The doctor checked her and left. Someone pulled open curtains so the sun spiked her eyes, and she tried to tell them she preferred the dark. "Open," she said, but she knew it was wrong. She couldn't find the word to say what she wanted, and the nurse nodded and smiled and said, "Yes. Isn't the sunlight lovely."

"Too sharp," Gladys said. The light burned her eyes. The light was cold like a knife, and she was glad to be dying.

Gladys let the Nazi in the house. So long ago, the first tendrils of memory frayed like old wire, so her brain said yesterday when she meant tomorrow, said awake when she meant asleep, said come in when she meant go away... So long ago, and he was there. She had been feeding the dog, and he was there with his white hair. She was on her porch, feeding the dog, but there was another porch so long ago, with Esther and Frantz, a scent of sulfur and tobacco, the flare of his light and Esther's laugh.

"Of course I'll marry you," he had said. Her belly was not yet showing, and Esther laughed—oh, she laughed—because she wanted them married.

"My favorite couple," she said. Gladys and Frantz. The three of them wove a fairy tale. Gladys would go first, before the baby started showing. Frantz could get the boat ticket and could get her out. Keeping the baby safe was most important, he said, and Esther agreed. "We'll come soon enough," she said. "Let me work on Muter," she said. All of them together, soon enough, in the United States of America. Frantz said it best, trying for what he claimed to be an American accent. "I'll get you all to the United States of America," he pronounced.

The fantasy they wove, the beautiful child of Frantz and Gladys, playing in the yard while the family laughed and talked. A happy accident, the baby, they said. Just a matter of telling Muter and Taa-Tah.

"It will be okay," Frantz said, breathing tobacco and onions into her mouth. "I love you."

The child was Aaron, but the child was the boy, the Nazi too. Maybe that was what Gladys thought. It was Aaron again, so she let him in.

Maybe she thought she could save him.

Maybe she forgot he was a Nazi. Maybe her brain said Jew when it meant to say Nazi.

Maybe she thought she could make him not a Nazi.

Gladys didn't know why she let the Nazi in, but she fixed it. She did. She fixed it. She realized he was a Nazi, and she kicked him out of the house.

Gladys married Ira. Gladys had Joseph. Joseph, who was supposed to be a rabbi and instead died in the backyard, hanging from a tree.

Gladys was ready to die. Gladys was ready to be somewhere better.

Chapter 36
Stephen
1990

Gladys made sure Stephen got extra helpings of chicken and mashed potatoes. "You're too skinny," she said. "Eat your greens," she reminded him, spooning wilted broccoli onto his plate.

Rachel's father nodded. "I swear your mother doesn't feed you. You can eat here any time."

There were sounds of silverware, and Rachel's father said something that made Rachel laugh. The kitchen smelled like the time he was sick in the hotel, and his mother microwaved him a can of chicken soup and kept checking his temperature and telling him she loved him. It smelled better than that.

Stephen shoveled potatoes into his mouth so quickly that the gravy dripped down his chin.

Gladys put a hand on his. "Slow down. You'll make yourself sick if you eat too fast."

As the sunlight faded, the sliding glass door became a sort of mirror in which he could see the ghost reflections of Rachel's family. Her mother, across from him, studied her food with tired-looking eyes, her back made wide by the window behind her. Rachel's fork glinted as she pushed chicken around on her plate. Gladys sat beside him, the lines and wrinkles of her face smoothed into a younger version of the Gladys he could see when he turned to look at her.

When he touched the place in his mind where his grandfather had died, the emptiness hurt more than the time the uncle burned him with a cigarette. It hurt more than anything. But Gladys touched his shoulder and spoke to him with that accent that sounded just a little bit familiar, and the lonely feeling receded. When he looked at himself there, with the ghost version of the family, he could almost believe he belonged there. He fit.

He caught Rachel's eye and offered her a smile. Her return smile wavered and melted as she turned away and seemed to gaze at her own reflection in the glass.

But later, after they had cleared the table and washed the dishes, when Gladys told Stephen to come and sit with her for a while, Rachel flashed him a much more genuine smile.

"You go practice your Hebrew," Gladys ordered Rachel. "Work on section five."

"Okay," Rachel said, and she skipped a little as she headed away in the direction of her bedroom.

Stephen followed Gladys into her room and accepted her offer to sit on her bed. Later, as she began a story about life in Germany, about the rise of Hitler, he sank to the floor and closed his eyes. He slept there that night, on the floor in Gladys's room.

His mother knocked on the door the next morning, while he was eating toast and peanut butter and laughing at a joke Rachel's father had told.

In the car, she breathed stale beer into his face when she raised her voice. "You can't just disappear like that!" she shouted. "You do know how your grandfather would have felt about you spending time with a Jewish family, right?"

He went back anyway. He went back again and again. He ate dinner and watched the reflections in the glass—they were a family eating together—the parents, the daughter, the grandmother, and the son.

Chapter 37

Rachel

2016

Rachel found Liz sitting on the bed in her childhood home. Liz was so engrossed in her phone that she seemed not to see Rachel standing in the doorway.

"I don't want to do this anymore," Rachel said, feeling as calm and centered as she ever had.

Liz glanced up and set the phone on the bed beside her. "Is it because of what I said in the synagogue? I could see it upset you. I'm just tired. It's been a whirlwind trip, and your family doesn't half do drama." She chuckled.

Rachel looked at the picture on the wall above her bed, a watercolor of two children holding hands and walking on a forest trail. *Had Mother said something about taking a watercolor class in one of her monologues?* "No," she replied. "It isn't about the synagogue. It's everything. It's long enough. I've waited long enough." Sadness about everything welled up in her, as did the shame she had carried around from Gladys and Stephen and the way it got all mixed up with her sexuality and her Jewishness and even how she reacted to those stalkers. It was always there, she realized, always there between her and Liz like a veil that kept Rachel from seeing clearly that Liz was not able to be any of the things Rachel longed for.

"But I came. I came to California for you, to prove how much you mean to me. I know I'm not perfect. But I love you."

Rachel kept her eyes on the window. She didn't need to look to know that Liz was crying. She could hear it in Liz's voice. "I believe you," Rachel said. "I actually really believe that you love me. But I deserve more. I deserve someone who can really be present. And you can't." She was tempted to go and sit beside Liz. They would hug. Her resolve would fade. She stayed in the doorway.

"I want to," Liz said. "I want to be the kind of person you deserve. I think I'm more afraid than I admit. Leaving Michael... it's a big deal. I'm not like you. My parents would freak if I told them I'm gay. Your parents... they let me sleep in your bed like we're a real couple. And my boys... I try so hard to be a better mother than my mother was."

"You are a good mother," Rachel told her, and she meant it. "You put being a mother before anything else, and you should. That's right." She meant that too. "But I want someone who will put me first. At least some of the time."

"You won't find that easily," Liz said, her voice sharp. "Everybody has other priorities by the time they hit their thirties."

"I don't mean it like that. I just... I want to feel valued, and I don't, Liz. I don't feel valued by you. I deserve to feel valued."

"Oh." Liz was openly crying and hugging herself. Her face had gone ruddy with emotion, and she looked as sexy as ever. "I don't know how. I don't think I know how to make you feel what you want to feel."

"I know," Rachel said. "I don't think you do either." And she meant that too.

———◉———

RACHEL SLEPT ON THE living room couch that night rather than share a bed with Liz. She dropped Liz at the airport the next afternoon, and they did not hug goodbye. Liz looked forlorn as she stood with her suitcase, watching Rachel get back into her car. Her last glimpse was of Liz shrinking in her rearview mirror as she drove. Then Rachel turned a corner, and Liz was gone.

Back at the house, Rachel found her mother in the kitchen, putting together some sort of fancy chicken thing. "I thought you guys were vegan now," she said with a laugh. "But you just keep making meat, and honestly—I hate to tell you, but Gladys was a better cook."

Rose laughed. "Yeah," she said. "Maybe that's why we became mostly vegan. I couldn't figure out Gladys's recipes. But you're so skinny, I keep thinking you need protein. And we're having company tonight."

"Who?"

"The Greens," Rose said. "You remember them? Mrs. Green got close to your grandmother. We thought maybe she could tell us something more about your father's relatives and what happened to them."

"You're really leaning into this, aren't you?" During dinner conversation the night before, both her parents had been animated, talking over each other.

"Come here," Rose said, her voice lilting with excitement.

Rachel followed her into Gladys's room. The curtains had been removed and the bed pushed against the wall to make space for a card table. Rose pointed at a notebook on the table. "Here's a list of the men named Frantz who lived in the town we think your grandmother came from."

Rachel picked up the notebook. Each name had a date of birth, an address, and a date of death or the words "still alive" written beside it. *Still alive.*

"We think this Frantz was a Hitler youth," Rose said. "See?" She pointed at the index cards. "Those index cards all have the names and any information we can find about them. Your father joined Geneaology.com. We're trying to find any other relatives who might know something."

As Rachel perused the list, Aaron appeared in the doorway. "I found something online about a Frantz Beckenbauer," he said. "He was a Hitler youth and later fought in the war but disappeared. He was rumored to have run away and joined the other side. That could be my father."

"Really?" Rose said. "Maybe your father was a war hero."

My grandfather, Rachel thought. She looked at her parents. Rose nodded and smiled as Aaron rambled on. *But what if he was some other Frantz? A Frantz who worked at a concentration camp or killed American soldiers when they tried to liberate Dachau?* Whoever he was, she realized, he had loved Gladys once. Gladys had been someone to love. That thought stopped her for a minute. She wondered how it would change her parents if they discovered he was not a Frantz who had acted against the Nazis. She wondered whether they would still be happier.

It would be fine, Rachel realized. It didn't matter how her parents reacted, because she was not a little girl. She could be okay no matter what they did.

"I was thinking," Rachel said, interrupting their conversation. "What if we invited Stephen for dinner as well? He might know some things. Gladys talked to him a lot."

―――⬥―――

AFTER DINNER, RACHEL sat with her parents and Stephen at the kitchen table. The Greens had not known much at all and had gone home early, but Stephen stayed and told story after story. He had overdressed for dinner in what she guessed was the only suit he owned. He smelled like he'd walked through a department store just as a clerk sprayed an entire bottle of cologne into the air. He had combed his hair over the bald spot in a style that reminded Rachel of her sixth-grade history teacher.

His frequent awkward glances in her direction had made her regret the decision to invite him, and she sidled away when he came too close and turned away from his gaze more than once. But her father was entranced when Stephen shared some of Gladys's stories about Frantz. They had already made plans to have him back again the following week.

"She said he was a clown. He would pretend to be characters from movies, and he did horrible fake accents. He wanted to be an actor," Stephen said.

Rachel had no idea if that was true, but she couldn't help smiling when both her parents turned to her and spoke over each other.

"You must have gotten your interest in theater from him," Aaron said.

"So that's where it comes from." Rose laughed. "You remember that time at your bat mitzvah..."

The landline rang. It had rung twice during dinner, and everybody had grown quiet and tense until it stopped.

Rose stopped mid-sentence. Aaron grimaced and leaned forward in his chair. Stephen pushed his chair back. "I'll get it," he said.

"No," Rachel said decisively. "I will." She went to the phone beside the kitchen sink and picked up the receiver. She pressed it to her ear.

"Prepare to die, you fucking kikes. Every one of you is dead!" the caller shouted, his voice slurred in drunken outrage.

Rachel shivered a little under a blast of air from the vent above her. She saw Stephen's eyes on her and tried to figure out what she felt as the words assaulted her, running together until she could barely absorb their meaning. *Is my body reacting? Do I want this?* Her heart raced. She counted beats until it slowed. One. Two. Three. Each word jolted her like a slap. "Jew rat. Christ killer. We're gonna purge all of you." She was aware of the tense silence at the table.

She hunted for words, something big and meaningful, some finale, a moment that would say, "This play is over."

"We aren't afraid of you," she said over the voice in the phone.

The man kept spewing. "You fucking bitch. I'm gonna kill you. I'm gonna find you and"—he paused for a coughing fit—"gonna find you and tear you apart. I'm gonna fucking abort you. You don't deserve..."

She laughed loudly enough to drown out whatever it was she did not deserve. The man's words came at her, but they were just sounds, not words with meaning. "I am not afraid of you. I'm done listening to you now."

"You should have been aborted!" he yelled.

She hung up then leaned against the cupboard next to the sink.

"We don't really need that landline," Rose said.

"Why don't you cancel the service?" Aaron replied. "We'll just use our cell phones."

Stephen stayed silent. His desire, more palpable than the smell of his cologne, consumed the space between them.

Am I aroused? Do I want him?

No. No, she did not. She did not want him, and she had not wanted him back then, in that attic when they played the games that neither of them really understood. A memory surged through her of the day she finally ended it.

"On your back," he said that day. They could hear an uncle shouting through the attic floor.

She dropped to her knees. Downstairs, they heard a thump, and his mother screamed.

"No," Stephen said. "On your back."

It was a new twist. She understood, even then, that the sounds below them meant his mother was being hit. Stephen flinched every time she grunted. "Lie down now!" he shouted in his *Hogan's Heroes* accent.

His uncle yelled, "You bitch!"

"Come on, bitch," Stephen said. "Do it, Jew Girl." His voice sounded harsh and a little bit dangerous. Not like Stephen her war friend, her bike-riding friend, the kid she played house with, but Stephen transformed and dangerous.

"Stop it!" his mother shrieked, and a door slammed.

Rachel stood. "No," she said. "I don't like this game anymore. I'm going home."

Outside, a car engine started. His mother began to sob.

Stephen hugged himself and shivered a little then, even though the small crack in the grimy window provided no breeze, even though they were both slick with sweat from the heat. But he let her leave. He was just a kid. They both were. She turned her back on him that day and descended the attic stairs. She stopped the games and walked out of the attic.

SHE FELT A RUSH OF grief. But that was okay. It seemed right, her sadness. She didn't need to cry. She just needed to let it be. The grief encompassed her. It bathed her family and Stephen in a warm glow. It reached out to Gladys in the nursing home, her uncle Joseph, her family who died in Nazi Germany, even Liz.

She nodded at Stephen. "I think I need to call it a night," she announced.

Her parents could cut the landline service, and the calling would stop. There wasn't much else to do beyond waiting for the people who had chosen to target her to move on to someone else.

Stephen pushed out of his chair and approached her. She could see the intention in his body, the way he tilted forward in preparation for a hug. She sidestepped so that his arms closed on air. Her stomach clenched with a pang of remorse when he dropped his hands but remained where he was, staring down at his feet. He had removed his shoes at the door, and she realized he was wearing Christmas socks.

Was that on purpose? Had he stared into his drawer and thought, "I want to remind Rachel of that night on the beach?" "I'm glad my parents invited you back," she offered.

He spun to face her and shrugged. "Me too."

"It was great having you," Rose called from the table.

"We'll see you next Sunday." Aaron stood and offered Stephen his hand.

Rachel fled to her room while they finished saying their good-byes.

She took her cell phone into the bathroom. While she was running bathwater, she looked at herself in the mirror. She had lost weight over those last several weeks. But she gazed into her own eyes, and she didn't turn away. There was nothing to unhappen.

She climbed in the bathtub and opened several texts she had received from Liz. She must have started texting as soon as the plane landed. She was trying to cover old ground, asking to meet.

Rachel thought carefully about what to write. *I'll meet you for a walk when I'm back in town*, she typed then deleted. *I don't think it's a good idea right now*, she wrote instead. *I think we need the summer apart. To let go.* She hit Send.

Her phone immediately began its tinny rendition of "I Could Have Danced All Night." She blocked Liz's number. She felt guilty, but she did it anyway. "Sorry," she said.

She deleted her Twitter account and made her Facebook page private. She deleted all the recent messages calling her names, attacking her. She didn't bother to read them. There was no need. She knew what they said.

After that, she texted Jo. "Do you still want to come? I ended things with Liz." Maybe they would date. Maybe she would date lots of people and explore her sexuality. No, that probably wasn't who she was. But she was open to finding out.

She googled synagogues in Pineville. She had no intention of joining one, but she was curious. She realized she had avoided anything to do with the Jewish community there. Hell, maybe there was a Jewish LGBT dating group. She laughed. That probably wasn't her scene.

The first two links were for synagogues: Beth Israel Orthodox Synagogue and Temple Concord Reform Synagogue. The next few links led to news stories:

Pineville Synagogue Vandalized.
Synagogue Defaced with Anti-Semitic Symbols.
March Against Hate Planned in Pineville.

The organizer of the March Against Hate was quoted in the first paragraph: "The people who hate us hate LGBTQ people and immigrants. They're racists and Islamophobes. This is a march and rally against all hate."

Rachel read the story. The march was planned for August. She would be back in Pineville by then. She considered the risks. The wrong parents might find out and complain to the principal or the school board. There might be more swastikas on her door. She needed a better security system or maybe a dog.

She followed the link in the article to the organizer's contact page. *I'd like to get involved,* she wrote. *I'm an actress. I could do a performance of some sort. I'd like to help.*

She would do a magic show, maybe. Something entertaining but pointed. She texted Pete. *I want to put a show together. I have ideas, some things I want to say. Will you help?*

Of course, came the immediate response, along with a smiley face.

She could hear her parents laughing out in the kitchen, and she smiled.

Acknowledgments

When I was thirteen, my local library gave me a poetry display. I still remember watching all those strangers stop in front of the poster boards to read my poems. I do not know the name of the librarian who set this up, so I cannot thank him or her directly. When I tell the story these days, I usually add a hint of humor, even a little self-deprecation, but that experience hooked me. I had something to say, and I now understood that other people were willing to listen. That librarian was one of many people who supported and encouraged my writing throughout my childhood and high school years, and it would be impossible to name and thank them all. So instead, I want to acknowledge all librarians, English teachers, and any other adult who takes an interest and encourages young people to express themselves through the arts. You make a difference.

I think of Daena Giardella as a midwife for creative people, and this book was born in the hundreds of hours of improv work I did with her. I cannot thank her enough for creating a non-judgmental space and holding the frame while I explored my characters and wrote entire scenes "on my feet." *Games We Played* exists thanks to those sessions. Thank you for teaching me to say yes.

Thank you to David Ebenbach for his early critiques and for urging me to follow my bliss and apply to the Vermont College of Fine Arts MFA in Fiction program. All the faculty at VCFA are amazing, and those two years changed my life. Ellen Lesser, Abby Frucht, David Jauss, Douglas Glover, and Robin Hemley are some of the people who particularly touched me either through workshops, lectures, or essays they shared during my time in the program. I want to especially thank Diane Lefer, who saw the dog in my novel and immediately understood what I wanted to say and how I could say it. Diane knew when to get out of my way and let me write and when to give valuable feedback that moved my work to the next level.

So many people waded through early drafts of this novel, listened to chapters or passages out loud, and gave me the space to talk out my ideas and changes. Some people even read multiple rewrites. I don't know how they did it. In no particular order, I thank:

The Cape Cod writing group: Margarita Cardenas, Helen Mallon, Maggie Powers, and Kitsy Stein. Special thanks to Kitsy and Maggie, who read an early draft all the way through and sent notes, and Margarita Cardenas, who read multiple pieces out of order and repeatedly reminded me that I could write other books and did not need to put every tangent and new idea into one novel;

The entire CNY Creative Writer's Café, with special thanks to Justina Bombard, Michael Canavan, Emily Glossner Johnson, and Karen Winters Schwartz, who read full drafts, gave notes, read revisions, and gave more notes;

The shrink group for wading through an early draft and giving feedback: Janet Jaffe, Nancy Lipsitt, and Irene Stern; and

My brother, Jeffrey Steiger, who read a draft and gave notes.

I thank everyone at Red Adept Publishing. I cannot say enough about how amazing my experience with RAP has been. Special thanks to Sara Gardiner for the most unflinching and brutal—I mean that in the best way possible—content edit I have ever experienced. She helped me turn the novel into a book I feel proud to release into the world. Whatever Sara missed, Kate Birdsall found in line editing. The ending is so much better thanks to Kate. The whole novel is better thanks to Kate, but I especially thank her for taking the time to understand Rachel deeply enough to know when something did not ring true. My RAP mentor, Erica Lucke Dean, has been supportive and helpful throughout this process. And of course, thanks to Lynn McNamee for giving my novel and me a chance.

I want to also acknowledge all the people who did not directly read or critique this novel but encouraged me, checked in, and took every opportunity to validate that my writing was worth pursuing. I can't possibly name everybody, but thanks to my family (blood and made), Barry and Jean Steiger, Brenda Steiger, Paul Bontoft, Julie Strempel, Irene Stern, Radell Roberts, and Rob Pusch.

Thanks to Claire Bobrycki for the excellent author photos.

As long as I'm thanking family, I should also mention my cats. I still have a version of this novel called *Novel Recovered from Kitten Incident.* You know what you did.

Thanks to *Women in Judaism, a Multidisciplinary e-Journal* for publishing an early excerpt of this novel under the title "Skeletons" in its 2007 issue.

Thanks to Vivian Dorsel for publishing my short story "Special" in the *Berkshire Review* (Volume 12, 2004). While this novel was a mere glint in my eye at that time, I'm certain anybody who read "Special" will recognize the heart of the story in Rachel's seventh-grade-magic-show performance.

I also want to thank the multiple doctors (good, bad, and indifferent) I saw when I was trying to get what I now know is my Common Variable Immune Deficiency diagnosed. I was very sick when I started my MFA program. I thought I might die, and that was a huge motivation for doing the MFA and writing this novel. It was the thing I wanted to leave behind. The bad doctors kept me sick, which motivated me to keep writing so I could finish before I died, and the good ones diagnosed me and got me healthy so I could finish and start on novel number two. Soapbox moment: If you have repeated infections and nobody is listening, please check out *Primaryimmune.org.*

When I started writing this novel, I worried that my white supremacist characters were too extreme. Then 2016 happened, and I worried they weren't extreme enough. I rewrote major sections in

2016 and 2017 thanks to our current political climate and the current administration, so thank you, I guess, for making my novel more relevant than I ever expected back when I first started.

About the Author

Shawne Steiger wrote her first story when she was seven. Over the years, she has been a pizza maker, dressage teacher, house cleaner, and therapist. The one constant in her life has been her writing, which is why, after years working as a trauma therapist, she applied to Vermont College of Fine Arts and completed an MFA in Fiction writing. After learning that she's happiest when writing, Shawne published short stories and essays in several literary journals.

Supporting her writing habit with her social work degree, Shawne frequently incorporates her understanding of how trauma affects people into her fiction. When not writing or working, she enjoys going to the theater, reading and travel. Luckily her love of travel stops her from fully realizing her aspirations to enter the realm of mad cat woman, since she's yet to find the perfect suitcase that will fit all her cats and still be light enough to carry.

Read more at https://shawnesteiger.com/.

Unlocking New Worlds

About the Publisher

Dear Reader,
We hope you enjoyed this book. Please consider leaving a review on your favorite book site.
Visit https://RedAdeptPublishing.com to see our entire catalogue.
Don't forget to subscribe to our monthly newsletter to be notified of future releases and special sales.